TEXTBOOK ROMANCE

KRISTEN BAILEY

Ebook ISBN: 978-1-80508-168-5
Paperback ISBN: 978-1-80508-170-8

Cover design: Emma Rogers
Cover images: Shutterstock

Published by Storm Publishing.
For further information, visit:
www.stormpublishing.co

ALSO BY KRISTEN BAILEY

Sex Ed

Five Gold Rings

Souper Mum

Second Helpings

Has Anyone Seen My Sex Life?

Can I Give My Husband Back?

Did My Love Life Shrink in the Wash?

How Much Wine Will Fix My Broken Heart?

Am I Allergic to Men?

Great Sexpectations

For teachers, everywhere.

PROLOGUE

Jack

There are things I fear in this world. Never being able to afford to buy somewhere to live. Exceptionally large and unpredictable spiders. Undercooking chicken. War. But right now, to that list, I'd like to add wedding seating plans. I don't like how they give you no warning, no chance to prepare. You just walk up to that easel, find your name and sit where you're told. That's when the panic settles in. Who am I sitting next to? Where they've placed me is going to determine how the rest of the night pans out, isn't it? Am I destined for an evening of indigestion and boredom? Have they put me next to the party animal who tops up everyone's glasses and heckles during the speeches? Have they sat me next to Grandma? Will I have to help her put her teeth back in?

'The Mandalorian,' a voice pipes up next to me. 'What's a Mandalorian?'

I look round at the woman standing beside me, elegant in a teal jumpsuit, her brown curly hair pinned back loosely, big gold earrings framing her face. She points towards the table nearest the bar with the coolest name on the board. Lucky lady.

'It's the Star Wars dude. Pedro Pascal. I thought all the ladies loved Pedro Pascal these days?'

Her expression tells me Pedro is not on her radar. 'I know Harrison Ford?'

'Yeah, he's a bit like him, but with a big helmet.' For some reason, I think it's a good idea to pull a pose like I'm firing a space pistol. I hope my suit forgives me for that. That might be the lone glass of Prosecco I've had. I didn't have breakfast today. I got up, threw on a suit and grabbed a couple of ginger snaps off a counter, certainly not enough to sustain a full day of drinking in this cool boutique hotel with its courtyard and fancy cocktails.

She looks at me curiously and raises an eyebrow. 'Gotcha. A big helmet?' she asks, though the blush in her cheeks tells me she immediately regrets that question.

'It's sizeable,' I explain, breaking into a smile. 'Very shiny. Not too large. You can't do anything with a large helmet. Very impractical...'

She grins widely, looking grateful that I'm playing along. I take in the angles of her smile, her dimples, the warm vibe about her.

'This is true.' She stands back as if she's assessing me in my Zara suit. A suit that looked much better on the model online. On me, you sense that if I stood too near an open flame, I'd go up like a roman candle. 'So, tell me, how do you know the happy couple?' she asks me.

'I went to uni with Ed. We shared a house at one point. You?'

'We teach at the same school. I'm Zoe.'

'Jack,' I reply as she puts her hand out to greet me. Married. Not that I was looking for a ring, but I can't help but see it as she does a very kindly gesture where she places a hand over the handshake. Like a hug shake. Her hands are super soft.

Zoe smiles at me. 'It was a lovely ceremony, wasn't it? Did you cry? I cried,' she tells me. 'But then I'm a crier.'

'I didn't, but it was certainly moving. They're a cute couple. Would you think I was weird if I said I was also particularly keen on her bouquet? It was very en vogue.'

Zoe pauses for a moment, still smiling. 'It was. So, tell me what else is trending in weddings, Jack?'

'A sage palette, Asian inspired appetisers and eco-friendly favours,' I say snootily, surprising myself. I really need to review my Netflix viewing habits. I watch far too many people getting married at first sight or saying yes to the dress.

Zoe laughs through her nostrils. 'You're very funny, Jack. Where are you sitting?' she enquires, scanning the print for my name. 'Jack...?'

'Damon,' I inform her.

'Jack Damon... Jack Damon. No, you're on...' We both squint our eyes, looking at the font of my table name then looking at each other.

'Fuck...?' I say, biting my lip.

Zoe bursts into laughter, putting a hand to my shoulder. It's nice that she's comfortable with me. I guess she's also had some Prosecco. 'Was he in Star Wars, too?'

'It's Puck,' pipes in another lady, joining us, looking resplendent in a floral maxi dress. She reaches over to kiss Zoe on the cheek. 'The printer did them dirty on the font. She likes Shakespeare, he likes Star Wars. It's their thing... You're not Brian,' she says, pointing at me.

No, I am not.

'Oh no, this is Jack,' interrupts Zoe. 'He went to uni with Ed. Jack, this is one of my colleagues, Beth. Brian's away with work so I'm flying solo.'

I earwig, assuming Brian to be the husband.

'Well, nice to meet you, Jack. I didn't realise Ed had friends. Do you have stories? Do tell.'

'Oh, I'm letting the best man tell all. He has a great one involving a fan.'

They both narrow their eyes. It's a good story. A tray of drinks does the rounds and we all take a glass.

'Well, here's to new acquaintances.' Zoe toasts, smiling. 'And the happy couple.'

We all clink our glasses and look over at the couple in question, Mia and Ed. Who would have thought Ed, king of the geeks, someone who wore old-man Asics at university, would bag himself such a gem? They're not the likeliest of couples, a bit of an opposites attract thing. But both of them beamed through that ceremony, and for both of them to have found that love and eternal friendship in each other is rather excellent. That's all you ever want for your nearest and dearest: happiness.

I turn back to the table plan. 'So, can you talk me through this table? I don't know any of these people,' I tell them.

Zoe looks at the list and widens her eyes at one of the names, then glances at me. She thinks I didn't notice.

'I saw that.'

'Saw what?' she says, taking a long sip from her drink.

Beth purses her lips, trying to keep in her giggles.

'They've put you with the ladies from the school office,' Zoe says. 'They are a kind but lively bunch.' She gestures over to a corner of the room where there is a lot of cackling and leopard print. One of them has a fascinator so large I think it could pick up radio signals.

'Seriously? Ed is one of my oldest friends – where's the camaraderie? Why has he set me up like this? Where are you sitting, Beth?'

'The Mandalorian,' she says proudly. Zoe high fives her.

'Why couldn't I be on the cool table?' I moan. 'You two seem like fun.' They both smile to be labelled as such.

'He's sat you next to Claudia,' Zoe adds. 'Maybe the set up was intentional? From what I hear, Claudia is newly single. Are you single?'

'I am. What's this Claudia like then? Is she nice?' I enquire.

'She's about your age, I reckon? How old are you?' Zoe asks.

'That's a very personal question,' I reply, jokingly. 'But I'm twenty-nine... and a bit. Yourself?'

'A lady doesn't answer such things,' Zoe jokes and gives me a look. I don't know what that look means. Have I offended her? She looks about mid-thirties, but I won't say that out loud.

'Well, age is but an arbitrary label that just denotes how many years we've been on the planet, no?'

'My knees say different,' Zoe retorts, laughing. I look down at her knees and she catches my eye, wondering why I would be looking her up and down. I can do that, no? 'Claudia, on the other hand, has very youthful knees.'

'Does she now?' I like the banter here, it's making this interesting. Zoe covers her mouth and places a hand on Beth's shoulder to steady her giggles. 'And what else do we know about Claudia?' I ask.

'She and her boyfriend grew apart...' Beth intervenes.

'How do you...?' Zoe asks.

'She's a big social media sharer. She also lost a stone eating nothing but carrots.'

'So she'll be useful later when I'm trying to find my Uber,' I joke.

They both laugh and I grin back, pleased to have brought some comedy to proceedings. They refuse to point her out to me, though. I hope she's not the lady with the giant fascinator. That'll have my eye out.

'Well, enjoy...' Zoe tells me, resting a hand on my arm. I like her. Why can't I be sitting with her? 'Come and find us on the dancefloor later?'

'Or the bar. I will see you at the bar...'

'Then it's a date,' she says, stopping slightly, hoping that wasn't too forward. It wasn't.

'I'll hold you to that.'

Zoe

I do like a wedding with entertainment, and nothing is more entertaining than watching people's dancefloor antics. Namely, some handsome young man I met at the table plan on the dancefloor with a group of women all thrusting and jiggling around him. To *Funkytown*. Poor guy, standing there like a human maypole, holding someone's handbag for them. Someone starts clapping and he's forced to do some sort of running man move. I like how game he is and how he joins in. I hope his suit forgives him for that. The newly single Claudia pats him on the bum and I see him cock his head to one side, his eyes wide like he's past the point of knowing what to do. Like he's in disco prison.

'Oh god,' Beth laughs, already half a bottle of red in. 'Should we go and save him?'

'Feel free. I'm happy observing for now. I hope this makes the wedding video,' I say, sipping at a glass of champagne. Beth is here today with her partner, Will, and I watch as they interlock arms, bopping their heads to the music in the background.

I haven't been to a wedding for a while now. My own feels like a lifetime ago. I wore lace and a tiara, we had lamb shanks as a main and a dancefloor of drunken uncles, one of whom did some breakdance move to Kool & The Gang and split his trousers wide open. Weddings just don't feel like they're part of this stage of my life now. When you're in your forties, all your friends have either done the deed, are having smaller, more discreet second outings or are living a resolutely single life. You get the odd evening invitation, or a forced invite from a younger cousin you've not seen for a decade. So it's nice to be here and absorbing all this wonderful loved-up energy in the room. It's a very well-thought-out affair from the sunshine colour scheme to the way we've been fed a steady stream of crisps at all stages of the day. I've always liked Mia. She teaches English with Beth, and I love how fearless and bold she is, how teaching in a comprehensive has never intimidated her. She looks out for Ed, always has done, and I've always thought they complement each other completely.

'Are you staying here tonight?' I ask Beth and Will as we pick on the last of the delicious wedding cake that Ed made for the occasion. I'd marry Ed for this cake alone. I wipe away the coconut crumbs on the side of my mouth so no one can tell I'm on my third slice.

'Oh no, we're going to get back after the last song. The plan was to have a banger of a night out without kids then tomorrow, nurse our hangovers while they watch *Bluey*.'

I have no idea who Bluey is, but it's lovely to see them let loose, thinking back to a time when my kids were that young and I craved the same. Just one night of freedom, to feel like a different person.

'Remind me how old yours are again?' I ask.

'Five and three,' Will tells me.

I smile. That time feels like a very, very long time ago. A time when you would come out, but you wouldn't necessarily relax. Your back would remain straight all night worrying about inane things like whether they'd climbed out of a window or given the babysitter a nervous breakdown.

'Beth tells me your kids are older. They didn't fancy being your plus one tonight?' he asks.

'Christ, Lottie and Dylan would have rather poked their eyes out with pins,' I laugh. 'The joy of teens. They'd rather hang out on TikTok... You wait. One minute it's Bluey and the next you're having to Snapchat them so you can ask them to come down for dinner.'

Will laughs. That wasn't a joke. We mainly communicate via mutually relatable memes that we share and tag each other in. They talk at me about people with initial names like KSI and SZA. SZA might be the influencer with the fragrances or then again, she might be in music. And even if it's music I say I quite like, that's not allowed. That's 'cringe'. So maybe it's a good thing they're not here, especially as the tempo of the music changes and the DJ mixes in a familiar beat. An old lady beat. Gram'ma Funk? Really? *I See You, Baby*. Groove Armada. I haven't heard this song in an age. Not since university at least.

'YES!' Beth squeals as the rest of our table looks up from their coffees.

'Was this you?' Will asks her, laughing. We were all asked to send in a song request with the RSVP.

'Of course!'

'It's a wedding, Beth. It's not a place for shaking ass,' I mention, thinking of my very neutral floor-filling request of the Bee Gees.

'I can't think of a better place to shake one's ass,' she says, pulling Will up. 'You too, Mrs Swift.'

I stand up reluctantly in my platform heels that I only wear three times a year and shuffle over to that dancefloor, an excellent stream of alcohol running through my veins. Mia is also on the dancefloor and waves when she sees me. She's not wearing a bra with that dress, is she? Oh, the days of not having to wear a bra, back when I didn't have to wear a firm support knicker to hold in all the lumps, bumps and unnatural valleys of my form. The last time I went bra-less was probably when I last heard this song. Warwick University in the year 2000. A club night in combats, a cropped top and a disposable camera I used to store in my leg pocket. Back when a good night out could cost you ten pounds and that included a questionable kebab and chips at the end. It feels nice for a moment to remember that time. It's nice, too, to see Beth and Will clinging to each other, jumping up and down and mouthing the words. So I dance. I mean, I do something that could be classed as such. It's a side-step with an arm pump that's in time with the beat and the flashing lights. Jack sees me from across the way and points at me. I don't know what that point means. It might be relief; he's been in disco captivity for so long and he finally sees a face he vaguely recognises. Claudia is also shaking her ass in ways that make it abundantly clear she's wearing a thong. Jack looks absolutely petrified.

'Help,' he mouths across the crowded dancefloor.

Oh behave, you're not being held hostage. As I thought, Claudia looks like she could be fun, and her knees seem to be well supporting all that shimmying. Maybe give it a chance. He opens his eyes at me, and I can't help but smirk and side-step over.

'Having fun?' I say as I approach them.

Claudia returns to a standing position and drapes her arms over Jack's shoulders. 'Of course, aren't we, Jackers?'

Jack has a nickname. I try not to laugh but just move my arms around like I'm doing a light breaststroke. He joins me, disco swimming through all the awkwardness. Purple disco lights are bouncing off his dirty blond hair; his green tie is slightly undone. There is something about him. I can't put my finger on it. He's classically handsome, a smile that sits between cheeky and intriguing, well-built, intensely blue eyes but at the same time something just clicks, and that surprises something in the recesses of my soul, which thought that impossible these days. He looks at me and puts his fingers to his mouth asking if I'd like a smoke. But I don't smoke. He's asking the wrong person. He widens his eyes at me again. Or... Oh. I nod.

'Claudia?' he says.

'Oh, I don't smoke. Awful habit. You two crack on... But make sure you come back, Jackers!'

I secretly smile at the relief registered on Jack's face as he turns away from her and takes my arm.

'Is she still looking?'

'Yes,' I tell him, glancing back at her face. 'But at your arse. Just keep walking, give her something to look at...'

He laughs, leading me away from the dancefloor and I grab my clutch as we pass my chair. We head out to a small courtyard outside the dining room of this city hotel, the early summer air cooling down slightly. It homes all the smokers, the vapers and a couple hidden in the ivy who appear to be snogging quite messily thinking no one can see them.

'I don't smoke, by the way,' Jack tells me.

'Yeah, I half guessed that. Jackers.'

'Rhymes with crackers...'

'And knackers...' I say, laughing, as we perch on a wall, surrounded by fairy lights. 'What do we do if she comes out here looking for you?'

'Then I'm prepared to go up to that man there, ask him for a cigarette and actually start smoking for the evening,' he tells me as I giggle in reply. 'Thank you for the save, Zoe.'

Given he's a tad merry, it's nice that he's remembered my name. 'You're welcome. I'm missing one of the only songs I actually wanted to dance to tonight, though.'

'Groove Armada. Classic. I'm sorry.'

I smile. He knows the song. Most people know the song, but his age makes me assume that he wouldn't. Like when I have to tell my children who Madonna is, and I feel like I've failed them in their pop cultural education. She was ICONIC, kids. She wore pointy bras! She danced with Jesus!

'Well, you explained to me what a Mandarin is so we're even.'

He smirks. 'You mean a Mandalorian.'

I click my fingers. 'Yes, that. Actually, I am sure my son watched that.'

'How old is your son?'

'Fifteen.'

He recoils in surprise. 'Crumbs, you don't look old enough.'

I laugh. I don't know why. Maybe because that was a compliment and you get to a point where you don't really hear those too often. I don't know whether to thank him, but there is something in his face that makes him look worried he's overstepped.

'Was that cheesy?'

'Kinda, but nice to hear. I think. Thank you...' I say, clutching my hand to my chest. 'I think we peaked earlier on with the helmet chat though.'

His laughing is a relief to me. He's easy company but I don't know how to say that without sounding weird.

'You asked before, but I turned forty-three in March,' I say, unsure why I feel the need to tell him this.

'Pisces?' he asks.

'Yes – you don't believe in all of that, do you?'

'I only say that because I'm a Pisces, too.' He holds his hand out for me to high-five it. I guess we are now bonded by astrology. 'Did you know that fish don't have eyelids?'

I cock my head to the side, chuckling. 'Is this your regular chat-up line? Did you use that on Claudia?'

'I'm not chatting you up,' he says, shocked. 'I'm conversing with an attractive woman about fish,' he adds, his nostrils flaring. I'll forget he called me attractive and that my cheeks are ablaze.

'I didn't know that fact, Jack. Then how do fish wink and flirt with other fish?'

'I don't know, Zoe. I will put in a call to David Attenborough about that.'

Handsome and funny. Twenty years ago, that would have been a dangerous combination. I don't really understand this pseudo-flirting that's happening here so I'm glad that my phone ringing interrupts the conversation. I look down to see it's Lottie. 'Excuse me, duty calls, I also have a daughter.'

He nods politely, putting his hands in his pockets whilst looking up at the sky and surrounding buildings. I like how his eyes are looking out for something.

'Lottie? All good?' I hear a light sobbing on the phone and my hackles immediately go up. 'Lottie, are you alright?'

'When are you coming home?' she asks tearfully.

'I can come home now if something is wrong.' Lottie's crying can be about a number of things, anything from a celebrity couple calling it quits to her fighting over bathroom space with her brother, but I can hear Dylan's low monosyllables in the background. Something's not right. 'You're both safe, yes? Tell me you're safe. No one's broken into the house or hurt you? You're worrying me.'

My volume raises slightly, and Jack stands up, hearing my change in tone, concern etched in his face.

'We're both OK. No one's broken in. It's just...' She breaks into a sob again. 'You told us Dad was away.'

'He's at a conference in Glasgow. He'll be back in two days. Is your dad OK? Did he call?'

'Then why did Melissa from my class see him in a restaurant in Richmond?' she blurts out.

'Why are you telling her on the phone, Lottie?' I hear Dylan tell her in the background.

'Who's Melissa? Maybe it was someone else. Your dad looks

like a lot of people. People always says he looks like Gareth Southgate,' I try and joke.

'I HATE HIM!' she screams down the phone.

'Lottie, calm down! Is this Melissa trying to shit stir? Who is this girl? Your dad is in Glasgow, I spoke to him earlier today.'

'He's not in Glasgow,' she whispers quietly.

And for a moment, I can't quite breathe. Something in my chest just ceases to move, to work, to beat. 'Lottie...'

'She sent me a picture.'

'A picture? Of your dad?'

'Yes.'

'Send me the picture,' I say, my voice shaking, trying to remain calm. Brian is in Glasgow. I'm certain of it.

'Lottie, you can't send her that. Lottie, please...' I hear Dylan crying. To hear him expressing that emotion kills me. And for a moment, I think about both my children, my babies at home, who've been fed some awful misinformation about the two people they're supposed to love the most in the world and how they're dealing with this together, on their own. My phone pings and I open the picture, staring at it for a moment.

'Mum? MUM?' Lottie shrieks down the phone. I don't answer. I feel a hand prise the phone out of my hand and my arm falls numb to my side.

'Hi, Lottie. My name is Jack and I was sitting with your mum at this wedding. I am going to grab an Uber and get her home to you, right away. Can you tell me your address?'

I hear Lottie's distraught voice on the phone, Jack trying to calm her down, repeating the address back to her.

'Yeah, leave it with me. You kids take care, OK? I've got her.' He hangs up the phone and looks over at me, his brow furrowed, his blue eyes staring into mine, searching for signs of life. 'Zoe? Are you OK?'

I can't quite get the words out. They're stuck deep inside,

my face frozen in shock. There's emotion that's aching to come out, but... I can't. I just can't.

'Was that your husband in the photo?'

I nod.

He looks down to the floor, as if he doesn't quite know what to do. 'Are you sure?'

I nod again. 'I know because the woman he was with... I know her, too.'

ONE

Four Months Later

Zoe

'I know someone who works in a sexual health testing laboratory. I could see if she could get us a vial of crabs and we could give them to him,' Kate tells me, peering over her glass of wine as we sit in my garden, trying to absorb the last of the late summer's rays. I would laugh but the thought of a vial full of pubic lice makes me grimace instead.

'No, you could not. That is so grim. How would I give them to him? Here, Brian – pour these in your pants?' I say in horror, half-laughing.

Kate shifts me a look, incredulous. 'No, silly. We'd have to break into his flat and sprinkle them into his pants drawer. Or maybe we could send him anonymous tainted pants. We could send them to that cow who was your supposed friend, too. There are ways and means. I'll ask for vicious blood-sucking crabs.'

I worry at how Kate has thought this through in such detail, but I also vibrate with laughter at my dear sister. Only a sibling would love you so ferociously and with such thought for how to seek revenge on your lying, cheating ratbag of a husband and his new lover. She pulls her hair into a bun, streaks of grey starting to colour her temples, her bright blue eyes matching mine. We sit together on this bench, around my faded garden table, remnants of cheese, charcuterie and wine corks littering the place. I re-arrange the blanket that covers our knees, looking up to watch as the sky starts to fade and the stars poke through. Kate leans over, lighting a candle on the table and using it to light up a cigarette.

'Give me a bit,' I ask her.

'You always told me it was an awful habit,' she tells me, scrunching up her face.

'It is.' Cigarettes always look unnatural on me. Maybe because I hold them with both hands carefully. I suck in the fumes and let them sit in my soul for a minute, hoping it might mask all that other emotion in there. Just one drag can't hurt. I cough and hand it back to my sister. 'I didn't realise there were different types of crabs.'

'I made that up. Actually, I don't know. I'll Google it.'

'The problem there then is if Brian lets on and reports us to the police, they'll look at your search history and then you'll have to go down.'

'I would do that for you, though. I would,' she says, resting her head on my shoulder.

'I know.' I rest my head on hers and cling on to her for dear life. My wonderful Kate. The older sister and the one who came here when life started falling apart, when I told Brian to get out of our family home, and who ensured we all got through these disastrous few months. The one who removed all traces of my husband in this house, who said things to his face that I didn't know how to, who picked up my children and held us close to let us know that even though our dynamic had changed, love was still there. She picks up a piece of salami and stuffs it into her mouth. The only problem now is that she has to go back to her life and work in Birmingham tomorrow. There was only so much living and working remotely she could do, plus her husband, Neil, told us her cats were starting to show symptoms of separation anxiety.

'I always thought I'd be excellent in prison. I'd be like Paddington. I'd make jams and encourage rehabilitation through arts, crafts and baked goods.'

I wrinkle my nose. 'Or, more likely, be the one crocheting ropes to start prison breaks.'

'That, too. I'd make crocheting street, you know?'

We both sit there, silently sipping at wine, looking out into my garden. Brian and I weren't in the least bit green-fingered so it's mostly lawn, whatever shrubs came with the house and some garden furniture that has seen better days, stuff that Brian didn't want when he moved out. That happened three weeks ago. He rented a van. Kate keyed the van before he left because that's what Kate needed to do. But it was a strange day of trans-actions and debate. He fought me for cereal bowls. I think that was the nadir of our breakdown, when he wanted just the three cereal bowls. What sort of animal breaks up a dining set like that? Who fights over the minutiae of life like that, like it's important? I wish we'd done more with this garden. There's an apple tree at the bottom that surprises me every year, yielding fruit even though I don't really give it any care. I also need to sort Dylan's broken goal that leans against the fence, maybe add something to attract birds and squirrels.

'Can I say something?' Kate says, tucking her feet under the blanket to make herself more comfortable. 'There were things about him I never liked. I feel I can bring these things up now.'

'Shoot,' I say, taking a big gulp of wine.

'He liked golf. I always think golf is for bores and twats.' I clink her glass. 'I also thought he needed better chinos, like a flat cut or something. There was a lot of bunching around the crotch area. Not that I was looking but sometimes it just looked like he was wearing a nappy.'

I giggle.

'And I didn't like how he got territorial over the barbeque in the summer. How he'd tuck a tea towel in his back pocket and then strut around with his tongs like he was Gordon fucking Ramsay, telling us about the marbling on his wagyu.'

I smile. The fact was, the kids used to tease him about that mercilessly. It became a family in-joke and a sort of pain stings through me to remember a time where we laughed off his preoccupation with the barbeque and the silly aprons he used to wear. I remember when Lottie strutted around the kitchen imitating him and he got grumpy and told us all to piss off, and we laughed even harder.

Kate senses my quiet and snuggles into me more. 'His allergies were also annoying, the constant sniffing,' she tells me. 'He used to roll his eyes at me when I told him about local honey.'

I nod. 'This is true. He was not one for alternative medicine.'

'And he was just too fond of Liam Gallagher. Like, you're allowed to like the man, he's a quality musician, but it was bordering on fanatical.'

Kate proceeds to bellow out a really bad rendition of *Wonderwall* that makes a bird fall out of a neighbouring tree.

'Someone's tuneful tonight. Is that the Pinot?'

'It's my hate for him, flowing through me,' she informs me.

I was never keen on Oasis. Sure, there were a few bangers there that I respected but it was all he played, and it made him look like some strange middle-aged fanboy. I always thought it a little hypocritical when he was a southerner, too. He should surely have an allegiance to Blur. I know I did.

'I don't think I can hear another Oasis song again,' I tell my sister. 'That makes me feel bad, though. My impending divorce is not their fault.'

Kate chuckles silently. 'You and all your bloody empathy. Only you would feel bad for hating someone you've never even met.'

'*Stop Crying Your Heart Out...*'

'Exactly,' Kate says.

'No. Just thinking back to when he used to play that song on repeat. Bloody droned on. Hated it.'

We both laugh. Kate catches my eye, studying how lost I really look. For the last month, she's been a real emotional crutch. We've slept in the same bed, she ensured I ate. I think at my very lowest, she helped wash my hair in the bath when I sat there sobbing. She's been amazing at finding words when I've needed them but also knowing when I needed silence to counter all that hurt.

'Do we need to burn something?' Kate asks me.

'Like some Oasis CDs?' I tell her.

'I don't think people own CDs anymore, hon. I was just thinking we needed to do something ceremonial to end your marriage. We can burn something, I could buy some old charity shop plates for you to smash? We could go on a CRUISE!'

She seems very excited by the cruise. I shake my head. People have been full of ideas. Friends have mentioned divorce parties, weekends away, meditation retreats with goats. But really all I've wanted to do is lie down in a comfortable tracksuit and stare at a ceiling. It is all so new, so fresh. I just don't know how to fix any of it.

Kate examines my face. 'Zoe. I can't tell you how the next few months will pan out, but you'll be back at work in a few weeks so at least you'll have some routine, distraction. And whenever it gets tough, you chuck those kids in a car and you come and see me, yeah? Neil and I have said it's an open house. It will be an Oasis-free zone.'

I nod, quietly, emotion close to edging into tears. 'Am I allowed to say that I'm scared, Kate?'

She grabs my hand over that blanket. 'It's allowed. He's not just hurt you. He's taken your self-esteem, your kindness and shat all over it. I will never forgive that shitspoon for that – never. And if I ever see that woman who was supposed to be your friend, I will have her.' If they were both here now, I have no doubt Kate would glass them with her wine goblet.

The friend's name is Liz. We used to go on spa days together. I made her a lasagne once when her mum passed away. She's tried to reach out via text. I didn't reply. Kate replied on my behalf with a singular middle finger emoji.

'Like a proper fight?' I ask Kate.

'I've seen her picture. She wouldn't stand a chance,' she tells me confidently.

I go quiet again. Do I want to hurt her? I want to shame her, both of them. I wish they would bring back scarlet letters. They've both acted terribly without thought for anyone else. My initial thoughts are sadness, rage, fantasies where I bump into them and just unload all my feelings onto them in a classy, non-violent manner that would make the crowd cheer. That would never happen, though. If I was faced with them now, I'd crumble and cry and roll into a ball on the floor. What has happened is so seismic. I just don't know how to cope, how to survive, how to move on from any of it.

'What will I do without you?'

'Survive. I have every faith. It's just the start of another chapter. I won't let this defeat you. You are too fucking marvellous.'

'So are you.'

'This didn't need to be said out loud, we knew this already.'

I nudge her, jokingly. She tops up my glass and stabs a toothpick into a couple of olives.

'Do you know what this feels like?' I tell her, a feeling

darting through me as I realise where I've experienced this loss before.

'Mildly drunk with a charcuterie board I feel we should have spent more time on.'

'How so?' I ask.

'The ones I see on Instagram have salami formed into roses,' she tells me, shaping her hands in the air. I look down at the table. We basically just ripped open packets and dangled the meat in our mouths. It wasn't entirely classy but hell, I don't know what that is anymore. 'Is that what you meant?'

'Yes, I was talking about cured meat,' I say, rolling my eyes. 'I meant, Brian leaving, the impending divorce... it feels like the time Ziggy died.'

'Ziggy, the dog we had when we were growing up? The one who used to hump the sofa cushions?' Kate asks.

The very one. He was the family dog that existed before I did – a tiny Border Terrier who liked toast crusts and lying at the end of my bed, keeping my feet warm. The sort of pooch that had a very human face, like he was an old man stuck in the body of a dog.

'I remember when he died, it was the first time I'd experienced grief. This is what this feels like. I feel like I'm grieving, like it's tying my insides in knots. I just need to...'

'Unravel...' Kate holds me closer. 'The difference being that Ziggy was the king of dogs whereas Brian is the king of shitspoons.'

'That's a very inventive term. Shitspoon.'

'I made it up especially for Brian.'

We both laugh quietly. It was only the two of us growing up and despite the distance and our differing personalities, she's still my person. We gravitate towards each other in times of need, we defend the other to the hilt, we can still sit here quietly and comfortably with each other and drink wine till we both pass out.

'How do you know someone who works in a sexual health testing laboratory?' I ask her softly.

'Zumba. She has stories.'

'I'll bet.'

'I can seriously leave you her number.'

'Stick it on the fridge.'

'That's my girl.'

Jack

I left university eight years ago and, every year since then, my friends and I have attempted some form of annual reunion to try to hold on to that time of our lives and all those precious friendships. In those first years, reunions would involve the pub. Actually, it wasn't just one pub, it was many pubs, and we'd drink and partake in recreational drugs, and dance and basically attempt to recreate our university experiences in Clapham, trying to reclaim the lost vestiges of our youth. I once slept outside a Tesco Metro after one of those reunions. I woke up to find a rat eating the remnants of my chips. Oh, the memories. Looking up at the newbuild house in front of me today, though, I feel like that's not going to happen this time, is it? I do hope there may be chips, though. I gaze at its very shiny red door, the Ring doorbell, the bay trees to either side and do you know what I see? I see adulthood.

'JACK ATTACK!' Sarah opens the door. I wish she wouldn't call me that anymore, but she does and flings her arms around me, looking vibrant and relaxed in a classy polka dot number. 'You found it then? Where did you park?'

'Oh, I walked from the bus stop.' I won't tell her I rang three different doorbells before hers, though, because all the houses on this estate look the same. Behind her, I can see the buzz of this small gathering in full flow. This is not the pub, we're not going to dance, are we? 'And I also bought you a housewarming gift. It's a money plant,' I tell her, hoisting it into the air. I carried that on a train all the way from London, so she'd better keep it alive.

'Gorgeous. Come in, come in...' I sense her looking around me to see if I've brought company, but that would be a no. It's just me and the plant.

Sarah and I were on the same course at university and lived together in a shared house. What I liked about her was that she came to university with a boyfriend and left with the same one, so there was no chance to ruin a perfectly good friendship by getting drunk and sleeping with her. She's reliable, sane but very sensible. You feel that she bought this newbuild with money she saved and a plan. We walk through the kitchen, and I wave at said boyfriend, Hakeem, who's wearing oven gloves and balancing serving utensils. This whole place is how I imagined our thirties to look, with its sleek counters and floors, and bifold doors that open out to the garden.

'Bowie's still going then?' I ask her. I look down. Bowie is her little Shi Tzu who I once dog-sat when she went on holiday and who took a Shi Tzu in my bed, on my pillow. Apparently, that was a sign of love. He looks up at me with curious eyes and I smile down at him.

'Of course,' she says, picking him up. 'You remember Uncle Jack, don't you?'

Bowie doesn't show any sign of recognition. Maybe if I left him a gift on his pillow, he might. I head outside, the sun flooding the patio, the furniture clearly straight out of its packaging.

'JA-AACK!' a chorus of voices chime in harmony and I put my arms in the air to signal that yes, I am here.

'Beer, mate?' a voice says, and Ed appears next to me, a BrewDog in his hand. If there's one thing I like about being older, it's that the quality of alcohol has improved.

'Always,' I say, putting an arm around him, relieving him of the beer. It was a university house of six and Ed was another comrade-in-arms, part of our motley crew who used to survive off toast, awful house parties and far too many afternoons watching quiz shows that made us feel clever. We loved Ed because he came to university with a full dinner service that featured six cereal bowls which is basically all we ate out of for two years. The last time I saw Ed was four months ago at his wedding. 'How's tricks? I am liking this tan on you. You look so healthy.'

'That's Florida sunshine for you.'

'Is Mia here?' I ask him, looking around the place, noticing the glimmer of silver on his ring finger.

'Oh, she's buzzing about...' he says, pointing to some sort of makeshift bar where she seems to be mixing large jugs of something. She spots me and waves animatedly.

'So... this is it...' I say, looking around this small garden space. Since our days at university, we've all splintered off in different directions, taken on different lives. Some of us moved home, some of us didn't. Sarah was one of those clever sorts who realised she'd get more for her money in Manchester. I inhale deeply. I'd be lying if I didn't say that in the past two or three years, these social gatherings have been more of a comparative exercise in who's the most grown up. Now that we were all thirty or approaching that age, it's an exercise in demonstrating who has achieved the most, who has made the right life decisions. God, I still have trouble working out what shoes to wear most days.

Sarah literally posted a video in our group chat of when she viewed this house. I know that on the stairs, she went for a Slate Sky carpet because she put a poll on our group asking us to vote. I won't lie, I think I may have gone for something with a little more character, but I see the pride in Sarah's face that she has made a nest and it's all hers. In the corner of the garden, a barbeque is in full swing and another of our friends, Rafe, stands there with a tea towel in his back pocket, posing with tongs. I hear him gabbling on about wagyu. I don't mind Rafe, but he went into finance and bought a flat in Canary Wharf, and often sends us pictures of him in yachts. It's only a matter of time before I get so drunk that I tell him I think he's turning into a wanker.

'She has an ensuite, you know?' Ed says, plainly.

We smile at each other. This was a big thing for Sarah which was probably fuelled from years of having to share a bathroom with people like us who used to steal her toothpaste. There are lots of Sarah touches about the place. She's big on candles, fairy lights, scented crap. There's also a sign in the kitchen. It's a picture of a cheese grater, and underneath it in cursive font BE GRATEFUL. Ed catches me looking and we stare at it together, clutching our beers, one hand in our pockets. It's how a man should stand at a barbeque.

'Did you buy her that?' I ask. Ed laughs into his beer. To be fair, if anyone is the most grown up in this place, it's young Ed here. Ed who is now married and entered into a legal binding agreement to share his life and worldly possessions with another. 'So, tell me, mate – how is married life?'

'Honestly? Pretty much like when we were just living together except we had a big party and I have photos as evidence.'

'It was a very good party.'

'I am glad you enjoyed it and many thanks again for the gift. Did you get the thank you card?'

I smile. I did. It was very Ed. Handwritten and very sincere, like his mum had told him to do it. He always had excellent manners.

'Did anyone else gift you a tree?'

'No. Mia's sister, who is not entirely pleasant, gave us a CD rack though.'

I laugh under my breath. 'Retro.'

'Who's retro?' a voice pipes in. Mia reaches out to greet me with a warm embrace and then puts her husband's arm around her shoulder.

'The music choice,' I say. We all stop for a moment. It's *Riptide* by Vance Joy which Sarah played on repeat at university.

'I once had a boyfriend who used to play this on guitar to me. He'd serenade me after sex,' Mia reminisces.

Ed looks at her strangely. 'And this was something you enjoyed? Do I need to sing to you after sex now?'

'Christ, no. It was desperately cringe. Just roll over and sleep, you twat. He thought he was a bit special, spliff hanging out of his mouth, a guitar covering his junk. It was not a special moment.'

There's good energy between Ed and Mia, the way the conversation flows, the humour. Sarah appears next to us with a tray of canapés. 'I MADE THESE!' she announces, excitedly. And even though I joke about this house and this life she has, it is hugely endearing to see her so enthusiastic about it all.

'What are they, lovely?' I ask.

'They're cucumber sushi roll thingies,' she tells us, and we all take one and bite into them, politely. I nod at her to indicate my approval and she links an arm through mine. That's the one thing about Sarah. I tease her mercilessly, but she's always held me close and looked out for me.

'I thought you were bringing your new girlfriend today,' she moans at me.

'New?' I say, a little confused. Ed and Mia lean in to find out more.

'Imogen?' Sarah says. 'The girl with the ring in her nose.'

'You make her sound like a bull,' I tell Sarah, nabbing another of her canapés. 'Sarah, we kinda called that quits in February. I saw you at Ed's wedding anyway. I was there alone. Keep up, love...'

'Well, you know. It's hard to keep up,' she jokes and Ed smirks.

Ed knows the reason I broke it off with Imogen was because I didn't get her twelve red roses for Valentine's Day, and she wrote me a very long WhatsApp message voicing her disappointment and outlining her future expectations on days of note in the calendar. One of the bullet points in her outline told me that one of those expectations involved me taking a week off on and around her birthday in October so I could dedicate my time to her.

'Well, my dear, we can't all be as lucky as you in love and life.'

'Any other prospects on the horizon?' she asks me. Sarah does this a lot. I don't think she does it to be cruel but rather out of concern. It's an all-encompassing question meant to enquire about my life in general.

'I've met a contortionist called Phoenix and we've joined a Hungarian travelling circus.'

She looks at me and shakes her head. 'And what will you do in this circus?' she asks.

'Lion taming, bit of juggling.'

Sarah huddles into me, rolling her eyes. 'More the clown.' We were both botanists at university and she left and went straight into a job in academia. I abandoned plants for family. It led to a variety of jobs, a house share and a string of makeshift relationships. I think she worried about me in that way, that I was off course, which meant I hadn't worked out what life was yet. I worried less and just lived life my way. It wasn't a linear journey, but I was fine.

'I mean, you'll get us in for free though, right? I love a circus,' Ed enquires.

'For sure.'

'Are you still in your house share?' Sarah asks. 'Last time I went there, there was a DJ mixing desk in the bathroom.'

'I am. I live with Ben and Frank, and we like a bit of techno when we're taking a...'

Sarah puts a hand to the air.

'BATH! When I'm taking a bath. You really think I'm quite uncouth, don't you?'

She shakes her head at me, laughing. 'But seriously, where are you working at the moment?' Sarah asks. 'Are you still an escort?'

Mia's eyes widen, choking on the bottle of beer she had put to her mouth.

'Not that sort of escort. I was a security escort. I used to drive an armoured vehicle. It paid very well.' And I won't lie, I liked the uniform. It made me look really hard. I don't say that out loud. I also don't say that I was petrified of what would happen if anyone ever tried to hold up our van. I'd have likely shat myself. 'I am just temping in a call centre for now. Pays the bills, you know?'

I don't say that with any shame. Work is work, but I can sense some disappointment in all their eyes that I should be doing more. They were all there when we graduated. They knew what happened and why I had to give up my own life for a while to help those I loved, but I think they always hoped I'd get back on track eventually.

'Sarah, I can see you silently judging me,' I tell her.

'I'm not... I'm just... How are Dom and the boys?'

Sarah always asks about Dom and the boys, my nephews, and secretly, I like how she's invested in them and understands the very closeness of our relationship.

'They're good.' I get out my phone to show them my screensaver. It's the four of us at Thorpe Park. It was quite possibly one of the best days out ever because there were no queues, so we got to go on most of the rides at least four times. However, given Sarah's line of questioning, I feel that might be too juvenile an admission to make.

I take another of her canapés. 'You never give Rafe the Spanish inquisition...'

Sarah turns her back to the barbeque. 'That's because we like you more. You're our little Jack Attack. We humour Rafe because we've known him for so long, but that jackass will be fine. We just want you to...'

'Sarah, you sound like my mum.'

She shakes her head and stuffs another canapé in my mouth.

'I think what they're asking is whether you're happy,' Mia intervenes, looking confused at some of the detail of the conversation. 'I don't know you well enough but you're happy, yeah?'

I nod. 'I know you all think that I don't have any direction. I still live in a house share, I have no career, no girlfriend. But I'm good, you know? Worry about things that matter. Climate change, that's bloody awful.'

'We worry because we love you,' Sarah tells us.

'I love you, too. It's why I came all the way to Manchester. Despite that really ridiculous sign in your kitchen...' I jest.

'Hakeem's mum gave that to us. I am obliged to display it,' Sarah whispers out of the corner of her mouth and we all laugh. There've been far too many reunions in these past years, too much time spent together, too many moments and shared jokes for us not to be friends anymore. Maybe, secretly, I love that they care.

'Hey, if you were thinking of a career change – our school is desperate for supply teachers. I think it's just short-term contracts but...' Mia tells me.

Ed bobs his head from side to side. 'It's an option. Pay is decent. You taught English for a while, you'd be a shoo-in. Plus, you'd get to see us every day.'

I smile. 'I'm not sure that's a selling point, mate.'

He laughs but it does trigger something in me. I wasn't an awful teacher, and I can handle kids. It would possibly be more interesting than the call centre where I have to hide my teabags and people shout at me a lot despite not knowing me. Perhaps a change is needed. Again. Ed and Mia seem to thrive in what they do and they found each other through teaching so maybe it's something to consider.

'DM me some details?' I tell Ed who puts a thumb up at me.

'Well, I think that would be amazing! You'd be so good at that, Jack,' Sarah says, enthusiastically.

I shift her a look. 'But what about the circus? I'm expected in Budapest. The lions...' I joke.

Ed laughs. 'He'd just be moving to a different type of circus, that's all. I think the kids would love you. Everyone loves you.'

I smile at all of them, looking down at little Bowie dry-humping my leg. Maybe.

TWO

Zoe

There is one thing they don't tell you when you become a teacher, which is that in all your years of teaching, you will be exposed to a ridiculous amount of cake and biscuits. I don't quite know where it all comes from. Half the time it's someone's birthday but most of the time, we seem to mark special occasions with baked goods – everything from the end of a half term to someone being promoted. Mandy is now assistant deputy pastoral care leader. Someone bake some brownies!

I look down now at the Tupperware in my hands that contains jam and coconut confections. It's the first day of term in a new school year. I'm not sure what I've done but I hope I haven't missed an email about a promotion. I look up at Ed in the middle of this crowded staff room, buzzing with activity as we all brace ourselves for the school year ahead.

'WHO CHANGED ALL THE PASSWORDS?' I hear someone scream from the corner. Well, it wasn't me. But I suspect it's the same person who keeps stealing the staff milk. Oh, it's good to be back.

'You've made me cake?' I ask Ed. Ed does this. He's chief star staff baker. I think someone in textiles made him an apron once.

Ed looks slightly flummoxed. 'I did. It's the same recipe as my wedding cake. Mia said you told her you liked the cake, so I thought... you know... since what happened... it's like a welcome back to school gift, to cheer you up...' he tells me awkwardly.

I pause and look down at the Tupperware in my hands. Crikey, he's made me divorce cake, hasn't he? Oh, Ed. He comes to hug me which is a very un-Ed kind of move and a few teachers surrounding us stop in their tracks. Ed is hugging. Something must be wrong. Jen from modern languages stands there, her mouth agape. As Ed backs away, she also comes in for an embrace.

'Hi, Jen, good summer?' I say, trying to joke, the container of cake still in my hands. I know she's had a good summer because of the bronze tan and the fact she's still wearing open-toe sandals.

'Something's wrong. What's happened?' she enquires, a concerned look on her face. Christ, I knew I'd have to say something eventually, but I thought I'd have time. But that's the problem with a staff room. Your business is never quite your own. The cake and the hugging has attracted a small crowd of six teachers, waiting. I don't even know one of them. I think they're new. Is this really how I'm going to introduce myself to you? Hi, Zoe Swift. I teach maths and I'm one of the school's official fire wardens. I'm also soon-to-be divorced and my husband is a cheating prick. Welcome!

'Are you leaving? You better not be leaving,' says Drew, the head of maths. We know he's the head of maths because Drew has a tie with mathematical symbols that I hope he doesn't wear outside of this school.

'I... just...' I mumble, trying to move away from Jen's embrace. I glare at Ed. *You started this with the cake.*

'I'm not leaving here,' I say. Drew sighs, relieved. I take a deep breath. 'I've left my husband, though. Actually, no, he left me. Less leaving, I told him to leave. Over the summer.'

The teachers surrounding me are all silent. This feels like the time Maxine from art stood on a stool in the middle of the staff room and told us she'd left her husband for a woman, but this didn't mean she was bisexual. We didn't know what it meant either or why she stood on a stool.

'Brian?' Drew asks, aghast. 'You and Brian? But you've been together for...'

'Since we were twenty, so you do the maths... Which is funny as we teach maths.'

Ed forces a laugh at my very lame joke. It's Drew's turn to grab me now. Lovely Drew who similarly has been married for an age to Louise. Brian and I used to go round to his house and socialise. Louise always made a very good moussaka, and she knew how to leave people to dress their own salads.

'You should have messaged us,' he says.

'All the staff?' I say, confused. The only time we ever copy all the staff in an email is when a student goes missing.

'Well, me, at least,' he says despondently. 'When?'

'Over the summer. I won't go into too much detail...'

Yet everyone stands around me, Jen especially which makes me think she wants that detail. It's too early for all of that. Plus, we have registration in twenty minutes.

'Am I allowed to say I'm slightly relieved? I thought you seemed stressed at the end of the summer term, and looked like you'd been crying yesterday during INSET, so I thought you were ill. At least you're not ill,' Jen says, chirpily. Drew rolls his eyes. Jen is like this. Even when the children have set off a fire alarm, blocked another set of toilets and are fist-fighting by the school gates, she'll stand there and tell us things could be worse. Yes, Jen. At least I'm not dead. What is one level above dead? Comatose? Just putting one foot in front of another, like some sort of love-crushed zombie. That said, I thought the concealer had been doing me favours with the dark circles under my eyes. Obviously not.

'Not ill...' I mumble.

Jen hugs me again. 'I need to go but let's have a cuppa later, yeah?' she says, the pity in her eyes piercing through, making me feel about a foot tall. The other teachers disperse (including the newbie) who are likely carrying this new staff gossip to their corners of the school. This is where it starts. If I could, after the summer I've had, I'd have just sat in a dark room and not come back here, shrouded myself in the shame of being dumped, single, alone. But needs must. I need the money to carry us through these few months of uncertainty while Brian makes a case for selling our family home. I need to try and show the kids I am fine. I need work to be a distraction from the fact a marriage I thought was strong and stable and forever was basically not. Drew and Ed stand there, still not quite knowing what to say.

'I literally said just give her the cake...' a voice says from behind us. It's Mia. Mia is different to Ed – she hugs everyone without notice or care and it's one of the things I admire about her. She bundles me into her arms. 'How are you, love?'

There's no sense of pity or curiosity there, either. It's a feeling she's here out of kindness and concern. More of this, please.

'I gave her the cake but then I thought she needed a hug. You told me to hug more,' Ed tells her, confused.

'Well, yeah. But give the girl some warning you're going to get in her space,' she tells her new husband, putting an arm around his waist. His arm goes over her shoulder, and she grabs at his hand hanging there. It's that sort of natural body contact you have with someone you feel completely at ease with. That's what love looks like. I remember that feeling. I hope they hold on to it for as long as they can.

'Well, I'm here. I didn't think I'd be capable of this a fortnight ago but here I stand, ready to teach,' I say, punching the air. I wish I'd said that with more enthusiasm, without feeling like my spine and shoulders are filled with jelly.

'Zoe, we can talk about a reduced schedule if that would help? If anything gets too much...' Drew says, kindly. 'I wish you'd said something before.'

'God, no... we're short staffed enough as it is. I'll be fine,' I tell him.

'Please, John from History had a full week off when his hamster died,' Mia says. 'Take the time.'

'I'll let you know if I need it, Drew. Thank you,' I say, turning to Mia. 'But... be honest. Do I look awful? I know I've lost a bit of weight, but do I look ill? Jen says I looked ill.'

'Jen is wearing a gingham maxi dress. She looks like she's going to teach on a prairie,' Mia says. Ed shifts her a look that says *I need to hug more, you need to bitch less*. Mia replies with a cheeky if contrite smile. 'You look like you're knackered.'

And with just one word, Mia sums up all that feeling perfectly. I wrap an arm around her.

'Thank you for the cake, lovely Ed,' I say, nodding to him.

'He made that especially. I hope you're sharing,' Mia says.

'My husband left me for one of my best friends, so no...'

Mia cocks her head to one side to see me derive some humour from something so bleak, a reassuring look that tells her I might be alright in all of this. Maybe.

'Well, how about an easy period two?' Drew tells me. 'I've been asked to settle in a new cover teacher, starting today. Maybe he can come in on your lesson, observe, he can help you out.'

I shrug my shoulders. 'I guess. We will mainly be giving out books and sticking. I'm not sure how much he'll get to observe.'

'He'll get to see one of my finest control thirty kids who haven't been in a classroom since July. He'll see plenty.'

Drew smiles at me. We've been down this street before, we've encircled the block several thousand times but it's kind of him to still have such unerring faith in me.

'Oh, I think we know him,' Mia suddenly says, excitedly, jumping up and down and clapping her hands. 'Did that sub start today?'

'Yes. Mr...' Drew checks a register in front of him. 'Jack Damon.'

Jack

'Sir, are you new, Sir?' a young lad asks me. I am not quite sure what to say. This boy looks about fifteen but the sort who knows the lay of the land in a place like this. If I say yes, he may use this against me. I feel like I need to gain his approval. I can't show fear. Do I fist bump him? Or maybe I shout at him for wearing trainers. My hands remain in my pockets. Shoulders back. Don't let him smell the first day fear radiating off me. He can tell I'm wearing a shirt straight out of the pack, can't he? I should have hung it up.

'How did you know?' I ask him, tentatively.

The young man swings his Vans rucksack over his shoulder, clocking my staff lanyard. 'It's the new style lanyard, innit? See?' he says, tapping his forehead.

'Like a modern-day Sherlock Holmes,' I comment.

'Man's got powers of reduction, innit?'

A girl next to him cackles, hitting him across the head. 'It's deduction, you muppet.' She looks me up and down and I put my hands over the mugshot to hide my very awful picture. It was taken by Claudia in the office. The one from the wedding who I think holds a grudge because I never returned to the dancefloor at that wedding. She just pushed me against a wall today. She didn't even say 'cheese.' I saw a flash and felt my nostrils flaring.

'Well, maybe you could do a new kid a favour?' I ask them. 'I need to get to the maths block.' Please don't send me to the bins.

'I guess you're not a geography teacher then?' he jokes.

That was actually quite funny, so I laugh at my own expense. 'No. But I don't get this numbering system. I'm supposed to go to X_5?'

'Yeah. It's over next to the sports hall, through the second courtyard,' he tells me. 'X classrooms on the bottom floor, Y floors on the top.'

'Like the maths, innit?' the girl interrupts. 'Someone thought that was funny.'

'Is it not funny...?' I ask.

'No, it should all be Z classrooms because maths makes me sleepy, you know?' the boy says, laughing and clapping at his own humour.

I laugh. That was good. The girl is less impressed, and I quite like her for it. 'Do you have names?'

The boy suddenly looks affronted. 'Am I in trouble for dissing maths?'

'No.' I put a hand out to shake his. He looks at it instead. 'I was actually going to say thank you for helping me and that it was nice to meet you...'

'Bobby,' he says, still looking at my hand, wondering if it's a trick or not.

'I'm Keziah.'

They stare at my hand then just flick nods at me. Did I win them over? Possibly not. I'm working against a school bell now and a sea of children all moving in different directions. I should have spent last night studying the maps in my orientation pack. I hope those kids gave me good info. We'll know in five minutes when I'm not in the maths block but staring into the canteen.

'KEEP TO THE LEFT, PLEASE!' a voice booms from somewhere. I can't even see where it came from. It could be played over a loudspeaker for all I know. I feel like I'm on the Tube with a thousand people who are all a foot smaller than me, all keeping left, all getting nowhere. Come and work at our school, Ed and Mia said. They joked it was like a circus, but I thought clowns and ringmasters as opposed to Piccadilly. However, it was a conversation that came at a perfect time. I had to admit the call centre was a little dull and uninspiring, and I'd spent many a day wondering where the breeze was going to take me next. It turns out it would take me here: Griffin Road Comprehensive.

I don't notice her at first. I think it's because I'm still preoccupied by the sheer number of children in this place but also because I'll all too aware of my dodgy timekeeping. I get to the maths block, noticing all those children slowly disappearing into other rooms, desperately trying to read the number plates off the doors. X2, X3... Is it organised like house numbers? I burst into X5 just as the classroom door is about to close.

'I'm so sorry, I got lost. This is X5, yes?' I mumble, taking off my bag.

'It is, Mr Damon. Welcome.'

I look up to see her face. You. I know you. My expression softens, a wave of relief overcoming me to see someone familiar. 'You... Zo— Swift?'

'ZoSwift? Yes, I believe that's my new pop name.' This raises a laugh from some of the kids, smaller versions of Bobby from before. I realise I'm just stood in front of the board, possibly staring in surprise. She looks less fancy without her wedding garb; tortoiseshell glasses are perched on her nose, her hair tied back from her face. She wears a jumper with wide leg trousers, Doc Martens, big earrings and bracelets up one arm. It's still stylish, cool and she exudes that warm energy I remember from the wedding. She's not going to be the sort who screams and throws pens at people. I hope. 'Would you like to take a seat, Mr Damon?'

'Sure thing. Where do you want me?'

'Maybe at the back? Terrill, do you mind having a partner for today?' Terrill doesn't look overly thrilled. I think he was hoping for a table to himself.

She smiles and walks up to me, putting an arm to mine and I exhale gently. 'Good to see you again, Jackers,' she says quietly. I laugh to myself as she signals to the back of the room. I do as I'm told, navigating the many desks, tripping over someone's PE kit as I do so. I really am making quite the entrance.

'Year Eight, this is a new member of staff and he's just going to observe our lesson today so be nice...'

'How, Miss?' a voice pipes up.

'Oh, I don't know, Harry – don't stare, let him use your calculator?' A murmur of a laugh tells me Zoe knows how to work this room. She looks comfortable here. There's no fear, this is her natural habitat.

'Do you not have your own calculator, Sir? That means you get an equipment detention,' the young lad replies.

'I do not...'

A once silent, well-behaved class dip into a collective 'Ooooh' and all their gazes fall on me.

'A detention?' I ask Terrill as I sit down next to him, getting a notebook out of my bag.

'Yeah, you have to stay here with Miss, after school.'

'That's not so bad,' I say, watching Zoe as she sifts through the room, crouching down to explain something to someone. You can see how that child appreciates the personal approach rather than being shamed for not understanding.

Meanwhile, Terrill gives me a look like I've just passed wind. This one will be tough to crack.

'Well, can I borrow your calculator?'

'I guess.'

'And what are we learning today?' I ask him.

'We're chatty chatty at the back there. Are you settled in

yet, Mr Damon?' I hear a voice command from the front of the room. She's not angry per se; rather, I think I see a glimmer of a smile that she's having to reprimand the other adult in the room.

'Yes, Terrill was just letting me use his calculator so I can avoid a detention,' I reply, putting a thumb up to the air.

'Well done, Terrill.'

'Can I give him an achievement point for sharing?' I say. The class giggles. Terrill looks pleasantly surprised.

'That's up to you. Mr Damon?'

'Yes, Miss?'

She smiles. 'You're still chatting...'

The class laughs. I nod and take out a pen, watching as she asks a girl in the front with impeccable French braids to hand out some worksheets. She's polite with her and lends a glue stick to another, joking that it's her favourite glue stick and she wants it back. When she talks, they're all quiet, they listen and it's like some sort of teaching magic. She doesn't talk down to them, she commands the respect naturally. I need to work out how she does that. I write the word RESPECT in my notebook and draw a bubble around it. I notice Terrill looking over at my page.

'Find out what it means to me...' he sings under his breath.

I laugh, perhaps a little too loudly.

Zoe looks up at me. 'I didn't realise bar charts were that funny, Sir.'

Terrill glares at me. If I dob him in now, I'll never crack him.

'I'm just excited, Miss. You know... it's maths!' I exclaim, a little enthusiastically. These kids will now go round the school and tell their mates about some excitable twat who was sitting in on their lesson.

'Well, I am glad. Just... keep it down.'

I'm glad she doesn't ask me to leave the room. Terrill side-eyes me. I think we may be friends now. He could have quoted the Notorious B.I.G. song to me and I would have got that as well, though. I'm down with the youth. I follow Zoe around the room again, watching the way she asks kids how they are, if they understand the work. It's all that warmth which radiates off her. I felt that from the moment I met her, when I shook her hand and she wrapped a hand around mine. Almost a sign, like I could feel safe with her. But every so often, she breathes in deeply and exhales and I also see a person changed. A look in her eyes, as if for a moment she's a bit lost and has to re-centre herself.

I remember that look. I remember it from that courtyard at the wedding when it felt like something inside her broke, like the calm serenity inside her was shaken up into a frenzy. After her daughter rang, I ordered us an Uber like I'd promised. I'm not sure why I went in the Uber with her, but I made sure she got home to her kids. She sat there glassy-eyed during that whole trip, the confused driver looking back at us every so often, trying to work out the dynamic. I think he thought we'd had a fight. I hope he didn't think I was the cause of the fight.

'Shit. I forgot my coat,' she said, at one point.

'I can go back and get it. I'll ring the hotel,' I told her. And then she grabbed my hand. Her skin was still soft, but her fingers were taut like wire.

'That's very kind. This is very kind of you. I'm so sorry. I hope you'll go back to the wedding. Enjoy the rest of your evening.'

I just sat there thinking, why are you thinking about me? In this very moment, your world is falling off a cliff and you're thinking about whether I might want to dance and eat a bit more cake. It was good cake, but I can get Ed to bake me cake any time.

'Are you OK?' I asked softly.

She didn't say a word. I don't think she could. I imagine she was still processing it all. I was trying to piece it altogether. So, Brian is the husband. He's not in Glasgow. He's been papped at a hotel with someone she knows. A friend? That's not good. That's bloody awful. I would not have handled that well. But she didn't break there. She just held on to my hand in the back of that taxi.

'It's the house with the blue car in the front drive, red door...' she told the driver and the car pulled up slowly. 'Here...' She went into her clutch to find her wallet. 'Let me offer you some money for the ride.'

'Don't be silly. It's on me. Get inside to your kids.'

'Thank you, Jack,' she replied. She remembered my name, and said it so sincerely.

I put a hand on her arm. 'Take care, Zoe. Please look after yourself. You don't deserve this.'

I don't know why I ended it like that. I should have ended on 'take care' or something generic and safe like 'good night' but it felt important to say that. It felt important to tell a person I thought was good that they don't deserve to be hurt, that despite all the love they put out into the world, when something bad happens to them, it's not because they didn't try.

She looked at me and for the first time that evening, a tear rolled down her cheek that she wiped away hurriedly. She smiled and let go of my hand and then exited the car, running lightly down the path towards her front door.

'Are we going back to the wedding?' the Uber driver asked me.

'Yeah, just wait a minute, mate,' I told him. I waited until I saw her figure through the glass panels of the door, her kids wrapped around her. She was where she needed to be. 'Let's go back to the wedding.'

'You alright, mate? Did she just dump you? I wasn't quite sure what was happening?' he asked. 'It's why I turned up the radio. We can stop for some chips if you've been dumped.'

I met his eyes in the mirror, half-laughing, half in shock. 'Nah, man. We're not together.' I like how he thought chips were the answer, though. 'She just got some bad news.'

'Oh. Shame, she seemed nice.'

'She did,' I answered. 'She really did.'

THREE

Zoe

'Hold up. Didn't you all go on holiday last year with them? This... *Liz.*' I like the way Drew says Liz's name. He spits it out with the venom it deserves.

I nod gently, cradling my gin and tonic. We've escaped into the local pub for a post-first-day drink along with most of the staff. If there's another thing teachers like to do, it's drink. We teachers of London comprehensives are fifty percent alcohol, forty percent cake, ten percent sheer grit and fortitude. Drew and I hide away at a corner table, away from the lively modern languages lot and the peacocking PE department, so I can share with him the details of my awful separation and impending divorce.

'Yes, turns out they'd been having an affair for about a year behind our respective spouses' backs. That holiday in the Algarve was where it all started, apparently.'

My eyes go a bit hazy to think where and when it would have happened. They used to do the odd supermarket run together. I'm not sure how you start some lusty liaison in the aisles of a euro-mart over the Portuguese custard tarts and Fanta Limon. But after the holiday, they didn't know how to stop, Brian said. I think of all Brian's words since, the vernacular he's used to describe their relationship – words like addictive, alive, thrilling. I remember my words back – words like selfish, mother, fucker. However it made him feel, it was still one whole year of lies. Liz's husband, Greg, dug deeper and found all sorts in the aftermath. Everything from proof of midnight phone calls, to Travelodge visits and a secret folder of photos including one with a dildo. I didn't want to see that, but Greg kept it all. As the kids at school would say, he kept those receipts.

'Well, he's a fucking swine and if I see him, I will tell him that to his face,' Drew says, taking a long sip of his pint. I smile gratefully, but can't imagine it, as Drew is gentle and not particularly athletic. But I like how he's defending my honour and picked a side. 'I messaged Louise. She says you are welcome at ours any time – she is distraught, but she wants you to know how much we love you.'

'I appreciate that, I do.'

'How are the kids?' he asks.

'Angry,' I say, with a stab of sadness, thinking of the effect all this has had on them. 'Not surprisingly, most of that comes from Lottie. She's refusing to see him.'

Drew winces. He knows my Lottie. He knows that the girl is a hotbed of hormones and opinion. I would be lying if I didn't say I liked the fire she's exuded in sticking up for me and how we've grown closer as a consequence, but I don't like seeing how hurt and sad she is about all of this.

'Brian's solicitor is telling me that as we're potentially sharing custody, she has to see him, but my solicitor is arguing that she has rights, too. If she doesn't want to see her father, then we can't force it.'

'Well, I think Brian's got to understand that much.' Drew puts a hand to mine. 'I'm so sorry, Zoe.'

'Oh, please don't apologise. Unless you're also having an affair with Brian?'

'No. I wouldn't know how to have an affair. Anyway, if I did, Lou would probably castrate me and feed my balls to the cat.'

I scrunch up my nose. 'That's an image I didn't need in my head, Drew.'

He laughs and for a moment, that sound is a relief. I need to balance out all this awfulness with something else, anything else.

'Are you OK?' he asks.

I really don't know how to answer. I realise that for a while, many people will ask out of obligation and then I will feel socially obliged not to make them feel uncomfortable and have to fill that silence with a stock answer. I'm here. I'm still standing. Just like Elton John.

'I'll get there.'

'We're maths people. We can find our way anywhere with the right co-ordinates.'

I can't help laughing. He made a maths joke which I find particularly funny but maybe that's the problem. Maybe I am boring. Maybe that's why Brian left. I find quadratic equations fun and that's not a huge selling point for any person.

'MATHS CREW! Why do you always hide from the fun?' a voice suddenly pipes up. It's the lovely Mia, and beside her a familiar face from this morning: Jack. I can feel the blush rise in my cheeks. For no other reason than I was not expecting to see him this morning, and there's possibly some shame at the idea of a complete stranger knowing my business and having seen that start point when my marriage completely unravelled. Here's someone who knows that I'm not OK. He is pretty much how I remember him from that wedding – the scruffy hair, the kind eyes – though he's swapped his shiny suit for flat front khaki chinos with brown, weathered boots and a light blue shirt with the sleeves rolled up.

'I'm doing the rounds with Jack here. Drew, this is Jack Damon – he's joined the study supervising team as a cover teacher. I believe you already know Zoe...' Jack and Drew shake hands while I try to work out what Mia knows about how I know Jack. 'Jack and Ed were mates at university, and we persuaded him to come and use his charms on the children.'

Jack catches my eye and smiles. After he observed my lesson today, we didn't have time to chat; we were busy shepherding children, then he had to run to another class. *Thank you, Mrs Swift! I learned a lot!* he shouted as he threw his satchel over his shoulder. It was hard to think of him as a teacher. He looked far too carefree.

'So did you teach before?' Drew asks him.

'I taught English as a foreign language in Italy, but I've been in between jobs since then. Mia and Ed think teaching may be the way forward,' he explains. 'I must say I learned a lot from Mrs Swift this morning, though.'

'One of our best, I'm not surprised,' Drew adds.

I punch his arm to downplay the compliment.

'You can call me Zoe when the kids aren't around,' I joke. 'Did you learn about sticking in worksheets straight?'

'Yes, and I learned about labelling my axes. You really don't like an unlabelled axis...'

For some reason, I giggle when he says this. 'This is true.'

Mia grabs a stool, dragging it to the table to chat to Drew about weddings and summer holidays. Jack stands there with his hands still in his pockets and I get up to face him, both of us smiling. I feel like I know him, but I don't. In fact, I want to hug him, but I have an inkling that might scare him.

'But seriously, thank you for letting me sit in. Very much appreciated.'

'You're welcome. Least I could do... you know, after the way you helped me back in May. I didn't know if I was ever going to see you again. But I'm glad I have and that I get to thank you again. In person. Less of a... wreck.'

There is a sincerity in his smile that makes this whole interaction less awkward. 'Don't mention it. To be fair, you saved me from the dancefloor, too.'

'This is true,' I say, pointing at him.

'Did you ever get your coat back?' he asks me.

'Oh yeah, someone from the hotel delivered it the next day.'

He laughs under his breath, grinning until I work it out for myself.

'Oh... you brought me back my coat?' I say, surprised.

'I handed it to a young lady at the door. Your daughter? I didn't want to make a fuss. I was also slightly too embarrassed to say I was someone you met at the table plan. And it was a nice coat. I didn't want you to lose it.'

I stand there for a moment to take in that kindness, slightly emotional because the coat is from Uniqlo and it's very warm.

'Don't get me wrong... I also went back to have some cake and get in the photo booth to leave some incredibly animated self-portraits with an inflatable cat. But at the end of the evening, I may have had a conversation with someone in the cloakroom and rescued it.'

'How did you know?'

'It was the last one there, so I had a punt.'

I still don't know how to respond to this man in front of me. It's like someone has sent him to me to help reaffirm my faith in people again. There are dicks out there but there are also nice people, nice people like you, Jack, who do deep dives into cloakrooms and return coats to their owners.

'It is my favourite coat,' I tell him, touching his arm. 'Thank you...'

He looks down at my hand. Was that weird? He thinks I'm touchy. I take the hand back. 'My pleasure... so...'

But before he has a chance to finish his sentence, a woman swans over and puts an arm over Jack's shoulder. 'JACKERS!' It's Claudia from the school office, possibly here to finish what she started at that wedding. Her stance with him is overly familiar, fuelled slightly by a half pint of Becks. Jack's face reads as a mixture of startled and at a loss of how to handle this.

'Good summer, Claudia?' I ask her, trying to intervene.

'Oh, you know. I hear you had an absolute shocker,' she says, bluntly. Jack winces at her lack of tact.

'It could have been better,' I reply meekly.

'I heard the news from Joyce. She thought something was up when you changed your social media picture, so she went to check your husband's profile and he's changed his picture to some selfie of him with another woman so we kind of assumed something had happened...'

Ouch. From a holiday romance to an affair to a social media partner. Is it terrible to say I think I preferred it all when it was a secret, when I didn't know what it was? Now it feels like someone ripping off a plaster incredibly slowly, revealing that messy wound underneath not just to me but to the entire world via Instagram. Roll up, roll up. Come and look at the car crash that is my love life.

'Was it an affair then?' she asks, seemingly unaware that I want the ground to swallow me up. 'I reckon my ex was cheating on me. Fuckers, the lot of them, you know?'

Jack stands there, his expression changing at being labelled as such, but I can tell he's also unimpressed by the way Claudia just wants to lay this all out bare here, in the corner of this pub with its patterned carpets and sticky tables.

'I... It was... It's just all quite fresh, you know?' I say, words lining the inside of my throat, but I can't seem to get them out. I don't want to put her in her place, I don't want to tell her anything else. I just can't talk about it all yet. But as I look around that area of the pub where the staff of Griffin Road seem to be gathered, enjoying their drinks, I also feel a sense of para-noia. Who else knows? How far has the rumour mill travelled? What misinformation lies there? Who else has seen this picture of Brian and Liz? And it feels exhausting, humiliating to have to face it all. 'I'm just going to excuse myself, guys, to the loo... Lovely to see you, Claudia. And see you again, too, Jack.'

I'm sorry, Jack. You'll have to deal with Claudia yourself this time. As I walk towards the ladies' toilets, I can feel all that emotion overwhelming me. It's like a crushing in my chest, an inability to make sense of what's happening, to single out a thought, a feeling. Occasionally that feeling springs out of my eyes, tears that could have filled the Thames by now, but some-times, it's just an intense sadness at how much has changed in a split second. Usually on a weekday like this, I'd rush home from work, I'd have a cup of tea. Brian would fall in a couple of hours later. Wine would be opened, pasta would be boiled, the kitchen would be a hive of activity where we'd laugh and share stories. Shouting at Dylan for leaving wet football boots by the back door, Lottie complaining I've not grated enough cheese. Piling on to sofas, more tea, slippers, my feet meeting Brian's on the footstool, sharing a throw and shouting at the television. Some warm vision of a routine has suddenly been ripped away from me. Gone. And it wasn't my choice. I didn't think it was awful. I loved it. I miss it intensely.

I enter the ladies' – grateful it's empty – and take to a stall to settle myself, resting my forehead against the door. Bloody Claudia. She's a sharer. Such is the way of social media these days that we all know the complete ins and outs of how her most recent relationship broke down, complete with screenshots of text fights and photos outing his cheating behaviour. I chose not to do the same. I didn't want people's pity. I didn't know how to post something with any type of angry edge. I sit on the closed toilet and get my phone out to read the text on the screen.

> How did your first day back go?

It's Dylan. Dylan has taken a concerned child stance with all of this. From a lad who was normally attached to a PlayStation, and who I saw occasionally when he was hungry, it's nice to see the empathy that was under the surface.

> All good. Have you gone straight to training?

Yeah, Max's mum is giving me a lift back. Love ya, Mum.

And an admission of love. Usually, I'd only see that when he wanted a favour.

> Love you too x

I stare at the message and then notice a conversation from Lottie from when I first got out of school.

OMG you'll never guess who I saw on the bus I saw Chloe but then I didn't talk to her because I don't want to because at the end of the day her mum and my dad got together and I blame her mum really because she was obvs unhappy in her marriage and so you think the way to get out of your marriage is to go after my dad? No way. Anyways, I blanked her and it was awks but to hell with that whole family if you ask me. ISTG I will go after Liz if I see her, like properly. LY mum. I'm going to go into town and get chips HMU if you need anything but still save me din dins xxxx

Lottie has all the words, all the emotions, and I worry about whether she's over-processing or actually doing the good and proper thing which is to express it all. They're both such different kids but, by god, the love I feel for both of them sits deeply in my soul. I'd move mountains for each of them. These are usually mountains of laundry but still.

I hear voices enter the pub toilet and I'm not sure why, but I move my feet up, just in case it's Claudia who's followed me in here to ask me more about the catastrophes of my life.

'It's fine, it's empty... Quickly...'

'Are you sure there aren't cameras? Could we get caught?' Christ, that's a man's voice.

I clutch my phone to my chest, still half dangling my feet in some sort of strange pose that I think must be doing wonders for my core. I should cough to let them know I'm here but strangely I can't do it and stay silent.

'You told me on our honeymoon that this was one of your fantasies.'

'Yeah, but...'

I recognise the voices. It's Mia and Ed from school and, from the sound of things, they have a reason to be in here that doesn't involve relieving their bladders or handwashing. I arch my eyebrows. They're young, they're consenting and married so it's really none of my business but I'm not sure I want to hear what that might entail or look them in the eye tomorrow in the staff room. Also, this might make me sound a tad old but... hygiene? I am quite a way off shagging someone in a public restroom, though I could be more tempted in a posh London hotel. The sort that have fabric handtowels and ylang-ylang in the soap.

I hear both bodies moving into the cubicle next to me and a body pushed up against the partition dividing us. Oh dear. Are they really? I hear a giggle and a zip unfastening. They are. It's breathy, that's for sure. Is that a slurping noise? What is she slurping? Face or... Oh dear. Oh, he likes that. She laughs. I can't be here. I slowly unlock the door. Please don't be a squeaky door. This is easy to do, just tiptoe out of here, don't breathe, don't make a sound. I tuck my handbag over my shoulder and make tentative moves out of the door to hear what can only be described as a low-grade grunt. Tiptoe quicker, Zoe. I don't just tiptoe, there are hand movements, too, like the Grinch, like I'm wading through air. When I get to the main door, some mischievous urge overtakes me, and I let it slam behind me to snap them back into the room.

'Your feet, they'll see your feet!' And I laugh at the sound of what can only be Ed climbing onto a toilet and then a crack of ceramics.

'You look like you're mid-dance move,' a voice tells me in the low-lit corridor and I swivel to see Jack standing there, observing me creeping out with my hands still in mid-air like dinosaur claws.

I put my hands down, smiling. 'I was drying my hands, obviously,' I say, blushing. Jack. Jack with his satchel. I like the satchel. It makes him look like some sort of earnest student. I imagine it's filled with sepia-paged books, a scarf and a leather notebook filled with bad poetry. He cocks his head to one side, that kindness in his eyes shining through again. There is something about Jack that makes me stop and take a breath.

'Don't think me weird,' he tells me. 'I just came to find you to see how you are. Claudia was a bit of a twat, to be fair. You seemed upset.' His expression and tone are warm, and I smile in reply. 'Are you OK?'

'I'm glad it wasn't just me being sensitive then. How did you extricate yourself from her clutches?' I ask him.

'I told her I was going out for a smoke. It's my go-to get-out clause with her now.'

I laugh. 'Well, that's kind of you, Jack – thank you. I just… It's very new. The separation. I haven't worked out how you reveal that sort of new information to people.'

'You don't. You tell her it's none of her business,' Jack says, matter-of-factly. 'Your private life should never be up for discussion like that.'

'Possibly,' I say, grinning at this young man's wisdom. I adjust my handbag over my arm, and lean round to poke my head out to the main pub area. It's time to leave, to remove the risk of getting drawn into more emotionally draining conversations. 'Enjoy the rest of your evening, I'm going to head back to my kids. It's good to see you again.' I put my hand on his arm, and he looks down at it, like last time. I forget that I don't know him as well as I feel I do. I retract it immediately, hoping I haven't made him uncomfortable.

'Or... maybe,' he ponders. 'I think I'm done here, too. HR made me complete five thousand staff training questionnaires today – I failed my fire safety quiz five times.'

'How does one do that?' I ask.

'The quiz told me if the school was on fire and a kid refused to leave that I should leave them. I plain refused.'

'You'd carry thirty kids on your back out of there?' I ask.

'Naturally. But to do that, I'd have to eat. Have you eaten?'

I shake my head.

'Well, if you could eat anything now that might make your life a little better, what would it be?'

'Nando's,' I say, without hesitation.

He smiles. 'Then let's get some peri-peri.'

'Let's.' I don't know what I've agreed to, but it would seem remiss to give up the option of Nando's. We stand there for a moment and smile at each other, in silence. I can't put a finger on what I'm feeling, but it's the opposite of rejected and emotionally forlorn. It's a good feeling. The silence is interrupted, though, by the door to the ladies' suddenly flying open, and there stands a very sheepish Mia and Ed.

'Jack, Zoe...' giggles Mia. Ed is a strong shade of blush. We all share glances and I look down to see Ed's chinos wet up to the ankle.

'You OK, mate?' Jack asks, smiling broadly.

'Don't even...'

'Diving for something, were we?' Jack asks and I laugh, loudly.

Jack

I've always admired people who order anything more than a medium at Nando's. Medium is a comfortable level of heat, it tingles the tastebuds and is a pleasant culinary experience. Hot makes me sweat around the collar; it's something I order in front of friends to appear brave and manly, but digestively and physically, it hurts.

I watch as in front of me Zoe digs into her hot chicken wings like it's nothing, no sweat moustache, no wincing, just an 'aaah' which makes me think this chicken is soothing her soul. To compensate for sticking with medium, I have ordered a whole chicken to myself, to make me appear more manly than I am. Look at me, I know how to do protein. I will be taking at least half of this thing home with me, though. I could put it in sandwiches, which is possibly the most mature thought I have ever had in my life.

'You look happy,' I say, through a mouthful of chips.

'Well, in the depths of my soul, there is still a sense of fracture and loss,' she replies plainly, 'but the chicken is giving me temporary reprieve. The heat is numbing the emotion.'

She doesn't even flinch. My eyebrows would be sweating at this point. There is something about her calmness, the serenity in her face. Beneath all of that, you sense this isn't the case, but she masks it well. We've found a cubicle in this branch with banquette seating, the premium seats, if you ask me. It's not a particularly busy night and I only know this as I haven't had to go in search for sauce bottles.

'Thank you for this. I think I needed it,' she says, smiling at me, licking peri-peri from the tips of her fingers.

'Chicken?'

'Just some space to breathe... Away from people and their opinions on my marriage ending. It's been a busy summer. I haven't had much time to myself.'

'I can also leave you alone with your chicken and chips if that would help?' I tell her.

She shakes her head, grinning. 'Don't be silly. I appreciate the company. I like how you're quite far removed from the situation, really. I don't have to explain too much to you. I know for a start you're on my side completely.'

'Team Zoe, obviously – all day long,' I say, stuffing a corn on the cob into my face. That probably did not look attractive, but I don't think she minds. 'But I take from all of this that Brian is gone?'

'Yes.'

'Good. Left you or thrown out? You don't have to talk about it if you don't want to...'

She doesn't look at me, her focus on her platter of chicken. 'A combination of both. He'll say he left but really, I couldn't bear the betrayal, the lies that kept unravelling. My big moment was when I took some scissors to his favourite jumper. I pretended the washing machine attacked it.'

I laugh as she pulls a face remembering it. 'Power move, you go, girl.' I put out a fist, she bumps it reluctantly. Her face warms to a laugh and I remember that look from the wedding. I like the way her eyes light up, the way she tips her head back slightly, so her neck is exposed.

'You said you know the woman?' I ask her.

'Knew. She will stay in the past tense as far as our friendship goes.'

'I hate her.'

'Thank you.'

'I also hate Brian.' She doesn't respond to that. I'm not sure if maybe bringing all of this up is too painful or that, deep down, she isn't quite sure how to hate her ex-husband yet. I guess it's harder to rearrange and suppress feelings like that. She stops to steady herself, running her finger along the edge of the plate.

She looks up at me. 'So, Jack. I want to hear more about you. I feel like I'm eating chicken with someone I don't know.'

'Like a blind date,' I suggest.

She chokes a little at the comparison and her cheeks fill with colour. 'Or not...' I smile with relief to notice she's not too offended. 'I'm just nosy. I remember you telling me you lived with Ed at university?'

'Yeah. He was a biologist, I was a botanist. He was an exceptional housemate.'

'I can imagine. He bakes a good muffin...' she mumbles, a forkful of coleslaw in her mouth.

I raise an eyebrow. 'Oh yes, an expert with muffins. Good rise, excellent distribution of fruit, good shape.' I don't know why I use my hands to demonstrate.

'Which is important.' She tries to contain her giggles and not let this descend into innuendo. 'So, a botanist. That means you're good with plants?'

'Well, anything that can be planted really. It's my thing.'

'So, you can tell me to sod off if it's none of my business, but then why are you cover teaching?' she asks.

I like the way she asks. Most people ask that question with judgement in their tone, but I can hear the care and curiosity in her voice.

'Oh, I guess since university I've drifted between jobs. I had to put family first for a bit. I once worked on a cruise ship for a month...'

'Were you in charge of the anchor?'

That was funny. 'I worked the casinos. I managed to get in some travel. It was fun.' I'll omit the part about how it was a huge orgy behind the scenes, and I suffered liver damage from the drinking. 'I also was a manager of a Zara. I still have my staff discount card if you ever need...'

'Continental, well-wearing knitwear?'

'Bingo. So, when I saw Mia and Ed over the summer, they told me that your school was crying out for teachers, and they said they thought I'd be excellent at it so... here I am.' There's a look in her eyes. I hope that's not pity. But I also sense some curiosity over what I've said about family. I see her pause, as if she's wondering whether to pry further. Either way, I don't mind that my route into adulthood has not been traditional. I have time. In my head, I feel I'm still allowed moments to free-wheel and try on different jobs before I settle, but I guess that can look unappealing. It can look like I have no staying power. 'And how long have you been a teacher?' I ask her, changing the focus from me to her.

'Literally, left university, got my QTS and have been teaching ever since. It's all I know.' I can hear hints of sadness in her voice. Given the age of her kids, you can tell that, unlike me, her life went in one singular direction and being caught off course has thrown her.

'It just means you're expert level. I bow to your greatness and years of experience.'

'And what do you know of my experience?' she says, smiling broadly.

There's a silence. This has descended into innuendo again, hasn't it? I remember this from the wedding. There was helmet talk, we've dipped into muffins and now we're chatting about her experience. She doesn't seem to mind the innuendo, it makes her smile, and I will also admit that I enjoy being a participant. There is something intriguing about her, that makes me want to keep sitting here, to find out more. It makes me think her husband was an idiot to let someone like this go.

'Well, I saw someone great today. Someone who knew exactly what they were doing, who knew how to take control, who had all the right words.'

She shakes her head, silently laughing to herself, and picks up another of her very spicy chicken wings, her teeth tearing at the flesh. I look at the curve of her jaw as she chews and she side-eyes me, pondering. I don't think she can quite read me. Is she here for my company or is she here for the chicken? I feel the pendulum swings in the favour of the flame-grilled wings; I'm only a sidekick so she doesn't have to sit on her own.

'I think you'll be a good teacher. The girls will like you, for sure... Younger ones who look like you will always have a head start with all the hormonally charged teen girls,' she tells me, looking over at me for a moment.

'Ones who look like me?' I enquire.

She narrows her eyes at me. So she thinks I'm attractive? 'Well, the girls have either you or Mr Lindsay in IT. He wears boat shoes and sweater vests. I reckon they'll be following you and your Zara knitwear around for sure.'

I laugh.

'Do you have a girlfriend?' she asks me. I shake my head. I sense she's asking out of curiosity rather than personal interest. 'Is this because you're still trying out different things? Like the job situation?'

It's painful to know I can be read like a book so quickly.

'That would be a yes.'

'Longest relationship?'

'Seven months, Cara Maddison. She asked me to move in with her. Before we'd had a chance to discuss it, though, she'd announced it on Facebook and made moving postcards that she sent out to all her family.'

She laughs, and to hear Zoe laugh, to see it, is deeply satisfying. I'm seeing a side of her that may be authentic and not steeped in grief. And yes, it's funny now but back then my friend, Sarah, misread it for an engagement announcement and bought herself a new dress.

A message notification beeps on Zoe's phone, and she looks

down at her peri-peri covered fingers, before reaching for napkins.

'Do me a favour, can you just reach into my bag and grab my phone?'

I am peri-peri free and retrieve her phone for her, placing it on the table.

'My passcode is 8624,' she tells me.

'Zoe, we've literally just met,' I say, in faux shock that she'd share something so private with me.

'I trust you. I know where you work,' she jokes.

I put the digits into the keypad and see a message notification from someone called WANKER. I hazard a guess at who that might be as every sinew in her body seems to stiffen. 'Is that his middle name?' I ask, trying to bring some levity to proceedings.

She takes a breath. 'Yes. It has Germanic roots. Very common in the Bavarian region.'

I am not sure what the message says but there is a strong urge to protect her from it, from him. 'Would you like me to read the message out? Let you know if it's safe?'

She looks at me and then shrugs her shoulders. I open up the conversation, trying not to see the message before where Zoe has sent him a middle finger emoji.

'Zo, Lottie has blocked me now. We need to come up with a way of sorting this. I am her father. I have rights. Please remind her of this. B. There's also a kiss at the end.'

Zoe exhales a huge sigh.

'Shall I reply?'

'No. Leave him hanging on read. It'll piss him off.'

Her eyes seem to change colour with anger, frustration, and I hate the way just a singular text is like a jab to the ribs and is so immediately affecting for her. There's the immediate instinct to take that feeling away, to bring that other Zoe back in the room. 'You OK?'

'Who knows? I hate that he's on my phone. The bloody gall of the man that he can end a text with a kiss, too. I'd rather kiss a wart-covered penis at this point.'

I put my piece of spicy chicken down. 'Well... don't do that. Shall I get rid of the message? Then the message isn't there. Shall I block him?'

She slumps her shoulders. 'No, I can't be seen to be petty. Lawyer's orders.'

'Maybe you would feel better if I was on your phone?' I ask her. I don't know why I said that. It's not like I'm going to go into her phone and beat the shit out of her husband, but it felt like the right thing to say.

'You want to slide into my contacts?' she enquires curiously.

'For teaching emergencies. You know, just in case I ever run out of...'

'Glue sticks?'

'Well, there's that, but it feels like you need to counteract the presence of the wanker with someone who...'

'Isn't a wanker?'

'Who cares. Who you can chat to whenever you want. And who buys you chicken.' She stops for a moment to look at me. I can't tell if that's confusion or amazement. 'Can I be the anti-wanker?'

'That sounds like something I'd use to clean my oven,' she jokes.

'I like you, Zoe, but I draw the line at doing your chores,' I say, holding a hand to the air. She smiles. I carefully create my contact. THE ANTI-WANKER. She looks over while I do this, still unsure.

'Can I also do something else?' I ask her.

I pick up a napkin and wipe a smear of sauce that was on the underside of her chin. She blushes, realising it was there. But the contact unsteadies me, to feel her skin against my fingers, to focus on her eyes up close. Is this flirting? I don't know, but there's something about her that I like, that I can't help but be drawn to, a light inside her that I want to get close to. Jack, I think you may have a crush.

FOUR

Zoe

'MUM! IS THAT YOU? MUUUUUM!'

It's the greeting I get whenever I walk back into this house. I often think that if a burglar walked in, they could literally just reply yes, raid the house and leave and the two teens upstairs would be none the wiser.

'No, my name is Juan. I'm from Deliveroo. Please can I use your toilet?'

'Number one or number two?' a voice says, weaving down from upstairs.

'Number two. I hope you have enough loo roll.'

There is a cackle from the upstairs landing and Lottie's head peers over the banister, her blonde curly hair hanging like curtains, the glimmer of her braces catching the light. The blonde is not from me but it's a glorious mass of curls that are either the best or worst thing about her life, depending on the humidity and whether her hair products like her. She swings off the banister in that way we've warned her not to do for years.

'I wasn't kidding, by the way...'

'About the big poo you need to do?' Lottie enquires.

I laugh heartily. 'About me being the Deliveroo person. I bring Nando's.'

Lottie squeals in excitement and hammers a fist on Dylan's door. 'Dyl – she brought chicken!'

I remember a time when Peppa Pig brought the same level of excitement. The door opens and Dylan appears in shorts and with wet hair even though it's autumn and I'm already in boots and a scarf. Dylan is one of those kids who just gets on with life – I never quite know if he's enjoying himself. He eats, he shares small details of his day, he leaves. He inherited the curls but they're sandy and usually hiding under a beanie. They thunder down the stairs, following me into the kitchen as I flick on the lights.

'Did someone load the dishwasher?' I say, surprised.

Dylan nods. The apt response here is to say I should divorce their father more often if it means they'll finally get round to those chores I've bugged them about for years, but even I know it's too soon for that. The kitchen is the hub around which this whole house operates, despite having their own rooms: their homework is still strewn about the island, the fridge acts as some sort of social noticeboard, their black puffa coats are hanging on the back of the bar stools. They grab at plates, taking their seats, both with one AirPod still hanging out of their ears in case they miss anything important on TikTok.

'I'm sorry I'm late. First day back and all that...' Lottie pushes some chicken my way. 'It's cool, I had some already.'

'With who?' she asks.

'A new teacher – his name's Jack.'

They both pause for a moment, and I realise the implication. Mother, that's a man's name. Dad's moved on and out, maybe I have, too. Except the answer there is no. It's far too soon, even if Jack was kind, spoke to me in innuendo and I liked the swing of his satchel. I look at both of their faces and feel that instinctive, urgent need to protect them. The day they found out about their dad is still fresh in my mind. A day of seeing such pure sadness from both of them. It still haunts me, and I am conscious that whilst I will never be able to protect them fully, I at least never want to be the sort of person who evokes that sort of emotion in them. I respond laughing.

'Not like that... he's a colleague.'

'Was he fit? Do you have a picture?' Lottie continues.

'You see, when I go out and eat, I don't spend my time taking selfies. I actually just eat,' I tell her, sarcasm in my tone to match all of hers.

She narrows her eyes at me, but I realise I haven't really answered her question. I need to lie. He is quite handsome. I did spend a great deal of time looking at his face, fascinated by his features, a little shocked at times that he was choosing to spend his time sitting across from me. You get the feeling he'd slide into the cast of some teen Netflix drama without worry. Good jaw. Do people still look at jawlines? I think this is an oft overlooked physical feature. You want something strong to frame the face and he had a good jaw. I can't tell my kids that.

'He was just a very nice young man... that is all.'

Nothing more. And that's not because he's over ten years younger than me but because romance and my love life are quite far down on my agenda at the moment. It feels like a complication, something I can't fathom. I wouldn't even know where to start with finding love, with nurturing any sort of romantic relationship. If anything, it feels absurd, bordering on hilarious.

'Was he like a dinner companion, accompanying your old arse to an early bird special?' Lottie continues. I flare my nostrils at her. These kids will always think me some sort of ancient relic who was born out of a pyramid, telling them stories of how I had to find public phones and carry metal money to contact my parents, and how I made mixtapes by recording songs off the radio. Nothing will ever convince them otherwise.

'Yes, just like that. He helped me find my glasses so I could read the menu...'

'That's nice. I hope he was respectful and called you ma'am,' Lottie says. Dylan laughs in reply, and I shake my head. Charming. If you want to know, he helped me remember what it was like to smile again, to laugh deeply from within. Sat across from him, over the peri-peri, he helped me feel human, reconnect to myself. But I guess they don't really need to know about that. They both continue to eat, content with my explanations. At the end of the day, I bought Nando's and I wasn't on a date-date so these small details don't matter. Dylan shovels some rice into his mouth, and I hang around them at the island, debating my next move. 'And all good? First days back go OK? New timetables work out alright?'

'Oh my god, I have Mr Weaver for chemistry and the man is literally the devil because if you so much as look out the window, he screams at you and he gave Lewis McFarland a detention for scraping his stool across the floor and I mean, I'd get it if the man could actually teach. He just screams and walks around with his pigeon chest like he owns the place and makes us copy things out of the textbook. I don't believe he's qualified. I think they need to double check his paperwork. And then, don't get me started, double PE on Monday morning. It's like the world hates me.'

Dylan smirks at me, as if to say, let's really not get her started. 'And you, Dyl?' I ask him to try and get a word in edgewise.

'Was alright. They've stopped doing those paninis at lunch, though.'

And that is all I'll get from Dylan until parents' evening when some random teacher will tell me he could contribute more to class but he's on track for a B in his pending exams which is Dylan all over – not excelling but coasting comfortably. He steals a chip from his sister which means they nudge each other on their chairs. She steals one back. This will either escalate to a headlock or they'll realise it's not worth the conflict. I try to act as peacemaker by stealing more chips and notice Dylan leaning into me, resting a head against my arm. I smile to myself.

Feeding time is suddenly disrupted by a key in the door, a familiar sound once upon a time, but now we all look up at each other in surprise, knowing who is there. I gulp quietly, trying not to let the panic reach my eyes.

'He really should ring the bell,' Lottie snarls, grabbing her chicken and heading to the small cupboard next to the kitchen that acts as a utility room, presumably to finish her dinner by eating it off the tumble dryer. Dylan looks up at me curiously, wondering what to do next. Leave or stay or squeeze in that cupboard, too.

I hear his footsteps in the hallway and turn to see his face at the doorway. That face. I've known that face for over twenty years; I've seen the lines carve themselves into his brow; I know his eye colour is hazel, not green; I know he can't quite grow a beard on the sides of his face so his stubble at times makes him look like Dr Strange. It's a face I've known and admittedly loved for years but to see it now, the emotion hits me differently. Dread. I dread seeing it because I don't know what emotion will emerge. Do I hate it today? Do I miss it? Do I want to punch it? He's come straight from work. I know this because of the shoes but every time I see him now, I see the parts of him that are only there because of me, that only I know about: a button I re-sewed onto a coat; a shirt I bought him for Christmas; a way he walks which makes me think he's using haemorrhoid cream.

'Brian...'

'Nando's? Is it someone's birthday?' he asks. No greeting, no acknowledgement. He puts a hand to Dylan's back, and I see him shirk from the physical contact.

'Just a back-to-school treat,' I say. I hate that he lets himself in here like he still has ownership over this household.

He glances around the place to see if anything's changed then casually walks over to switch on the kettle. 'You didn't reply to my message. Where is Lottie? Can we chat?'

'I was busy.' I was eating chicken with a fit younger bloke. Tell him. But I don't. 'I guess I'm free now, though.' I lower my voice so that Lottie won't hear. 'You just need to go easy on Lottie. Give her time.'

'How much time? She's been angry with me all summer. This can't go on,' Brian says, opening a cupboard to retrieve a mug. I hate how natural the movement is, how he knows where everything is in this place. Maybe I need to move things around. I hear the tumble dryer go on in the cupboard and I smile.

'Are you saying she's not allowed to be angry?' I ask him. He makes himself a cup of tea and paws through some bills and letters on the counter.

Dylan gets out of his seat and takes a mug from the cupboard. I see him avoid eye contact, not saying a word, but making a cup of tea and placing it in front of me, an arm going to my shoulder.

'Thanks, Dyl,' I say, putting a hand to his arm.

Brian takes some of the junk mail and places it in the recycling bin. Once upon a time that would have been fine, but again, his presumptuousness riles me. I may have wanted to read about getting some new double glazing. He turns from the bin to confront me, his mouth puckered in the way he does when he's stern and wants to start a fight.

'Well, I don't know what you've said but you have to help me.'

'What I've said?' I repeat.

'I am not the enemy here. I am her father, and she is my daughter. Nothing's changed there.'

'Nothing's changed?' I repeat back at him, hoping he can hear how idiotic he sounds. You ripped the arse out of their world. You abandoned us, so we sit here, almost grieving you, the life we had. You were there when they were born, we had such dreams for them and the life we wanted to give them and you've taken that away from them, our beautiful children. But yes, nothing's changed, Brian.

'If you were a good mother, you'd want to help me fix this.'

'If I was a good mother...' I repeat slowly. What was that word Kate used? Shitspoon. I want to reply but instead I hear a sound from the cupboard that sounds like someone throwing something. Just not at the dryer, we need the dryer. I don't have words for Brian, just deep disappointment that he doesn't realise that something like this, to have found out in the way she did, would be world-ending for Lottie. For our daughter, a child. Before that, Brian was a pitch-perfect father – his emotional intelligence and connection he had with both kids made me so proud. Now? Now it feels like he's embedded in his own affair, and it feels selfish, it feels miles away from the person I knew and loved.

'Also, in two weeks we have those tickets for that concert in Manchester. I'm making plans. She was part of those plans.'

She was before you callously flaunted your affair in public. All these sentences play out in my head. In some alternative reality, I have the sass, the confidence to tell him what I think, but I need to maintain some sort of calm. In the face of him misbehaving so badly, I can't run riot with my emotions too, and confuse the kids even more – I need to be reasonable in a wholly unreasonable situation.

'We were looking forward to it... Right, Dyl?' Dylan doesn't look up but nods, half-heartedly.

'Is she here? Can I go up and see her?' he asks. He heads

into the hallway and starts shouting up the stairs, treading each step carefully.

I open the door to the utility room where Lottie's face is like thunder. 'No!' she loud whispers at me.

'Just hear him out?'

'I will literally shank him with a chicken bone.'

Dylan can't help but smirk. 'Well, you wouldn't because you have super weak forearms.'

She sneers at me from beyond the laundry basket, almost barricading herself in there.

'Just don't touch my clean sheets with your chicken fingers... You were looking forward to Manchester?'

'I was.'

I squeeze into the cupboard and squat down next to her, seeing her eyes well up. 'Lottie. He's still your dad. For all that's changed, he will always be your dad.'

'But he's also a wanker, too.'

'Well, yeah...' She smiles and throws her arms around my neck.

'Can I say that to his face?'

'Only at Christmas.' I grab her face and look into those hazel, not green eyes. You're so angry and I get it completely and I'm almost grateful for it, but I can't have you hold on to that emotion forever. I don't like how this has transformed my bright bouncing teen into this seething ball of resentment and confusion. That's not a way to live, to grow up.

'What is she doing in the cupboard?' Brian says, returning to the room and seeing us there.

'Laundry,' she shouts out. 'Idiot.'

'Lottie, you can't talk to me like that,' he argues, trying to look over my body to catch her eye. I wouldn't try, Brian. With the anger steaming off her, she'd turn you to stone. 'Why have you blocked my number?'

She shows me a chicken bone that she pretends to stab into mid-air. I put my body in the way so Brian can't see it.

'I'll do what I like. I'm allowed to be selfish in this very moment – I must have learnt that from you.'

My bold and fearless Lottie. It was the only way I ever wanted her to be, but this courage is all so barbed, so hurtful and that's less good. I put a finger to my mouth, urging her to stop.

'Why are you being like this?' Brian pleads.

'No idea.' She's brave but by god, she's sarcastic, too. It's the best weapon in her arsenal.

He tries to enter the cupboard. She throws a bottle of Febreze at him. Brian should be grateful it wasn't the iron. He stops for a moment, and I look up at him. You know why she's being like this. You've known this girl all her life. She needs time, she needs space, she needs to trust you again because no one in this room does at this very moment.

'Look, the tickets are booked for Manchester, and I'd really like for us to go together. It'd be good to get away. I... Please, Lottie...' he whispers.

I see her on the verge of screaming a hell of a lot of expletives, but she stops to see tears welling up in my eyes.

'Dyl, talk to her. Please, mate. Look, I'll go,' he says, hands to the air, admitting defeat.

Dylan doesn't reply. He just sits there, and I hear Brian's footsteps leave the kitchen and the front door softly shut. I notice Dylan walk over to the sink with his father's half-drunk cup of tea. He throws it down the sink, puts the cup in the dishwasher and returns to his seat.

'Can we leave the utility room now? Maybe... Please...?' I ask Lottie and pull her up to her feet, putting an arm around her as we walk back into the kitchen, and sandwich Dylan into a reluctant hug, trying to gloss over that awkward interruption.

'I don't want to go to Manchester, he can seriously stick Manchester up his backside,' Lottie exclaims.

'He's a massive arsehole but I'm not sure an entire city can fit up there,' Dylan mutters and we all laugh. It's his first and only words on the matter but at least they were funny. They both cling on to me so tightly and I'm not sure I've felt a hug this tight since they were tiny and it was thundery outside, a time when they used to cling to the very bones of me.

'Remind me what the tickets were for again?' I ask them both.

'The 1975.' It was a Christmas gift he'd given them way back when he was still the hero in both their lives, a trip they planned together to include shopping and dragging Lottie around a football stadium tour.

'But we won't go now, Mum. It's not right.'

'Why not?' I ask them, parting the hug.

'Because he's a twat and it wouldn't be fair to you,' Lottie tells me.

And I exhale loudly because as much as I love their allegiance, I would be a terrible parent to punish Brian in this way, to get in the way and affect his relationship with his own kids.

'Or maybe, you go. Try and have a nice time. You love The 1975.'

'We love you, too,' Lottie says. 'Possibly even more.'

I shake my head, laughing at her.

'He did a shit thing, kids, but he's still your dad.'

'We're only bound by genetics. I can make choices if I want to see him or not. I saw a TikTok about toxic parents,' Lottie mumbles. 'He made a choice. He doesn't want us. He doesn't want this...'

'Lottie,' I say, pushing her curls away from her face. 'He just doesn't want me.' The words escape out of my mouth so very quietly. He stopped loving me, not you. The emotion would hit me at that moment, but it's interrupted by Dylan clawing his arms around me, squeezing me so very hard. This is when the emotion kicks in. To have my big gangly son envelop me like this and tell me his love still perseveres, that he still wants this, he still needs me. The tears well up in my eyes. Thank everything for the both of you.

'Hate him,' Lottie says, pushing us away.

'We don't use the word hate,' I tell her.

'Then I am not keen on him,' she retorts, echoing a time when she was little and I said she wasn't allowed to hate broccoli. She spies my phone on the counter and picks it up, starting to scroll through it. I close my eyes slowly.

'Lottie, you're not posting passive aggressive memes on my Facebook again, are you?' I ask, panicked. She did this in the summer. I had to delete a lot of things.

'Chill your boots, Mother. I am just doing...'

Her fingers move mercurially over the screen until I hear a familiar sound which lets me know she's connected the phone to the speaker in the kitchen. And then a song starts blasting through, one I only know because I spend a lot of time scrolling through my Instagram Reels at night trying to sleep. Lottie pulls me to my feet.

'Come on. We're dancing this shit out.'

'Don't swear,' I snap.

She ignores me. 'Dance. You too, Dyl.'

Dylan rises to his feet. We used to do this a lot, the four of us. Some kitchen dance break around bubbling pots, the windows all steamed up, chopping boards full of half-peeled carrots. It's like she's doing this to prove we can still do this as a trio.

'And it's better now,' she says, throwing her arms around in wild abandon. 'Dad can't tell me my music is unlistenable noise and try to make us listen to Oasis.'

Brian did do that. You can't dance to Oasis. He wasn't a graceful dancer in any case. It was like dancing with a turkey who had limbs. Dylan joins in reluctantly, the dancing more restrained, but he looks at me the whole time, waiting, hoping this might help. It does. I sway and pump to whatever this viral pop track is about being back on seventy-four. Whatever happens next, we keep dancing. I feel Lottie's arms around me in a strange hugging sway when suddenly my phone pings on the counter, breaking the music for a few seconds.

We look down as a message appears from The Anti-Wanker.

'Who the hell is The Anti-Wanker?' Lottie says. I smile, too shocked by his name coming up to even try to hide the message from them. 'And why is he sending you a chicken emoji?'

Jack

She's not replied to the emoji. I may not have thought that one through. I'm not even drunk. I just went home with half a chicken in a bag, and wanted to end the evening on a nice succinct message that would make her smile. I wanted her to know that I enjoyed her company. I should have just said that. Emojis are immature and lack a certain eloquence. She'll think I'm an idiot.

I sit here at my kitchen table staring at my phone, willing her to reply at least, but nothing. Damn. My phone starts ringing, and I jump a little at the interruption. I look down at the name of the caller. We're safe. I click to accept the Facetime.

'UNCLE JACK!' shriek two faces into the screen and I laugh at the sight of the very snotty insides of my nephews' nostrils.

'George, Barney. To what do I owe the pleasure?'

'We're shopping with Dad and we're bored,' they tell me. To prove this point, they show me around the supermarket, going up close to a lovely row of tinned vegetables, just in case I'd never seen sweetcorn like that.

'But you're helping your dad, yes?' I ask them. George makes for quite an erratic cameraman – there's quite a fair bit of heavy breathing and shots of the floor. I am so glad to be witness to this, especially when they zoom in on my brother's arse hunched over a trolley, examining a very scrappy list.

'Daaa—ddd.'

My brother turns around. 'What the... are you filming me? You didn't record my fart, did you?' I see Barney keeling over with laughter as my brother, Dom, grabs the phone and suddenly sees my face. 'Bloody hell... Boys!' I hear them howling and running off down the aisle. 'STAY CLOSE!'

He returns his attention to me. It's a Dom face I know well, one that looks like he's trying really hard to work out a tricky sum.

'Well, I didn't hear a fart.'

He laughs, rubbing a hand across his stubble, his brown hair slightly frizzy at the edges. 'They're out of chopped tomatoes. I can just chuck in passata to a bolognese, yes?'

'Yes, you can.'

I smile. Back when the twins were very little and owing to quite sad circumstances, I lived with Dom for a bit. We had no effing idea what we were doing but we thought as long as we knew how to cook a decent bolognese sauce then we'd survive. I swear they now eat it at least once a week. He refers back to his list, chucking things into his trolley. The way he holds his phone, I'm getting a wonderful view of the supermarket ceiling and as before, the insides of his nostrils. 'How are you? Sorry about the boys. Were you in the middle of something?'

'Nothing. Just got in from school actually.'

'Oh god, yes. First day. How was it?'

'Interesting. You good? The boys back today?'

'No. I have two more days for my sins... Boys, why on earth

do we need that much Weetabix? Are we feeding another family?' I see him wave his arms around, not quite telling his twins off but standing there in disbelief.

'It's all fibre, Dom.'

'Yeah, Dom,' Barney says playfully, and I laugh.

'Jack, I have to deal with these two hooligans.'

'Hooligans?' I hear a ten-year-old voice protest.

'Text me the highlights of today. Come round for tea,' he tells me hurriedly. I salute him and hang up. Highlights? Well, there was chicken. I open up my messages to see if Zoe has replied. Still nothing. Double damn.

'Mr Damon, good evening to you...' The back door to the kitchen opens, the lights flash on and in steps Frank, one of my housemates, carrying a strange selection of Tupperware. Frank works in town, in IT, which means we have excellent Wi-Fi connection, and I think the printer we own as a household may be stolen. Frank only left home a year ago and his mother still worries about him, so he often appears with a week's worth of meals that she has prepared for him, so he won't waste away. Her legendary over-catering means that we all share in these gifts, and I tell you, the lady can do extraordinary things with rice. Frank likes a sensible coat and haircut, and knows the maths to split bills in the right way.

'Francisco. I see your Ma has been busy?'

'Indeed, she made that glutinous rice for you again,' he says, unloading the boxes onto the table and into the freezer. They're all labelled immaculately. 'She also thanks you for soaking her Tupperware.'

'Well, I'm glad my skills have been noticed.'

'I hate that she likes you. Possibly more than me.'

'Not hard, mate,' I joke but his mum bought me an expensive bottle of Johnnie Walker for my birthday, and I know for a fact that she only gave her son socks. It was like some sort of dowry for taking in her son.

Frank pulls up a chair at our very wonky kitchen table, the legs made even with coasters and old flyers. This is the style of our kitchen – everything has been fixed and made liveable through gaffer tape and our very mediocre DIY skills. Every night we say a prayer for the fridge that was last checked electrically in 2015. Frank doesn't tell his mother this.

'Why were you sitting in the dark?' Frank asks me, leaning back and grabbing a fork from one of our drawers.

'Oh, I was contemplating something.'

'Is it the teaching? How did your first day go? I told you the kids would be wild and unforgiving,' he says. He did tell me that. I sometimes go to the corner shop with Frank and if groups of kids walk in, he always looks terrified and dodges them in the aisles, hiding behind the beer fridges.

'Not that. Still finding my feet. I think the kids like me, but I also think they like the fact that I'm a sub.'

To be honest, I hadn't really thought too much about the teaching. I'd taught English before in Italy on what was meant to be a sun-kissed, post-uni trip where I imagined myself staying in a villa and riding my bike around long stretches of sandy roads with a linen shirt half undone. I never fulfilled that fantasy. Instead, I got stuck in a two-bed flat in Naples with a landlord called Mario who was an actual plumber, I shit you not. In comparison, the students I had back then were also a bit more willing to learn. Two of the classes I stood in front of today looked like they'd rather be anywhere else. There were a lot of paper airplanes, people secretly playing Candy Crush and one girl who stood up and started to French braid her mate's hair.

'We were horrific to the subs,' Frank tells me. 'We locked one in a stationery cupboard once and the rumour was it started the onset of her alopecia. I've always felt awful about that,' he adds, wistfully.

'Not you, Frank,' I say in shock.

'I was a bad boy once upon a time,' he jokes. He looks at me carefully. 'Normally by this point, you've started to help your-self to my food – I thought you liked my mum's noodles?'

'I've eaten. I had a Nando's.'

'Like a welcome meal?' he asks.

'Sort of...' Maybe that's all it was. Just two people eating chicken, me acting as some sort of dining companion and her welcoming a new colleague into the fold. I shouldn't read too much into things. Like when we said goodbye and she reached out and touched my arm. That was her just being nice; she does that. It's just an arm. It was just chicken. With a really nice, attractive person who gets my jokes.

Frank puts on the kettle and scrambles around looking for a clean teaspoon. In the meantime, the back door opens again to reveal our third housemate, the one who completes the holy trifecta in this house. 'Gentlemen! I have returned.' Ben and I used to work in Zara together back when he was balancing out being a TV extra. He now works in television production with a sister who's a low-level celebrity chef, so he keeps us stocked in cookbooks and regales us in stories of the Z-list celebrities he's encountered. He inhales deeply. 'Frank, did your mum fry us spring rolls?'

'Yes, she did,' Frank says, pushing a Tupperware in his direction.

Ben takes off his scarf and sits down. 'I love your mum. Can I marry your mum?'

Frank furrows his brow. 'But you're gay.' Frank is like this, very black and white, not a lot of lived experience. I think this is why Ben and I took him under our wing. Ben's always loved that he has the same old man name as his dad. A boy like that needs saving from his naivety.

Ben laughs. 'I'm still gay, my friend. I was just being face-tious, but I have great admiration for the woman in any case. Does she really deep fry them, just for us?' he asks. 'Does she do television? I think the public would love her.'

Frank shakes her head. 'I think she air fries them now. And no, please do not put her on television. She'd be a liability, she has no method.'

'The best sort of cook then,' Ben replies. 'So how are we? How was the first day of school?' he asks me, putting a hand to my shoulder and shaking it around. 'Were the kids nice to you?' Ben is also house mother – he likes to check in on us and make sure we're well, and this genuine concern for my wellbeing is probably the reason why we're still in each other's lives. He sits down as Frank gets another mug out for him to make a second cup of tea.

'His colleagues took him for a Nando's after work,' Frank adds.

I take one of his mother's spring rolls. They are undeniably crisp; she could win awards for these. I go over to the counter with half of my Nando's chicken as an offering to this little feast.

'Were they lady colleagues?' Ben asks, knowing there was a time many moons ago when I slept with two people we worked with at Zara and had to move branches. I nod. Frank looks supremely confused that I seem to have moved so quickly on my first day. 'Already? That will get you a reputation.' Despite the lecture, he puts his hands under his chin to take in the gossip.

'One colleague. Her name was Zoe, she works at the school.' I smile a little too widely to say her name, playing back all our little conversations today, remembering the way her eyes changed shape as she laughed.

Ben rewinds his mind. 'Hold up. Zoe, the one from the wedding with the cheating husband. No actual way!'

That's the thing about Ben – he remembers everything. It's why he's on bin duty in this house. Frank places a cup of tea in front of him and offers him more of his mother's food.

I nod. 'The very one.'

I told Frank and Ben this story. It must have been when I

came back from the wedding. I was slightly drunk, and I think they were knee deep in a binge watch of *Bridgerton*. They both eat a bit more slowly as they take in the next instalment of drama. 'Did she dump the husband? What happened? I hate the man and I don't even know him. Does he have a name?'

'Brian. And no. I think he left her so she's just in the aftermath. Trying to work out what to do next.'

'And are you what she's going to do next?' Frank asks innocently.

My jaw slackens. Ben chokes on some noodles, laughing. 'Francis! You made a joke! But yeah...' he says, turning to me. 'Are you?'

'I don't know. I think after tonight, there's something... Possibly a spark, but I can't quite read it.' As I say the words out loud, I realise there's some feeling for her emerging, possibly a desire to act on it – but is that wise?

Ben picks up his phone. 'Shit name, Brian,' Ben says. 'Can we stalk him on social media and make his life hell? I can send him dozens of private messages pretending to be from Only-Fans and jeopardise his new relationship.' I like Ben's willingness to invest such hatred in someone he's never met.

'Or not.'

He spies me glancing down at my phone. 'What are you waiting for?'

'What do you mean?' I reply, innocently.

'I know that look when you're waiting for a text, to see if someone's going to reply.'

'I am just conscious of the time. I need my beauty sleep. My hours are different these days.'

Ben narrows his eyes at me. 'What's her last name? This Zoe?'

'Zoe Swift,' I reply, a little too quickly.

He moves his fingers with mercurial speed over his keypad. 'Found her...'

'You have?' Even though we've only just met, even I haven't done the social media stalk yet. Frank and I peer over Ben's shoulders. The Facebook profile is very private which is a given when you're a teacher, but I like the profile picture, some golden hour shot that hits her face with all the right light. We look through the limited photos she has chosen to share plus a few posts that pop up telling me she's donated money to a dog's home and someone who ran a 5K in aid of a local hospice. I knew she was kind to her very core.

'She's very attractive,' Frank says plainly.

'Right?' I say, relieved that it's not just me.

'No, Frank has a point. I'm getting a Rachel McAdams vibe. I like the hair,' Ben says.

'And Rachel McAdams is like, what... thirty?' I say.

Ben shakes his head. 'How old is Rachel McAdams?' he asks Siri on his phone. We all arch our heads over his screen. 'She's forty-four. And quite frankly, it's criminal how as an actress she has been overlooked when Ryan Gosling did so well out of *The Notebook*. How old is Zoe?'

'Forty-three. She's forty-four in March,' I say again, a little too quickly.

'Older can be good. Some of the best sex I've had has been with older lovers. They know what they want, they have less hang-ups,' Ben mentions. Frank keeps quiet. The difference between my two roommates is that I suspect Ben has played the field whereas Frank stands by the gate of that field quite content, not really knowing how to play at all.

'You make her out to be some sort of cougar style MILF,' I say, conscious I'm defending her honour. 'She's just a nice soul and maybe someone who doesn't realise that about herself.'

Ben smiles. 'There's a story here on her profile. It's public. Do you want to see it?'

'Will she know I've seen it?' I ask tentatively. 'I don't want to look weird.'

'It's my phone, I'll just look like some random person who's come across her profile.'

I nod, not really sure if I should be delving into her life like this. But the video that comes up makes me smile. It's her half dancing to Jungle in her kitchen with two teenagers that I will assume to be her children. Her hair flies about and it's obvious she doesn't know she's being filmed. It reminds me of the woman I met at that wedding. *Three is the Magic Number*, says the text over the video.

'Those are some old kids, though. When you said she had kids, I assumed they were smaller. The boy there has more facial hair than Frank,' Ben says, studying the video. Frank strokes his upper lip subconsciously.

'They're thirteen and fifteen,' I add. I like how they look after their mum in the video, how they sing along completely out of tune and get their mother to join in. Those look like two kids who adore her completely.

'So Brian really is a shit then. Can I put that as a comment?' Ben asks.

'No, you can't,' I say, trying to downplay my horror at the thought.

Ben looks over at me, holding on to a spring roll in his hand. 'You're staring at your phone a lot. Did you send the older lady a picture of your...' He fiddles with the spring roll in his hands. Frank seems distraught at the comparison given his mother must have rolled that with her fair hand.

'No, I did not.'

'Then our boy is crushing,' he says out the corner of his mouth. Ben would know. He's known me long enough that when I meet someone I like, I procrastinate. I try to reason whether it's a good idea and, in this case, the cons list is incredibly lengthy. But sometimes it's hard to ignore a spark. Sometimes there's a person who shines so brightly in the corner of your eye that your attention keeps moving towards them.

'I am not crushing, leave me alone,' I reply, flaring my nostrils.

'Never,' Ben says, pouting his lips into a kiss. And his eyes still follow me as I look down at Ben's phone, Zoe's video still playing on a loop. I can't help but smile as I see her dancing.

FIVE

Zoe

'Wait, did he send you the chicken drumstick emoji or the real chicken?' Mia asks me, messily eating a sandwich and stealing her husband's crisps on the staff room sofas. Behind her sounds the familiar ping of the microwave, the boiling of kettles and the whispers of conversations as our colleagues recount the horrors of their mornings. This is how we endure the teaching profession – we share and relate whilst we heat up last night's leftovers, trying to find some humour in everything. I hear about how in physics, a child tried to escape out of a second-floor window. How in French, a child tied someone's shoelaces to a table and they're now in medical with a fat lip.

'The real chicken,' I tell Mia.

'So, basically he sent you a cock.'

I widen my eyes. I mean, Lottie had questions, too, but then we also got into a semi-argument because it turns out that when I was dancing like a bloody loon around our kitchen, trying to copy some viral dance routine, she was filming the whole thing and putting it on social media with public privacy settings and it was watched. Not only by my friends but from the looks of it, random strangers called Ben that I don't even know.

'Also, rewind there. You both went on to Nando's? Like on a date? How did I not know about this?'

I shrug. 'It was a week ago. We've all been busy,' I explain.

Ed's eyes widen at this point. 'Jack's literally just started. Did you have relations with him?' Mia clings on to Ed's arm in response to his politeness.

'Oh god, no... He was just good company. It was nice. He's nice...'

They both sit back on the sofa opposite me with curious looks, still chewing their lunch. Mia narrows her eyes. 'Ed, I don't know your mate well enough. Is he nice?'

'The implication there being that I would be mates with a complete idiot,' Ed replies. 'He's a good person.'

'What was he like at university? Did he get about?' Mia asks him.

'He once shagged a girl in our kitchen. I had to disinfect the whole kitchen, even the countertops,' Ed recalls casually. I choke a little on my cheese sandwich, surprised that he's decided to lead with this particular memory. 'I mean, I wish he hadn't. I prepared food on those countertops. I rolled dough, I had raw meat on there...'

'Quite,' Mia replies.

Ed blushes at the innuendo which, knowing Ed, was not intentional at all, but which makes Mia snort with laughter. She nudges her husband playfully.

'Was he dating this girl?' I ask.

'Oh no, he never really did girlfriends. He's a bit of a...'

'Jack-the-Lad?' Mia says, finishing his sentence.

'Not even that. Girls like him. He's got that thing all the kids talk about... rizz?'

Mia squeezes his arm, impressed that he's expanding his lingo. I think I may know what Ed's talking about, though. I feel

I've seen the rizz in full flow. It's certainly made me a little giggly in ways I shouldn't be.

'He's personable. Never cruel, not the sort to not call someone back. He was always very kind. He once made the local paper at university because he saved a bag of kittens that he found in a skip.'

Mia cocks her head to one side, doe-eyed.

'Yeah, except he brought them back to our student house and they were absolutely feral. This is why Jack has a scar above his eyebrow, because one of them attacked his face. I remember the night it happened – it literally jumped out of a houseplant like a very small tiger.' Ed turns his hands into claws, mimicking said cat.

I notice Mia studying everything he's saying, and I appreciate the concern she's showing in trying to weigh up Jack's character, almost as if she's checking he's good enough to be taking someone like me to Nando's. 'So, what we're saying is that he's a nice enough bloke, likes cats, possibly slightly commitment-phobic, some sexual experience under his belt,' Mia concludes.

'Pretty much. He likes his music, we used to like a fry-up on a Saturday morning, and he'd drag me around vinyl shops...'

Mia nods in approval.

'Oooh... And if you wanted to know the person responsible for me wearing better fit jeans, then this is the man. Before I met Jack, I used to buy my jeans from supermarkets.'

Mia gives Ed a look. 'I must remember to shake his hand next time I see him then. What about the job thing? Why all the career changes? Is the work ethic poor? Does he have issues with punctuality?' she continues. I appreciate this deep dive into his personality on my behalf.

'Oh, that's all because of his brother...'

Mia and I sit there waiting for him to expand on his answer.

'Ed, I've met this man a few times and you've not

mentioned this. What about his brother?' she says, turning to him, worried.

'I told you he had a brother. His name is Dom. Anyway, when we graduated, we all had plans, but Dom's wife passed away from cancer. She was super young, like in her mid-twenties, and he was suddenly alone with two young kids, so Uncle Jack moved in and helped him find his feet.'

I put a hand to my chest, sitting back on the sofa to hear it. Behind all that boyish charm is someone with real heart, with a warming back story that runs deep. I can't help but be moved by it all. Mia grabs a throw cushion and slaps her husband with it. 'Ed! You did not tell me that!'

'I didn't?' he replies. Mia looks incredulous. 'He did that for about three years. Moved in, did part-time jobs to help look after them and then after that never really found his stride.'

I sigh, understanding where all Jack's mature empathy comes from. It comes from a good sincere place.

'So, in essence, a decent human but a little lost?' Mia summarises. She smiles at me when she says that. It's sweet of her to think I'm in a similar situation. I'm not lost. I've been bloody deserted, marooned, stranded.

'So... circling back to Zoe,' she continues, trying to lighten the mood again. 'Was his subconscious talking when he sent her the chicken emoji?'

Ed shakes his head from side to side. 'It could have been pure coincidence. He could have sent her the chicken drumstick instead.'

'Which would have also meant he wanted to bone her...' Mia replies, which makes Ed laugh.

'I really do not think Jack wants to bone me,' I mumble, almost unable to repeat that sentence out loud. It feels like a ludicrous notion.

'Who doesn't want to bone who? What have I missed?' a voice says, coming over to take in the gossip. It's Beth who I haven't seen in an age. Such are the first weeks of school, filled with departmental meetings and time spent locked in the copy room trying to remember how to copy things on both sides of the paper. I give her a hug as she comes and sits next to us on the big staff room sofas, offering her canteen chips around.

'The new teacher, Jack, went for a Nando's with Zoe and then he sent her a chicken emoji.'

'Zoe!' Beth shrieks. 'You're dating? Already?'

I raise my hands to the air to halt all the gossip in full flow. Beth was one of the first people who found out about the split from Brian as I knew her sister had gone through similar, so I asked her for advice. She's been a pillar of wonderfulness ever since. She sends texts to check in, sends me books on Amazon and occasionally just leaves Kit Kats in my staff pigeonhole. These are the small things that have helped tremendously.

'Nooo, it's nothing like that,' I say, though the truth is I'm still trying to work out what it is. It's not like I haven't thought about Jack since the cock emoji, it's just not because of the cock. There is something about the distraction and attention I've received from him that feels like a tonic, that makes me not think about the disaster zone that is my life. That said, the flirtation behind it makes me deeply embarrassed. I don't know how to flirt, I've not flirted in years and not with someone who looks like that. 'I am so far away from dating, like miles away, but I was just confused by the emoji, so confused that whenever I see him around school, I've taken to hiding behind doors and pillars. Seriously, I thought the aubergine was the penis emoji.'

'Aubergine, baguette, lipstick, cactus, snake, mushroom, rocket, chicken, banana...' Beth reels off. We all stare at her. Mia offers her hand up for a high-five. 'I went to the student cyber safety seminar last month, I took notes. So I'm confused. Jack sent you a sex emoji and you're not sure about him. Is he a dick? Ed, is your friend a dick?' she asks him forthrightly.

'He's a very nice person. I've known him for a while,' Ed says, defending him. 'Is it an age thing?' he asks me plainly.

Mia elbows him sharply in the ribs. 'Rudeness. Zoe's in her early forties. She's in her prime. One of the best racks in the staff room,' she says, almost as if she's seen my bare breasts and can pass comment. I blush. They only look decent because I wear a bra, Mia. 'I wouldn't blame Jack for fancying you. I fancy you,' she says, blowing me a kiss.

Beth looks supremely confused. 'Oh. So we're saying Jack may fancy you? I mean... of course... but you don't want to go there?'

I try to ensure my intense confusion doesn't show in my face. 'God, no. I don't think I'm ready for... that... him... all of it...'

Beth smiles warmly at my confusion. 'Or... you know? He's young, you're freshly single. Maybe you just have a rebound fling to do some healing? Apologies, Ed. I am sure your friend has feelings and I'm not saying use him, but if he's flirting, flirt back a little? Have some fun, Zoe. You deserve that more than anyone I know.'

I laugh under my breath at the idea that this is even an option. This whole conversation has got out of hand. I just wanted to check in on emoji meanings. From the sounds of it, this man likes to shag on kitchen counters, and I don't think mine are stable enough for such action. 'You are all hilarious, but I will find my fun elsewhere, thank you.'

'Like another teacher?' Mia says. 'I hear Vivaan from Chemistry is on Tinder.'

'He also wears a bum bag, Mia,' I tell her.

'Handy for condoms and such,' she retorts, and we all sit there giggling. Even Ed. This is all I need for now. This is fun. This sort of conversation that's removed from all of my sadness, from my crapbag ex-husband, that means I laugh, loudly, in a way I didn't think possible.

'Look, I don't think Jack and I are a feasible option. It's just he was also there when it all happened, when I first found out about Brian, so it's been nice to know he's an ally.'

All three of them sit there squinting their eyes, like they're trying to work out this very complicated plot twist.

'He was there? How?' Beth asks.

'At the wedding. I got a call from Lottie during the reception and it all unravelled and he just happened to be there and called me an Uber and made sure I got home safely.'

Mia and Ed look absolutely devastated. 'You found out your marriage was over at our wedding?' Mia asks me.

I nod, suddenly sad that I've divulged that news to them. However, before she has the chance to dig further for information, we suddenly hear a lot of shouting from the corridor beyond the staff room doors. Everyone in the room freezes, wondering who might take this on. I mean, we all have sandwiches to eat. Ed and Mia look to each other, then rise to their feet, swinging the doors open to see a group of boys running in one direction.

'OI!' Mia screams after them. The boys don't stop. They exit the staff room and Beth and I look at each other. She looks down at her well-earned chips and I notice the way her body sinks into the sofa.

'I'll rock, paper, scissors you for it,' she says, but I get up. 'This one's on me,' I say, stealing one of her chips. I head out the doors watching as Mia and Ed try to cut off a group of boys at the top of the corridor. I would put a fiver on who at least three of those boys are, such is the joy of this school. To be fair, the majority of the kids are great. They keep their heads down, they know the value and privilege of education. It's a small sliver of dicks who spoil it for everyone else. The one thing I've learnt, though: don't waste your energy running after them. I descend a staircase trying to listen out for voices and footsteps. The boys' toilets. They like to assemble in there. They like to vape in there which is why we had to have a fire drill last week in the rain. I head towards the door and hear voices inside. I can't go in there. Do I knock? But before I do, the door opens. Jack. He looks me in the eye, mildly surprised to see me standing there, and smiles broadly.

'Mr Damon...' I suddenly feel a bit more relaxed, but I hope his ears aren't burning. I know where you've had sex. I need to act normal. 'That's a fetching hi-vis vest you're wearing,' I say, pointing at him. Four boys filter out of the toilet and past us, mumbling 'Sir,' and 'Miss' as they escape. He salutes all of them before turning his attention back to me.

'I didn't know how much power the hi-vis gives me. I may just wear this all the time now.'

'Just a hi-vis?' That was the wrong thing to say, and an image floods my mind. That image shouldn't be there.

He smiles and raises an eyebrow. 'Well, I do believe that's not in the staff dress code, Mrs Swift. It would cause quite the stir. How are you anyway? I haven't seen you for a while. All good?'

I nod, not knowing whether to bring up the chicken emoji. 'All good. How is lunch duty? I see they've roped you in for the fun stuff.' I reach over to him and pick off what looks like a piece of lettuce from his shoulder. I shouldn't touch him, but I can't just leave that there.

'You have a warped idea of what is fun. There were salad wars, lettuce was thrown. Is there any more iceberg in my hair?' he asks. I scan along his hairline until my gaze lands on his eyes again, and a small scar above his eyebrow.

'Just a bit of frisée,' I tell him, picking something off above his ear. 'The type of lettuce, I mean – you have zero frizz in case that was a concern.' He finds that unusually funny and I feel the need to mute his response. 'I've just found out something about you actually.'

He cocks his head to the side. 'I expect that is Ed telling you university stories. Don't believe any of them.'

You had sex on a kitchen counter. We start ascending the stairs towards the staff room. 'Something about a cat. The one who gave you that scar on your eyebrow.'

'That scar was from a really tough street fight in which I stopped an old lady from being mugged.'

I raise an eyebrow at him.

'Damn Ed, ruining my street cred. It was a feral kitten I saved from a skip. His name was Sushi because he was ginger with little white paws.'

'That's kind of adorable.'

'I know,' he says, a broad grin creeping across his face, his hands adjusting his hi-vis.

'I was talking about the cat's name, not you.' He laughs loudly and I think this is what I like about Jack. It's not quite flirting, but it just flows so very well. I like the thin veil of innuendo in our conversation which entertains me even though I know it won't go anywhere. We stop in a stairwell that overlooks a playground and watch groups of kids huddled in the mid-autumn air, nibbling on sandwiches, gazing at phones, trading in banter and play fights.

Jack turns to me, looking like he might be taking a long breath. 'Anyway, while I have you here. I just want to say that if ever you need a peri-peri friend again, I quite enjoyed our chicken date last week.'

'It wasn't a date,' I say, almost reprimanding him. 'It was company. And while I have you here, I liked the chicken emoji, by the way. Keeping it classy.'

At least I've handled the chicken-sized elephant in the room. It's dealt with, we can move on. I've drawn a line under what I think about the foundations of this acquaintance.

'It's because we had Nando's – the chicken,' he replies.

'The cock,' I whisper, for some reason looking down at his

crotch in case he didn't get the message. I shouldn't have looked down.

'OH my GOD...!' he shouts and two girls at the other end of the corridor turn around. 'I just sent a very innocent chicken. You thought I was sending you a...?'

It's my turn to go bright beetroot now.

'Oh dear, it's just... I shouldn't have raised it. The cock...'

'You shouldn't have raised my cock?' he laughs.

And for some unknown reason, I push him. I cup my hands to my mouth. 'I shouldn't have pushed you. Oh, my days, stop saying cock!'

'You said it first!' he says, bent over laughing. I am lucky the corridor is clear and those two girls have moved on. 'So that's why you didn't reply?'

'I didn't know what to do with it.'

'The c—'

I put a hand up before he has the chance to say the word again and turn this into innuendo. 'I was embarrassed because I didn't know how to respond. I didn't understand what you were hinting at and, deep down, I really didn't know if perhaps this was some sort of pity flirting.'

Jack steps back for a moment in shock, his expression changing. 'Seriously? No, it's not like that at all. I think you're kind of...'

I put a hand to the air. 'Sad and damaged? I know.'

His brow stays furrowed. I mean, there is truth in that. Have Ed, Mia and to some extent Beth put you up to this? Just go and flirt with the sad old divorcee, boost her self-esteem, make her feel happy for a short moment. Because I don't really understand otherwise why you, a handsome and obviously intelligent young man would be here, talking to me, making me laugh. Why would you want to enter my sad, complicated life? Why would you want to be another complication?

'Zoe...' he says, brushing against my arm, but I back away.

He looks up at me, confused.

Why does he say my name like that? For a moment I look into his blue eyes and feel petrified at how it makes me feel.

'THIS WAY!' a teen male voice suddenly roars, and the moment is interrupted by a stampede of boys running towards us.

'Keep up, Mr and Mrs Rogers!' one of them screams, his bag hanging off his shoulders.

'BOYS!' I yell but this does not deter them.

I spy Mia and Ed not too far behind at the end of the corridor. When they reach us, Mia stops to put her hands to her knees. Ed stands next to his wife to support her.

'This is why I go running,' Ed tells her.

'I'm seriously going to yack,' she says, turning to us. 'Some help, guys. I can't even...'

And one last look and smile before Jack heads off to join in with the running.

I'm not going to run, obviously. But I really don't think I should be looking at Jack's arse as he runs away from me, should I? Who the hell am I?

Jack

'Well, Mr Damon. I'm pretty sure this is the best turnout we've ever had for homework club,' Drew, the head of maths, tells me, looking at the half-full classroom in front of me. 'Well done, everyone.'

I know Drew teaches maths so it shouldn't be hard to figure out that the room is eighty percent girls and I have a feeling that the reason half of them are here, not to toot my own horn, is to come and check out the new male teacher. For the past forty-five minutes, I've seen little homework – they've mainly been using this computer room to check their social media, look on YouTube and barrage me with questions. I have a feeling I may also have been part of a series of Snapchat fan-cams. If they have posted them, I hope they've used the right filters.

'So where do you live, Sir?' a girl asks me.

'Did you want a specific address? Maybe a whatthreewords to my front door?' I say, sarcastically. This is apparently funny. 'I live in London.'

'Boring!' the girl answers. According to the register, this girl's name is Hayley and I have no idea how she's keeping her eyes open as her upper lids are weighed down with fake lashes. As with the majority of girls in the school, her school skirt is rolled up so it resembles more of a belt and on the desk is what I thought was a pencil case. It's not. It's a make-up bag filled to the brim. I've been around women. I know how much Gucci lip oil costs. Yet even just to have those thoughts run through my mind makes me realise how I've made the leap into judgemental adulthood in just one week of being here. Because, in reality, being in this school has really rehashed many unpleasant memories of what it was to be a teen: learning how to live in new skin bubbling with acne; raging with hormones; covered in a light mist of grease and Lynx Africa. Trying to work out a style, what you like, what you don't. Being asked to choose subjects that determine the rest of your life, hoping you get things right, most of the time getting it wrong. And for once, I feel infinite amounts of empathy for all these kids. I want to shout clichéd mantras at them about 'powering through' and 'you got this' without sounding condescending, without sounding like the enemy.

'Sir... is this right? I don't know if this is right? Could you check this is correct?' a voice suddenly says.

It's a mixed bag in here today. There are the Year Elevens, here out of curiosity, but also some of the new Year Sevens who I suspect are actually here to do some homework. I head over to the front desk where this little one is sitting. Her pens are labelled, and her school jumper is possibly two sizes too big.

This is someone here to do some work and make me feel like I'm earning my overtime. I peer over at her book, the date and title underlined.

'I'm no geography expert but that looks good, like it may make sense. Hayley, do you do Geography? Maybe you could help...' I point to the keen bean, Year Seven.

'Bonnie, Sir.'

'Could you double check this...?' Instead of sitting there chatting about nails. Maybe this is how I make this crowd work for me.

Hayley moves over and Bonnie's body tenses, looking absolutely petrified. 'Yeah, that's good, Bonnie. I like your highlighters,' she says, peering over her desk.

'They smell fruity,' she says, still scared.

'Really? Can I?'

Bonnie smiles and just like that I've given Hayley a small little friend she can adopt for her last year here. I'm all about building student relationships. I hear a camera phone click and turn to see three Year Nine girls giggling. Do I pose? Do I confiscate the phones?

'It was Isla, Vee and Polly,' a boy says at the back, slightly older from the looks of it. Here to do homework by the appearance of the books out in front of him.

'SNITCH!' one of them screams.

He sticks a middle finger up at them and I try to get in between them so it doesn't break down into a full-on fight.

'Girls, I don't appreciate it. Phones away, please. Thank you for looking out for me...' I wait for him to give me his name.

'Gabe.'

'How's the homework going, Gabe?' The lad looks up at me cautiously. I can't quite figure him out. The black trainers in place of school shoes tell me there's rebel in him but the majority of rebels wouldn't give the time and care to do their homework. I look down and see it's maths. 'Who's your teacher?'

'Mrs Swift.'

I can't help but smile to hear her name but think back to that conversation I had with her earlier, during lunch break. It was sad to hear all that self-deprecation, to hear her feel like any attention I'd given her was forced or born out of pity. I'd text her to tell her differently, but I know she's scared of my texts now. That'll teach me to text in emojis.

'What do you think of Mrs Swift?'

'Best teacher in this dump,' Gabe answers without hesitation.

'Mate, I'm literally stood right here in front of you,' I joke.

This makes Gabe crack a smile and he sits up, shoulders back, leaning back in his chair to look me up and down. 'Well, I don't know you, do I?'

'You may be right, though. I've met Mrs Swift, she seems nice.'

'She's not up her own arse, you know what I mean? She wants us to do well. She gets to know us. I respect that.'

I nod, wishing Zoe was here to listen to this appraisal. 'Well, keep it up. I'll tell her you were singing her praises.'

'Just don't make me look like a suck up, yeah?'

I laugh. 'I'll try.' I look up at the clock. 4pm. My hour of goodwill but decent overtime pay is done. 'Well, everyone, our time is up here. If you are planning on coming again when I'm hosting, I beg you to actually do homework. You can do Snapchat and attend to your make-up needs at home.' The girls roll their eyes at me, but I hear the scrape of chairs as they all gather their giant puffa coats and bags and head for the door. 'Have a good evening, everyone.'

'You too, Sir.'

'Bye, Sir.'

'Love you, Sir.'

I don't know who said the third one, but it wasn't Gabe. Does it feel nice to have amassed a small fan club in my short time here? Yes, but it's also petrifying as I've just done my safeguarding courses. I'll have to go home and look at my online presence. I went on Tinder once. I need to check I'm not there anymore. I also should possibly delete any incriminating photos from drunken lads' holidays in my late teens in Ibiza. I go around the room picking remnants of pens and bits of torn-up paper off the floor to see Gabe still lingering at the back of the room.

'You alright, Gabe?' I say. He helps me rearrange some chairs, studying me closely.

'So, are you like a real teacher?' he asks me.

'Well, not really. I'm just cover. I went to university with Mr Rogers in biology. That's how I heard about this job.'

'He's a g.'

'He is.'

And then a moment. It feels like he wants to tell me something, but he can't. It's possibly because we've just met and he barely knows me, but experience tells me that sometimes it's easier to share secrets with people you hardly know.

'You good, Gabe? How you getting home?'

He lugs a sports bag alongside his school rucksack. 'Got to get the bus to football, innit?'

This might be my in. 'Where do you play?'

'Club or position?'

'Both.'

'Hampton and Richmond for their academy. I'm a centre back.'

'I thought you had a Van Dijk quality to you...'

I see this boy relaxing as he laughs, snapping his fingers at me. 'Wash your mouth out, man. You're in London. The quality is all Reece James.'

I shake my head. 'Well, now you've let me know you're a Chelsea fan and I am frankly disappointed.'

He smirks at me. 'And who do you support, Sir?'

'Brentford.'

And he laughs. Hard. 'You poor thing. Night, Sir. I'll say a prayer for you.'

I laugh, saluting him, and ensuring I've left the room in good order before gathering my coat and bag and turning off the lights. Did I bond with him, or did I possibly shame myself in front of a fifteen-year-old? Who knows? As I head down the corridor, the place almost feels ghostly; the animated bones of this school, usually full of life, are still and quiet, almost calm. I go down the stairwell and notice one classroom where something seems to be happening. I head down there to have a nose. It's not as busy a classroom as mine was, a group of maybe ten students sat there, but I flinch to see the teacher in charge of them all. Zoe. I haven't seen her since lunch and I'm not sure how to continue that conversation. There are definitely things to say, though. I stand at the doorway until she notices me. As she does, her expression changes.

'Mr Damon, anything we can do for you?' she says, as her students start to pack away their things. I can't read that face. Is she angry with me? She seems a bit more serious than usual. She probably thinks I've come to hassle her. I've possibly pushed things too far. At the end of the day, she's a woman who's in relationship turmoil and I've maybe been too flirty, too full-on. Though, hand on heart, I really did think I was sending her a chicken.

'Oh, I was just in homework club, and I noticed a light on. Hello, Mrs Swift,' I say, putting a hand up to acknowledge the children in the room. I lean against the doorframe, satchel hanging by my side.

'Were you looking to join STEM club, too, Sir?' asks a boy at the front.

'Is there space?' I joke.

This seems to soften Zoe's expression. 'There is, but unfortunately you've joined us a little too late. We were just about to pack up. Guys, you were awesome – please remember to sign up to our STEM trip to Winchester in November. Letters went out today. There's a Rubik's Cube competition involved.' I'm not sure why because I can't do a Rubik's cube, but I put my hands up in the air to show that I think that's truly exciting. Zoe and all the children look at me curiously. 'I will see you next week. Please can you put all the equipment away before you go, and have a really lovely evening.'

This wasn't like my homework crowd. This is a lovely younger attentive group who do as they're told. Not a phone or giggle in sight. They all gather their things.

'Didn't I have you for Tech today?' asks one boy as he comes to the door. Possibly but they've put many kids in front of me this week and I couldn't recognise half of them in a line-up. They all have the same haircuts, bags and they're all either called variations of Jayden, Emily or Harry. 'Yes, you did very well.'

'Was he a good teacher?' pipes in Zoe.

Please don't tell her I couldn't control the boys in the back who didn't do any work and it took me five minutes to make the PowerPoint work.

'He was alright,' he says, fist bumping me before running off. I will take that as validation.

I see Zoe laughing to herself as the rest of the kids politely take their leave. I stand there, hovering by the door as she gathers worksheets and puts things away.

'You're still here, Mr Damon,' she says as I dare to step into her classroom. I may as well make myself useful. I head over, handing her some pens and mini whiteboards. There's something warm and lived in about her classroom. I like how she covers the pockmarked walls with pictures of isosceles triangles and maths words like OBTUSE. I paw over some handwritten thank you notes on her noticeboard from past students, ones who write long notes and draw lots of hearts and kisses.

'I don't mind helping you tidy up. So, this is STEM club?'

'It is. Seriously, if you wanted to sign up, there is space. There is always space,' she laughs. She blows her hair out of her face and reaches up to her forehead to find her glasses. 'Those two boys sat at the back. One of them can't speak a word of English. He has no clue what I'm saying and just claps a lot. The other I think just sits here waiting on a lift. Talented doodler, though.'

'It's a nice extracurricular club to have. You could have someone in here who ends up working for NASA as an engineer and it'll all be because of your STEM club.' She chuckles heartily at this, shaking her head. 'They all seem to like you anyway. There was a boy in homework club who was very complimentary about you, by the way.'

'Name?' she asks.

'Gabe?'

She smiles. 'Well, that's a pleasant surprise then. Nice lad.' She watches as I continue to help tidy her classroom, lingering when maybe I shouldn't. 'You don't have to do that, you know.'

'I do. It's helpful. You can get achievement points for that.'

'You know teachers don't get those.'

'We don't?'

She laughs and I watch as she shakes out her curls and puts her coat on. 'Well, thank you, nevertheless. Don't let me keep you from your evening.'

I don't know whether that's code for her telling me to get lost, but I stay, my hands in my pockets, unable to go or do anything but watch her packing up. 'Let me at least walk you to your car safely?'

She stares at me hesitantly, but I get a smile. 'Christ, the school isn't that bad. But OK then.' She walks towards me and turns off the lights to the room, hiding herself in her scarf. Do I bring up the cock/chicken thing again? Do I continue that conversation or pretend it never happened? For once, it suddenly feels awkward between us and even though I barely know her, it's never been like this. We walk out of the maths block, and I hold a door open for her as we walk across the quiet empty courtyard.

'So, how are you getting on... one week in? Have the children scared you off yet?' she asks me.

'Quite the contrary, actually. I've met some lively ones, don't get me wrong, but it's quite an eye opener. We never caught up with those boys, by the way.'

'Oh, they're too smart for that,' she explains.

'Would it be bad if I told you that I was one of those boys at school?'

She laughs. 'No, I can imagine that. Did you smoke in the toilets then?'

'No, I smoked in the park, behind a bush like everyone else. Were you STEM club material then?'

She looks affronted. 'I was. I had braces and I loved maths. I was a good girl.'

'Really?' I say.

She stops before she replies, hesitant to have this descend into innuendo again. 'Feels like a lifetime ago, though. I'm at some strange juncture now where platform heels and Nirvana t-shirts are making a comeback. Hard to have your school years referred to as vintage,' she explains.

'You focus a lot on your age,' I say, almost telling her off.

'Says the person who didn't get my Nirvana joke...'

'I know who Nirvana are. Seminal grunge and why Dave Grohl is the man he is today. I'm just saying you're not that old. If we'd just met, I'd say you were in your thirties.'

'Well then, I'll take that. My moisturiser thanks you,' she replies, almost gulping to have to absorb a compliment.

'Plans this evening?' I reply.

'Same old, same old. Kids, pasta and multiple cups of tea will feature, possibly some lesson planning and replying to emails. You?'

'Nothing.'

'Oh, to be young.'

'There you go again,' I tell her, my tone changing to tease her.

She narrows her eyes and gives me a look. 'Jack, I don't think you realise you have all the youth, none of the responsibility. You could do anything you want tonight. You could go clubbing, take in a film, eat a kebab on a bench without fear or judgement.'

'So could you,' I tell her.

She scoffs at the suggestion. 'The most exciting thing I might do tonight is to buy some chocolate at the petrol station when I fill up my car. I have a very boring and sad life,' she jokes.

'You need to stop saying things like that, you know,' I retort, frowning at her. For some reason, she laughs away my attempts at telling her off.

She reaches into her bag to get her car keys. 'Well, it is the truth. Ed and Mia's wedding and my Nando's with you were kind of the highlights of my social calendar. As we head into autumn, I'll start to hibernate like a small bear. My social life will mainly be pyjamas... and before you ask, not matching sexy pyjamas.'

'Who wears matching sexy pyjamas?' I ask, trying to contain my laughter. 'I don't.'

'People. I see them in films. Kardashians. I bet none of them wear sheep print pyjama bottoms with an old hoodie and big fluffy slipper socks.'

I stop in my tracks. 'No way, I was going to wear exactly that same outfit when I got home,' I tell her cheekily.

And she laughs, punching me on the arm again like when she pushed me before, bemused that this conversation is happening. I need to tell her I don't mind doing this, to chat, to just be by her side and get to know her better.

'Are you OK, Zoe?' I ask her, still dawdling next to her as we walk across the decrepit school tennis court.

She looks over at me. There is something there. From having seen this since the very beginning, it makes me feel she isn't. I saw a light go out almost straight away when she found out the news. I look into her eyes, imploring her to tell me.

'I don't know... I feel very lost,' she tells me, her breath shuddering as she exhales.

'Understandable. Can I just say something? It was based on something you said before.'

'Shoot,' she says. We both are still mid-amble – moving from tennis court to the low-lit corners of the bike sheds and school car park.

'I just... I wanted to say... Before, you said that I was talking to you because I felt sorry for you, and I just wanted to say that's not the reason at all. I wanted to clear that up.'

'Oh...' I see a blush rise in her cheeks. 'Well, that's...' I stop by the bike sheds and get out a key, starting to unlock my bike. 'Hold up, you ride a bike to school?'

I look up at her. 'I feel judged. I can't afford a car in London plus it's very eco-friendly of me.'

'It's an honourable and fine way to travel.'

'It's a second-hand mountain bike, Zoe – it's not a horse.'

She cackles in reply. How would I park a horse here all day?

'Where's your helmet?' she enquires.

'And we're back on the helmet talk again...'

She laughs again, tipping her head back because it would

seem that's what we do. We engage in back and forth that flows so very nicely, I make her forget, we find each other funny.

I stop for a moment to watch her. 'You like a swerve, don't you?' I tell her, smiling.

'Excuse me?'

'I find when I try to say something nice, you change the subject or downplay the compliment.' It hasn't gone unnoticed. And the fact she can't see what makes her so lovely is really starting to make me ache. No one should feel that lost.

She furrows her brow for a moment. 'I guess I...'

'I just need to say something, Zoe... I talk to you because I like you.' And I don't know why but she starts laughing again. I'm not sure that was funny. Was it? It's not a joke. And a look – one we both can't quite shake. 'You make these jokes about being old and boring but you're not. The Zoe I met was charming and interesting and I didn't see an age, I saw a person who made someone she'd just met feel completely at ease. And even when you were at your most hurt, you still exuded warmth, your empathy just shines through...'

She stands there, and I am not sure how she feels or whether she wants to reciprocate but I hope she's taking it all in. I see some emotion in her expression that makes me think she hasn't felt that way about herself for a long time, something thawing.

'I apologise if that made you feel uncomfortable. That wasn't my intention, but I just wanted you to know that...'

'I... I...'

I've mucked this up. I'll probably get fired for harassment. At least thank me or tell me I'm funny. Instead, she fumbles and drops her keys. We both bend down as I help her to retrieve them and our hands meet, both of us pausing for a moment at the brief contact. As we stand up again, our security lanyards entwine themselves around each other and I reach down trying to disentangle ourselves, both of us giggling. Her hands go to mine, and I can see her eyes searching for answers until they land on me. And she reaches towards me in the dim lights next to the bike sheds, her lips meeting mine. I kiss her back, reaching inside her coat, my hands reaching around to the small of her back, pulling her in close to me.

SIX

Zoe

I stand there at the front door, knocking lightly. I don't know why lightly because it's only 5pm but I hope she's in. The door opens and Beth is there, still in her work clothes, holding a tray of fish fingers and chips in a hand with an oven glove.

'Zoe? Oh man, have you been crying? Shit, come in,' she says, panicked.

Beth lives a few streets down from me so she felt like the person I could turn to in my hour of need. Quick cup of tea, tell her what happened, find reasonable solutions, and go home to my own kids.

'I'm not intruding, am I? Is it dinner time? I don't want to spoil time with your boys,' I say, tucking my bag under my arm, looking down the hallway at her lads who are sitting at the table.

'God, no. Come in,' she says, leading me in and rushing back into the kitchen. 'Joey Joe, I said a little blob of ketchup. Like a coin.' I look down at his plate, at a large coaster-sized ketchup tsunami. Beth looks at it, too, and shakes her head.

'Well, it's all vitamins. Boys, this is Aunty Zoe – the one who works at Mummy's school. Take a seat...'

'Hi, Aunty Zoe!' Joe chirps. He pats a chair next to him, looks up at my face and hugs me. I'll take that hug, you beautiful blond little boy. I watch as Beth empties the tray of beige food onto their plates, helping herself to a fish finger in the process and offering me one. I don't say no. Maybe a fish finger is the answer, but even that sounds rude. I just sit there and look into space picturing what just happened, literally forty-five minutes ago.

Beth studies my face as she breaks up Jude's food with child-sized cutlery, giving me a moment to compose myself. She gets up, moving around the kitchen and takes a couple of wine glasses out. This is why we like Beth – this was not a time for a cup of tea. But I will also admit to liking Beth's house; it feels like a throwback to mine, toys scattered around the place, the fridge doors filled to the brim with toddler art and very small items of laundry just hanging off airers. It makes me wonder how Lottie and Dylan were ever this small.

'Is it Brian? Has he been a ding-dong again?' she asks, smelling the top of a bottle of half-drunk rose wine in the fridge, checking if it's acceptable to serve to guests.

'A what now?' I ask her, laughing. She passes me the glass and I take a large swig from it. The boys chuckle over their dinners.

'Oh, Joe got told off in school for calling someone a B-E-L-L-E-N-D, so Will and I are trialling alternative terms for stupid people.'

'Well, not Brian for a change, though he still remains the biggest ding-dong known to man.'

'Ding-dong,' Joe says, sniggering.

'I just...' I fumble for the words, wondering how to put this. 'Jack. You know Jack? From the wedding and now he's at school, and he's teaching. The one we were talking about today.'

She nods slowly.

'I K-I-S-S-E-D him. Today. Just now. By the bike sheds,' the words explode out of me, and I emit a sound that's half laugh, half shriek. I cover my mouth. I've told someone. Joe and Jude look very confused by me as does Beth, who stops for a moment not knowing whether to laugh or cry or be shocked.

'By the bike sheds?' she says, incredulous.

I'm still laughing and nod, not able to stop.

'Hon, then why are you crying? Did something else happen?' she says cautiously. 'Was he...'

I shake my head, smiling, reliving every single moment in my head, taking a huge gulp of rose to steady myself. I kissed him. I made the move. A move I hadn't made since I was at least twenty. Since first getting together with Brian all those decades ago. And the feeling was exhilarating, bizarrely strange. And I think about Jack's words. His compliments. Maybe it's because I haven't heard those words from someone of the opposite sex for an age. And those words chipped away at the core of me, some hardened core that refused to believe I was worthy of compliments anymore. You are just someone's mum, someone's teacher, someone lost in time and space who fumbles through, surviving. And so to feel seen makes my eyes well up. Unless Ed and Mia did pay him to say it, then I won't speak to them ever again.

Beth smiles, taking a sip from her wine glass. 'Are you just a bit emotional then that you've had a K-I-S-S and it's been a really long time and it was really nice?'

I nod, still a little wordless. She beams back at me. Joe offers me a chip and I don't refuse. I dip it in his puddle of ketchup. I feel like there's a jet stream of emotions running through my veins. I kissed him in the dark corner of that bike shed. I don't know whether I was supposed to do that. Maybe he was just trying to show me some sincerity. But I got caught in some emotion that I didn't think I was capable of feeling anymore. It was one of those kisses that brimmed with urgency, a feeling I got myself swept up in, the sensation of his lips pressing against mine, a hand to my back, pulling me in so our hips touched. I remove my scarf as I feel the colour rise in my cheeks.

'And did anything else happen?' Beth asks.

'God, no. Actually, I panicked. Like, we had a moment but then I remembered that there are cameras there...'

Beth giggles.

'I'm serious. Remember when all those bikes started to go missing? How will I look at Kev the caretaker ever again? I could lose my job!' I say, panicked.

'Zo, have you met the PE department? They're feral. I think they're the reason we had to steam clean the sofas in the staff room. You just had a little K-I-S-S by the bike sheds. Did you use...' She sticks her tongue out at me, and I let out a little yelp, nodding. Beth can't control her laughter and Jude giggles in return. 'And how did you leave it?'

'I panicked. I told him there were cameras and literally ran to my car... and you know I don't really run and then I sat there in my car and cried for twenty minutes before I thought to come here because if I went home to my kids then they'd want to know why I was crying, and I'd have to lie.'

Beth puts her bottom lip out. 'Oh, Zoe. Joe-Joe, give Aunty Zoe a hug again.' Joe does as he's told, and I bury my face in his hair which smells all fruity like kids' shampoo. I really shouldn't cry in front of this little one. I'll be known as Crazy Aunty Zoe. 'You cried because you're sad it happened?' Beth continues.

'Not at all. I think they were happy tears. I think it just unlocked a lot of emotion I was keeping down. Emotions about me and how I felt about myself. Maybe. I think I was also shocked. I haven't K-I-S-S-E-D anyone for a long time. I think I was still surprised I worked or that I knew what I was doing. And all that emotion I felt. It was like...' I take another long sip of wine to steady myself. It was like electricity running through me, like in all those Avengers films that Dylan has made me watch. I felt charged, full of power, a power which had previously been taken away from me and I didn't know what to do with any of it.

'I mean, the bonus is he's kind of cute, Zoe,' she says. Joe scowls at her. 'Not as cute as you, though, bub.'

Joe beams at her.

'But twenty-nine? Really?'

'And? Technically, you're both millennials so it's allowed, by law,' she says, helping herself to some more of Jude's chips. 'Can you imagine Brian's face, though, when he finds out? I'd like to be there. Could you plan it so I'm there?' she says.

I open my mouth in laughter but more so in shock. Jack is the first person I've kissed since Brian, and I hate that Brian even comes to mind in a moment like this; that he'll always be the person to which I compare everything. Technically, I'm still married. It feels almost wrong. But it would also be the best comeback to all his shithousery. Could I use Jack like that? I wouldn't want to take advantage of all the empathy and kindness he's shown me so far. Not that I would know how to take advantage of him at all, and suddenly the thought of this progressing further than a kiss makes me a little hot under the collar again.

'I can't even fathom taking this further, Beth. I haven't done this, anything like this, in an age. This is beyond my frame of know-how.' I'm not even joking. I was stood in my STEM club thinking about my evening ahead. I thought about the half a tiramisu I was looking forward to finishing in my fridge. I was thinking about picking up bread and milk on the way back home, watching *Ted Lasso*, bringing a glass of water to bed, arguing with the kids about their phone and sleep habits, not before changing into my pyjamas and watching Instagram videos on my phone of either cats falling off chairs or someone showing me three-ingredient air fryer recipes that I will marvel at and save but never recreate myself. That was me, that was my life, and it was mundane and routine, but the predictability was a comfort. Then along came Jack. Like a bloody human grenade. 'What do I do now?'

'Text him? He gave you the C-O-C-K emoji, maybe send him something? You're asking the wrong person, though. Seriously, Will and I text to tell each other to buy milk. I can ask my sister, she's very good at online flirting.'

I shake my head. Is this what people do now? Back when I first dated Brian, we sent each other suggestive messages on our NOKIA 360s but now there's a different world in front of me. It's pictures, emojis and GIF-based. I'd have to do so much, most of which would involve a heavy amount of hair removal.

'Maybe I'll just leave it for now. I'll revel in the novelty,' I tell Beth, slightly more level-headed, not trying to get too ahead of myself.

'Can I just say, though... look at how this has ignited something in you. Look how much you're smiling. That's a very good thing. You're one of the loveliest people I know so don't think you don't deserve this – just enjoy it for what it is,' she says, holding up her glass. I hold my own up and the boys join in with their plastic beakers filled with diluted squash. We all smile at each other. 'To Zoe!'

'Ohhh-eee!' Jude shrieks and we all take sips of our drinks, laughing as the front door opens.

Beth peers down the corridor. 'It's DADDY!' she cheers, the boys joining in with their hands in the air. I remember moments like that once upon a time ago and I see the boys' faces light up.

Will sees my face and waves. 'Zoe! To what do we owe the pleasure?'

'Oh, I just thought I'd pop in for chips and squash,' I say as he comes into the kitchen, kissing the top of his wife's head and high-fiving his boys.

'And what's new?' he asks.

Beth and I look at each other knowingly. I don't know how to explain any of this.

'She kissed someone called Jack by the bike sheds and he sent her a picture of his ding-dong,' little five-year-old Joe repeats plainly. It would seem he does, though.

Jack

Let's get this straight. She kissed me. I didn't overstep. I was sincere about how I felt. I saw someone who was so hard on herself, whose self-esteem was in the absolute gutter, and I wanted to lift her up, make her feel worthy and believe those things about herself. But then there was a kiss, and it was the sum of those small physical moments of our hands touching, looks, proximity, and it had enough spark to have burnt those bike sheds down to the ground.

And I didn't quite know what to do. So now, I stand here in front of the door of this flat and knock loudly over the music. I hope they're not having a party in there because I, for one, will be upset that I haven't been invited. The door opens and Ed is there in tracksuit bottoms, looking slightly annoyed that some-one's caught him in casual clothing.

'Jack? Were we expecting you?' he says, welcoming me in and putting an arm around me. 'MIA, DID YOU INVITE PEOPLE TO DINNER AGAIN?' he shouts into the kitchen.

Mia pops her head around the corner. If Ed has gone casual, Mia looks ready for bed, wearing a giant Snoodie. 'JACK! No, but come in, you plonker. Come and save me from Ed who's explaining the importance of grade boundaries to me,' she jests, not before planting a big kiss on her husband's cheek to make it up to him.

I stroll through their flat, a place I've visited before, but which is very different to the house I currently inhabit. It really does feel like the next stage of adulthood with the prints on the wall and the stainless-steel kitchen. I also notice all the house-plants and examine a fern by the window that I do believe I bought for Ed myself. It still lives. This doesn't surprise me. Whilst a good majority of us came to university to escape, to discover, to drink cheap alcohol, it always came as a shock to me how concerned Ed was about his learning. To the point where sometimes I think he came innocent and left in exactly the same state. He was always a reliable sort, the only man I knew at university who had his own sandwich toaster and who cleaned it after every use.

Mia grabs a beer from the fridge for me, turning down the music as I take my coat off and sit down on an armchair, admiring Ed's matching throw cushions.

'To what do we owe the pleasure then?' Ed asks. 'Do you want to stay for dinner? We're having baked potatoes, but I can put in another and grate some more...'

'I kissed Zoe Swift by the bike sheds,' I tell them, clutching on to my beer, my mouth a little dry to have said that out loud.

Ed pauses for a moment. I'm not sure whether it's because I interrupted his baked potato talk or he just doesn't know how to respond. Mia, however, punches the air in delight. Their reactions are so different that I really don't know how to feel about the situation. Mia comes over and hugs me and all I can say is that her velveteen Snoodie is extremely soft. It's like hugging a very large rabbit.

'I knew it, knew it, knew it! You kissed? What else happened?' Ed shifts his wife a look as if disapproving of her urge to find out all the salacious details. If anything else followed on, it doesn't feel like Ed wants to be party to it, but it was just a kiss and one that was quite extraordinary. Sometimes kisses can be like that – they can be filled with longing, a sharing of something so intimate that it imprints itself on to you and you imagine what will follow, what could be. I can still feel the touch of her lips on mine.

Ed remains quiet, looking at me. He plants himself on a neighbouring sofa and Mia goes to sit down next to him.

'You're mad?' I ask him, taking a long sip of beer, fearing his judgement.

'Not mad, just, she's been through a lot. I think I feel a bit protective towards her.'

Mia rests her head on her husband's shoulder, curling her legs up towards him.

'I know, mate, and I don't want to hurt her, I really don't.'

'So how did you leave things?' Mia asks excitedly, putting a handful of peanuts in her mouth and offering me some.

'I have a feeling she was kind of freaked out.' There was a moment when she backed away from me and just looked at me in shock and I couldn't read her expression at all. Did she like that? Or not?

'There are cameras there,' Zoe said. 'We have at least three bikes stolen from here a month.'

I didn't know how to reply to that. Could we talk about the kiss? We just kissed. I, for one, found it quite amazing and I wouldn't mind doing it again.

'I have to go,' Zoe mumbled, clutching on to her keys so tightly that I could see her flesh go pale. 'The cameras...' she said, pointing to two corners of the bike shed, her eyes darting around before she pulled a scarf over her mouth and literally jogged out of there towards the darkness and her car. I wasn't quite sure what that meant so I stood there for a moment. I just hope those cameras got my good side.

Ed grimaces. 'Who kissed who?'

'She kissed me,' I reply.

They sit there opposite me, trying to work out the details of the kiss, trying to decide if whatever we've started should persist for the greater good.

'Are you a shit kisser?' Mia asks, wincing. 'Ed, snog your friend and find out.'

Ed laughs it off, but her comment leaves me slightly paranoid, and I put a hand to my mouth. Was it a breath thing? I did have onions for lunch.

'Maybe she was just slightly overwhelmed by the moment. When Mia first kissed me, I wasn't really sure what was going on. She took me by surprise. I had food in my mouth. I could have choked,' Ed informs me.

'He loved it really,' Mia replies, blowing her husband a kiss. 'Ed's right. Knowing Zoe, she's probably been with her husband for so long that she was likely just a little shocked that it happened. Plus, you're easy on the eye, so it was probably just panic.' Ed glares over at her. 'Not as easy on the eye as you, though, love. Obviously. Did you enjoy it?'

'Very much so,' I report, trying hard to keep my cool. Mia smiles at me knowingly, though. She knows that kiss was felt in my very core. It's all I've thought about for the last hour.

'I mean, the other option is that she's kissed you and worked out it's too soon and she's not ready and if this is the case then I suggest a gigantic step back. Give her space and time to sort out what she wants.'

I nod. These two combined are quite a knowledgeable pair and it all makes a lot of sense. Let her decide. The kiss was the litmus test, and we shall see where it goes from here.

'So, what do I do now?' I ask them.

'Just don't send her another cock emoji,' Mia says, her finger pointed at me in warning.

'It was a chicken. And how do you...?' I frown at them. Their eyes move in different directions.

'She may have said something earlier today in the staff room. She was a little confused,' Ed confesses. 'How did you not know what that emoji meant? Even I know that, and I didn't start using emojis until a year ago.'

I shrug. I've given myself an education today, though. I know not to send sushi emojis as well.

'Also,' Mia says, leaning forward. 'You didn't mention to us that she found out about her husband at our wedding. She said you were there.'

'Yeah,' I say hesitantly. 'I wasn't sure if it was my story to tell. But yeah, when she got the call from her daughter, we were chatting outside. So I share a lot of hatred for Brian and I don't even know the man.'

Mia suddenly sits bolt upright. 'Oh my, if this goes further then, Ed, remind me to take some sort of group picture with Jack and Zoe and I'm going to tag the fuck out of it for Brian. Yes?'

Ed nods reluctantly.

'Have you met Brian before?' I ask cautiously. 'What am I dealing with here?'

Mia pulls a face at the mention of his name. 'Bit boring, to be fair. Met him at a couple of Christmas parties. Old man denim, the sort who looks like he's into golf. Like, between you and him there's no comparison. You're like...' She studies my face. 'Young Ryan Gosling vibes. He's a football pundit in sensible knitwear.'

Ed smirks which makes me think her assessment is pretty accurate. I'll take young Gosling. Your wife has excellent judgment but then she did choose you.

'I wouldn't worry about him, though. He's made his bed and I do not think Zoe would go back there,' Mia continues, shaking her head.

'Yeah. I think this is all about Zoe moving on. Let her make the first moves if this is a thing. Maybe take her out for coffee, a drink, dinner... don't go too quickly. Let her get to know you properly. For her, she'll have major trust issues. Someone she was with for years did the most awful thing so just go slow,' Ed adds.

Mia smiles at her husband still looking out for his colleague and takes Ed's beer bottle, helping herself to a sip. 'And... I don't want to be presumptuous but if this is a thing, then maybe just lay down the parameters. Is it a rebound thing? What are the expectations? Because she has kids, you know, and I think whatever she feels, they will always come first for her,' she adds.

I nod, sincerely. I hadn't even thought that far ahead but even at this stage I know it's important for me to do the right thing by her.

'I also don't know you well enough but, if Zoe's just some conquest, someone to add as a notch on a bedpost or if you are a complete shit to her, then I will come after you and I will kill you, and Ed knows all the lab techs so we'll make it look like an accident,' she tells me, a little harshly, with the finger pointing at me again, her eyes tense with a fire that tells me she's not messing around.

'She's not joking,' Ed mumbles. I don't know whether to be scared or whether to be impressed that Ed married someone with a bit of spark. I've never been more scared of someone in a Snoodie. But all this love that they have for Zoe makes sense. I get it.

'I promise, I will look after her,' I tell them, throwing some sort of Scout style salute to the air.

'Like, if it goes next level, give her some proper orgasms, yeah? Something that will make her forget that complete bellend of a husband of hers. How's your technique?' she asks nonchalantly. I do applaud how much she cares about Zoe in a multitude of ways.

'MIA!' Ed says, exasperated.

'I'm just saying... when you say "look after her" then do it properly. It's no less than she deserves after what she's been through,' she continues, throwing her hands in the air.

'I'm sorry about her, I really am,' Ed says, glaring at her but laughing at her audacity at the same time.

But they both have a point. Whoever Zoe was going to choose next was going to have mighty boots to fill, not to replace her husband but to restore her faith in men, in relationships, to let her know that love and all its complication is worth it. I'm not so arrogant to say I'd be able to do that, but after that kiss I know I'd at least like to try.

I take a large swig of my beer and watch the couple in front of me. I think I'm starting to come round to wanting something like this – the sort of affection they have towards each other. The way the laughter between them flows so effortlessly. And for a moment, I picture this with Zoe.

'Also,' Ed says, looking thoughtful. I await his next pearls of wisdom. 'Did you want to stay for that baked potato because if you do, I'd need to put it in now...'

Mia and I laugh. Oh, he was being serious.

I don't stay for a baked potato. Mainly because they do take a long time to cook but I know Frank's mum is making her legendary crispy belly pork for us and I am, in these situations, dictated by my stomach. However, I'm grateful that both Mia and Ed were able to sound me out.

As I head out of their flat and locate my bike I replay that scene in my head again. The moment her body relented, and I felt it fit against mine, the softness of her skin against my cheek. I unlock my bike and hear my phone ping in my pocket. I go to retrieve it and see a notification on my home screen. It's from Zoe. It's an emoji of a chicken. I laugh.

SEVEN

Zoe

> It'll be fine, Zoe. Here if you want to talk it out
> this weekend x

I look down at the message and smile, resting my elbow on the countertop of my kitchen.

It's been over a week since I sent the chicken, since Jack replied with a laughing emoji, and since then all that's happened is an exchange of messages, a conversation. We don't mention the kiss, we just continue that line of witty exchange via messages instead. Sure, I have to look up my emojis to ensure I'm not sending anything remotely vulgar, but I like that feeling of hearing my phone pinging, or seeing he's replying after I message him, and I like those three dots that tell me he's writing. I like how sometimes he's the last person I speak to at night, and he tells me to sleep well. I have no idea where it's going, but there's a warm buzz that comes with the novelty of our conversations, the idea that there's no pressure to be anything other but myself with him. And at a time like this, I am grateful to him for the distraction as today starts the first weekend where I will be without my kids.

'Mum, where are my black trackies?' Dylan asks me. I smile and point to the laundry room where I washed and dried said trackies in preparation. Even though he has three other pairs, it's only those ones that will do. He grabs them and gallops up the stairs again. I take a long sip of wine. Manchester is what's happening. I finally got Lottie in a position where she would agree to go on the trip. Granted, my plan was based on good old-fashioned bribery and blackmail, but I also assured both of them that they could go with my blessing even though I knew it would hurt my heart beyond belief to not have them round like some sort of security blanket. Whether I'm married to their father or not, they are not pawns in this situation and my desire will always be that they remain unscathed in all of this. So, it's a Friday night, they're packing and I am readying myself for their departure. I will not cry.

A head pops round the door. 'You know it's not too late. I can stay if you want. Or maybe you could come, too?' Oh, Lottie. She shuffles over in her Ugg boots and wraps her arms around me. I see parents who do this a lot. They go on holidays despite their marital circumstances, all part of some big, blended family. Maybe one day I'll get there, but not now. If I went now, I'd likely push Brian in front of a bus. I won't tell her that. I stroke her head and kiss her forehead.

'Lottie, I'll be fine. You go. I think that's part and parcel of how our new situation will work out. We just won't do things as a four anymore.'

'And I hate him for it.' She scowls. All at once, I feel all that sadness and grief in her tones. I hate to admit it, but we were a good foursome.

'Just try... That's all we're asking. Push the hate down because you're going to be sitting in a car with him for four hours now.'

Her deadpan expression and flared nostrils make me giggle. 'And like we said, I think if you asked him to buy that North Face coat you're after, I reckon he's so desperate to get in your good books he may buy it for you. I'd seriously milk it.'

'Pandora stuff, too?'

I open my eyes and nod at her, and she smiles. Little Lottie. Even though it's the biggest cliché you'll hear, I remember when she'd sit on my knee at this countertop and we'd eat toast together on a Saturday morning and I'd help her drink her milk, holding a beaker to her mouth that was as big as her tiny face. Now she's all limbs, a mane of hair and this wondrous human I get to unleash on the world. She comes over to embrace me again as I hear a key turn in the door, and I stiffen. That sound feels like an annoyance to me now. He's here. Lottie doesn't let go and I feel a lump in my throat already starting to form.

'Hello?' his voice thunders through the hallway. 'You ready, kids?'

'Lottie,' I whisper. But her hug gets tighter. 'We're in the kitchen, Brian,' I call out. The front door shuts and I hear him walk through.

'Evening, all! Ready, Lots?' he asks her. How is he so sprightly? Lottie is silent and shrugs her shoulders, looking over to me, confused at having to leave me but still wanting to show her allegiance. I get it, little one.

'Dylan's just upstairs,' I tell him. 'Actually, can I ask a favour? Now that you don't live here anymore, please could you ring the bell rather than letting yourself in? Just so we respect each other's boundaries.' He stares at me for bringing it up, now, but it felt like as good a moment as any to say he can't just come into my house and treat this like his home when it suits him. 'I mean, I wouldn't just walk into yours and Liz's house without asking.'

He looks mildly confused, like I'm speaking another language. 'But we're co-parenting, it's different,' he tells me.

'It isn't really – you don't live here anymore,' Lottie adds. 'I agree with Mum.'

Brian goes to the doorway of the kitchen, refusing to answer and as he looks away, Lottie winks at me. 'DYLAN!' he shouts. 'Let's go, bud.'

I look Brian up and down, sipping my glass of wine. It's strange how the external has hardly changed. His leaving didn't prompt him to go out and buy a new wardrobe or go for a radical new haircut. I remember finding those brown boots with him in a sale, telling him to buy them, they'd go with everything. What is strange is how internally, everything is different. The value he placed on me, our family, our life. He felt that Liz was worth more than that. It still hurts that I never saw it coming. That in the space of mere months, life changed so very quickly. I quickly swipe away the painful feeling that flashes up and remind myself I'm better off this way. I will be better off. Then I picture Jack and think of the kiss, and my stomach is a riot of butterflies.

'Plans for the weekend, Zoe?' he asks me casually, bringing me expertly back down to earth.

I was going to hoover and maybe start a box set, you shitbag.

'Oh, I've got marking to do and then I was going to meet someone for lunch.' I'm not but I have to pretend I have a life, that there may be the possibility that I might be doing something exciting with my life, like tapas.

'You're still letting work seep into your weekends then?' he says casually.

'Well, that's my problem now, eh?' Is this why you had an affair? Because I'd work at home at the weekends? Are we blaming my career now? Maybe it's easier to do that than blame your lack of integrity. I look over at Lottie. Civility, civility, civility. I want to throw a mug at his smug head. Dylan appears with a rucksack at the door, and I look down at Lottie's trolley bag that I know includes two changes of shoes should she need them. Dylan can barely look at me.

'So...' I say, trying to control a waver in my voice. 'Have a truly excellent time. Send me some pics to let me know you're having fun. I guess I'll expect you back on Sunday evening at some point.'

'Depending on the traffic. We'll get dinner enroute. I thought we could go for a Wagamama.'

The kids turn to look at me. Wagamama was always something we did as a four, boys one side of the bench, girls the other. Crispy squid and edamame to start. Shared jokes over katsu and ramen. You absolute shit, Brian.

The kids know as much and come over to envelop me in this double-sided hug that seems to be our new thing. Let's sandwich Mum to let her know how much we love her. Brian looks on quietly as I hear Lottie crying.

'Hey, hey, less of that. You will have so much bloody fun, you won't even know I'm not there.'

She shakes her head as Dylan stands next to her, looking at the floor, and I'm reminded of little people going to school for the first time, being removed from me and what they know, and feeling completely unsure and unsettled about that situation. And it breaks me to see them like this, but it also makes me want to glass Brian. Keep it together, Zoe.

'I love you both madly. And souvenirs, yeah?'

'A Man City scarf maybe?' Dylan jokes.

'Wash your mouth out, kid. Know your manor,' I say, putting on a London accent. The sound of him laughing is a relief. 'Lottie-Lots, just try,' I whisper into her ear, holding her close and kissing her head. And I would hold her forever like this if I could, but I can't and I feel her grip loosen as she stands away from me. I wipe her cheeks and smile.

As they gather their things, I can hardly look at Brian even though I can sense he's trying to catch my eye. For what, Brian?

To gloat? I hope you choke on your gyoza. Instead, I focus on the kids and lead them through the hallway, reminding Dylan to do up his coat and passing them sneaky ten-pound notes into their palms.

'Love you, Mum.' That's from Dylan and those are the words that may very well end me.

'Love you, too, Dyl.'

And I watch their bodies as they bundle into Brian's car, small arguments over shot-gunning the front seat, and wave at the car maniacally as they reverse out. And then they're gone. I walk back into the house, closing the door softly, the very haunting silence being my only company, as tears fall softly down my face.

I don't notice the doorbell at first. My tears took me to the sofa where I thought I'd just have a moment to weep and hug some pillows. Maybe I'd have a drink and do something I normally wouldn't if the kids were here, but then I don't remember a time without them. Maybe I'll finally get round to watching *Bridgerton*. Then I notice the doorbell. Maybe I ordered food and didn't remember. More likely it's next door asking me if I've seen their cat. They really need to put a tracker on that beast. I head to the door and notice two figures standing there. Jehovah's Witnesses? If this is the case, I might listen to their spiel just to have some company on a Friday night.

I open the door and before me stand Mia and Ed.

'Oh, Zoe,' Mia says, noticing my damp face and swollen eyes. She enters the house and throws her arms around me.

'Why are you here?' I ask, surprised to see them.

'Well, Jack mentioned you'd be on your own and he was worried about you so...'

I smile to hear Jack's name, kind of glad he's not here to witness this strange meltdown of mine. 'Well, that's very sweet.

Come in, come in. I'm sorry I'm such a wreck, though. I'm literally still in work gear and I haven't got anything in. We could order some food?' I tell them, using a tissue I had up my sleeve to dab at my glowing nose. I lead them into the house, hoping they haven't seen the shadows of tearstains I've left on the cushions.

'Did you have plans? Tell us if we're in the way and you'd rather be alone,' Mia says, looking around the place.

'I hadn't really thought about what I'd do. I was just going to potter...' They both look at me curiously, Ed nodding like an ally who knows how a good potter is soothing for the soul. Mia looks less impressed as they both take a seat on my sofa. 'You spoke to Jack then,' I quiz them. To be fair, with the kids out of the picture, Jack would have been the perfect distraction for this weekend, but I still debated if it was too soon, too complicated, too scary.

'He said you've been texting,' Mia says, unable to contain her glee. I smile back at her. 'Am I allowed to ask what that is?'

'I don't quite know... You know about the kiss, don't you?' I ask them.

'There was a kiss? Really?' Ed says, with a shocked expression. This is why Ed does not teach drama. He can see my raised eyebrow and looks sheepish. 'He did come to us for advice.'

'And what did you advise him?' I ask tentatively.

'We said you've been through a lot, to go at your pace and maybe don't snog again on school grounds,' Ed says.

'You kiss me on school grounds,' Mia replies, indignant.

'Yeah, but not a full-on snog with tongues.'

I widen my eyes. Either Jack went into detail or that CCTV footage got out. Could you see my tongue? That's bloody awful.

'Was that the right advice?' Ed asks.

I nod. It's spot-on, though I don't really know what my pace is. Like glacial slug speed. Is that something young Jack is willing to hang around for? They both sit there politely, waiting for me to react, to say something. 'So, do you want to hang out tonight? I have wine, we could just get drunk?' I ask them, hoping they won't just spend the evening staring at me.

'Actually...' Mia says, fidgeting in her lilac Converse. 'We're here for other reasons. You're allowed to say this is a shit idea but actually it was Ed's.' She points to her husband and he takes over.

'Look, at our wedding we were given a lot of random gifts and one of them was a night in a hotel in London. It's a spa hotel, the stay comes with treatments and food and... well, we're probably never going to use it...'

'Ed doesn't do spas,' Mia explains. 'He has concerns about hot tubs and fungi.'

Ed nods. 'Legitimate concerns. So, we just thought... Well, we also felt bad that you never got to enjoy our wedding properly because of what happened with the phone call about your marriage ending, and, well, it's a tough weekend, and you've been through so much... we thought you'd like it? Like a gift to you,' he rambles.

'Really?' I say, surprised by the kindness of the gesture. 'To check in tonight? But...'

'But... your kids aren't here so you can't use that as an excuse. You literally just have to bung some stuff in a bag. We phoned the hotel and they've got space. We'll also throw in a lift. Ed is an excellent driver,' Mia says. 'You don't have pets, do you? We'd even look after them if you need.'

I feel my bottom lip tremble at the loveliness of it all. A spa? All I can think of is a bathtub I won't have to clean before I get in it, a bed I wouldn't have shared with my ex-husband at some point, a clean room free of memories of my kids, my family. It's wonderful to suddenly feel so elated by the idea.

'Are you really sure? If someone gifted it to you...' I say.

'It was Ed's aunt. That's probably why we'd have to take

you, so we can take a photo in front of the hotel to prove we've been,' Mia confesses. 'But really, I think this would be good for you.'

I go up to them, hugging them both tightly. It's strange when these big catastrophic life events happen. People hover around you waiting for you to fall, to catch you, but really what saves you is the singular gestures, whether those be unexpected chocolate bars, hugs, text messages or re-gifted spa trips. It's the sum of all these gestures that keep you afloat.

'And, I mean, it's a couples' package – just in case you wanted to invite anyone else along?' Mia tells me. Ed elbows her sharply in the ribs, and they exchange a look.

I laugh. Not tonight.

Jack

'THIS WAY! YOU'RE RUNNING TOWARDS THAT GOAL!' I shout across the football pitch at the many little people all herded around the football, drawn to it like magnets. They don't care if they're running the wrong way, they just want a touch of the ball. Little Vinnie charges towards the wrong goal, scores and then does some Ronaldo-style goal celebration like he's the king of the world. I double up in hysterics to see him, then blow the whistle around my neck. 'KIDS, COME INTO ME!' I signal. Do they listen? Do they hell. They all continue to run around in circles while I blow the whistle three more times. Little heads start to get the message and herd in my direction, three of them wearing Manchester United gear which makes me shake my head. 'WHO HAD FUN?' I yell.

They all scream something in return, some of them punching the air. I am really not sure how much football they learned but they got a run out and look incredibly excited about life. 'Are you coaching us Sunday, Uncle Jack?' asks a little familiar auburn head in the middle of the pack.

'No, George, your dad is taking that.'

'Boooooo!' cries out his twin brother, Barney, and I smile because essentially that's validation that, as a coach, I'm pretty awesome.

'I'm just helping out for the night because your dad is stuck at work and said he'd pay me in McDonald's.'

This makes this ten-year-old crowd laugh. 'What do you get at McDonald's, Coach Jack?'

'I get a chicken nuggets Happy Meal with a strawberry milkshake. And the toy, not the book. I'm no geek.' I get more laughs. Maybe I'm teaching the wrong age group. 'Before we leave, please take your water bottles and don't leave until you see your mums or dads.'

Some of them come up to me to fist bump me and say their thank yous and for one brief moment in time, I know what it feels like to be Pep Guardiola after a training session. Such respect. One day, I hope one of you plays for England and remembers that time I made you run around all those multi-coloured cones, wearing mouldy bibs that were two sizes too small.

In the car park beyond the gates, I see Dom running from his car, still in a work suit. He greets parents and heads over to me as I pack the equipment away. 'Oh my, I owe you, little brother. Were they good? Did they listen?'

Dom is my only sibling, one of the few people I look up to. He was always the hero, always looked out for me, so it made sense that I would return the favour. Even if that sometimes takes the form of the occasional training session and babysitting, which basically is an excuse for me to play video games and induct those kids into the world of stuffed crust pizzas.

'They were all amazing. If they win on Saturday, we can hope that's because of my excellent coaching.' I turn and see George running so fast in circles that he falls over. Maybe not.

'We haven't won a match in two seasons, Jack. We were beaten 16-0 last week,' he tells me painfully.

'Ouch. Why haven't they sacked you then?' I joke.

'Double ouch. Because I'm a volunteer and no one else will do it? Unless you...' he says, hinting at me. 'I bet they liked you. I'd buy you a McDonald's every day.'

'Healthy.'

'They do salads now.'

'The answer is still no. I love you, I love George and Barns, and I will help out anytime, though.'

He sticks his tongue out at me as we walk towards the car park, and I heave the giant bag of balls and equipment over my shoulder across the astro pitch. It's a huge community pitch on the outskirts of South London where we grew up, herds of excitable kids being chased by exasperated coaches under the floodlights, the mid-autumn air starting to bite. I won't lie, it brings back fond memories of when I used to play, when our dad used to coach us and our mum used to stand there in her big red beanie with her Tupperware of cut-up oranges, getting overly excited every time her son had possession of the ball. 'I'm still going to get a McDonald's for this, though, yes?' Needs must.

'You strike a hard bargain... just not tonight. I've got to get these two to Cubs to tire them out. Bank that Maccy's for another time.' I flare my nostrils, unsure whether to just ask for the money. I stop at their family motor and wait for him to open the boot so I can deposit the kit. 'Anyway, we need a catch up. Come over for lunch one Sunday. I want to hear more about how the new job is going. I always thought you'd be a decent teacher.'

'You must have witnessed my fine command of the children tonight,' I joke. 'It's all good. A little manic learning the ropes but I'm meeting some nice people.'

He nods in the way that Dom does. I gave four solid years to helping him out with his boys and there's gratitude there, but I think he always hoped that once I moved out, I'd find my own path. He's another who doesn't quite understand why I'm still drifting and haven't picked a vocation in life.

'And do you think they might take you in? Train you up? I hear you can do that these days? Train on the job.'

'Hold up there, sparky,' I tell him. 'We'll see. I'm not sure teaching is for me.'

He rolls his eyes. 'Jack-of-all-trades. Master of...'

'All of them, you cheeky bastard!' He smiles at me, knowing he's legally not allowed to hate me. 'By the way, I got the boys' birthday party invite. I'm there. What do I bring?'

'Yourself and a big fucking box of Lego. That Ninjago shit. Are you bringing a girlfriend?'

'That would be a no. You still dating that school run mum?'

He flares his nostrils. 'Kind of. This is why we also need a catch up. She's into stuff.'

'In bed?'

'I need tips. I can't search for it on the internet because I put in that child protection security software. If I look it up at work, I'll get fired.'

'Then I am intrigued,' I say, laughing. Then I pull a face. 'Is it to do with wee?'

Dom laughs loudly so his breath fogs the air. George runs up behind him, throwing his hands around his waist. 'What are you talking about?' he asks, his cheeks all rosy from the cold and the activity. 'Do you need a wee, Uncle Jack?'

'YES,' I say, attempting to be convincing by jogging from foot to foot. 'I was also discussing birthdays. Your dad said to buy you a puppy... what colour do you want?'

'REALLY?' Barney squeals.

Dom shakes his head at me. I hear the sound of male voices swearing behind us on another pitch and we instinctively cup our hands around the boys' ears. The other joys of football that I had forgotten about. I look over at the pitch and the majority of them don't look much older than eighteen. Some match is in full flow, the soundtrack provided by a row of spectator dads obviously knowing better than any referee. My attention is drawn to one of the boys at the back.

'I know him. I teach him,' I say, pointing him out to the twins. It's Gabe from homework club. I watch him take on a lad and put in the most perfect tackle to dispossess him. 'NICE, GABE!' I don't think he heard that, but Dom did, and he smiles.

'I don't think teaching is for me,' he says, mimicking my voice. That's not what I sound like at all. 'You crack on and watch the football. I've got to run. What do we say, boys?'

They bundle themselves into my arms and I smile broadly to be a part of that uncle-twin sandwich. 'Thank you, Uncle Jack. Love you.'

'Love you, too, buds. Be good. Think about a name for that puppy.'

They laugh. My brother does not. He bundles them into the car, and I wave them off, not before my attention is taken again by the football happening on the pitch across the way. I gave up football way before that age, being more distracted by girls really, but it's nice to see Gabe so invested in it and excelling in something he's obviously good at. I go up to the railings where he's playing, a final whistle blows, and it would seem his team are celebrating so I will take that as a win. I clap my hands and watch as Gabe heads over to the side of the pitch to talk to a parent, before catching my eye.

'Mr Damon, what are you doing here? You watched my match?' he says, a tad cautious.

'I was coaching my nephews on the other pitch. Just caught the last few minutes. Class tackle, by the way. I knew you were giving Van Dijk energy...'

He cracks a laugh and then I think I get something, possibly approval. It's the fact I'm in my adidas football boots that I wear once a fortnight for five-a-side, isn't it? The tracksuit makes me look like I know what I'm doing. I'll take that. I hope he tells people at school that I'm cool. I could do with the boost. Although Dom thinks differently, I'm still on the fence about teaching. Maybe it's the culture of being a sub but a lot of the kids presume they can doss in my lessons. I peer into other lessons and kids are sitting there, taking notes and learning. In mine, I'm begging them to just write the date down and not climb out of the windows.

As I turn away from the pitch, I see a girl in a fluffy bomber coat run up to Gabe to share her excitement of the win with him and I smile. She takes a selfie of them as he hangs an arm off her. Oh, young love. Why does it involve so many selfies, though? But I know what it means to feel the excitement and butterflies of a new relationship and I suddenly think of Zoe. It's been a very reserved week since our kiss. I went with Mia and Ed's advice and I'm being a gentleman and respecting her space. So, we talk, we keep it PG, I don't dip too much into innuendo. But that doesn't mean I feel any differently, that the kiss we shared hasn't opened some floodgate, that I don't think about her constantly. I've not sure I've ever craved someone so much. The intrigue about what that kiss could mean haunts me and I'd be lying if it's something that hasn't come into my mind every night before I go to sleep and have a wank, as crass as that sounds. Needs must.

As I stand there, I contemplate my next moves. It's Friday. God, I should be going out, right? I would if I wasn't so tired and it's too late to do the ring around and make plans. I should have just asked Dom for a tenner for that McDonald's or invited myself around to theirs. Maybe Frank's mum will have made us something to eat? I could wash my hair and start a show. Hold up there, Jack. That may almost be too exciting.

I look down at the last message I sent Zoe a few hours ago. Her kids were heading off with their dad this afternoon and I told her all would be fine and offered my services for a chat should she need it. She saw it but didn't reply. Was that too forward? I didn't want to suggest that with an empty house I could be someone who could fill that space. I hope she's alright. She was worried about her kids going off with their dad and I could feel the stress radiating off her, and all I really wanted to do was offer her a hug. Could I just go round, hug her and then go? That wouldn't be weird.

A message pops up on my screen.

> Jack, you free tonight?

Like some saviour, someone who knew I was destined to be alone tonight comes to the rescue. Ed.

> Can be? You out tonight?

> We've ventured into town for some drinks.
> Come join?

He drops me a pin. It's actually only five Tube stops away so do-able once I have a quick shower, but the location is a tad confusing.

> Are we getting massages? Spa hotel?

There's a pause.

> We just had dinner here and we're hanging around. It's a nice bar. There are free nuts.

> You are full of innuendo tonight. Stop flirting with me.

> I can't. Are you coming? This is not innuendo by the way. Mia needs to know if she has to nick a chair from the next table.

To be honest, it could be just what I need. Not sure I could handle something too raucous this evening. Just a civilised drink with mates with some sort of bar snack involved because my own brother couldn't shout me a burger.

> I can be there in an hour?

Excellent. See you in the bar. Wear nice shoes because I don't know the rules in these establishments anymore.

> Can't wait

I text him, then I send him the chicken emoji. He doesn't reply which is no fun.

EIGHT

Zoe

Would you like to know the last time I stayed in a hotel? It was on holiday – the holiday which was the starting scene of the affair that destroyed my marriage. We flew to Seville with the plan of driving down to the Algarve and we spent a few days in this gorgeous hotel in the old town with sprawling Andalucian archways, green palms and a rooftop pool. The kids had their own room so that meant Brian and I had our own space and whenever that happened, we usually had sex to celebrate the occasion. I can't remember the sex. Is that awful? I don't think you're supposed to remember every single sexual experience when you're married, but I do vaguely remember Brian's face hovering over me, his eyes closed like he was concentrating really hard. After he came (and I had to finish myself off), he wrapped a towel around his waist and sat on a chair by the hotel balcony, one leg cocked up on the frame and I could see his balls just dangling down as he perused the room service menu and told me there was no way he was going to order a ham sand-wich for ten euros. Such is marriage. There is no need for mystery or to hide one's naked self. You let it all hang out, quite literally.

I stand by the hotel room door now and stare at the bed. I guess the management assume there's still a happy couple set to arrive because the bed is covered in rose petals and there are two towel swans, kissing, perched on the pillows. I sigh deeply. Is it terrible to want to ring down and request a hoover? However, there is also a bucket at the end of the bed with a bottle of champagne and a note to the newlyweds. I bin the note, take hold of that bottle and uncork it in one swift move, pouring myself a glass. It's a spacious modern hotel room but with the heart-shaped lamps and dimmed lights, there is a considerable amount of love everywhere you look. Why is there a pole in the room? Oh. Maybe I can get drunk enough and pretend to slide down it like a fireman. I chuckle to myself. I don't know if this loved-up boudoir will make me feel worse, but maybe I just need to value the gift of space, privacy for one glorious night.

I remember this used to be the dream. When I was a young mother, I fantasised about hotel rooms, but not for sex: for escape, for rest. I longed for eight hours' uninterrupted sleep, room service, a bed I wouldn't have to make and a bath I could swim in where toddlers wouldn't invade the space announcing that they needed to do a poo and required an audience. And maybe this comes twelve years too late, but I kick off my shoes and feel the hotel carpet underneath my toes, sipping on my bubbles. Maybe this is exactly what I need.

My phone pings, and a selfie of Lottie and Dylan pops up. Obviously taken in a motorway services, and not including their father. I hope he hasn't abandoned them there. I smile at the stupid faces they're pulling, grateful for the fact they have each other. If nothing else, the last months have brought them closer together. Before, their relationship was filled with absolute love, where they'd joke about teachers from school, bond over

TikToks and sweets, but then yo-yo to fights where it would sound like one of them had committed actual bodily harm when really all they'd done is stolen a hoodie.

> Love you idiots, completely x

They don't reply. Deep breath, Zoe. I distract myself by nosing around the room, opening drawers and wardrobes that I'll likely not use, and then look out at the view, peering over the Thames, the dark of the city closing in over the skyline. I need to take a picture for Mia so she can share it with her aunt. Mia and Ed have outdone themselves tonight. Mia helped me pack, slipping a bottle of wine and a box of chocolates into my bag, and they drove me here to the door. I need to take lots of photos but also steal some toiletries for them as a thank you.

When I get into the bathroom, I take a step back, chuckling to myself. This really is a couple's suite extraordinaire. To the middle of the large bathroom is a circular hot tub style bath, the likes of which Ed doesn't trust. Next to it is a remote and I press on some buttons to see that it also lights up and plays what sounds like smooth jazz. Is this how couples bathe these days? People have had sex in that bathtub, haven't they? I now share Ed's worries. I once read an article in a women's magazine about someone who got pregnant from a hot tub. The sperm just hitched a ride on the jet streams into her fanny. As there is no man around, however, I remain undeterred. I give it a quick rinse and fill it, adding some of the free jasmine and honey bubble bath, fiddling with the remote. There's at least thirty jets in there. I'll allow for a bit of light bubbling and these lights are making me giggle so I'm going to go with a disco pink Barbie style glow. I then go to my hastily packed bag and remove my toiletry bag to get ready. The one thing I quite like is that I can make a mess here, can't I? I'm not sharing this room. I can literally kick off my shoes, pee with the door open, de-robe and drop my knickers in the middle of the floor without shame. I do just that.

I rest my champagne glass on a shelf next to the bath. Should I read in there? Or perhaps bring my phone? Not to take selfies, naturally, but to have something to do? I look around the room and take the hotel manuals and menus in there so maybe I can plan my evening. I'm picturing room service and watching something in a robe. As I get everything set up, I look at the large mirror in that bathroom, catching sight of my naked form. I pause. Having a teenage daughter has always made me quite conscious of how I judge my body, wanting to keep the discourse as positive as possible. These pink Barbie lights are actually quite flattering but there are still the curves and blemishes that have come to be, the pendulous quality of my breasts when I lean in certain ways, the soft lines of my stomach from having housed two children. I never used to have hang ups. Pilates helped. Ageing was a privilege rather than something to fight but having been discarded in the way I was, I sometimes have had periods of paranoia and compared myself to Liz. Blonde Liz who did wild swimming and who had those type of smaller boobs that just stayed where they were post-children. In the Algarve, she wore two-piece swimsuits and short dresses that showed off her tanned legs. I think about a time in the Algarve when she and Brian would have had sex for the first time. I bet he didn't sit in the corner afterwards showing her the curvature of his hairy forty-something balls.

But hell, now is not the time for any of that. Come on, Zoe. You're on your own in a hotel room without having to share that space, without having to dwell on any of those intrusive insecurities, so I tie my hair in a loose bun and get into the safety of the bath, looking down to see those lights really illuminate my pubes. They look like that sort of bioluminescent algae. I'm not sure that's a good look. I retrieve a razor, wading through the bubbles of the jets and feel one of them hit a place it shouldn't. I jolt and giggle to myself. This bath is huge. I feel my legs bob up and I float with all those lights and bubbles, glad for one moment that I don't have to share. This is all mine. God bless you, Mia and Ed. I wade over to the manuals and menus and open those up, too. There better be a club sandwich option. If I'm here for the night, then I also want to know about all those little things that will make my heart sing. Like a breakfast buffet with an egg, pancake and waffle station. I feel a smile creep across my face. I didn't know how much I needed that until now.

A message pops up on my phone. I doggy paddle over to see who it's from.

> Well, how is it?

> > I don't deserve you as friends. It's amazing. I think they were expecting you though. There are rose petals on the bed. I'm drinking your champagne.

> Drink away. Rose petals are a bit cheeseballs. Ignore them.

> > I have. I'm in the bath. It glows.

I maybe won't tell her about my cosmic algae pubes.

> Look, Ed and I are just grabbing dinner at the hotel restaurant. Do you want to join us for a drink in the bar in a bit? Say an hour?

> > Least I could do for the joy of this room. See you in a bit xx

Jack

'Can you believe that's what he did? It's not hard, you know? It's a decision we should make together but he just goes and does that without my input. And I was like, no. And he says I'm overreacting and I'm like, "*Overreacting?* You ain't seen over-reacting!"'

Oh, the Tube on Friday nights in London. Sometimes I wish I could bank half the things I've seen on here (I once saw someone with a pig on a leash) and some of the snippets of conversations. The two girls in the seats opposite me continue.

'I can't believe he did that, hon...'

'Right, he can eat his poxy pizza on his own as far as I'm concerned. If you don't ask me what toppings we're getting, then you can piss right off.'

I look down and smile to myself as one of them goes into her clutch to retrieve some mascara and re-applies it using her phone camera. It's a packed carriage tonight filled with the last of the work commuters and others headed out for the night, some hiding tins of alcohol in their pockets, full of energy and optimism for the night ahead. I know those nights out. It starts with the best of intentions where you head for dim sum and a bar but usually ends with you rolling out of a nightclub at least one hundred quid lighter, studying the night bus schedule because you're worried a taxi will bankrupt you. London really needs to sort out its capacity to look after its inhabitants past midnight because seriously, it's just kebabs and random buses getting us through.

I look back up and the girl opposite is smiling at me. Oh dear. I wasn't smiling at you with your big fur coat and platform shoes. I was smirking at the ridiculous notion that you've had a row with your boyfriend over pizza. Row over the important things in life, not a bit of pepperoni. Do I smile back? I can't. It'll lead her on. Instead, I squint my eyes and pretend to read the ad above her about bleeding gums and the importance of mouthwash.

Next stop: South Kensington

You see girls, I'm quite grown up now. I'm headed to a hotel. These days I frequent hotels with bars, with drinks that may have fancy garnishes. I'm going to lean against a bar and delight in conversation against the backdrop of alternative trip-hop. There will also be free nuts. It feels very mature and I'm suddenly grateful to Mia and Ed for the invitation. Maybe the two of them have elevated my social standing. I'm now a pseudo-teacher, I'm going to establishments that have dress codes about trainers. With my thirties knocking on the door, this all feels very grown up for a change. I wait for the Tube to lurch forward before rolling to a stop and skip off, headed towards the escalators.

My phone pings as soon as I'm at ground level.

> Are you nearby?

I exit through the barriers before replying.

> Yeah, just round the corner. You got a table?

> Kind of.

So we'll be propping the bar up instead. Must mean the bar is packed but sign of a decent evening ahead if a good crowd is in there. As I approach it, I know we're in different territory as there is a doorman, a reception full of people sat on velveteen sofas, a smooth marble floor with modern mood lighting. My phone still in my hand, I go to ring Ed.

'Hello?' There's an interference on his phone that doesn't quite sound like he's in a bar.

'Ed, mate. I'm in reception. You here?'

'Oh... Look...' The noise continues but I hear a siren in the background. He's not here, is he?

'Ed, are you driving? Have you guys left?' I say, my disappointment palpable. That's worse than being stood up and not a matey thing to do. I don't know whether to be angry or not.

'Look, this wasn't my idea. It was Mia's so blame her...'

'You were the one who suggested the hotel.' I hear Mia's voice over the hands-free.

'I really don't know what's going on, guys, but I'm here. Are you coming back?'

'No. Look, can you see the signs for the bar? Just head there,' Ed tells me. 'I want to say trust us.'

'Ed...?'

'I'm sorry, mate.'

And with that he hangs up. What the hell, Ed? If anything, I'm more surprised that this is coming from Ed, who's normally more reliable than this. I look at my watch. I wasn't late. Did they maybe get so randy that they had to head home for a shag? I mean, we're in a hotel if that was the case. I poke my head around the corner to look at said bar. Is it a vibe? It's a bit generic. Cushioned cubicles, low lighting, a man on a piano. It's the sort of place a travelling businessman comes to have an over-priced whisky. Well, I guess that person is me now. One drink to at least make the journey worthwhile. But as I head over to the bar, I see a person walking this way, weaving around tables searching for someone until her eyes land on me. She pauses for a moment before realising what's happening, a large smile creeping across her face. She heads towards me.

'Were you looking for Mia and Ed, too?' I ask her.

She nods. My heart races to see her, wearing a black dress with buttons all down the front. 'I was. I can't believe they ditched us.'

'Unforgiveable behaviour.'

She looks different, lighter but fresh-faced. 'Seeing as we're both here... drink?'

I beam. 'I would like that very much, Zoe.'

. . .

'So, this was like a set-up? I didn't realise Ed was so Machiavellian,' I tell Zoe as she sips on her gin and tonic, laughing. We've managed to secure a little booth by the window and she's sitting opposite me. It's like an upgraded version of our dinner date at Nando's.

'I think his wife may have had something to do with it,' she explains, which makes a bit more sense. Well, I don't think I care who is truly responsible because for now, I like the company and the fact Zoe didn't freak out to see me. We take this slowly. If it's just drinks, so be it. She cradles her hands around her glass and sighs deeply. 'You'll have to forgive me. I've had two glasses of champagne.'

'Before I arrived?' I ask, bemused.

'Oh no, in my room. My set-up also came with a room here that they told me was a wedding gift they wanted to pass on to me,' she admits.

'You have a room?'

She can barely look me in the eye but giggles. 'Oh, it's some sort of honeymoon suite. It has a pole.'

'Like a straight pole as opposed to a Polish person?' I joke. 'Just standing in the corner.'

She bursts into laughter, and I will admit to loving that sound, completely. Zoe and I look at each other. We kissed, you and I, and I loved that feeling. I really did. I don't know how to tell her that but there's a prolonged moment of staring into her eyes where I can hardly breathe. What is wrong with you, Jack?

'Thank you also for checking in on me this afternoon,' she says, trying to break the intensity.

'My pleasure. How did it go?' I enquire.

She shows me a selfie of her kids on her phone. 'That's the last I heard from them, but I think I just need to let them go and put some trust in Brian that he'll look after them.'

'Which must be hard when your trust in him is so broken,' I add.

'Bingo.' That sad look re-enters her eyes and I feel desperate to take it away.

'Well, I know it's hard, but I hope you get a moment for yourself this weekend. Have you booked in any treatments?'

'I'm not one for facials,' Zoe says before widening her eyes and realising the other meaning of the word.

I hold my drink in my mouth, trying not to spit it out in hysterics. 'Zoe! Look at you lowering the tone of the conversation in this very swish bar. I'm appalled.'

She laughs again. I made that happen. And she cocks her head to one side, deep in thought. Please don't be overthinking this. That kiss had chemistry, we are both attracted to each other, let's see where this can go. But I won't go there without you. She leans across and I bend over that table to meet her.

'We need to talk about the elephant in the room, don't we?' she says, smiling.

I pretend to look around for said elephant. 'Or not. Whatever you want to talk about is fine with me. The weather's turned, hasn't it?'

'It has. It's fresh.'

'Indeed.'

We both smile. She takes a deep cleansing breath. 'The kiss was unplanned and spur of the moment and I'm sorry I put you on the spot like that.'

I don't answer, but I know my face expresses my confusion. 'Never apologise to me. It was a very pleasant surprise.'

'Pleasant?' she asks. 'Pleasant is a word for wine. Like it was pleasing on the palate.'

'Maybe the kiss was pleasing on the palate?' I joke.

'JACK!' she squeals, then she looks serious again, like she's trying to get her thoughts straight. 'This is... I don't know what this is, but I'm not sure if it's the best idea. We work together now. You're...'

I put a hand to the air. 'Don't say young.'

She smiles serenely before explaining herself. 'Then you have a very free, uncomplicated life and mine is less so. It comes with a very new separation, kids, and I'm a big bag of confused emotions. I just don't think it's fair... to you.'

I smile and lean into the table further, placing a hand on hers.

'This is you being nice again. Thinking of other people and not yourself. What do you want?' She sits there in silence, looking down at my hand. 'I mean, we can talk about the weather. If that's what you want. We can chat about the probability of it raining tomorrow. We can finish up here and I can leave you, in peace. We can just keep chatting. We can forget that kiss ever happened. If that's what you want.'

'I'm just... the other option. I don't know how to do that...' she mumbles.

'What would the other option be?' I ask curiously.

She shakes her head at me, laughing. 'You know. It's like in a film. I'd give you a wink and my hotel key, and then we'd get handsy in the lift and then you'd come to my room... and it would be a complete debacle.'

I roar with laughter. 'It would, would it? A debacle? That's a word.'

'Jack, I've had sex with the same man since I was twenty-one years old. I don't know what you think I can do or what you expect but I am terrified of you.'

'Of me?' I smile. 'Little old me?'

'Little?' And we both burst into giggles, still leaning over that table, our heads inches away from each other. 'Zoe, all I would expect is to be able to share space and time with you.'

'Space and time... Like a maths equation.'

'Exactly. Would you like me to say something about angles now? I know maths is your thing. Maybe square roots?'

And I can't describe that feeling I get when I make her smile and laugh like that. It's addictive, to hear that sound and see her face crease into all those lines, to know I've done that. She stops laughing to lean over and downs the rest of my whisky. She chokes a little and then steadies herself.

'That was neat.'

'It was.'

She looks me in the eye, nervously finding her words. 'You should come and see the bathtub, at least. It lights up.'

'It does? Cool.'

And she nods, getting up from her chair, waiting for me to follow.

NINE

Zoe

FUCK.

It's the only word that echoes in my head as I stand here in this lift with Jack. I can't even look at him. If he touches me, I won't know what to do. I may implode. I still don't know what this is. He's just coming to look at the bathtub because admittedly, it is very funny. I am being presumptuous here. He might get in that room, look at the view, have a peek in the minibar and not really fancy it. And then we'll possibly shake hands, and he shall go home. I am, however, super grateful that I had a long soak in that bath and had a shave and a tidy. I only hope that when goes to look at that bathtub, I gave it a rinse. Of all the things for my mind to be preoccupied by right now, those are the thoughts. He's looking over at me. I've seen this scene in a film. They kiss in the lift and then the door opens and an old woman peers in disapprovingly or someone pushes an emergency stop button and stuff happens. Stuff. I really hope that bath is clean. I look back over at him as he puts his hands through his hair. He's in his trusted brown boots, a black shirt with a few buttons undone at the neck, a grey wool coat, jeans that fit a little too well. I should stop looking at his legs, thinking about what his legs look like.

'Why do you look so nervous?' he asks me.

Because I'm worried there are my old armpit hairs straggling in the bath.

'I'm not nervous. You're just coming to see my bath.'

He smiles. There is something about his smile. Before, I noticed a nice smile, one that belonged to a handsome face but now his smile is a whole feeling, a conversation, and it makes me smile in return, it makes me hold my breath for a few seconds.

The lift door opens, and he puts a hand out so I can lead the way. Fuck. Room 224. He walks a step behind me and I reach into my pocket, rubbing my thumb against the key card. You can do this, Zoe. I put the key card into the slot and the light pings green. I've seen this scene in the film, too. I open the door, he backs me onto the wardrobe and then we lead a trail of clothes to the bed.

I don't give Jack a chance to do that.

As soon as I open the door, I just don't turn back. I march quite meaningfully into the bathroom, kicking some knickers under a desk on my way, so I can have a look at the bath before he does. I don't know what he's doing but I can sense him behind me, softly shutting the door.

'Well, this is it. The disco bath,' I tell him, not even looking him in the eye, picking up the remote. 'It has a dimmer switch and jets and stuff,' I say, like I'm trying to sell him the thing. He chuckles to look at it whilst I scan it quickly. Not a hair in sight.

'It's impressive,' he admits with a nod.

'Right? I feel bad Mia and Ed missed out on this.'

'How do the jets work?' he asks me.

'To show you, I'd have to fill it up. Did you want a bath?' I ask him.

'With you?'

I make a very strange sound at the suggestion, a kind of snorting wail a scared deer might make. 'I meant if you wanted to road test it, solo, not with me. I mean, I could fill it up so you could see what it does but if you just wanted to see what the jets do then I don't want to waste the water because, you know...'

'Know what?' he asks me, trying to suppress a smile.

'Polar bears and ice caps and stuff,' I say, trying to maintain some order in this room, in my thoughts.

We both stand there in the bathroom, looking into the empty bath and burst into laughter. I don't know what this is. Even less so when Jack puts a hand out, looking for mine, slipping his fingers around mine. I don't flinch. I let him hold that hand.

'Can I suggest something?' he says.

Please don't say sex in the bath. I still can't bring myself to look at him.

'Do you remember when we first met? At the wedding? There was a moment when I thought you really looked relaxed and happy. On the dancefloor.'

'I was suitably lubricated.'

That was not the thing to say. He tries to hold in his laughter. I put a finger to the air to stop him from saying what he's thinking.

'So, let's have a dance...' he says.

'Here?' I ask.

'We could both get in the bath?' he suggests. 'But I suspect we'd break it.' He gets his phone out, connecting it to the speakers in the room, opening Spotify and handing it to me. 'I'll even let you choose the song.'

Just him and me, dancing in this very empty room. I am not sure how much that will help. I might have to turn the bath lights on to add some atmosphere. OK. I remember I quite liked dancing with you. Let's see how this works. Jack peers over my shoulder as I try to pick a song. He takes off his coat and boots.

He checks a bottle on the side of the bath. I wasn't an animal, I didn't finish the bottle, so he pours what's left and has a sip, offering me some, too. I am conscious that his hand is on my shoulder. Got it.

'RAYE?' he says, as I select it. 'The lady has good taste.'

'Well, you know,' I say, a little too confidently.

I press play and watch as he downs his drink and takes the coat off my shoulders. He takes my hand, pulling me into the main part of the room. He pretends to lunge, warming up, and I laugh. But he's not wrong. Maybe I should lunge, too? The beat suddenly kicks in and he nods to signal his approval, moving his hips and arms, shoulders going. OK then. I'll be game. I kick off my shoes, feeling my shoulders rotating, and start swaying from side to side. I can do this. Is it sexy, alluring dancing? I don't quite know what that looks like, but I can't seem to stop smiling because I don't quite think his dancing is sexy either. He pulls faces, he looks strangely comfortable, silly even and it encourages me to do the same. He opens his eyes at me and puts a hand out, spinning me under his arm but that's the move, isn't it? As I spin, he pulls me in close to him. That was smooth. I can't look at him, so I angle myself to look over his shoulder. Crap, that's close. Can he hear my heartbeat that closely? I have no idea what to say, what to do, but I feel all of this a little too much. I feel something I've not had run through my body for years and I don't know what any of it means. I rest my head on his shoulder, closing my eyes.

'Please fuck me,' I whisper. Oh, shit.

I stand back from him, the music still playing, and my eyes widened, mortified that I let my subconscious out. I put my hands to my mouth. 'I'm so sorry, I really am. I don't know what just came over me. That was...'

'Kinda hot, I'm not going to lie.' Jack stands there smiling. He catches my eye for a moment and my face feels hot, a sensation deep in my chest that feels like it could consume me. He walks over to me calmly and tucks a curl behind my ear. 'What would you like to do?' he tells me, his face centimetres away from mine. 'I can leave if you want?' His cheek brushes against mine. I shake my head, until my chin rises and I press my lips gently against his. His kiss in return is sweet, light, like he still doesn't want to pressure me into this, like he cares, and the intimacy of it floors me.

'Stay,' I whisper. 'There are things I'd like to do...'

I don't know this Zoe. I don't know her at all. But she kisses Jack harder with more urgency and he leans into it, pulling my body into his. I've never felt a kiss like this, the spark of it, some chemistry that draws me to him. My hand moves to the back of his head, grabbing his hair as he moves down my neck across the top of my cleavage before pulling my dress down and part of my bra, his lips finding my nipples. I can't cope with the intensity of it, my body shuddering in pleasure and surprise, sighing gently. He returns to my lips, and we step backwards slowly before falling onto the bed, both of us laughing as we bounce into the mattress.

He looks at me for a moment.

'So, what would you like to do?' he asks me, kissing the underside of my chin.

'Can I be honest?' I say, as his hands move down to my stomach, along the curve of my thighs. 'I'm not quite sure.'

He smiles but then he looks at me intently, his hand reaching down and lifting up the skirt of my dress, his fingers running along my thighs. I feel the pleasure of it down my spine and I arch my back. He maintains eye contact and I feel his fingers creeping up until they're near my underwear. I can feel his fingers stroke gently against the material and I gasp which makes him laugh gently, and he kisses me again which makes me part my legs a little further. When he pushes the material to one side and slips his fingers inside me, he inhales deeply with me, and I can't bear to contain that feeling anymore. I moan loudly, my body shaking, trying to remember what this is. And as his fingers glide inside me, I don't know whether to laugh or cry, but all I know is that it's time to let go. It's time to feel all of it and fucking enjoy it.

Jack

I wake up that night at about two in the morning, my body spooned around Zoe's and the curve of her shoulder rested against my chin. Through a gap in the curtains, I can see a slice of the River Thames twinkling, shapes from the room reflected in the window. I kiss Zoe's shoulder gently and hold her close to me, putting a hand around her waist and trying to doze back to sleep.

'You're up...' I hear her mumble.

'I'm sorry. Is it pressing against you? Did it wake you?'

I feel her body shudder with laughing. 'Go to sleep, Jack.'

I kiss her shoulder again. 'I can't. I think I'm in some sort of state of hyperarousal.'

'That's a clever way of saying you're horny.'

'I'm horny? I believe you were the one who initiated the second time.'

'And the third time...'

I feel her body shudder with laughter again and my arms hold her tighter, my hands wandering around her midriff. There were points where I could tell she was self-conscious about her body. You saw it in the way she asked to dim the lights, the way she scrambled for the covers, but she didn't need to feel that at all. I guess I saw things through a very different, adoring gaze. Maybe caressing her stomach will convince her of that much. Our feet meet at the bottom of the bed, the sheets twisted around our bodies.

'So, is this how you normally are when you have sex? So...'

She goes quiet.

'You were pretty insatiable.'

She turns to me, her face grimacing. 'I'm sorry. Was it a bit much? A bit full-on? It may have been the alcohol.'

I smile and give her a kiss to placate her. 'It felt good to be wanted, to see you enjoying yourself. I may need some sort of intravenous fluids, though.'

'I may need a massage tomorrow. I think I pulled something in my calf.'

'Well, you were the one who wanted to attempt that position,' I say, smiling. I run my fingers along her arm, liking the softness and feel of her skin, the way our legs are still messily entangled. I like how she seems so comfortable next to me, how her face shines in some sort of sex afterglow. 'So, was it OK? Are you OK?' I ask her and, again, she looks up at me, curious by my concern.

'I mean, it was alright,' she says, and she tips her head back laughing. I put a hand to her waist, tickling her until she squeals. 'It was pretty extraordinary. Thank you.'

'The pleasure was all mine.' Our eyes meet and there's a smile. Only the two of us will know what ever happened here and it's nice to have that shared secret with her, only her. 'So formal. It was anything but...' I say, kissing her collarbone.

'And given that your frame of reference is larger than mine, was it OK for you? Really?' she asks.

I cock my head to one side. 'It was pretty fucking fantastic. I don't know why' – I say, my kisses working down to her stomach – 'but you really turn me on.' I love how kissing her makes her body tense, how her nipples harden under my tongue. I loved the way her body gave into me and shook when I was inside her, the way she exhaled in relief, my hand holding down hers above her head, not letting her move, getting her to relent to the feeling. I love that I could do that for her. But there's something about being with her that keeps me here. Lying here with her just feels right, there's no sense of panic or worry, it feels strangely calm.

'Can I ask a question?' she asks.

'Shoot.'

'Like, how many people have you...'

'Slept with?'

'I'm sorry – is that weird and awkward? I don't want to slut shame you.'

I laugh. 'It's actually not that many – about twenty. Would it be ungentlemanly to ask you for your stats?'

She puts her hand up to the air, all her fingers outstretched. 'I met Brian when I was at uni so, you know, it's not that many.'

'Well, it didn't show in case you were worried. You know, sex is sometimes about energy. Get the right partner and none of your experience or history means a thing, really... And I think we had very, very good energy...'

She smiles because she knows that much to be true. There were moments where I glided my body over hers, the way we fit, a moment when I was behind her, an arm across her breasts and she interrupted the sex with a tender kiss, slowing down the action so we could both take it in. It was some sort of synergy laced with laughter, passion, a sensuality I don't think I've felt for the longest time, if ever.

'What's your favourite colour?' I ask her, an immediacy within me to know much more about her than I do already.

'Yellow. Yours?'

'Green.'

She nods. 'Is this what we're doing now? Is it question time?'

'Why not? We're both naked with nowhere to go. Ask me something.'

She pauses for a moment. 'OK. I've not dug too much but Ed filled me in about you and what happened after you graduated from university.'

I smile, instinctively grabbing at a pillow under me to get comfortable. 'And there was me asking about your favourite colour.'

'We can do that. What's your favourite chocolate bar?'

'I'm partial to a Snickers but no, we can go deeper. I don't mind. What did Ed say?' I ask, curious at the information that's been traded around the staff room.

'Just that you put your life on hold to help out your brother. He mentioned nephews.'

I shrug my shoulders and scrunch up my face. 'They're Barney and George – they're both nearly ten. And yeah, I had a sister-in-law, Amy, and she died when the twins were literally babies, so I moved in with Dom and helped him out for a bit. I actually saw them tonight before I came here.'

I look across at her. I can't tell if that's her eyes welling up but she's silent, studying my face.

'You lived with them? Do you have any other siblings? Your parents?'

'Just Dom. Parents sadly both deceased.'

She squeezes my hand at that point. 'I hope someone has told you that you did a really wonderful thing there... for your brother.'

It's my turn to be silent. I guess, in a way, the boys did, though everyone these days seems to be more preoccupied by the fact I've never moved on from it. However, I saw how much Amy's death devastated my brother. I heard his tears, loud, raw, pained. Plus, those kids are still kids. It always seemed a safer option to stay close if they still needed me. There were times I went further afield but I always gravitated back to them.

'I'm just thinking back to when we first had that Nando's and you never mentioned it. You alluded to family, but you gave off more of an impression that you just bounced from one thing to another. You didn't say why...'

'I never did what I did for the glory. He's my brother. It was the right thing to do.'

She continues to study my face.

'Plus, we'd only just met, we were eating wings, I didn't want to talk about anything sad like that to someone I just met. And you were going through your own things,' I say.

'Or maybe you're just modest. You love your family. You also experienced their grief and trauma; you prioritised them over yourself, and that speaks volumes about you, Jack.'

I take a deep breath that someone I barely know just summarised it all, and I don't quite know how to take it, to have someone read you and elevate you like that. And strangely, I think back to other women who I've shared similar pillow talk with. Times when we've just chatted shit. I once had a woman lie next to me and list out everything she'd eaten that day. She couldn't believe she'd eaten three bags of crisps.

'You've gone quiet,' she tells me, concern etched in her face.

I shake my head. 'Can I go deep then?' She furrows her brow and I laugh. 'In conversation...'

She nods.

'You need to promise me something next time?' I ask her.

'Presumptuous,' she says, narrowing her eyes.

'Are you trying to tell me, you were just using me? Like a one-night stand? I am devastated. I thought you were different,' I say, kissing the side of her exposed neck.

'You had a request,' she asks, a little nervous laugh telling me I may be asking for something beyond her sexual prowess and knowledge.

I pause for a moment to take in her face. In my early twenties, I had a lot of one night stands to fit around life being an uncle to twin babies. I sought out sex to sate a physical need, rather than look for relationships. This could be because I saw how Dom experienced real loss – maybe I was too scared to get too close to anyone. But being here with Zoe sparks a different sort of feeling.

'You're fucking beautiful. Just know that I think that much. I hope you can feel that way about yourself, too.' And I feel her body relax, I see the shallows of her throat gulp deliberately. She scrunches up her face, trying to downplay what I just said. 'And don't you dare swerve that,' I say, putting a finger to her lips.

'Just give me time to take all this in. It's just... I was with someone for a fair few years. And now there's you and you're...'

'Don't say young.'

'A different sort of package, shall we say? It's new and it feels...'

'There are issues with my package?'

'Surreal. Like, while you had a little doze, I've just been lying here, contemplating whether that happened or whether I had some out-of-body experience.'

'I will take that as a compliment.'

She laughs again but there's still a bewilderment in her eyes, not really knowing how to label this. Maybe we don't have to.

'Do you have anywhere to be tomorrow?' I ask her.

'No? You?'

I shake my head. 'Then have a sleep. Let me hold you. I'll be here when you wake up if you still want me here and we can make stuff up as we go along? Maybe?'

She nods, curling her body into mine. 'Maybe,' she says, her eyes closing. 'They have a breakfast buffet here. There's an omelette station...'

'That might be the sexiest thing anyone has ever said to me,' I whisper into her ear and she falls asleep, in my arms, her curls resting against my arm. I kiss the top of her head protectively, but I'm wide awake, wondering what the hell I might be feeling.

TEN

Zoe

I NEED ALL THE DETAILS BECAUSE JACK IS NOT REPLYING TO HIS TEXTS.

I stand in this rather large hotel bathroom and look at myself in the mirror, just wearing my knickers and Jack's t-shirt, looking over Mia's message. I splash my face with water. I don't know how to answer her. Maybe I should tell her I don't know what she's talking about. Jack? Didn't see him. I'm not wearing a t-shirt that smells like him. I haven't inhaled the t-shirt. I just had a lovely time in my giant bathtub and ordered pizza and cheesecake for one in my hotel room and watched Graham Norton. What did you think happened, Mia? I didn't have sex FOUR TIMES with Jack. I didn't get naked with him. His penis was nowhere near me. He didn't have my nipples in his mouth. I certainly didn't come so hard that I apologised profusely to the furniture in the room because I was in some complete state of shock.

I stare into the mirror at the woman standing before me. My

curls have always been unmanageable but now they're frizzy and unkempt. This doesn't quite feel real; that I have to cup my mouth so Jack can't hear me laughing, tears filling my eyes. You just had sex, Zoe. With a really good-looking young man. I'm torn between telling the world but also just wanting to savour that moment on my own for a lifetime. Look what you did, Zoe Swift. Fucking well done, girl! For some reason, I feel myself punch the air and do a little dance to myself, all in full view of this bathroom mirror. Maybe I should thank Mia and Ed for being so very sneaky, for leading this horse to the water so she could have a long cool drink.

I don't quite know what to do now. We woke early, had lazy morning sex. Again. And since then we've been lying there, chatting. He showed me a scar on his left leg from a school snowboarding trip. He went through his social media to show me the time when he was nineteen and bleached his hair. In return, he asked me questions. He asked me about some woman who I almost forgot existed. I remembered my favourite ice cream is coffee and my favourite holiday was back when I was at university when I went with Kate to Marrakech and we nearly bought a monkey from a man who had it hidden in his trenchcoat.

> Jack? Jack from school? Is he OK? Why?

I reply to Mia.

I'll keep her hanging for a little while. I feel I need to tell someone, though. Beth? Kate? Maybe I'll ring down to reception? I re-open the bathroom door and stand there watching Jack as he lies half-naked in bed, the sheet over his waist, flicking through the brochures from the hotel spa as his head rests in his arm and the curves of his bicep appear clearly defined. I did that. Christ. And I bite my lip trying to hold in my giggles. This still feels like an unreal experience that he's there. He stops reading to look up at me and smile.

'Have you had any texts from Mia yet?' I ask him, propping myself up against the doorframe.

'Just Ed. I'm ignoring him. I texted my housemate, Ben, to let him know I'm alive, though,' he says, holding his phone up. He pouts. 'You're out of bed,' he says, patting the space next to him.

'I was just going to have a shower, freshen up. I fancy breakfast,' I inform him.

'By my calculations, breakfast will be available for another hour or so,' he says with a cheeky glint in his eye. 'I have a feeling you haven't had a chance to languish for a while.'

'Languish. That sounds like something people do when they're dying of typhoid.'

'I find it can be a wonderful means of restoration.' I would focus on his words, but he moves in the bed so that I can see the curve of his arse through the sheets. I'm not sure what's come over me, but I want to bite it. I don't think that's right.

'I just need a moment to... regroup...' I tell him. 'Outside of that bed.'

He laughs. 'Well, did you want to do anything outside of here? We could grab some food? Maybe go for a walk.'

And for a moment, I stare into space thinking of life beyond this room. A panic comes over me to think of my kids. How I've not really thought about them for the last twelve hours and I don't know if that makes me feel guilty. How I quite liked being here with Jack in this little sex bubble, how it's provided escape, connection, joy – something I so desperately needed. I just don't know how this exists outside of these four walls. I sigh deeply.

'Breakfast, first. I need coffee,' I say, reaching down to take off his t-shirt and throw it at him. I guess if we're going to be seen outside of this bubble, it starts with the omelette station.

. . .

I guess there's a certain sort of clientele I would expect to see at a hotel breakfast buffet. We're in Central London so I assumed tourists, some families and possibly a businessman enjoying some grapefruit segments with a laptop open trading stocks with Tokyo. However, as I walk into this very well-lit room, I see a wall of fruit displayed to the right and remember we're in a spa hotel. The order of the day is resting in jacuzzis, wellness and mud packs. It means that the clientele of this particular breakfast buffet is ninety percent women.

'Mr and Mrs Rogers, welcome,' the waitress tells me as I give her our room number.

Oh, shit. I'm supposed to be married. Will it matter that we're not wearing rings? Maybe that's just not our bag. I feel Jack reach down for my hand and we follow her through the restaurant, several pairs of eyes on us as we head for a table by the windows that reach from ceiling to floor, revealing a bright London day to us, the clouds clearing over the skyline.

'Everything available is on our menus today. Can I point you towards our detoxification tea? It's a brilliant start to the day and our granola is made in-house. Let me know if you need anything else,' she says.

I nod and her eyes bounce between the two of us supposed newlyweds. We didn't make much of an effort in terms of make-up, dress and hair, we just seemed to be living off some sex afterglow where nothing else mattered. Jack just threw on a t-shirt and jeans whereas I literally have last night's dress on and some hastily applied mascara, my hair bundled messily on top of my head.

I open up the menu. 'There was us thinking we'd get a big greasy fry-up and it's mainly egg white omelettes and chia seeds,' I joke.

'*Salvia Hispanica*,' Jack says.

'Is that like Huevos Rancheros?' I ask.

He laughs. 'It's the Latin name for chia seeds. They're a flowering plant in the mint family, native to Mexico.'

'He studied botany.'

'The lady remembers correctly.'

He looks over at me and smiles. He has that sort of youth on his side where he doesn't look tired, more sexy dishevelment. All I know is that we stood next to each other in the lift down here, both of us facing forward, catching our reflections grinning at each other and for a moment, I didn't really care what I looked like. However, being in this room now, the feeling is different. There's a large table behind us that look like they're on some girls' weekend. All of them look rested, like they've been steamed and massaged to within an inch of their lives. One of them wears the sort of leggings that define the actual crack of her buttocks, her stomach is on show, and she rests a zip-up hoodie over her shoulders.

'You don't look relaxed?' Jack asks me, studying my face.

'There's a lot of women in here,' I mumble, looking down at my menu. I've never seen a longer smoothie list.

Jack scans the room. 'You are correct. It's me, the omelette man, two waiters and the gay couple in the corner.'

'They could be friends, even brothers.'

'He's got his hand on his thigh. I'm going with couple. Oh dear,' Jack says. 'They caught me looking. Say something funny.'

'Something funny?'

Jack laughs and takes my hand. I guess to signal to the gay couple that he's attached, fake married even. I giggle in return.

'So why are all these women making you stressed?' Jack asks.

'I sense some of them looking, trying to work us out, possibly checking you out?' I say. And just like clockwork, the lady with the very revealing leggings walks past our table, and I glance up to see her trying to catch Jack's eye. I don't know how to react but Jack snickers as she walks past.

'You noticed that, too?' I say, pulling a face.

'Zoe. You think I'm going to dump you at a breakfast buffet for someone wearing indecent leggings?'

'Well, no... but...'

'Because I'm looking at her and it screams high mainte-nance, attention seeker. She's videoing the buffet which tells me she's some sort of influencer. I don't think I'm meant to be with someone who takes selfies with fruit salad.'

His gaze doesn't move from mine, and I smile back. 'I am going to see if they do some sort of coffee in this place. Can I get you a cup?' he asks sweetly.

I nod and watch as he leaves the table, several pairs of eyes following him as he does. I wonder how this looks to other people. Do we appear mismatched? Do we look married? Are they judging me? I try to work out the big group behind us and see one of the group is wearing a big badge on her jumper with a '40' on it. It's a birthday gathering. The lady on the badge looks up at me and smiles. That was me three years ago. But it wasn't. Kate took me to Zurich for the weekend. And I think back to a time when Brian gifted me a card that told me he couldn't wait to be around for the next forty years, and he gave me a bracelet with my birthstone in it. We then went out for a posh dinner. I had sea bass. I need to get rid of that bracelet.

'Coffee for the lady. I also peered at our options. There is a nice-looking Eggs Benedict, lots of avocado, too, if that's your thing,' Jack says, returning to his seat. 'I also got you some fresh orange juice. They have that machine where you can see them squishing the oranges.'

I smile to see how that's provided him with so much amuse-ment. I take a polite sip, just as two people walk past wearing just robes and the hotel slippers.

'At least we put actual clothes on,' Jack jokes. 'You still look like you're on edge,' he says, adding some milk to his coffee and stirring in some sugar.

I shrug my shoulders. 'It's just an interesting experiment to be out with you. In public.'

'I like it. It feels like we're doing something normal. I can see how you take your coffee. I can learn a bit more about you.'

He leans in over the table, and as much as I want to kiss him, right here, right now, it still doesn't feel quite right to do that here. People are eating, for a start.

'Poached eggs. If you want to know something about me, I love a poached egg,' I tell him.

'Then that's where we'll start. Stay here, get comfy – let me. With smoked salmon, English muffin, spinach?'

I'm not sure how that was written on my face but that sounds perfect. I nod and he wanders away again as I take in the view.

'Well, she's obviously older?' I suddenly hear a voice coming from the other table. My ears tentatively turn to the conversation as I pretend to sip my coffee. I can only suppose they're talking about me. I spy bottles of organic champagne on the table which tells me they're here for the health but also the mimosas with the freshly squished oranges. Someone tells the woman to shush.

'Maybe he's a kindly cousin or relative that's taken her out for the weekend,' one of them cackles. 'I don't think they're together, together.'

'Maybe she's rich. Like he's a toyboy.'

The lady with the big 40 badge catches my eyes and blushes hard, trying to quieten down her friends and family. I try to focus on the river and streets below. And I think about what they would have said if it had been Mia and Ed here. Knowing what I do about Mia, she would shut them up, for sure. There would be an orange juice massacre. But what if it was Brian? They'd leave us alone. We'd look like a couple in their forties enjoying a weekend away. We'd have blended into the background, and they'd move their attentions elsewhere. I'm not sure how I feel to suddenly be so visible.

Jack returns to the table, and I see eyes following him.

'All ordered, they will bring it over. I also went for a seed sprinkle which I apologise for but your man at the egg station said something about omega-3 and I was sold.'

'He's not wearing a ring. I don't think they're together,' a voice drifts in again.

Jack raises his eyebrows to hear it. Given his back is to them, it's far easier for him to signal his disapproval in his face.

'What else have they said?' he whispers.

'All sorts,' I say, trying to hide my face. 'They think I might be super rich, and you are perhaps my toyboy.'

'Rude. Are you rich, though? Could I hit you up for some Armani?'

I laugh but he studies my face, and I see his eyes change to realise my sadness at it all, that this group of women feel it appropriate to shame me. He turns around in his chair. Whoa, don't do that.

'Morning, ladies. Just checking, do you have any spare sugar on your table?' They all stare at him for a moment before someone hands a white ramekin over. I feel every inch of me freeze. What is he doing? Please don't. 'And happy birthday,' he says to the lady in the badge. 'Is that why you're all here?'

A girl who can't be older than her mid-twenties chimes in. 'Yeah. That's my Aunty Jade.' She pushes her chest out and flutters her fake eyelashes.

'Well, we hope you have a lovely weekend. Are you enjoying it? My wife and I think it's amazing here.'

They all turn their gazes towards me.

'Yeah, it really is,' Jade with the 40 badge says to break the incredibly awkward silence. 'How long have you been married?'

He turns to me and takes my hand. 'Oh, five years today.

Taking the opportunity to get away from the kids, shag each other senseless and chill in the spa, you know?' I can't seem to breathe. Someone who I think might be Grandma in their party seems to expel orange juice through her nostrils. The table is silent. 'Best woman I know,' he tells them, gripping my hand even tighter. 'Enjoy your breakfast, ladies. Thanks for the sugar.'

He turns back to me, and I notice that cheeky glint in his eye again. The same one I saw a few times last night when he was lying next to me, on my bed. I could very well die of embarrassment, right here, right now, but I think I don't mind it. The table behind is silent and a waiter suddenly appears with two of the exact same orders. It's Eggs Benedict but it seems to be served on a bed of cress.

'Amazing, thank you,' I tell the waiter.

'You're welcome, Mrs Rogers. Can I get anything else for you?'

I laugh as he says my fake name and he pulls a face.

'Don't mind her, my wife gets very excited about smoked salmon,' Jack intervenes.

I smirk. 'I do.'

The waiter looks less impressed and disappears. I watch Jack as he cuts into one of the eggs, poached to perfection. The yolk drips down the salmon and he looks back up at me.

'Well, eat up, Mrs Rogers.'

'Really?'

'Yeah. I told that table I need to shag you senseless and we have to follow through on that,' he says, biting into a piece of toast and raising his eyebrows at me.

I guess we do.

Jack

I think I may have broken Zoe. I don't know whether it was the seed sprinkle or wanting to prove to her that my gaze was solely focused on her but after breakfast, we came back here and as soon as we walked through the door, I led her to the bed, undressing her slowly, paying attention to every part of her. I don't know if she quite believes what's happening, whether she trusts me entirely. This is understandable given what she's been through but for now, I just want her to know she's safe with me. I won't hurt her like her husband has. Never.

For now, she sleeps a little too peacefully, and I arrange her curls on the pillow, slowly running a finger down her spine. She doesn't flinch. Maybe not broken but it's good to see her resting. I see her phone suddenly glowing on the bedside table. It's someone called Kate. I think that's her sister; she mentioned her last night. The phone glows until it goes to voicemail. I ignore it, but then it lights up with a text and I can see a message.

Zoe, pick up. Really important xxx

I glance down at Zoe as her chest rises slowly against the mattress. I look at her phone notifications and see messages pinging in from Dylan. That's her son.

Please pick up, Mum. Please xxx

Have you heard from her?

Mum?

At least twenty notifications have come through in the last hour when I believe we were in the throes of smoked salmon and then some pretty intense orgasms. A call comes in again from Kate and instinct tells me to answer it. This is not a great idea.

'Fuck me, Zoe, where have you been? You always answer your phone.'

'Hi, ummm...'

'Who's this?' the voice says abruptly.

'I'm Jack, a friend. Zoe can't come to the phone right now. She's in the toilet.'

'Has she been in the toilet for the last hour?' Kate snaps back at me.

I'm not quite sure how to answer that. 'Can I take a message?'

'I don't know anyone called Jack in my sister's life. Who are you again?'

'I'm a work colleague.'

'Where does my sister work?'

'In a school, she teaches maths.'

I see Zoe stir in the bed and look up at me. She points at her phone, confused. I cover the mouthpiece. 'It was ringing, I didn't want to wake you. It's your sister. I think something's happened...'

She sits up immediately, taking the phone. Given Kate's volume, I hear everything clearly.

'Where the hell have you been?' Kate shrieks at her. 'Check your messages, now.' She switches the phone to speaker and scrolls through her phone, her expression changing, the colour from her face draining.

'What the actual hell?' she mumbles.

I don't quite know what to do but I move out of bed and put some clothes on. This feels like a situation for clothes.

'Before you have an actual heart attack, she jumped on a train to Birmingham. She's on the phone to Neil now and we've told her to stay on the line until she's with us. We'll pick her up from the station in an hour and then I'll drive her back to you guys.'

I see the tears welling up in Zoe's eyes and she wipes them

away with the palm of her hand. 'What the hell was he thinking?'

'Who knows with that man anymore? If I see him, I will literally stab him. Hang up here and call Dyl. He's panicking. I'll let you know when I have Lottie. Just bloody pick up your phone, yeah? And who the hell is Jack?'

She looks up at me. 'I went to school to work on a project thing. He's a colleague.'

She mouths sorry to me. Kate doesn't respond to that. 'Love you. All will be fine. Just breathe.'

Zoe nods and the line goes dead. She sits there in bed, a hand to her mouth and it's the same Zoe I saw when she first found out her husband had been cheating on her. The sadness kills me.

'I'm sorry I picked up your phone. I should have just woken you up. Are you OK?' I ask her.

She doesn't look like she wants to get into the practicalities of that situation, but I can see her mind running through a million different thoughts.

'Can you get me some water?' she asks. I nod, heading to the desk in the room and pouring her out a glass. She walks over to her suitcase, looking for clean clothes and tying her hair into a bun again. I see her scroll through messages, tears rolling down her cheeks. She starts to make a call, puts the phone to speaker again and I sit on the edge of the bed, eavesdropping.

'Mum? God...'

'I'm so sorry I didn't answer, Dyl. Are you OK? Please tell me you're OK?'

'I've just shut myself in my room. I can't believe Dad did this.'

'So Liz wasn't there when you arrived?'

'No, last night we went out for dinner and then this morning, she just appeared at breakfast. Turned up to the Airbnb with pastries and coffees and Dad announced she was going to spend the rest of the weekend with us. That's when Lottie totally lost it.'

Tears start to properly flow from her eyes. I don't quite know what to do but I put a hand to her back. She tries to hold it together so Dylan can't hear how upset she is.

'Understandable. And then she just left?'

'Stormed out, screaming and crying.'

'Well, I don't want you to worry because it turns out she rang Aunty Kate and is currently on a train to Birmingham.'

'She what?' Dylan says, half-laughing. 'How did she wing that?'

'Have you met your sister before?' she jokes. 'Aunty Kate will go meet her and bring her home, make sure she's safe. Dylan, I don't know what to say. Do you want to be there? I can come and get you. I can book a train for you or get a car to bring you back home. I'm so sorry he's done this.'

And that's when her son starts sobbing and Zoe totally loses it.

'I'm so sorry, Dylan.'

'I don't want to be here, Mum. I don't want to do this alone.'

Zoe nods and I see her eyes frantically working out what to do. I signal to her requesting if it's OK for me to talk. She stares at me, but I know what I have to do.

'Hi, Dylan. My name is Jack. Your mum and I work together, we've been in school today working on a project. Look, let me help. I've got friends in Manchester who I can call. What I'm going to do is get them to pick you up and drive you down to Birmingham so you can find Lottie and your Aunty Kate and then she can drive you back home. Does that sound like a plan? Have you got an address there?'

Dylan pauses for a moment. 'Mum?'

Zoe scans my face. 'Yeah, it's fine. We can trust Jack. It's a good idea, then at least you'll be together.'

'I think it's called Spinners Way. There's a Tesco Express downstairs.'

'Then that's good. I'll give them a call and get them to pick you up from outside there. Their names are Sarah and Hakeem. They're really nice, just stay on the line and we'll give you all the details you need.'

'OK.'

Zoe looks at me as I escape to a corner of the room to ring Sarah. Sarah will get involved because she's nosy but also has a halo of solid gold when it comes to people needing help. However, if I have to, I will refer to the time their dog pooed on my pillow. I see Zoe trying to calm her son down, emotion lacing her voice, and all her focus and attention is on him. Is it strange to say that makes her all the more attractive? That maybe shouldn't be at the forefront of my mind right now.

'Sir Damon, to what do I owe the pleasure?' Sarah says down the phone.

'Hon, I need a favour. You don't happen to be free today?'

'Yeah, all OK?'

And as I explain the situation to my friends with bribes of more free pet-sitting, I hear Zoe in the corner of the room. She's on the phone but quite obviously not with Dylan anymore and there is a strength and ferocity there, unleashed.

'How in the hell did you ever think that was a good idea? So you just let her leave? You didn't follow her? She is THIR-TEEN. I couldn't give a flying fuck about Liz right now. Why aren't you with our son? Well, he doesn't want to be there, so I've got someone picking him up. *WHO*? It's none of your business. He is old enough to be able to state what he wants, and he doesn't want to be there. Have enough respect for YOUR children to let them make their own decisions... I don't care about your rights as a father... If you're so concerned, then speak to a lawyer... Have you banged your head or something? I DON'T GIVE A FLYING FUCK!'

And I sit there listening, half giving Hakeem directions but also witnessing Zoe really let go. I suspect she's not spoken to her husband like this since all of this has happened. And he deserves this. When you set fire to your world, you shouldn't be allowed to not feel some of those flames up close and realise what you've done.

And all at once, I feel relieved and proud that she's able to tell him exactly what a complete and utter dick he has been.

ELEVEN

Zoe

I once watched an episode of *Grey's Anatomy* where a man had a brain tumour that changed his personality; he acted so irrationally that he went up to a bear when he was camping and got his brother completely disembowelled. Sometimes, when I think of what Brian could possibly do next, I consider that maybe he did have some sort of traumatic brain injury that triggered all of this. Maybe he was hit by a golf ball or hit his head on one of the rafters in the loft. If not, maybe I could hit him in the head. I think I could manage that quite easily.

Lottie is many things: she's independent, she could talk her way out of a paper bag. She's shrewd and streetwise but by that same measure, she is thirteen and the idea of her just walking around the unfamiliar streets of Manchester, on public transport with just her phone and the clothes on her back, makes me slightly queasy. Anything could have happened, she could have ended up anywhere, with the wrong people. I look down at her text.

> I hate dad. I am going to divorce him myself.
> I'm coming home. I'm going to Aunty
> Kate's xxx

It was sent before she got on the train. So casual, so bloody confident. It's the sort of thing you wish you could bottle up and sell. I kept texting her to tell her how much I love her, and she just replies in rants with abbreviations I still don't understand. I can't be angry because I get it. What was Brian thinking? This was supposed to be a weekend for him to repair his relationship with his children, not a chance to throw Liz into the mix. He's lucky Lottie didn't bare her teeth and just go for her. It's only by the grace of the universe and sheer miracle, she is now safe with Kate and my heart can rest easy.

> Who were those people? And who the hell is
> Jack?

Brian messaged me when Dylan was collected.

Oh, he's just the twenty-nine-year-old man I fucked five times in the space of twelve hours. Who knows where my clitoris is, gave me multiple orgasms after breakfast and who has helped me sort out your mess. YOURS.

I didn't message him that, but I was close. So close. In the meanwhile, I am also aware that the sex bubble has burst. A magical twelve hours in this room came to an end when the curtains were opened and real life flooded in. Jack and I are showered and changed and sit on opposite sides of the room, trying to work out the logistics of getting my kids home. And I guess most blokes would have left by now but Jack stays. He keeps offering me drinks. He gives me updates on where his friends are with Dylan. He disappeared for half an hour but returned with doughnuts. It's a special sort of person who understands how a stressful situation needs fried dough, sugar and jam.

> They've just dropped me off. I'm safe. They
> were really nice.

As soon as Dylan's message drops, I exhale deeply. Not that I didn't trust Jack's friends but at least my kids are reunited and with someone they know. A FaceTime suddenly comes through, and I panic. I have to chat to all of them but I'm still in this hotel room. I jump up from my chair and run towards a blank wall that I can try and blag as home or school.

I press accept and as soon as I see both of their faces on screen, relaxed and safe on Kate's sofa, I start crying. They both stare at me, looking confused.

'Why are you crying?' asks Lottie. 'Where are you?'

Independent it would seem but not particularly empathetic.

'I'm at school, Lottie. I can't believe you. I don't think you realise that you got on a train. On your own. Anything could have happened to you,' I try to explain to her.

'Yeah, but it didn't. There was no way I was going to spend a minute longer there. With him,' she sneers.

I'm not going to waste my anger and worry on her, but I sigh, shaking my head. 'And you, Dylan, you OK?'

He forces a smile. 'Hakeem and Sarah were really nice. Hakeem has season tickets for Man City, he said he'd take me to a game if I wanted.'

He'll never talk to me about his dad and how this really makes him feel and I don't want to force it, especially when we're not in the same room. 'Then I'm glad.'

'I'm going to feed them, Zo, and then we'll drive back. You OK?' Kate says, drifting into view. I see her eyes scanning my surroundings.

I nod. 'Thank you,' I mouth quietly.

'No worries, sis. They're safe.'

I hang up before the kids have a chance to see me cry again.

I throw my phone on the bed and then perch on a corner of it, my head in my hands. They're safe, that's all that matters.

'Can I give you a hug?' Jack asks me, walking over.

I nod and stand up, allowing myself to just curl into his body, to feel his arms wrapped around me and unlike last night, when the feel of him was electric and filled with some sort of potent charge, it now just feels warm, comforting and I am truly grateful for it.

'Can I send some money to Hakeem and Sarah? Have you got an address? I can send them some wine,' I tell him, still in hold.

'It's all taken care of,' he tells me quietly.

'Thank you.'

'It's all good.'

We part for a moment and Jack studies my face. 'I'm sorry. I must look a state.'

He shakes his head. 'Still beautiful, just a bit puffier.'

I laugh and encourage him to sit down next to me. 'Talk about real life coming in and interrupting proceedings quite rudely. I'm sorry. Thank you. Seriously. For your help, for all of... this.'

Jack smiles, resting a hand on my thigh. 'Well, despite the interruption, I enjoyed *this* very much. And to be honest, I don't think I could have done what we did for another twenty-four hours. Maybe this was the universe telling us we needed to pace ourselves.'

I smile broadly.

'Please don't worry about me. They're your kids and they deserve all your attention. They really do. I know how much they mean to you.'

I'm pleased to know he's been paying attention to that much. 'And where do we go from here?' I ask him, curious. 'Not that I need labels or anything like that, but I don't want to misconstrue anything.'

'Well, I would like to see you again, Zoe. I really would.'

And I furrow my brow. This is not a simple boy meets girl story, this is messy and it comes with baggage that is still packed, that is still heavy and in the way. I know he doesn't see the age gap but my practical, numbers-based mind dwells on it a little too much. Despite all his compliments, the spark, the very good essence that I feel underpins who he is, I still question whether it's worth his time.

'You'll likely see me again. We work in the same place.'

'I mean, I would like to see you naked again.'

I pause. 'I think I would like that, too.'

'You think?'

And we both laugh as he grabs one of my hands, kissing it. 'You just come find me when you need me. I'll be here, waiting.'

'Naked.'

'Well, not at school. I hear that's frowned upon.'

I get an Uber home. Jack and I said our goodbyes in the hotel room with a prolonged kiss and a lift ride down to the lobby filled with charged looks and hesitation. When I got home, the house was grey and empty, echoing the cold drizzle that had started to fill the air. I unpacked my bag, put on a load of washing and had a long shower. It was strange. I carry no shame about what happened last night. I feel guilty I missed my kids' calls when they needed me, but I keep experiencing flashbacks to moments of intense joy, feeling echoes of Jack's touch, moments that make me smile wildly. It happened. I just can't let anyone know, not now, and especially after everything that the kids have experienced this weekend.

As soon as Kate's car pulls up to the drive, I run out into the driveway. They come and find me, and both of them nestle me into a long, prolonged hug. I feel complete. I feel an overwhelming sense that all is right again with the world.

Kate suddenly joins the hug. 'Come on. It's drizzling and I need a big cup of tea. Kettle on, please.'

We all disperse, the kids getting their bags from the car whilst Kate throws her arms around me. 'You're all flushed, rosy. Are you coming down with something?' she enquires.

I don't quite know how to answer that. That could be the stress of this morning or the orgasms. 'It's the change of the seasons, isn't it?' It was definitely the orgasms. 'Were they OK on the drive?' I ask her.

The kids get inside the house, disappearing to the loo and to take their bags upstairs, and I follow, watching their tired bodies mooch around the place.

'Quiet. I think Brian's been trying to text and plead his case. I could hear them conspiring in the back of the car. He's been attempting to make them feel guilty about the concert tickets and Lottie told him where he could stick them.'

'Sometimes I do think she's your child,' I tell her. She replies with a smirk. 'I had a screaming session with Brian before. I can't believe he did this...'

I lead her into the kitchen and Kate stops in her tracks as she takes off her coat. 'Hold up. You screamed at Brian?'

'Yeah?'

'You've not done that yet. You've been all reserved and upper hand. Good for you. You needed to do that.'

As I fill up the kettle, I glance at myself in the reflection of the window. I did do that. I gave that man both barrels and I did not hold back, and I wonder why. What changed? What gave me the confidence and the power to do that?

'He's driving back tomorrow morning,' I tell Kate. 'For "crisis" talks.'

'Well, I'm not going to talk to him,' Lottie tells me as she enters the kitchen, going through the cupboards on the hunt for biscuits and snacks.

'Can I stay?' Kate asks. 'I can give him a crisis worth talking about.'

Lottie laughs at her aunt and comes to snuggle in next to me. 'You look different, Mum.'

'I thought that,' Kate says.

'I did one of those nice Korean face masks last night whilst I watched *Reacher*,' I tell her, swallowing hard to have to lie. 'Anyway, we still need to talk about you wandering around the North of England and getting trains on your own.'

'Are you angry?' she asks me. 'Dad was pretty furious.'

I look at her face, thinking about all she's been through in the past day, all the emotion that bubbles away inside her and I'm not sure how my fury will help. 'I'm just... I don't know... Relieved that you're safe.'

'I did everything you've ever taught me to do. I sat next to an old woman who smelt of soup. I kept a key in my hand in case I needed to stab someone.'

I turn to Kate. 'It's like your genes literally jumped into my child.' I bundle Lottie into my arms. 'But you also abandoned Dylan...'

'Yeah, I felt bad about that,' she admits.

'How is he?' I ask her.

She shrugs, and I can hear echoes of him crying again on the phone. It brings a lump to my throat.

Dylan enters the room. 'I'm fine. I just don't walk to talk to him for a while. Is that OK?' I nod and he puts an arm around me, grabbing my shoulder. He also clutches a large brown paper bag. 'I don't need anything else. But this was an excellent idea, Mum. Love you.'

He puts the bag down on the counter. Nando's? I check the receipt in case Dylan has just accepted delivery of a neighbour's dinner. Right address and by the looks of it, a fair bit of wings – all at differing spice levels. My phone pings, and a message from The Anti-Wanker appears with a chicken emoji. I laugh out loud and Kate narrows her eyes at me. The kids scurry around the kitchen, getting plates, locating phones and washing hands whilst Kate comes and stands next to me.

'What's the deal with this chicken? This better not be from Brian,' she whispers.

I shake my head. She looks down at my phone, opening it up to see the notification on my screen. Her jaw slackens.

'You weren't at school today, were you? When I called?' she whispers.

I side eye her. 'Later. I'll tell you later.'

She widens her eyes at me, and I can't tell if that emotion is horror, surprise or happiness.

Jack

'Uncle Jack!' the boys scream as they see me, thundering down the stairs. 'Did you bring food?' they ask me.

'Yes, I was presumptuous and brought takeaway. How are we feeling for chicken, lads?'

'Are there chips?'

'Are there chips? Of course.' The children and my brother cheer, arms in the air. I am a hero.

Dom comes up to me, grabbing the bag. 'Absolute legend. Literally nothing in these cupboards. Otherwise, we'd be having toast. What's up with you – you look knackered?' he tells me.

'Charming. I was out last night,' I tell him, following him into the kitchen.

'Oh, the joys of a night out. I hope you didn't come here to brag about the size of your hangover,' he moans. 'Lads, clear the living room table and get *Ninja Warrior* on.' The boys do as they're told.

I won't lie, Dom doesn't keep a very tidy house. There are solo shoes that lie around the place, stacks of letters from school that sit on the kitchen counter, football kit that hangs off every available radiator space. But I've also never met someone so invested in loving his boys. I'll always remember his words to me: now Amy's gone, I have to try and love them twice as much. I tried to help him with that, and I don't think the boys want for anything in that respect. He doesn't sweat the small stuff, he's learnt to prioritise his time by giving what he can to those lads and they always seem especially buoyant about life. So I don't judge. I let him get on with it and prop him up every so often when he needs it.

'I'm just being a decent and loving brother,' I tell him.

'Do you want money?'

'No.'

'Are you moving back in?'

I moved out several years ago when the boys started school and I convinced myself that Dom could survive without me.

'Also, no.'

He looks at my face. 'Jesus Christ. You're coming to me for life advice.'

I don't answer.

'Little Jack has life dilemmas. Is it work? Did you hit a child? Do you need legal counsel?'

'No.'

He gets out a selection of mismatched plates, grabs the ketchup from the fridge and starts piling up the chicken wings and chips. 'Then the only thing left is either your health or your love life...'

'The latter...'

I see his face rise to a broad grin. 'Then if this is you coming here looking knackered because you've had sex all night, you can leave.'

I laugh, stealing a couple of chips. 'You can talk! Didn't you say last night that you needed help because your new school mum squeeze is into weird things?'

He looks through the hallway to ensure the boys are out of earshot and closes the door to the kitchen slightly.

'God, yes. Her name's Kim. She's into sexting. Because obviously as parents, none of us have time to meet up and shag in real life. She wants pictures and all. I have no idea what I'm doing.'

He says it so matter-of-factly, I can't help but snigger. 'Well, I love you, man, but I draw the line at taking pictures of your cock for you.'

Dom laughs, snorting a little, and it makes me smile. After everything he's been through, it's always been nice to hear that sound, to level him out with a bit of joy. These days he's some life-beaten dad who forgets to cut his hair, who wears the same five T-shirts because they still fit and who I suspect just gets a lot of joy from a nap on the sofa and an uninterrupted shower. The man is owed.

'I can give you some tips.'

'I think she wants more than the tip,' Dom jokes and we both laugh because deep down, our sense of humour never really developed past our teens.

'Always erect, no one wants a picture of a flaccid penis. Try lying down, instead of standing up. It's all in the angles and the lighting.' He nods, taking it all in. 'Also, never include your face in the pictures. Protect your penis and your identity.'

'That's a good slogan,' he chuckles. I open a drawer to look for serving utensils and pull out some shin pads and what looks like part of the vacuum cleaner. Dom looks upon it all and turns his palms up to the air. 'In my head, it's a reliable filing system.'

I turn to look at the kitchen fridge, at old pictures drawn by the lads. Back in the early days, people newly acquainted to our family assumed Dom and I to be gay as we popped up in all the boys' drawings, all holding hands. Then they'd find out the truth and Dom and I always got the sighs, the glassy eyes. So you're raising those boys together? Like some 80s sitcom? And we would nod. I'll be frank, I always thought it would get us both laid more but it never did.

I look over as Dom gnaws away at some chicken. Again, I like seeing the joy in his closed eyes and happy chomping sounds. He looks up mid-chew. 'So, tell me of your love life woes then. I can't for the life of me think why you would need me for advice.' He sounds confused. 'Beers are in the fridge.'

I extract two bottles and find the bottle opener to crack them open. He sups furiously at the top of one and clinks it against the neck of mine.

'I've met someone. She's older.'

'Older than me?' he says hesitantly, the lines around his eyes creasing.

I nod.

'Does she have her own teeth?' he says, mocking me.

'Shut up. She's forty-three.'

He pauses for a moment, unsure of what to say. 'That's acceptable, I guess.'

'It just comes with complications. She's just split up from her husband, there are kids in the picture.'

'How old?'

'Thirteen and fifteen.'

He puffs out his cheeks. These are not reactions that instil a lot of faith that he approves. He fiddles with some sauce sachets, putting a hand to his semi-receding hairline that I'm not allowed to talk about. 'Jack, is it weird that I don't quite know what to say?' he tells me, taking a seat at his kitchen table. I can't quite tell if he's shocked or indifferent.

'Well, you're not angry. I thought you might just laugh it off and warn me off her.'

'Do you love her?' he asks, his tone going big brother, semi-serious for a moment.

'God, no. I've just met her. I don't know. The sex was pretty unreal and we click, there's something there. I can't quite put my finger on it. I feel like we bring out something good in each other. Maybe.'

He laughs under his breath, staring at me. 'That's quite mature for you.' And I smile because that's how it feels to be with her. It feels grown up, comfortable. It's her sitting on the edge of the bed and not playing games, just asking me what this is and us wanting to do right by each other. I'm not sure I've had that clarity in any other relationship.

Dom looks out through the hallway and into the living room, his eyes fixed on his kids. There's always a way he looks at them that speaks of gratitude but also looks completely overwhelmed by emotion. 'Jack, the more and more I think about love, I have no clue what it should look like. For me, it was supposed to be me and Amy raising those boys and waiting for them to get big, adding more children to the mix and just existing together for an eternity, but hey, life had other plans, eh?' I glance at him for a moment. All that grief hit Dom especially hard, and I always worry about when it will rear its head and jab him in the guts again. He's dated since but he never talks of anything serious. I don't know if perhaps he's scarred for life or his heart just belonged to the one person, but you can tell how much he misses her, how he thinks about her daily. 'J-Lo is fifty and I'd tap that in an instant,' he adds.

From heartfelt sentiment to slightly inappropriate. 'Dom, she'd eat you alive. You don't even know how to take a picture of your willy.'

And he chuckles again, studying my face. 'Is she nice? Clever? She's not like that girl who wrote you her list of demands, is she?'

'Her name was Imogen, and it was a list of expectations...'

'Yeah, you were well rid of that one,' he says, still talking about her with mild disdain.

'She is nice. Her name is Zoe.'

'Well, you deserve nice and that's all I'll say. I just...'

I can see him mill through his words wondering the best way to phrase his next sentence. 'When you left us and the boys, it was almost a relief to me. For the longest time, I thought we'd held you back. Every day I wait to hear that you're going to fly somewhere, do something amazing, but you just stay close.'

'Armed with chicken, though,' I add, and then I frown. 'I went on that cruise ship once. I travelled.'

'And you came straight back.'

'I'm a homebody.'

'You... I don't know how to say this... Sometimes I wish you were a little more selfish with your time, your dreams, your life. You invest a lot in people, you're nice and loyal to a fault. I will always respect that. But when I hear you might get with a woman who's got a ready-made family, I worry it will just ground you again when really...' He pauses and gazes at a photo of his wife on the fridge. 'You have all the time in the world.'

He looks at me wondering if he's crossed a line.

'I'm just living in the now. Taking it one day at a time. I haven't thought about the future really,' I say, aware I'm trotting out some old, tired lines.

'I bet she has, though. With kids, it's what you do – you have to put them first. Shit, are you going to be a stepdad?' he jokes.

My eyes widen. 'Dom, I only slept with her yesterday. I haven't really thought that far ahead.'

'Then why did you come to talk to me?'

I pause for a moment. Maybe because this did feel different to the very random women I usually date for a few weeks before it fizzles out. Zoe is real, she has a quality about her that speaks to something in me. I think of times looking at her yesterday and feeling so relaxed yet so charged with an emotion I'd rarely experienced before.

'She had a bit of drama with her kids, her ex was being a

dick and she dropped everything for them. I don't know. It reminded me of you.'

He punches me in the arm.

'How complicated is the situation with the ex?'

'Together for twenty years, he ran off with her mate.'

'Ouch. Is he huge? Could you take him?'

'Easily.'

'I'll back you up. I'll bring the boys.' We both arch our heads into the living room where the twins jump off the sofa in the same way you see pumas jump off rock faces. Yep, bring them.

'Well, just look after yourself, you know. Protect your heart. It's a good heart,' he tells me.

'I'll try.'

'Have you sent her pictures of your ding-dong yet?' he enquires.

I laugh. 'No. I had sex with her five times in twelve hours, though.'

He widens his eyes at me, and I can't tell if that emotion is horror, surprise or happiness.

TWELVE

Zoe

'I think if I had sex five times in a row, my fanny would just give up on me. It would go into shock,' Kate tells me, sipping at her tea.

'It wasn't in a row, we had breaks in between,' I tell her.

'Were there biscuits involved?' she enquires, giggling. She looks down at her phone at the picture on Jack's Instagram, still trying to work it all out. She's confused? How the hell does she think I feel? 'At the end of the day, I think it's all karma. Life doled you out something a little shite and then in return, you were sent this Jack boy.'

'Don't call him boy,' I tell her.

'Hon, I've got bras older than him.'

I punch her in the arm, and she laughs, almost falling off her stool. Kate stayed last night as we all nestled into our sofa with spicy chicken and a rather violent vigilante thriller film that I think the kids needed to watch so they could work out some of their frustrations. Kate told me she wanted to stay for the moral support and needed to rest after driving, but I think she stayed for the gossip. As soon as Dylan took himself off to bed, she asked for every last detail. She lay next to me last night, still foraging for details, she woke up with me to keep digging. You slept with someone over ten years younger than you? How many times? He looks like that? At one time, she actually applauded.

And now we sit here, making our way through rounds of toast and tea as we wait for Brian to make an appearance, the autumn sunlight flooding the kitchen, the house silent. Such is the way when you have teenagers. I remember a time when I dreamt of this, when the kids were little and I'd be sitting in the front room watching *Peppa Pig* at six in the bloody morning. But now, they sleep. They don't emerge until lunch and the silence is an empty echo, almost preparing you for the moment when they will eventually fly from this nest.

'You know this will be the absolute best thing to show Brian when he gets here, right? I might get this guy's image put on a mug that says THIS IS WHO MY EX-WIFE FUCKS NOW.'

'Don't do that. That's not why I slept with him. You know that, right? It wasn't for revenge.'

'Oh god, I know that. But don't you want to brag, just a little bit...?' she says cheekily. I reach over and rub at toast crumbs that seem to have accumulated on the corner of her lips.

'No. And when he's here, don't say an absolute word. Don't pop up in a doorway like some strange puppet and announce it.'

She puts jazz hands to the sides of her face. 'Guess who Zoe's shagging, Brian?'

I giggle a little, choking on my tea, a little worried, however. Please no. She looks at me completely bemused.

'I am happy, though. If anyone needed this, it's you,' she says beaming, shaking her head and still slightly in disbelief. 'When can I meet him?'

I grimace at her. 'Never.'

'Ouch, are you ashamed of me?'

'No, I just have to work out what it all is. If it will happen again or if it's just...'

'Fucking,' she says, gritting her teeth. I find an oven glove and throw it at her. 'Oh my, you're, like, living everyone's middle-aged fantasy.'

'And what would that be?'

'Oh, I love Neil. I don't see myself with anyone else except that dopey bastard but sometimes I do think about having a lover. I'd live alone, have a bed to myself, not have to worry about sharing space and picking up someone's pants but at the end of a phone, I'd have a young, handsome lover to call upon who'd sort me out.'

I put a hand to my chest in shock. 'You make Jack sound like a gigolo.'

Kate cackles in reply. 'That's one word for it. But this boy isn't boyfriend material, is he?'

I can't answer. There is something there. A very potent spark that is hard to ignore. I like how his presence pushes me to let go, to be spontaneous and react. But in real life, outside our bubble, I guess if I wanted to consider something more with him, I'd have to put a lot more thought into what that would look like, how that would work.

'Stop calling him a boy...'

'Kid?'

I shake my head at her, just as we hear a light knocking on the front door. At least he's not just letting himself in anymore. There's a feeling in response to that sound. It used to be sadness, pain, but the feeling has transformed a little. I don't fear it as much.

Kate looks at me carefully as I get off my stool. 'You OK?'

I nod and walk to the door. I see his figure hovering by the glass, opening it slowly. When I do open it, he stands there, his eyes bloodshot, pulling the collar of his coat up around his neck. 'Zoe.'

'Thank you for knocking, at least.'

He shrugs his shoulders and follows me into the kitchen. When we get there, Kate seems to have disappeared. Hopefully not waiting to jump out of a cupboard and tell Brian that I'm shagging someone new, though the thought makes me grin.

'Is that Kate's car in the drive?' he asks me.

'Yeah, she dropped the kids off yesterday and stayed.'

Brian's eyes search around the kitchen area and through to the living room to look for her.

'There's coffee in the cafetiere if you want. Help yourself.'

It doesn't feel right to serve him anymore. He opens the cupboard, taking a mug and pouring himself a cup. Always black, no sugar. I can't read my feelings here. It almost feels like apathy, and to feel that towards someone I once was married to feels strange. Where the hell is Kate? I then hear the sound of the dryer whirring into action. Like aunty, like niece.

I take a seat at the counter and watch him take off his coat, putting a hand through his hair. It's the eyes that keep me quiet. I've not seen them like that before. Has he been crying? But there is a real melancholy there and I'm reminded of when his dad died five years ago and the raw grief he experienced. By that same measure, I remember how I propped him up at that time. I remember experiencing all those emotions with him, through him. How strange to suddenly feel so disconnected to him.

'I'm so sorry, Zoe. I really fucked up.' It's such a complete sentence to describe the last six months that I let it sit there for a while so we can both absorb it. 'Where are the kids?'

'Have you not met our kids before?' I say, looking at the clock. It's nine-thirty. 'You'll be lucky if you see them before midday.'

He pretends to laugh, both of his hands around his mug, his shoulders slumped over. 'How are they?'

'They're so bloody angry with you. I mean, they were pretty

angry already so it's like you just added another layer of wrath there.'

'I just thought...'

'Or didn't. I can't see how that situation was well thought out at all.'

'But it's Liz, they know Liz,' he says, trying to defend himself.

'Brian, they knew Liz as a family friend. *My* friend. Someone who used to sit in our living room and drink wine. To them, she has a whole different persona now. It was far too soon to even attempt to do that, to present them with some different dynamic, one which basically replaced me.'

He looks down at his coffee to take that all in. I can't believe how coherent I am. 'It's not like that. No one will replace you as their mother. They adore you.'

I won't argue that, but I adore them just as much, and I remember a time when Brian did, too. When he put their needs above his own. It was perhaps that shift in him that broke my heart the most.

'I don't know how to repair any of this, Zoe. I really don't. Even before Liz arrived yesterday morning, everything's changed. The way they talk to me, Lottie's sarcasm, the way Dylan's body stiffens when I try to hug him,' he says, a lump in his throat.

'You didn't just betray me, Brian. You betrayed them, too.' He can barely look at me. 'I don't want them to hate you. I never want that, but it will take time for them to trust you again. You made a decision to break this, and I don't think it's a quick fix.'

He looks uncomfortable to have to be told that much but then his judgement can hardly be trusted these days.

'Phase Liz in if you must but I think it will take even longer for them to accept her.'

'Have you completely poisoned them against her?'

'Fuck off, Brian.'

He flinches in shock to hear me swear because I rarely do. I take a sip at my tea to hide my shock that I've done that myself.

'How is she?' I ask, almost too casually.

'She's also having trouble with her kids. Eldest won't talk to her. Her youngest has started truanting from school.'

It's almost as if he's asking for sympathy. I hope he doesn't mind if I have none to share.

'Well, I hope the sex is worth all of that,' I say, again shocked at my ability to be so acerbic about it all.

His back straightens for a moment. 'It's not just sex, Zoe. I love her. I love Liz.'

And he comes right back at me with some very sharp barbs indeed. My face goes numb to hear it. And not because he stopped loving me or because that feeling of love moved to someone else but because I don't think I'll ever understand it. I don't know if that is love. To hurt all those people in the wake, to irrevocably ruin all those kids and their perceptions of family, their parents, to act so completely and utterly selfishly. That seems to me to be the very opposite of love.

Brian tries to reach over to hold my hand and I pull a face, retracting my hand as far from him as possible. 'That was cruel. I'm sorry,' he says, appearing contrite at least.

I laugh under my breath. I've heard that word so many times that it's started to lose its impact. The utility room door suddenly opens, and Kate stands there holding a basket of folded towels. Brian does a double take to see her standing there, knowing she would have overheard most of our conversation.

'Kate?'

'Brian.'

The last time these two met, it was on our driveway. She had just keyed his delivery rental van and he'd come back to confront her and she said he was lucky that she didn't key his balls. My neighbours heard that and I think we all winced thinking about what that would entail. She now holds on to some very new, important information about my love life and she really, really needs to shut her face about it.

Kate gives Brian a look and then shifts her gaze on to me. 'What fabric softener do you use? Your towels smell gorgeous.'

'It's Lenor,' I tell her. 'It's a limited-edition jasmine range.'

Brian sits there awkwardly, waiting for Kate to pounce.

'I guess I should thank you for driving the kids back yesterday. I appreciate you were there to...'

'...pick up the pieces of your piss-poor parenting?' she replies. I suppress a smile at the glorious alliteration in her reply.

'Be there for them,' he mumbles in reply.

'Well, I bloody love those kids like they're my own so, of course...' she tells him, plainly.

'And the people who picked Dylan up from Manchester? Are they friends of yours? That bit confused me. Who's Jack?'

I glare at Kate who can't seem to hide her glee, clutching on to her basket of towels. Don't you dare. This is not a case of tit for tat. Though I did partake in his tat quite a fair bit last night. I pull a face, also trying to hold in my laughter. Brian yoyos between the both of us, trying to figure out this shared joke.

'I know Jack through work, he helped me co-ordinate it all,' I say, possibly a little too unconvincingly.

'Well, I'm glad he was there to give you some help.'

'That's not all he gave her,' Kate says out of the side of her mouth. I close my eyes. I don't think Brian heard that. She was far too slick, far too absorbed in her own sense of humour. I should glare but I grin, broadly. 'I'm going to put these towels away,' she says, taking her leave.

Her back to Brian, she widens her eyes at me cheekily and I follow her gaze as she leaves. When I turn back, Brian is looking at me strangely. He heard that, didn't he? Bloody Kate.

'You seem different. Have you changed your hair or something?'

'I washed it?'

We both laugh, studying each other's faces. There is something about him that I miss, possibly. He was a huge part of my life. I will always hold on to that. We share children for a start. But I think the emotion might be moving on. I think I might have started to swim again – the water is warmer, I don't feel like I'm drowning anymore.

Jack

Hi

Hi

Thank you for the chicken.

I didn't send you any chicken. Is this your way of thanking me for the sex? I guess we can call it that.

You're funny.

I try. How are your kids? Home safe? You OK?

All good. They're home, they're safe. I'm sorry I didn't message you before this. It's been quite the weekend.

It has. I'm glad the kids are at home with you. I also feel the need to thank you too, you know? Thank you for taking a chance on me.

That's my favourite ABBA song.

Who's ABBA?

You are funny.

Will I see you tomorrow?

Yes. Meet you in the copy room?

> I'll be there. Naked. Next to copier 1.

It's a date. Also, are you free in two weeks?

> She's planning ahead.

It's just that I've got to go to Winchester with my STEM club. I need to take another member of staff.

> I can be available.

It's paid.

> You don't have to pay me for my company.

I wasn't planning to. But log the hours as overtime.

> First we call the sex 'chicken'. Now it's 'overtime'.

I'll put your name down then.

> Please do. I'd like that very much.

Thank you again, Jack. Can I say that I'm glad our paths have crossed?

> You can say that. I like hearing it x

I put my phone down on my chest with a huge smile on my face, sipping at a cup of tea whilst I lounge in my front room. I'm glad Zoe messaged first. I'm glad that despite her family dramas, I still linger in her thoughts because she lingers in mine – and she wants to keep seeing me. In two weeks. I can wait two weeks and in between I'll get to see her at school, every day if I'm lucky. I don't think I'll mind that one bit.

I left Dom and the boys last night and crawled back here to pass out. Dom still thinks this place is some single man's twenty-four-hour party palace when, in reality, I came back to Frank playing *Call of Duty* with a set of online friends I don't think he's ever met in real life, and Ben in bed with a box set and cold meds. I can hear them both through the ceiling now. One sniffing for his life, the other yelling like he's in the middle of actual warfare, trying to get someone to cover his six. It's midday and strangely, I feel a little lost. I don't know if I'm tired or need to do some laundry. The answer is both but for now, I will continue to lounge, put on some mindless television, scroll through the corners of social media where I can keep updated on current affairs but also see what all my friends had for dinner last night. Such is my very single life. My phone ringing gets my attention.

'Hello hello.'

'Jack Attack,' Sarah replies, very calmly.

'I owe you.'

'You do.'

'Sorry I didn't call yesterday. I should have checked in and done that properly. It's been a strange twelve hours.'

'No harm. Can I say, though? What a nice young man. A sad young man but very polite.'

'I wouldn't know. Did he say much to you?' I ask her.

'Hakeem just distracted him with football talk. They created their dream team. Once I requested Jack Grealish so I could just stare at his calves, I was cut out of the conversation.'

I laugh. 'What a way to cheapen and sexualise a very good footballer. I am disappointed, Sarah.'

Sarah is silent which makes me wonder if she's waiting for me to volunteer more information or whether she knows already. Perhaps the old university hotlines have been burning.

'You've spoken to Ed, haven't you?' I ask.

'We may have had a conversation. His new wife is fuming, by the way, that you haven't updated them on what's happened there.'

'Really?' I say, defensively. 'The Ed and Mia who quite brazenly set me up.'

'You slept with her, didn't you?' she asks.

'A gentleman never reveals...'

'Gentleman? Who's that then?' she jokes. 'Did the lad get home? Is he OK? I kept asking him that, but he didn't really reply, and I didn't want to dig.'

'He's with his mum, he's home. It was a family matter and I've left them to it.'

I'm not sure how much more to tell her.

'Then we did a good thing then, eh?'

'You did. Thank you.' I knew I could call Sarah and she'd help. She was the reliable sort at university, the one who you'd call if you were stuck in the kebab shop and your payment method had been declined. Of course, this never happened to me. And despite a small feeling of judgement over my life choices, there is friendship there. Friendship without question.

'Well,' she says, shifting tone. 'Seeing as we're talking favours, I may have something I'd like to lay down at your door. If you're interested?'

I sit up on the sofa. 'Is it Bowie? Did you need another dogsitter?'

'I've been offered a job. It's quite a big conservation project out in Borneo, they want to me to lead it and project manage. It's the dream job, it really is...'

'Amazing, mate. So how long would I have the pooch for then?' I ask. I'd have to lay down some proper ground rules to the mutt. Keep off my bed, stop humping my leg, but we could make it work. I'd have to work out if Frank is allergic. I'm sure the nephews would love him.

She stops and laughs. 'You idiot. They want me to build a team to go out there with me. And strangely, your name was right at the top of my list.'

I stop for a moment and look blankly at some cooking show I've been gawping at mindlessly. Borneo. Conservation. The words make me sit up. I'd never really sought out work like that for myself since I left university – those jobs always felt like pipe dreams for further down the line. But there was a time when I planned to use my degree to do fieldwork somewhere. I just never got beyond that. The idea fills me with some prickles of curiosity, excitement.

'The pity recruit,' I joke.

'Hardly. I believe you graduated with a First. There was a Jack I once knew who was fascinated by this type of ecosystem. Orangutans, Jack. There would be orangutans.'

'Are you trying to use monkeys to tempt me into a job?'

'Yes.'

'Sarah, I'm flattered but...'

'It's a five-year project,' she interrupts me. 'I'm going to send you an email with all the particulars and links to the village where we'd stay. It's right on the water. We'd have to sort visas and...'

'Hold up there, sparky. Seriously. Is this your way of trying to sort my life out? I am very capable of finding a job for myself, you know?'

She laughs at the end of the phone. 'Puurlease. I work at a university. I am surrounded by dozens of botanists who'd jump at the chance to come out and do this sort of work. It's once in a lifetime stuff. I asked you because you're my friend but also because you are who you are.'

'A pain in the arse?'

She cackles in reply. 'Well, there is that. But you adapt to your surroundings, you're not put off by challenges and you're a people person. The team would be better with you in it.'

I exhale gently to hear her compliment. Sometimes I can't think as far back as my degree – it feels like a lifetime ago. But I remember Sarah and I used to talk about the work we would do;

a couple of young idealistic tree-huggers with aspirations to explore and save the world.

'I really hate blowing smoke up your arse, by the way. It feels very unnatural,' she tells me.

I laugh. 'Sarah, are you being serious? What about your newbuild? Hakeem?'

'We'd rent it out. Hakeem will tag along. It's all very new but I can't let this go. It's a big deal.'

'How long do I have to decide?' I ask tentatively.

'So you're considering it?'

My phone pings and I hold it away from my ear to see a text from Zoe.

See you tomorrow x

I have to sit there and take a moment. This isn't normally what happens in my weekends. Normally, I lie here and realise I've spent a whole hour scrolling through TikTok and that Monday is around the corner. All that time has passed without anything happening until now. And now, life is offering up forks in the road. 'I just need to think about a few things.'

'Well, don't hurt yourself, hon.'

I laugh.

THIRTEEN

Zoe

I walk into school the next day and Mia is waiting in the staff room for me, arms crossed, basically tapping her foot in the same way we do when we're waiting for kids who are late into our classrooms.

'Is your phone broken, you absolute cow?' she tells me.

Ed comes rushing over from the staff room fridge. 'I am so sorry about her, I am so sorry we did that to you. It was all her idea. I told her it was such a bad idea. I told her you'd never trust us again and we work with you. We'd have to see you on Monday...'

I look at both of them, po-faced, shaking my head.

Ed looks absolutely mortified. 'Did you at least enjoy the room? I'd have understood if you felt it appropriate not to stay. Did you stay?'

'I stayed.'

'Then that's a good thing... isn't it, Mia?' Mia looks like this isn't the information she wants but there's a sliver of satisfaction in stringing her along, to make her think she's not as clever as she thinks she is.

'And did anyone stay with you?' she asks me, impatiently.

'What? No. You got me that room for myself, didn't you? I mean, I went down to the bar to meet you for that drink, but I may have missed you, no?' It's only then that I can't seem to control the smile emerging and Mia comes over and hits me across the arm, a joyous emotion creeping across her face.

'You are hilarious. So it worked? The plan worked? ED! IT WORKED!'

Ed shakes his head. This does not bode well for Ed – Mia will be incorrigible now. It's like we've unleashed a criminal matchmaking mastermind into the world.

She pulls me to the sofa and asks me to sit down.

'You have five minutes before I have to go to my room and set up for the day,' I tell her. 'We met, we chatted. It was lovely.'

'*Lovely*? I didn't put that plan together for lovely,' she says, wrinkling her nose.

'He's lovely.' She sits there and shakes her head. 'I'm not sure what you want to hear?'

'Did he at least make you come?'

'MIA!' Ed says.

'She said I only had five minutes.'

I sit there laughing, watching them argue over me but my eyes are secretly wandering around the room looking for Jack. I don't think he's in yet. It feels a bit schoolgirly to be searching him out, to feel all that excitement in my bones to want to see him again. I realise the great irony in this and laugh to myself.

'Zoe, I can only apologise,' Ed says, turning to me.

'Ed, it's OK. Your friend is lovely,' I say, putting a hand on his arm. Ed smiles back at me, relieved. I sling my bag over my shoulder.

'We'll get more details later, yes?' Mia asks and I shake my head, laughing.

'But thank you, you crazy, wonderful woman,' I say, hugging her.

And Mia does a little dance as I head off to my classroom, the magnificent sound of her whooping with joy echoing down the corridors.

As I walk across the courtyard to the maths block, I try and get my head around what's happened in the space of just a few days. I feel a little disoriented to think of all the things that transpired. This isn't what my weekends used to be about; they used to be about watching football matches on cold pitches, laundry, marking, planning the groceries for the weekend. Now I feel like I've played out a full four-part series in mere days. It started with me as a single parent crying over the absence of her kids; it moved on to highly explicit scenes of me shagging someone over ten years younger than me, and it ended with me killing demons. Demons called Brian who wear terrible chinos. As a young Year Seven child smiles and waves at me as I walk past, I wonder if it all happened to another person. I smile to myself in disbelief.

'You look different.' It's a voice that weaves in from the end of the corridor as I enter the block. It's Drew. Do I dare tell Drew? He'll think me mad.

'Good different?' I say back to him.

He nods. 'Good weekend?'

Drew, I came so hard on Saturday morning that I thought my nipples were going to fly off. I smirk to myself. That's not Monday morning maths talk.

'It was alright. We still having that departmental meeting?'

'No, Sharon is stuck in traffic. You just look... I don't know the word... I think it's rested.'

I don't know how to reply to that so put a thumb up in the air. As I walk in the room, though, someone is sitting at my desk, in my chair, waiting. It's that cheeky relaxed stance he always seems to take, sleeves rolled up, bag slung across his shoulder, that look in his eye which shows he knows exactly where he should be. I bite my lip to try and hide my glee in seeing him.

'Mrs Swift. Good morning.'

I look down at my desk and see a shiny red apple. 'Is that for me?'

'It is,' he says, looking down at it.

'That's old school,' I tell him, my grin making my cheeks hurt.

'In return, I was hoping you could help me.' A group of students walk past my room, and he immediately stands up.

'Mr Damon, of course,' I say, trying to remain calm. 'Was it a maths related problem?'

'More of a teaching one. I was hoping you could show me something.'

He needs to stop smiling at me. I need to stop visualising this man naked. I've seen him naked. There was a point where I had his penis in my mouth. A blush rises in my cheeks. I take my bag off, putting it on a nearby desk and walking over as casually as I can to put my coat and scarf on the back of my chair. As I do so, his arm brushes mine and I momentarily stop breathing.

'Can I ask what's in that cupboard? To the back of your room?' he asks.

'Oh, it's stationery. Books, paper. I have a very good guillotine in there.'

'For paper?'

'Yes. For paper. The one for heads is over in History.'

He laughs. 'Do you possibly keep a supply of paper clips?'

'Paper clips?'

'Yes.'

'Well, I guess we could take a look?'

He nods.

I walk over to the cupboard and allow him to follow, feeling his presence behind me. As soon as I close the door behind us, he turns my back on to it, and kisses me, intensely, passionately. His lips are pressed firmly against mine, hand to my inner thigh. And all good sense leaves me completely as I kiss him back, allowing him to push his body to mine, feeling the warmth of his skin on mine, that faint spark that always sits between us ignited. He pulls away and leans his forehead against mine.

'Good morning, Mrs Swift,' he says, breathily.

'Yep,' I say, unable to return the greeting.

'I know I said the copiers but it's busy in there and I don't think I'd have been able to do that.'

'That.'

I seem only capable of answering in monosyllables at the moment. He sighs and tenderly kisses me again before scanning the shelves and picking a jar of paperclips, throwing them in the air and winking at me.

'Just what I needed. Thank you, Mrs Swift. I appreciate it.'

'You're very welcome, Mr Damon. I have lots of paper clips if you ever need them.' I exhale, trying to retain some sort of sensible calm but laughing under my breath.

'I see you also have a lot of protractors.'

'Did you have angles to measure?' I ask him.

'Always.'

And with that he comes in for one last kiss before pulling away and I feel his hand leaving mine.

This is awful. This is what we tell the kids not to do – the ones who couple up and rendezvous by the toilets, by the bike sheds – and suddenly I realise I kissed this man by the bike sheds, too. I'm regressing into my youth, I need to remember how old I am. I mean, I know that because I feel that even more when I'm with him, but I need to remember my codes of teaching and how to be a responsible adult. This is why when I am on school grounds, I should always have some level of good sense. I am a mother. No more. I step back from him and take a deep breath to compose myself.

'Paperclips,' I whisper for no other reason than it's the only word I can think of at the moment.

He laughs and I push at the door but as I do, I'm very conscious of someone standing in there, waiting for me. Shit. I shut the door pretty much in Jack's face so he can't follow me. That can't happen. You stay in the cupboard with your paperclips. Having to think on my feet, I grab at a box of glue sticks.

'Gabe? Morning, how are you today?' Am I flushed? Am I flustered? Have I got lip gloss smeared all over my face? Did he hear the kissing? I hope not because that's not really a sound that anyone should want to hear.

'I'm good, Miss. Sorry, is someone in there? I heard talking...'

'Oh god, no,' I say, hoping Jack heard that. He really has to stay in that cupboard now. 'I was just talking to myself, running through my day.' Because that is a better option than saying I was in a cupboard with another member of staff, the fact that I just stand in cupboards and talk to myself. Gabe gives me a look and smiles. He's a good kid. I have a number like this – they're a bit older and have floated through school but suddenly have got to Year Eleven and realise they need to leave here with something, anything. I wish they'd got to such realisations earlier in their school career, but at least I now have something to work with.

'How are you? How was your match last week? Did you win?' I ask him.

Gabe looks shocked that I remembered. 'Yeah, we won. Two-nil. I got an assist. How about your lad?'

I like how Gabe remembers small details of our conversations. 'He didn't play this weekend.'

He nods. 'Actually, Mr Damon was at my match. You know him?'

I let out a small squeak at the mention of his name and try to style it out with a very forced cough. 'Oh yeah, the new sub. He was there?'

'He was taking training for some other kids.'

I smile. Of course he was. He's a young, good-looking man who's terrific in bed, saves kittens from skips, and volunteers his time for grassroots football. I really need to start hearing bad things about this man to make me think he's human.

'Is he a proper teacher?' he asks me.

'Define proper,' I say, trying not to laugh, praying Jack can hear this.

'Like you.'

'I don't know. He's just doing some cover work. He may stick around, may not. Whereas I've been here so long, I sometimes sleep in the school gym.'

'Do you, Miss?' he asks, shocked.

'That would be a no, Gabe.'

As he didn't get the joke, I get the feeling that he is preoccupied. In fact, that cool confidence that often just oozes from him is absent, so I revert back to his language of football.

'Well, I'm glad to hear it was a win. Local derby, right?

Again, he seems shocked that I remembered. 'Yeah. It's just... Do you have a minute to chat through something?'

I stand there with my multipack of glue sticks, staring at the cupboard door. Jack will be alright, it'll only be for a moment. He won't starve and you can get phone reception in there.

'Of course, take a seat.' I urge him to close the door first and pull up a seat for him next to my desk.

'Is everything OK?' I ask him. He puts his bags down and starts fidgeting, picking at his nails that are bitten down to the skin.

'There was a scout at that game. A good one. Someone from Fulham wants me to come along to training and see if I like it there...'

'GABE, that's fantastic news!' I tell him enthusiastically, slightly confused at how despondent he appears.

'It is, it isn't. I don't know...' he mumbles. 'It's a big step. I don't know if I'm ready for it. Plus, they, like, train three times a week and I've got exams coming up. It's a lot of work.'

'Are you just worried about the balance?' I enquire.

'Yeah. I'll have to get a bus to Fulham training because my mum and dad work. I want to leave here with some GSCEs in case the football don't work out. And Fulham might not even like me...'

I shake my head at him. 'Well, you can shush that sort of talk for a start,' I say. 'A lot of what these places look for won't be skills, a lot of kids they take on want hard work, commitment and from what you're telling me now, I see that in mountains.' He takes a big sigh and tries to summon up a smile. 'Let's change that language about. Let's say Fulham *love* you, let's say the football *will* work out, you *will* leave here with GCSEs. I am manifesting that shit for you.'

'You swore, Miss,' he reminds me.

'I know, it was for impact. Don't tell anyone,' I say, putting a finger to my lips.

'I just don't think there are enough hours in the day, you know?' he tells me.

I lean forward in my chair. 'Well, as your maths teacher, I am saying now that you will leave here with at least something in my subject. I will be sure of that. Even if I have to come to your training and shout out equations over the sidelines.'

'Yeah, don't do that, Miss,' he laughs. The lad already thinks I'm a little mad for talking to myself in cupboards. 'So you think I can do this?'

'I have every faith, Gabe. Keep it positive. Give Fulham a go, show them you're an absolute baller. These sorts of opportunities don't come up that often so sometimes you've got to seize them with both hands and work hard – not think you can't do it because you're...'

'Scared.'

'Exactly.'

He nods. 'Facts... facts. Did you use the word "baller", Miss?'

'I did.'

He laughs.

'Hon, have you spoken to your parents about this? What about your form tutor?' I ask him.

He shakes his head from side to side. 'My parents are a bit overexcited about it. I don't like my form tutor,' he tells me plainly. 'But I like you.'

He realises what he's said, and I try not to smile too much. 'Well, that's very kind.'

'Just in a teacher way, yeah. Not like I *like* you, because that would be well weird,' he explains, the grimace on his face confirming that statement. 'You believe in us and stuff. I don't have anyone like that in my life.'

And I stop for a moment feeling sad but almost slightly relieved that I can fulfil that role for him. I can't say I have any experience of what it means to be an elite sportsperson, but I have always felt this lad wears a lot of that pressure on his young shoulders and doesn't quite know how to carry it. Maybe it's from being a mother or having lived in this job for the longest time but you worry about all these kids like they're your own, all you want is to see them succeed.

'They will meet you and love you, I'm sure of it. If you're coming unstuck with work and it starts to get too much, you know where I am. We can always chat more.'

'Come unstuck. That's funny,' he says, and I look down to see the box full of glue sticks still in my lap.

His mood seems lifted, his body lighter, and he gets up from his chair. 'You're a real one, Miss.' I shrug my shoulders, not really knowing how to answer that.

'I'll catch you later, Gabe,' I tell him as he leaves the room, closing the door. I stare at the cupboard, watching it opening gingerly as Jack's head pops around to see if the coast is clear. I shake my head at him.

'Paperclips,' he says, holding the box over his head. 'Found them.'

I'm not sure I can handle what this tryst entails. From stolen kisses in darkened corners to having to snap on my teacher face, all of it makes me feel giddy, in a good if unfamiliar way.

'I'm glad, Mr Damon. Did you get everything you need in there?' I say, trying to remain cool and professional.

He stops for a moment. 'I did. Thank you for your assistance, Mrs Swift. You're a real one, you know.'

He laughs. I would laugh if I had a clue what that actually meant.

Jack

She bought me a Snickers. After I kissed Zoe in that cupboard, I went to the staff room and there was a Snickers waiting for me in my work pigeonhole. I remember telling her I liked Snickers in a passing moment, our heads on the same pillow and I remembered staring at it, smiling. There was a Post It note attached saying *For the Anti-Wanker x*

And I thought about how Zoe went out into that classroom and told a confused, stressed young man that he was amazing, and she had complete belief in him. I thought about how she does that, she raises everyone up on some sort of pedestal and watches them, content to just prop them up. It made me think I'd never met anyone like Zoe before in my life. A person who put that sort of energy out into the world. I then thought about the kiss. I thought about hotels, and it meant I went to my Year

Eight French lesson distracted and basically let half of them engage in a paper ball battle which meant no one left knowing how to conjugate irregular verbs in the present tense.

Since then, five days have passed since I kissed Zoe in that cupboard. I'd like to say it was a complete moment of spontaneity but really, I woke up that morning and I had an ache to see her before the day started. Not that sort of physical, sexual ache but just a feeling like I missed her, that seeing her face would make this Monday morning feel a thousand times better, so I stole an apple out of the staff room fridge and I went to search her out. Since then, it's been five days of messaging and random gifts appearing in each other's pigeonholes. It's turned into some lovely innocent form of courting because we work in a school and we have to keep things appropriate, but it's built an intensity there, too, a string of messaging that has become quite sexually explicit. It makes me smile to think of her blushing at the content – content that includes pictures of my ding-dong. However, sitting in that cupboard, listening in to her conversation with Gabe, one thing also worries me and that's what she said about me – 'he may stay, he may go' – and I start to wonder what she means by that. Does she worry that I'm taking this to be some mindless fling to help her get over her husband? Does she anticipate me leaving? Because I guess I could. Sarah's job offer is still on the table and the option is there in a way it hasn't been before. Zoe also spoke of opportunities, grabbing them with both hands, and her words echo so very true. But how could I do that to Zoe now? Given everything she's been through, I don't want to hurt her again. Maybe I just need to let her know I'm serious. All these feelings I have about her, the esteem in which I hold her, feels serious.

I'm waiting now in a local shopping centre, a zig-zag network of escalators overhead, low-level instrumental music in the background, surrounded by the buzz of a Friday night as people finish work and begin their weekends. This may not be the ideal date but at least it'll prove to Zoe that she's not just a fling in my eyes.

'Hey, stranger.' I hear her voice behind me and grin, spinning around to greet her. She looks relaxed, happy, scrappily trying to rearrange her curls. I reach in to kiss her and whilst she doesn't flinch, I also sense some caution. We're kissing. In public. We've done this before but there are far more people in the vicinity. There may be children around that we both know. She looks me in the eye but also spies the bag hanging from my arm.

'We're doing gifts?' she asks, curiously. 'Is that a contribution to my STEM club?'

I laugh. 'Not quite. You wore trainers?' I say, looking down.

She looks down at her New Balance. 'You know I'm not hugely sporty, yes?' she says, still trying to work out the boxes in my bag. 'You haven't given me much in the way of clues here. Is this one of those puzzle escape rooms? Is that for someone else?' she asks.

I told Zoe to meet me here. Let's just have a date, spend some quality time together, I told her. Her kids had both agreed to spend an evening with their father – just him alone, this time – but I sensed that after what happened in Manchester, she still wanted to stay close. Just give me a couple of hours, I asked. She now looks at me suspiciously.

'It actually is.' But before I have a chance to let her know what's happening, two people bomb us from behind.

'UNCLE JACK!' Barney shrieks. 'YOU CAME!'

I think Zoe may be shocked. I can't quite work out if she's impressed by this ambush or not, but she ensures that it doesn't show in front of my nephews. To the rear, Dom appears, carrying a couple of shopping bags and some helium balloons. 'Barney, George, Dom – this is my friend, Zoe. I hope you don't mind that I asked her to come along today?'

Zoe laughs to herself. 'I'm so sorry for the gatecrash. But I guess happy birthday?'

The boys high-five her but I can see Dom working it all out, slowly. It's the older woman. I'm trying to gauge if she was what he expected. He realises he's probably left it too long without saying anything and snaps his manners into place.

'An absolute pleasure, Zoe. God, the more hands the merrier. I've got eight more boys showing up – it's going to be chaos.'

He gives the supermarket-bought cake to Zoe to carry while he hands me a bag full of what look like some version of party bags.

'Dom. What are these?'

'Oh, I forgot party bags, so I had to improvise and stuff them with things I found at work,' he tells us, trying to corral the boys in the right direction. I look down. Some lucky kid is getting a full set of neon Post It notes, what looks like some vending machine crisps and some multicoloured paper clips, which makes me smile. 'I hope you're a huge fan of Laser Tag then,' Dom asks Zoe.

I'm not sure about the look that Zoe gives me next. I think she's mildly amused, but I also hope my smile is going to persuade her that this is far more interesting than a restaurant pizza or an overpriced drink in a generic pub. She looks at me and then down at the boys. 'Well, I hope you like being beaten, kids, because birthday or not, you're all going down...'

I thought I'd seen bedlam before. I've travelled through train stations in Asia, and I've even been at the canteen in Griffin Road Comprehensive, but nothing has quite prepared me for Laser Tag with a group of thirty kids on a Friday night. Because it's not just the nephews celebrating their birthday today, we all seem to be lost in this neon maze with Lewis who is turning eight and Kai who is turning nine and all their little friends, too. Some of whom seem to have inhaled some Haribo beforehand so they will be absolutely feral and take no prisoners. One of them eyeballs me in his glowing vest and slides a finger across his throat. Well, I'm sorry. You may be close acquaintances of my nephews, but you're going down first.

'Right,' says a very bored teenager who's been sent to brief us. 'I need to remind you of our house rules. Please remember there is no eating or drinking in the arena and if we hear any foul language then I am afraid that we will ask you to leave.' I am not sure why he looks at the little girl at the front when he says that. 'No running, no biting, no kicking, no phones, no climbing and please do not lie down on the floor. ARE WE READY?'

'Yes!' cry a number of small children.

The bored teenager suddenly summons up a roar out of nowhere. 'I SAID, ARE WE REEEEEEADY?'

'YEEEEESSSSSS!' they all reply.

The tension and energy are palpable. It's like a scene out of *Gladiator* when the doors are going to open and the slaves have to fight some tigers except all the slaves are tiny and in tracksuits and there's a techno soundtrack. There will be blood. Behind these children stand six less enthusiastic adults – family members who've been asked to supervise, many of whom against their will except for one particularly exuberant dad who came in sports gear, a makeshift headband and who you know has eyes on the leaderboard. Mate, you are also going down.

A door suddenly opens, and all the children disappear into clouds of dry ice and flashing lights, their screams fading into the darkness.

'This feels like the ship out of *Alien*,' Zoe says next to me. She has a point. Exuberant sporty dad runs in, his laser gun held close to his body like he's in actual battle.

I watch a girl immediately shoot him. 'Come get me, you giant dick.'

Zoe laughs as we stroll through this strange, darkened maze of terror. 'So, give me your line of reasoning here... why you thought this date was appropriate,' she jokes. She doesn't seem annoyed or angry but slightly bemused to be finding herself in this position on a Friday night. In a hoodie, leggings, a glowing vest and armed with a laser to take on a bunch of hyperactive kids.

'I thought, in my mind, it could be fun. Something a little different.'

'Dom seems nice.'

'He makes a shit party bag, but his heart is the right place.' We allowed Dom to sit this one out so he could sit outside, put candles in the cake and enjoy forty-five minutes of relative peace before the children emerged again. 'That vest is super hot, by the way – just saying...'

She pushes me, which at first I think is a little aggressive until I work out she's pushing me out of danger from incoming fire. The speed with which she returns shots and manages to accurately take out an eight-year-old leaves me mildly aroused.

'Zoe? Methinks you've done this before...'

'I have a son. Of course.' She pulls me to a corner of that arena, behind a padded cushion. 'The strategy is to let the kids do all the running. You just find a corner, take a defensive stance and then shoot them whilst they're running in circles.'

'So, you're like some expert Laser Tag strategist. Just impressive on so many levels...'

'I've just been around the Laser Tag far too many times.'

As we wait there in the corner, I stand close to her, my breath on the side of her neck.

'I'm trying to work out if you're just wildly inappropriate or you're one of those people who enjoy risky situations?' she says, jokingly. 'You heard the briefing, I don't want the shame of being barred from this place.'

'I didn't hear anything about being thrown out for kissing.'

'I'm thinking more about what you've got pressed up against me...'

'Zoe! How rude. That's just my laser,' I say, holding up my gun. And a laugh illuminated in purple, pink and green but also one that makes me think she's not too angry with me for bringing her here.

'FOUND HIM! FIRE!' Our hiding place is suddenly invaded by George, Barney and a couple of friends who bombard us with lasers, so much so that my laser vest seems to be having its own epileptic fit. I fall to the floor, pretending to die and one of them puts a foot to my back and seems to celebrate my demise. I hope that's not one of my own nephews.

The music cuts out. 'Can the gentleman lying on the floor please get up?' someone announces over a tannoy and I return to my feet. The music starts up again and the boys run away to plan their next attack. I turn around and Zoe has disappeared. Damn, maybe this was too much. I start tiptoeing around this place. I am sure I had a fever dream in a place like this before. It's like *Lord of the Flies* meets *TRON*. I get to one corner, to see exuberant-headband dad hiding from an elevated position and taking on a herd of kids who can't seem to see him. I approach quietly. I take that evil fucker out.

'WHO? DAISY? IS THAT YOU AGAIN?'

I smile and escape again until I get to a corner of this place, listening to Barney's voice from around a corner.

'If you had the choice, would you rather have an eye in the middle of your head or two noses?'

Oh, Barney. I take a swift glance around that corner to see that Zoe is with them, and I start to wonder if she's been taken hostage or defected to heavier artillery. I hear her laugh and smile.

'One eye, obviously. Is it a giant eye?'

'It would take up at least half of your forehead.'

'Still the eye. Imagine having all those nostrils and having to pick all of them – it would take up most of my day.'

All the boys in that corner laugh and I beam. I know her.

'So are you like Uncle Jack's girlfriend?' one of them asks her.

It's a little painful for young George to be so forthright but it's also the beauty of those little boys. 'So many questions... Hold up?' There seems to be a break in the conversation to have a full-on laser attack with some other people in this arena. All at once, I feel a little ashamed. I should probably join in and help defend their position, but I don't want to reveal myself and not hear the answer to their last question.

'Yeah, yeah... RUN, YOU PUSSIES!' That was certainly not Zoe but also not my nephews and I feel that again, I may need to advise Dom on the company that his boys keep. I stand with my back to the padded cushions.

'So... are you his girlfriend?' Well done, George, for keeping that line of interrogation going.

'I'm just his friend. Why do you ask?'

'It's just we've not met any of Uncle Jack's girlfriends before.'

'Really?'

I pause for a moment, hoping these boys don't shame me. It's true. I don't think anyone's lasted long enough, but also this felt like a step to introduce my lads to anyone. They're essentially my family, my people, the ultimate litmus test. In the back of my mind, they're also part of the reason I've not acted on Sarah's job offer yet. I know I would possibly miss them too much.

'He must really like you if he's brought you to Laser Tag,' Barney adds, and I hear Zoe chuckling.

'Indeed. You both must really love your Uncle Jack.'

'Of course. He's the best. Did you know he can burp the alphabet?' George says, and this is when I spring up. Less of that, especially as they have a story about the time I tried to light a fart. Let's not kill the illusion.

'FOUND YOU! I can't believe you took Zoe hostage!' The boys all take aim.

'She came of her own volition!' one of their friends shouts. He knows the word volition, so I'll allow the boys to be friends with him.

'It is true. When you were on the floor, I thought you had died.'

'So you left me?' I say, a hand to my heart.

'I am sorry, they also lured me with sweets.'

I shake my head as she smiles at me, the techno still ringing in our ears. This must be something if I still feel all these immense feelings for you amidst this absolute bedlam. The boys around her start to flee in different directions as I try to get close to her again. However, as I walk, my vest starts to glow again, and a little girl stands behind me.

'I GOT THE PRETTY BOY! SUCK ON THAT, LOSER!'

FOURTEEN

Zoe

'Hold up, let me take a picture,' Jack tells me, holding his phone up at me in the street. What I want to say is please don't put this online, but there's still some residual joy in what I've achieved tonight. I've also had a drink so I might be slightly merry. I hold the gold plastic trophy to my face and pose, quite uncharacteristically. 'Perfect,' he says, looking at the picture on his phone. I peer over to have a look. I look less jubilant, less like a grown woman revelling quite embarrassingly in the fact that she came top of the leaderboard at Laser Tag. Was it a good evening? You know what, I think it was. You forget how little children are balls of energy, but also mildly hysterical, and it was fun to experience that madness for an evening, to see Jack's nephews so very excited about their birthday. I only wish I could get that excited about a birthday again.

'Your nephews are very sweet, by the way,' I tell Jack as he walks next to me, tucking into a piece of cake wrapped in a paper napkin. It's that time of night when the streets next to this shopping arcade have started to buzz with the activity of people on the search of a night out: restaurants filling up, people dashing up escalators towards cinemas. The party is now over, candles have been blown out, kids have been picked up by parents, and Barney and George have been wrestled into Dom's car.

'They are the best. Mad as a box of frogs but brilliant.'

There is something in how he talks about them with such love, how he embraces the energy and isn't scared of it, that is endearing.

'So tell me more about them. You moved in with them when they were...'

'Four months.'

I am silent to hear that, mainly trying to process the fact that their mother would have died when her children were so young. I am imagining him just jumping into a house with two tiny babies and the maturity and heart that would have taken.

'They were teeny tiny, like puppies. I could fit one in each arm,' he tells me, acting it out.

'Would you do it again?' I reply.

'Have a baby?' Jack says, laughing. 'Well, that's quite a jump forward in our relationship but...'

I blush, realising what I've just said. 'Christ, no. You know what I mean...'

'Do I?'

'Well, maybe this is as good a time as any to ask if you want your own kids,' I ask boldly. I guess it's important for clarity here given the different stages we are in our lives.

He shrugs. 'I have no idea. If fatherhood crosses my path, then I would take that on, but there's no plan.'

I nod. There is no plan. He says those words so easily. I remember being his age and my life was mapped out so certainly. I was pregnant with Lottie, a small house, the seeds of a career just blooming. But I guess plans don't always have endings. Six months ago, would you have told me I'd be eating birthday cake on the high street with a man who isn't my husband? Maybe not. Maybe I do just need to live in the moment like Jack does. He urges me to take a bite of cake from his slice and I smile. He does this so naturally and I'm quite taken with the familiarity of it, how he doesn't care what people think, how I take a bite and he wipes some sprinkles off my lips.

'So where to now?' he asks.

'Soft play?' I ask.

'How do you make that sound kinky?'

And we both laugh, his breath gently fogging the air, and I watch his profile, the angles of his jaw, the way he playfully pushes an elbow into me. 'You want to sleep over tonight?' I say, my voice a little shaky as I know exactly what that will mean, and he smiles to himself, almost looking a little smug that his Laser Tag seduction may have worked. It did. I won't say that out loud.

'And you've made that sound quite innocent,' he mentions.

I don't know how to tell him what I have planned will be anything but. I grin but my thoughts are suddenly interrupted by a voice.

'Zoe?'

I don't know where the voice comes from to start with, and I'm not sure why I recognise it, but I stop for a moment, Jack slowing down beside me, and I turn towards a pub we've just walked past. It's a busy thoroughfare so I look around before my gaze stops at a group of people drinking outside, on one woman especially, her hand wrapped around a glass of red wine. I don't quite know what to say. Liz. It's Liz. She's surrounded by a couple of friends who from the looks of their haughty gazes have been fed a different sort of narrative about who I may be. I stand there and let them stare me down, their eyes shifting between myself and Jack, wondering why I'm in trainers on a night out with a slight Laser Tag sweat moustache when they're in a collective uniform of skinny jeans, heels and smart wool coats.

'What are you doing here?' she asks me.

I've not seen Liz since it all happened. I didn't see the point. She reached out by text, but I didn't know what there was to say. *It's fine, you have Brian. I hope you have a lovely life together but you're a bitch?* The problem is there is so much to say. It used to be me sitting there with her, sipping wine, and do you know what we used to do? We used to bitch about how our husbands didn't load the dishwasher properly. How do I go into this? Do I ask her how she is? How do I bring up Manchester? *So, why exactly did you think it was a good idea to show up there?*

'I went to Laser Tag,' I tell that small group, looking down at their table of tiny cheeses and olives. That was a poor conversational opener.

I think one of them laughs at me under her breath. 'Oh, is it like one of those evenings where they open it up to adults? I've heard about this bar in London that does that – they have ball pits, and you can get cocktails.'

I nod, Jack standing there trying to work out who these women are from the awkwardness that sits there in the air like mist.

'You know Tina, right?' she tells me. I nod. Tina is a schoolgate mum I've met at cosmetics parties where I think she once harangued me into buying a body scrub that cost forty pounds and gave me hives. Tina looks me up and down.

'Hi, Tina. How's Phil?' I enquire politely.

'He's fine. He just got a Tesla.'

Beside me, Jack laughs before realising that wasn't funny.

'Do you have a Tesla?' Tina asks him, slightly annoyed.

'No. I'm not a fan. I'm Jack, by the way. Hello, everyone. I, too, was at Laser Tag. Why don't you show them your trophy, Zoe?' he tells the women sitting there.

I turn to Jack, smiling, holding up my trophy. This impresses these women less. I can't quite look Liz in the eye. I can only think she said my name out loud to usher me over and shame me.

'Well, I'm Liz and this is Tina and Fran.'

'Liz,' Jack repeats quietly.

Shit. He knows. This is Liz. The Liz. And it's a strange thing but five minutes ago, I felt comfortable, confident, like it was just him and me but now he's met Liz, and I worry irrationally that like Brian, he'll look at her, with her heels and her blonde hair and her Pilates core, and maybe he'll see what Brian saw there, too. But instead, he stares at her, almost in shock.

'You're the one who...' he mutters. He points his fingers around in different directions before realising he's said too much, and turning to me to say, 'Is she your friend who had that unfortunate incident with the fillers?'

I smile to myself as Liz reaches up to her face.

'No, that's someone else,' I inform him, trying to maintain my composure.

'How do you know each other?' Liz asks, defensively. I feel every cell in me tense up. Hey Liz, you know you went and ensnared Brian behind my back? This is Jack, he's my consolation prize and personally, I think I got the better deal. The man has abs. I know for a fact that Brian doesn't. He has a furry stomach like a large kiwi fruit.

'Zoe and I work together,' Jack tells her.

'So, you're a teacher?' she says, continuing to pry.

'I am. I teach... chemistry. We should actually go, Zoe – the others are waiting for us at the restaurant.'

I was never quite sure how the situation would pan out when I saw Liz again for the first time. I somehow imagined I'd be braver, angrier and bring some attitude to the situation. I catch Liz's eye, and I can't quite read that emotion. I think she's trying to maintain some sort of upper hand by not overreacting or creating drama. It's happened, let's all move on and be super civil.

'You're going out?' Liz asks me.

The inference from that being I wouldn't go out, that I would still be sitting at home, crying over being all alone.

'Yeah, we're having tapas and then we're off to a club,' Jack adds.

'A club?' Tina says, like she can't quite believe that's possible for someone like me.

'Yeah?' Jack says. 'Have a good evening here with your wine and your olives.' I don't know why this makes me laugh under my breath. He turns to me. 'Come on, Zoe.'

'I'm sorry, by the way... I really am,' Liz suddenly pipes up.

I stop in my tracks to hear those words, turning around to see she's stood up, hovering over the table. Tina has a hand to her arm, as if she's telling her to sit down. Fuck off, Tina. Liz texted those words to me, too. I can sense Jack looking at me, anticipating my next move. He's seen me at Laser Tag at my most ruthless. I've won trophies. I smile. I inhale deeply. 'No, you're not.' My voice is calm, soft, almost resigned. One day, for the sake of my kids I will have to likely speak to you and possibly even forgive you, but that moment is not now. You made a choice that took my life away. I don't think you get to apologise for that.

I put a hand on Jack's arm, and he looks down at it and, smiling, gives me a playful wink. Let them gossip. It'll be a hell of a lot more interesting than their shitty Tesla talk.

'But...' Liz mumbles.

I don't say anything more. I turn to walk as Jack quietly salutes his goodbyes. Mercy me, that felt bloody good. Just keep walking.

'Are they still looking?' I ask as we move away.

'Yes,' he says, smiling. 'Do you want me to grope you or

something? I can put a hand on your arse. I'd be happy to, in fact.'

'No. Just act semi-natural.'

He swings his arms next to him quite randomly and I double over giggling.

'Expertly done, Mrs Swift.'

'Really?'

'Yes. Plus, you are far more attractive than her,' Jack tells me.

'Whatever,' I tell him, looking down at my casual leggings Laser Tag vibe.

'No competition. She and her coven were giving off witchy crone vibes. That's not hot.'

'That's not, is it?' I ask as we head off the main thoroughfare and turn a corner towards the car park.

He shakes his head and slides his hand into mine, knowing that we're out of sight from curious eyes. The darkened street is quieter and he pulls my arm playfully towards a doorway, pushing his body into mine.

'I mean, do any of them have a trophy for Laser Tag?' he jokes. I shake my head, but he looks me straight in the eye, trying to check the emotion.

'I don't know if that went well,' I tell him.

'Oh, it did. You made her squirm. It was fun to watch, though I was frankly waiting for the slap. I'd have slapped her,' Jack informs me. 'Are you OK?'

He still looks me in the eye, and I can feel his concern. What I want to say is that I'm OK when you're around. You make me feel stronger, like I can take on the world, I feel lighter. In these last few months, when my world has been upended, you've come in and put the table the right way up, re-arranged the chairs. You've sat down with me and held my hand and are re-filing all my emotions so they make more sense. I have no idea what this feeling now is, but you make me feel incredibly cared for and, for the moment, it means everything. After twenty-odd years of giving, of sharing my life, it suddenly feels like I have something just for me. I put a hand to his face and he kisses it, looking me in the eye. There are no words for this so I kiss him, adoring that feeling when his lips press against mine and he smiles, kissing me back. I will never tire of this. It's possible that this is my favourite thing to do with him, the intimacy and immediacy of a kiss. It's the opposite of marriage, it's everything that was missing. I hardly remember a time when Brian and I would kiss like this. There were light pecks on cheeks, never drawn out and intense like this. Jack pushes me into the wall next to that doorway, one hand to my face and another reaching down to my back. My body reacts and relents to his touch as he looks around to hear footsteps.

'Zoe, I really want you,' he murmurs, his hands still reaching around me.

'Here?' I say, giggling.

And that look enters his eye, I know that look. I love it. He takes my hand and we roll further in the shadows of that doorway, sheltered from the street, and he whispers into my ear, 'Maybe the naughtiest thing we can do is fuck literally two hundred yards from where that woman is sitting.'

As soon as the words leave his mouth, I exhale slowly, immediately aroused. I don't do this. I sit at home and watch boxsets. I'm not illicit and wayward. I'm not sure I have the balance. But that look, that glint in his eye urges me to let go; it tells me to have some fun with this. Brian and Liz did – now it's my turn. The tension between us builds and he kisses me, pinning me against the wall but reaching down to pull down my leggings and knickers with one fell swoop. As soon as the cold air hits my skin, I sigh but then feel the warmth of his hands against my thighs, his fingers stroking me gently. I moan, biting my lip, trying to restrain myself as I feel his cock pressed against me. He undoes his trousers, turning me around, my hands flat against the wall as he grabs tightly on to my hips and slides into me. And I can't read this emotion at all. It's fear, it's complete disbelief that I'm doing what I'm doing at this very moment, but it's also the way he's not lost in this event. He leans into me, the warmth of his breath on my neck, putting a hand over mine and squeezing it tightly, doing his best to make me moan so loudly that even from this distance Liz might be able to hear.

Jack

So let's get this right. I am not a sex in the street kind of boy but after seeing Liz, the olives and her witchy minions outside that bar almost shame Zoe, I felt we needed a response. Zoe is sometimes too calm, too measured, which is pitch perfect in the moment, but I knew she also needed a release, to do something a little vengeful. I'm not sure if it was very classy to have sex perched against a wall behind a key-cutter's but I also wanted to prove to her that I want her, that I choose her, that in a moment of being confronted with the woman who was the other option, she didn't even register in my mind. All I saw was Zoe.

'Tea,' she says, pushing a mug across the kitchen counter. And now we're here, with Zoe following through on the promise of a sleepover. In her home. This feels like next steps and she knows it as she's starting to look a little tentative. I'm just fascinated how we've gone from pretty intense sex to a very civil cup of tea within forty-five minutes.

'That's a good colour of tea,' I tell her, sipping politely.

'Why, thank you. I think it's quite hard to get tea wrong, though,' she says, reaching to the top shelves of a cupboard to obtain some biscuits.

'You'd be surprised. Dom is awful at tea – I've seen him share one tea bag between three mugs before. Criminal.'

If I thought I'd seen Zoe in her natural habitat at school, I was wrong. This feels like her domain. I scan her fridge, looking at the certificates, reminder letters and magnets that decorate it. My eyes are drawn to a Polaroid picture of her and her kids. It's not a Zoe I've seen yet, maybe only in that Facebook video her daughter posted, but it looks relaxed, a little goofy as she pulls a face. I go to the fridge with my cup of tea and examine it properly.

'Where was that taken then?' I ask her.

She arranges some chocolate chip cookies on a plate and comes over. 'Oh god. Don't. I look ridiculous there.'

'You look happy.'

'I took the kids to Brighton for the weekend. It's our thing. In the summer, we take the train and spend the day on the pier, eating chips, riding bumper cars. I've done it ever since they were little.'

'They're lucky. Those are nice memories to have. You're a good mum.'

She scoffs at the suggestion.

'Zoe, you're swerving again,' I say, annoyed at her.

She shrugs her shoulders. 'I think it's just most mums don't know if they're doing a good job. We muddle through, we do our best. Come at me in ten years to see if those kids have got through life and are decent members of society, then I'll know if I've done my job.'

She looks at the photo with me and I see a more misted emotion in her eyes.

'You're worried that the separation has scarred them a bit,' I say.

She swings her head around in surprise that I've read her so instantly. 'Well, yeah. But maybe that's Brian's weight to bear in all of this.'

'True. I mean it, though. I've only seen glimpses of you as a mother, but I see your concern for them, I've heard how you talk to them. They're lucky to have you.'

She bites into a cookie so she doesn't have to absorb the compliment and nudges me in the ribs. I guess the other thing from glancing around this place is seeing how they've carefully removed all traces of Brian. I expected a photo or a bill with his name hanging around, but nothing. I'm glad that he doesn't linger but I am curious about someone who'd throw this away so quickly, especially over someone who just gave me some pretty unlikeable vibes. Zoe goes round to take a seat at her kitchen counter as I continue to move around the kitchen, taking in all the details: a pair of her dangly earrings in the fruit bowl, a pile of exercise books on the counter, a mug by the sink with a big yellow Z, a spice rack running low on cinnamon. I go and take a seat next to her.

'Having a good look around then?' she says, sipping her tea thoughtfully.

'Just piecing it together. Will I get a full tour in a bit?'

She laughs. 'Yes. I suppose you want to see the bedroom.'

'Presumptuous,' I say, taking another sip of tea. 'But yes.'

'That can be arranged.'

'Wonderful.'

I help myself to a cookie. She looks at me thoughtfully, perhaps less tentative than that night in the hotel.

'So... have you had sex in public before then?' I ask her, sipping on my tea casually. She chokes a little on her biscuit, refusing to look at me.

'I had sex on a beach once on holiday,' she admits.

'Sandy. I got a hand job at a festival once.'

'In a tent?'

'No, in a crowd. I was off my face.'

She laughs under her breath. 'Who was on the stage?'

'A DJ. Is that awful? It was a very long time ago.'

'Was she facing you?' Zoe asks, frowning, trying to work out the logistics of it.

I get up out of my stool, standing behind her, just off-centre.

'It was sort of...' I guide her hand down to my crotch. 'She didn't have eyes on the situation.'

'Then how did she manage to move her hand? Her arms must have been super bendy?' she says, mimicking the motion.

I look down at her hand and smile. 'I mean, if you wanted to simulate the situation for your own curiosity, you could put some light trance on.'

She laughs but fumbles around looking for the buttons on my jeans. I can be game for this. I pull my trousers down, my penis pretty quick to react in this situation as she manoeuvres her wrists, trying to find a position, giggling as she twists her arms around and her fingers are wrapped around my cock. I won't lie. This is better than the festival situation as back then that girl was so drunk, I was scared she was going to yank my nob off. I lean forward, putting my chin to her shoulder.

'Was it like this?' Zoe whispers.

'Yeah... keep...'

But as she slides her hand over me, there is suddenly a sound, a knocking at the door and the sudden shrill sound of the doorbell. I jump back, Zoe's eyes widening.

'MUM! ARE YOU IN?' a voice echoes through the hallway.

We both look at each other, the colour from Zoe's face draining.

'I thought the kids were with Brian tonight,' I whisper.

'That was the plan. Shit, shit, shit...'

I hear Brian's voice. 'Liz said she saw her in town, out with some school people. I don't think she's in. Look, just...'

'Then why is her car here?' Lottie says plainly. 'Just use your key if she's not in.'

Mild panic descends on Zoe's face, and I know what I have to do. I pull up my trousers for a start. Zoe flaps her hands around, looking around for places for me to hide, looking down at my erection. That'll go in a minute but really not soon enough for me to be meeting family. She heads for the patio doors and unlatches them. 'I am so sorry. Just hide out behind the shed and I'll come find you. Is that OK?'

I don't want to add fire into an already flammable situation so do as I'm told. I am pretty sure what Zoe doesn't need is for Brian and her daughter to find her wanking me off in the middle of their kitchen. I creep out and do as I'm told, just in time as I hear voices in the hallway. I scamper in time to take cover behind a shed, the back door still open.

'MUM! You are in!' I peer my face around the corner of the shed to see Lottie throw her arms around her mum's neck. 'Why were you in the garden?' she asks.

'Oh, I thought I saw a fox.'

I laugh to myself. I am the fox, I'll take that. And for the first time, I see Brian, in the flesh, charging towards the door in some sham show of masculinity to take on this urban fox. I sneer to see him. 'I don't see anything,' Brian says, looking out to the lawn. I wonder if I should just jump out and give the twat the fright of his life but hell, it's not the time. I'll just stand here in the shadows of this very mediocre garden. There's a lot of shrubs. They could do a lot more with this space, you know?

'Why are you both here?' Zoe asks them.

'I forgot my retainers,' Lottie says. 'I'll just go and get them. Did you have someone round?' she asks, and I pat myself down thinking of whether I've left any evidence in that kitchen. The second cup of tea. Shit.

'Beth came round for a bit.'

Lottie exits the room and I see both Brian and Zoe standing there, silent. I watch them cautiously. I can picture a time when they would have matched and it seems bizarre to think that their coupling only ended recently.

'Liz said she saw you in town,' Brian says, trying to start a conversation.

'Yeah.'

'How was it?' he asks, apprehensively.

'Oh, we had wine together, hugged it out and traded in stories about you.'

'Really?'

'No, Brian. We didn't.'

I laugh. Well played, that woman.

He moves around the kitchen, looking curiously at the small gold trophy sitting on the counter. She puts it in a drawer.

'You weren't out for long then?' he says, almost mocking her. It feels like he and Liz deserve each other. Zoe bustles around the kitchen, emptying mugs and putting them in the dishwasher.

'It was only dinner in Wimbledon, headed back early.'

'I guess that's handy.'

'Excuse me?' Zoe says, a little surprised. I smirk to myself. Oh, your ex is very handy.

'That it was local.'

'Yes, very handy,' she repeats, looking out the back window, almost searching for my shadow.

'Are you still looking for that fox?' Brian asks, his gaze following hers. 'Do you want me to go out and take a proper look?'

'No,' she says, smiling. 'Just leave him be. He's harmless.'

'You say that but once they get in the bins... I know what you're like.'

'Brian...'

'Zo...'

'Not your house anymore.'

And I pause for a moment. He knows what she's like. It's condescending to say the least, but I guess there is truth there, too. Here's someone she's known for years, a marriage and a history that will always have some hold over her, and for the first time, I feel a little worried about how I will ever follow on from that.

Lottie bounds back into the room. 'Got them. Let's go, Dad. You OK, Mum?' she asks, putting an arm around her again. It's a nice image, one I've only imagined. I've heard Lottie's voice on the phone but she's as I imagined, a confident young lady who loves her mum to pieces.

'I'm good. You and Dyl have fun and I'll see you tomorrow.'

She ushers them into the hallway, and I stand there in the lowlights coming from the house, wondering how I fit into this life of hers. I think I could. I think I could eat breakfast at that kitchen island, I could wake up here and help her with the bins so the foxes don't get to them. I hope she might let me.

FIFTEEN

Zoe

'Hold up, he took you where?' Beth asks me, taking the register for me as we load up this minibus to Winchester.

'Miss, what happens if you've forgotten to pack your lunch?' Bonnie asks me.

'Then you'll likely be sharing my tuna and cucumber roll. We'll think of something,' I say, turning back to Beth and lowering my voice. 'He took me to Laser Tag.'

'How old is he again?' she jokes.

I narrow my eyes and shake my head at her. Yes, it was an unconventional date, and I seriously thought my Laser Tag days were behind me, but it was pretty easy to work out the intention, and what he wanted to do was introduce me to his family which, according to those bouncy nephews of his, was quite a big step for him. In any case, the cake was good and despite my limited experience in the dating pool of late, any date that involves cake is a good thing. Beth looks at me; she's intrigued but also trying to work me out. Whereas Mia thinks she's wildly smart for orchestrating this set up and Kate feels it's what I deserve for having been treated so badly by Brian, Beth is still trying to work out if this is a good or bad thing. She's not the only one.

'I take it the date didn't just end at Laser Tag, though?' she asks me.

Oh no, we shagged in an alleyway, I gave him half a hand job in my kitchen, hid him from my husband in my garden and then we did indeed have sex. In my bed. I can't really say that with children peering in and out of the school minibus.

'No,' I reply, smiling, and she laughs under her breath.

'Well, then I'm slightly in awe. I was telling my sisters about you at lunch and you are their new hero.'

I chuckle in disbelief that stories of my escapades are being told around tables like some sort of urban legend. Did you hear about that mumsy teacher who got dumped on her ass and then hooked up and found happiness with someone fourteen years younger than her? Yeah, I can't quite believe it either.

'And so what do I have to do?' Beth asks.

'Oh, Jack was at the house and Brian and Lottie dropped by and so I had to think on my feet and say you'd dropped in for a cup of tea. So, if that comes up...'

'I will be a very convincing alibi. I take it your kids don't know?' she asks.

'God, no. One step at a time. A lot of people don't know. I just haven't worked out if it's a rebound fling or something more...' And the fact I'm still debating this makes me feel guilty. Because meeting Jack's family felt like something bigger, more important than I was expecting and I'm not sure if he wants me to reciprocate. I feel the longer this goes on for, the more feelings are going to be involved and people might get hurt and with what I've just experienced with Brian, it feels like it could get too complicated. 'Can you imagine the things my Lottie would say if she met him?'

Beth scrunches up her face, nodding. 'So do you think fling

because he might not stick it out or because you're not quite ready for serious yet?' she asks me.

It's the ultimate question. 'Both?' I suddenly sense his figure appear from around the corner and I stop for a moment, trying to stop looking so damn happy every time he's in my immediate vicinity. Beth turns to see why my stance has changed and laughs to herself.

'Stop it,' I tell her.

'I know that look.'

'I'm just excited about my impeding STEM trip.'

'Yeah, whatever, Mrs Swift. I am going to love you and leave you,' she says, peering into the bus. 'Have a lovely time, everyone!' She leans into me. 'Have fun, Mrs Swift.'

'Miss Callaghan, Mrs Swift,' Jack says, trying to act normal but brushing against my hand intentionally. I hold my breath as he does this. He can't do this all day. I won't cope. His school look hasn't changed bar a backpack this time. I hope he read the letter and packed a waterproof coat, lunch and a pencil case with a calculator.

'I did say eight o'clock, Mr Damon. It's five minutes past eight.'

'I am sorry.'

'Well, to make it up to us, you can drive the first leg to the services.'

'Deal,' he says, putting his hand out so I can shake it.

'Be good, kids,' Beth jokes, interrupting this little moment, allowing Jack and I to part ways and get this trip on its way. It's like a day out with ten children tagging along who are bloody good at Rubik's Cubes.

'Morning, everyone!' Jack says, waving to his passengers, before settling into the driver's seat where he plugs his phone into the cradle, connecting it to the minibus stereo. He starts the engine and presses a few buttons until music starts blasting through the speakers. I can't seem to control my reaction and have to put my hand over my mouth, looking out of the window.

'Is this RAYE, Sir?' asks a voice at the back.

'It is! It's my new favourite. I had a dance to this a couple of weeks ago,' he says, smiling to himself as he grapples with the gearstick. With who, Mr Damon? Pray, do tell.

'Let me know if you have any requests. Just no Oasis.'

I stop for a moment and look at him curiously.

'No Oasis?' I ask.

He starts reversing and the ping of the minibus starts to echo through the carpark. 'Just can't stand them.'

'Ditto,' I reply. 'Ditto.'

I'm never sure what these school trips will be like. I suppose I hope that there'll be a singalong on the bus and the children will be brimming with excitement about a day away from school and some provision for adventure and alternative learning. What really happens is that you're terrified that you have sole responsibility for these kids. What if I lose one of them? What if one of them wanders off? What if the bus breaks down on the motorway and we have to live in a layby forever? Never say that I'm not an optimist. It's been a hell of a drive and one that's now taken us to Fleet Services where we've stopped so the children (and I) can relieve ourselves, and the children can get excited about us allowing them to buy super expensive sweets.

'Boys with me then,' Jack announces to the bus as children clamber over each other. I look at my watch. I've scheduled fifteen minutes for this stop which also allows me to buy more coffee. Jack turns to me smiling. 'You OK, Miss?' he asks me. I don't know why he looks so well. I want to say it's youth without sounding condescending, but he just looks like he's rolled out of bed and done nothing more than thrown on a shirt, trousers and boots. He gets out of the bus and stretches his hands over his head, revealing a slice of stomach and the waistband of his underwear. I avert my eyes to avoid blushing in front of the kids but exhale coolly to know I've seen a hell of a lot more than that. 'When I'm in there, can you just check Maps again? I might come off the M3 early if the traffic is still bad,' he tells me, before herding his small group of boys towards the services building. I have control over his phone. That feels like next level intimacy – my kids won't even let me do that much – but I do as I'm told, studying junctions and red lines on maps. As I scroll, however, a message pops up.

> You keep ignoring me and it's bloody infuriating.

It's from Sarah. I should ignore it. Not my phone. Not my boyfriend in reality, so it's bad for me to even feel a hint of jealousy or interest in any of this. I will just assume it's the same lovely Sarah who delivered Dylan back home safely to me.

> I need to tell them as soon as possible so please make a decision.

My interest is well and truly piqued now. A decision about what? Jack hasn't mentioned anything to me. I wonder if it's important, something he has to reply to now. Maybe it's as simple as a party invitation and she needs to know for catering. If this is the case, then I feel her fury as people who don't RSVP are galling. Maybe I have found that one thing about Jack that's vaguely annoying.

> And I'll say it out loud, if you don't take up this opportunity then you're bloody stupid. Just bloody say YES.

Does this mean he's turned down an invite to a really good party? Instinct tells me probably no. I shouldn't get involved. I shouldn't even tell him I've seen this. I should look up directions and routes and just mind my own business, but I open up his messages and scroll up. Shit. He'll know I've read this. I'll just say I have fat fingers and plead ignorance. I look through the message chain – a lot of it is Jack just ignoring Sarah, but I come to one message from about two weeks ago.

> This is what I was talking about last night. Please please consider it. I'm not asking you because you're a mate but I really think you'd be amazing at it. S

I follow the link and it takes me to a page detailing a conservation project in Borneo. I scan the page and find a small news box talking about how a Dr Sarah Jarvis is leading a small team of botanists to conduct some research out there, and I put two and two together like the good mathematician I am. Jack has never mentioned this. He took me to Laser Tag, we've kissed in a stationery cupboard, and had sex in that time but this was never something that came up. The messages track back to the weekend after we first slept together. I guess I am just a casual thing, so this is maybe something not to discuss with me. But I can also understand why he wouldn't mention it to me as it would involve him leaving. Leaving me. By that measure, though, is this why he hasn't said yes? Is it because of me?

'Miss. Is there a shop at the university? I said I'd buy my mum something.' I can't seem to answer. 'Miss?'

'I guess we can find something, Bonnie. We need to find you a lunch, too, don't we?' I tell her.

'Is something wrong, Miss?' she asks, sensing a change in my mood.

I shake my head. It feels like life encroaching on that lovely bubble I have with Jack again. Maybe that's what holds me back from liking him too much, talking too much about what our future looks like because, deep down, I was also a bit hesitant that it would go anywhere. Not that I viewed this as a fling. It was certainly starting to feel like more than that, but because in our lives, I see huge forks in the road. I don't want to give my kids even more emotional upheaval in trying to understand a new relationship. I don't want him to feel like he had to jump into my life and fit into it, rather than live his own. He's too good a person for that. I think when you've seen your own life fall apart, you don't wish that for people you know, for people you care about. You only want good things. I watch as I see him and his group exiting the services and scramble around trying to ensure that it looks like I haven't been snooping on his phone. That wasn't a good move in any case. I put the phone down on his side of the bus as the door enters.

'All good?' he asks me.

I nod. 'Right, our turn, girls. Did you want anything? A coffee maybe?' I ask, attempting to play it cool.

'I'm good.'

'Oh... by the way, when I was looking at your maps, a message from Sarah came up.'

'Oh, cool,' he says, taking his phone and going through his messages. I watch him as he reads the messages then writes a reply. I wish I could ask the young boy behind him to peer over and see what he wrote. I really do.

Jack

I don't know about these kids but I am learning shit loads today about science and maths, *and* I've seen a boy solve a Rubik's Cube in twelve seconds. I seriously double high-fived him. I'd never seen anything so incredible. I think he appreciated the celebration but was slightly confused by my overexcitement. This exhibition is happening in a series of university buildings and for this last part of the day, we've allowed them free rein in this science centre, praying that they will make their way back to us.

'Please, please, please. You have half an hour and then we need to get back on the road. Please go round in pairs. Don't attempt to go into the student union bar and *please* don't lose my clipboards,' Zoe tells them all. They all hang on her every word, nodding. I can't lie. We have the well-behaved maths crew, but I guess that's better than dragging kids around a castle where they don't want to be. They all disperse in different directions and Zoe breathes a sigh of relief.

'It's been a good day. Chill. Here,' I say, handing her a cup of tea and putting a hand to her back. I rest the hand there a little too long, but she doesn't seem to mind. It's been a strange day like this where we've had to keep an acceptable distance from one another so as not to scare the children – any brief contact has, therefore, almost had to be planned, appear to be accidental, though it makes me clench my fists in frustration. I follow her as we settle on some stairs that open out to a huge quad dotted with trees, benches. It's a perfect spot to people watch and take a well-deserved breather, the early winter sunshine a welcome relief. I watch as she pulls her scarf over her face.

'Are you cold? Do you want to go inside?' I ask her. 'Or maybe I can sit closer to you? We can share bodily warmth.'

She shakes her head.

'Are you just worried about another sex debacle?' I ask her and she laughs in response.

'Here, at least get close enough to have a crisp,' I tell her, offering my pack over to her. She puts a hand in my packet, our hands grazing, and I see her smile.

'Thank you, Sir.'

'There are no children around. I believe you can just call me Jack.'

She smiles. I'm not quite sure but since the minibus, Zoe has been a tad quieter. I'm not sure if it's fatigue or the stress of having to keep eyes on all these kids but she stares out into the quad now, looking at all the students rushing to lectures and the curved sprawling architecture of the modern buildings.

'It's super fancy here, eh?' I say.

'Very. It's certainly very different from a London comprehensive,' she says, studying my face. 'Tell me how you met Sarah again – wasn't it at university?' she asks me, out of the blue.

'Yes, we were both botanists – proper plant geeks. Why?'

'Oh – you know, being here I was just curious. There's so much I don't know about you. University to me feels like it was a lifetime ago. I can't believe this might be Dylan in a few years.'

She seems pensive and I desperately want to hold her hand. 'So you were a numbers geek at uni?'

'Yep. I loved the maths. But I had a terribly blunt fringe, too. That was a mistake,' she jokes. 'Why plants?' she asks me. 'Botany?'

'When I was little, I was very into rainforests. I remember I had one of those fact files for Christmas and I knew all the names of the trees and the animals, and I became a bit fixated. That's not very sexy, is it?'

She breaks into laughter. 'I don't know. It shows a passion for something, it shows you care. I see it with your nephews, too, Dom. In how much you care for them.'

It feels good that she sees that in me. 'I'm good with trees, actually. It's my specialist subject. Go on, quiz me.'

She leans back, giggling. 'The man is telling me he's good with wood.'

I cock my head to one side and point to a tree in the vicinity. 'That is a London plane tree. From the *Platanaceae* family.'

'Impressive,' she says.

'You have no idea...'

She's quiet.

'Actually, when I was at your house last week, I was looking at your garden.'

'It's a shit garden,' she replies.

'It needs some TLC, but you've got an amazing apple tree at the end of the garden that's doing well. You've got good soil back there. It's a good place for trees to flourish.'

We look out to a young couple who seem to be chasing each other around the quad. The boy catches up with the girl and he swings her around, before he kisses her.

'God, I want to kiss you,' I tell her without looking at her.

She leans forward, resting her elbows on her knees and putting the edge of her thumb in her mouth. I look over at her, seeing her mouth curl to a smile.

'You know, when I came to your house after the boys' party last week, I keep thinking back to little moments of that evening.'

'Moments?' she asks me. We both still look down the steps, trying to appear like we're engaging in a normal, decent, educated conversation but the temptation to tease Zoe in this very moment is far too great.

'That moment when you were sitting on top of me on the edge of your bed and I had your nipple in my mouth. I keep thinking about the expression on your face.'

'Jack...' she mumbles, looking over her shoulder in case a student is standing there.

'I keep thinking about the shape of your mouth when you moan. How I love running my fingers over your lips, down your neck...'

She doesn't reply but I see her fidgeting on the spot, crossing her legs and hovering her drink over her mouth. Every moment with her seems to be etched in my brain at the moment; there's an addictive quality about being with her, near her and I can't compare it to anything else, any other person I've been with.

'Did you like that, Zoe?'

She nods.

'And I really loved putting my hands on your lower back and feeling the wave of your hips, the movement over me...' My mouth goes dry, every sinew of my body raging to know she's right next to me and I can't touch her. 'Being inside you... feeling you tighten over me.'

She exhales loudly.

'I love all of it, all of you.'

I said that, didn't I? She doesn't reply and I'm almost glad she doesn't.

'Too much?' I joke.

'I don't know how to reply. I'm literally sat here on these stairs on a school trip and my nipples are rock hard,' she says, gritting her teeth. 'I hate you.'

I laugh, side-eyeing her, almost wanting to break her. I hope you don't.

'But you know what, something I remember so clearly was you hovering over me, kissing my cheek very gently, just here,' I say, running a line along my stubble. 'And your face lingered there for a moment, you stroked my hair, and it was gentle and affectionate and I think a lot about that kiss, too.'

'I love kissing you,' she finally says.

'You *love* it, do you?'

'Don't put words in my mouth...'

'Well, what else can I put in your mouth?'

'Now that was too much,' she says, cackling.

She looks over at me and the temptation is too much. I take one of her curls and tuck it around her ear, looking her in the eye. And this is what makes her so attractive to me. The way she studies my face in a way that no one has before. I think of girls who used to tell me before that they thought I was relatively fit or that they liked my hair, but she seems to look beyond that. In fact, I don't think she's ever said anything like that to me, just comments on that sort of skin-deep appeal. She says it with her touch, her looks – a quiet appreciation of it all. Always a look like she's searching beyond all of that, too.

'Have you ever thought about going back into botany?' she asks.

The question comes out of nowhere. I don't think it comes from a place of judgment and I'm not sure it's one of those statements that questions my direction, pushing me towards different goals. Maybe she is concerned about my age, maybe my line of work isn't worthy enough. The truth is, I'm studiously avoiding thinking about how there is an offer to return to that line of work, trying to gauge if it's right for me.

'Why do you ask?'

She bites at her thumb nail. 'I guess I'm just thinking about what ifs. Like, if life had been kinder to your brother, maybe you'd have tried a different line of work.'

'Possibly. One day. I don't think too much about that. If the right job came along, then maybe I guess I'd take it up?'

She's quiet and looks down at her shoes.

'I hope you would. I really do.' She takes one of my hands and does that thing where she wraps her hands around it, shaking it so it can appear civil, like a gesture between colleagues. It makes my chest ache and I think about Sarah's messages before and my response. I can't go now. I want to stay. I want to be here. With her.

SIXTEEN

Zoe

'YOU'RE TOO DEEP!'
'STAY IN POSITION!'
'FINISH! FINISH! WHY DIDN'T YOU HEAD IT?'

I've stood on the sidelines of many a football pitch, ever since Dylan was a tiny little thing and his jersey used to look like a dress, but I'm not quite sure why everything seems to sound lewd to me at the moment. I stand there and pull my scarf over my mouth to hide my grin. It's not a sexy look, football sideline clothing: a big, padded coat, a bright beanie, scarf and insulated wellies – anything to keep warm, dry and pretend you enjoy being there.

'This tea smells like wee. The number fifteen on the other side is fit. Smell my tea, this smells like wee, doesn't it?' Lottie pushes a Styrofoam cup in my face.

'It doesn't. Maybe that smell of wee is you. What will the fit number fifteen think?' I tell her. I joke with her, but this talk of boys has become a more recent development and all it does is compound on all the other worries I carry as a parent. Pick a nice boy. Please. I know too many kids in my school that are your age, and I would stab some of them through the nads before I'd let them near you and I'm the ultimate pacifist.

'Number fifteen has a mullet,' I observe.

'Everyone has a mullet at the moment. Get with the programme, Mother.'

'If you brought that home, I would point and laugh.'

She shakes her head at me and threads an arm through mine. 'I'm so cold.'

'You should have a worn a coat... perhaps, just maybe...' I tell her, absolutely no sarcasm in my tones at all. It's a sentence I repeat to these kids ad nauseum – I bet they'd listen to me if it went viral on TikTok or it came out of the mouth of someone cool like Zendaya, though. It's nice to have Lottie out with us today. She used to stay in on football mornings but since everything has happened, she tends to stay close. I think she still feels some residual guilt for having abandoned Dylan in Manchester, so this is her sisterly way of making it up to him.

'GOOD KICK, DYLS!' she screams. A man a few feet away from us turns around and sneers at her. Naturally, Lottie doesn't respond to this well. 'He can wind his ugly old man turkey neck in.'

I pull her closer before she has a chance to throw her cup of wee-smelling tea at him.

'Talking of ugly old men,' she says, looking past me. I follow her gaze, watching as Brian makes his way up the pitch, shaking hands with a few of the dads he knows and engaging in conversation with them. This will always be the messy part – there are so many threads of our lives that are entwined, that I will never be able to unravel. We've been friends with some of these parents for years. We've had dinners together, drunk in pubs and traded messages on WhatsApp groups and, naturally, what's happened has frayed those threads. I mean, it's not about taking sides, but I feel there are different versions of our story that have been made available and I don't think I have the energy to let people know which one is the most accurate. Brian turns to us, and I put a hand up to greet him without smiling. Lottie ignores him. I am not sure what to say. Please acknowledge your father? They've spent a few evenings together since Manchester, but the trust is still lacking. Dylan tells me she comes at him with a battering ram of sarcasm. Does that secretly please me? Possibly, but I'll never say that out loud.

'He should have said he was coming,' she says, side-eyeing him, her nostrils flared.

'And there was me thinking you were here for Dylan to show him what a good sister you are.'

'You're mistaken, I'm here for the post-match McDonald's,' she tells me, fake smiling.

Brian and I have not drawn up arrangements or battle lines when it comes to the kids yet. There are talks of co-parenting, doing what's best and investing a shared interest in things like parents' evenings, concerts and sports matches but it's ensuring the kids are open to this arrangement, too. Ever since Manchester a few weeks ago, he's learned that being their father is a privilege, not so much a right, and he has to start rebuilding after all the damage he's caused.

'EDGE OF THE D! EDGE OF THE D!' one dad shouts.

Lottie giggles from behind her tea. 'Did that man just shout at him to go edging on his D?'

I pull a shocked face. 'Lottie! Yes, he did. Can I ask how you know what that is?'

'Mother! Can I ask how you know what that is?'

And yes, there is deep anxiety there in me as a mother but we both laugh.

'What's so funny?' a voice suddenly pipes up, sliding into the conversation. We both stop laughing and I pray that Lottie keeps this civil and doesn't repeat that comment about edging.

'Nothing,' Lottie says, returning to the football. 'You're here.' It's less a question, more a statement.

'Morning,' I say, trying to keep things civil. Brian always comes to these matches with his trousers tucked into his boots which gives him farmer vibes. He keeps trying to catch Lottie's eye and she's doing a very good job of dodging it.

'Score?' he asks.

'Oh, they're behind one-nil but there's time to turn it around,' I inform him, not really knowing what emotion matches my mood.

We stand there taking in the football. I wish I really knew what was going on so I could shout out something constructive, but Dylan looks like he's running in the right direction at least.

'I was thinking that maybe after this... our post-match McDonald's ritual – maybe we could all go together?' Brian suggests.

As soon as he asks, I realise that this isn't my call at all. Would I be able to drink my strawberry milkshake with him in the vicinity? I guess we're at that point where him being present doesn't cause me such anxiety anymore. Lottie looks over her shoulder.

'Will Liz be there? Is she hiding in a bush, waiting in your car?' she says pointedly.

Touché, Miss Swift.

Brian who would normally reply with anger knows now not to respond as such. 'No Liz, just the four of us.'

Lottie is silent but I notice her attention taken by the football for a moment. 'YES, DYLS. RUN, DYLS!'

We all look out on to that pitch and Dylan is on a break, running towards goal. The defender's nowhere near him, just him and the keeper. Lottie grabs on to my arm, jumping up and down, tea everywhere. I'll never understand that feeling as a parent. You feel it when they've been up on stage and repeated their lines perfectly, when they win a race on sports day, when they receive a certificate in a crowded room. Part of it is some form of relief that you feel on their behalf but all that pride, all that happiness, all that love just courses through you, making you rather giddy. Well done, that kid. He threads the ball through the keeper calmly and you see the net ripple as it hits the right-hand corner. Dylan turns and runs to the centre circle, roaring with joy, a rare moment of pure emotion that he just exudes into the air. There's a loud cheer from our small crowd but mostly screaming from Lottie as she puts her hands to her mouth and does a loud whistle.

I don't say a word. Mostly because I can feel Brian gripping on to my arm in excitement. He looks down for a moment, realising he's overstepped and takes it away, but we share a look. Despite everything, we made these two human beings and by god, aren't they just the best things? Brian takes a step away and I look out on to the pitch, Dylan surrounded by his teammates but his eyes scanning over the sidelines to see us together. He looks to his dad who puts a thumb up and then he looks at me, a tear rolling down my face. I'll have to tell him it was the cold.

'What's number fifteen's name? What's his Snap?' Lottie asks Dylan as we walk back to the car.

'You're so grim and embarrassing. No,' Dylan grunts in reply, flicking mud from his boots at her.

She screams. I'd intervene but I mostly watch in amusement at how much their relationship see-saws like this. Once the play fighting starts then I'll intervene. Brian walks beside me, a perfect silence helping me keep some distance. Both children have agreed to Brian joining us for a McDonald's and I guess we'll see how that goes but I'll look forward to seeing Lottie upgrade to a large merely out of spite because he's paying.

'ZOE!' a voice suddenly sifts in from behind me. I don't

turn around immediately because the voice is young and I don't recognise it, but I hear footsteps and they call me again. I turn. I know you.

'Barney?' I am not quite sure if Barney was playing football today or mud wrestling with a bear, but he comes over and I put a hand out before he has a chance to hug me. Brian stops beside me, pouting as he tries to figure out who this child is. He's not in the age group I teach, not a relative or neighbour and I suddenly watch my own kids stop to turn to figure this kid out, too. Oh dear. I have to think quickly here. 'Look at you! Have you been playing football today as well?'

'Yeah, we lost, though, but only by eight-nil this time which Dad says is better than last time, so we are getting better,' he replies gleefully, clutching a muddied bag of Haribo in his left hand. 'Did you come to watch me?' he asks.

'Oh no, I was here watching my son play. This is Dylan,' I say, pointing over to him.

Barney raises his chin. 'He's big. How old are you?'

'Fifteen,' Dylan replies curiously.

'How old are you?' Lottie asks him.

'I'm ten. Zoe came to my party. She's really good at Laser Tag.'

I can't quite breathe. I can tell people have questions. Mum, is this what you do now when we're not about? You go to the local shopping centre and play Laser Tag with random children? But before I can answer, someone approaches us, a huge bag of footballs hauled over his shoulder.

'Zoe?'

'Dom! Hey...' He leans over for a hug and my kids don't quite know where to look. 'I just bumped into Barney, and he was telling me about your game.'

'ZOE!' another little voice interrupts. It's George. My kids' eyes bounce between these two little kids. There are two of them, Mum. What's happening? The problem is you think I'm probably friends or more with this man and his twin sons. I don't know if the truth is worse. 'Were you here to see Uncle Jack?' George continues.

Even the sound of Jack's name makes me blush. Mainly because last night I was sexting him at midnight. What we have remains the most illicit yet charming of liaisons and still not something to talk about here.

'Oh no, this is my son, Dylan, and we came to watch him play football. This is Lottie, my daughter and this is...' I don't know how to label Brian anymore. He's still legally a husband, not quite an ex, not quite a friend. 'This is Brian.' He's just Brian.

I notice Dom's tired brain and memory sifting through the details of my family arrangement and trying to piece it all together, trying to show them all some civility. I guess he'll know as much as Jack has told him. He pauses when he goes to shake Brian's hand that tells me he knows something about our relationship. Brian seems cautious if very, very curious. I need to say something.

'No one ate the oranges I brought, Dom. I'll have to eat these all myself now,' a voice sounds and I know who it is immediately. He did tell me he was going to watch his nephews play but I didn't think to ask him where that would be. I inhale deeply to hear his voice but can't quite focus knowing all my worlds have collided on this very muddy, cold football pitch. 'Zoe?' he says, a huge beam hitting his face to see me. I see him coming in to hug me but I angle my body so he can't get close. I won't be able to cope with the spark of that physical contact. He senses something's up and looks around. Yes, Jack. Look who's around. Oh, shit. And with that he just puts a hand to my shoulder.

'Look at you in your football gear.'

'I look like a Womble, Jack. I know.'

He laughs before we realise where we both are, and the many pairs of eyes we have on us.

'You're Jack?' Dylan says out loud.

Dylan has spoken to Jack on the phone. He knows it's Jack's friends who gave him a lift to Birmingham, but I guess he expected someone different. Someone older? Because there are no farmer vibes here. It's a tracksuit, football boots and a long puffa coat, a beanie stylishly finishing off the look.

'I am. Dylan?' Jack puts out his hand and Dylan goes over to shake it. 'I remember your mum telling me you played. How'd you get on today?'

'We won two-one.'

'And Dyl scored,' Lottie adds. 'I'm Lottie,' she says, less keen to offer out her hand. Her eyes study him cautiously.

'Of course. I've heard a lot about you.'

'All good, obvs.'

'Obvs.'

She laughs in response which is a relief given it's Lottie. She scans him up and down, assessing the 'fit' as she does. Jack looks at me, waiting. I am not quite sure what I'm supposed to do. This doesn't feel like the time and place to fill you in on how we are all connected. I look down at Jack's nephews, standing by their dad, stuffing sweets in their face and carefully watching all these exchanges. Please, boys. Please don't say I'm Jack's girlfriend and that I told you I'd rather have a giant eye than two noses.

'So, Jack is a teacher at my school, Dom is his brother, and these two cuties are Dom's boys,' I explain for clarity. 'I did go to their party, and it was brilliant.'

'You went to Laser Tag?' Lottie asks me, curiously.

'I returned a favour. They needed more adults to supervise.'

Dom furrows his brow. He can see George about to say something and hands him another bag of sweets to divert his attention. I notice Brian taking it all in quietly. I can tell he can't quite believe that cover story. 'You're the Jack who helped Dyl in Manchester?' Jack turns to Brian and whilst they've never met, I know he's worked out who he is. Please, Jack. Not here. Brian outstretches his hand, and I may have an aneurysm. 'Then thank you for helping him out, mate.'

Mate. God, you wouldn't be calling him that if you knew the things he'd done to me, that we'd done to each other. For a moment, a cold winter's morning feels positively balmy, my scarf feels like a noose.

'Brian,' Jack says, still gripping on to his hand. Please let it go. Their eyes meet.

'Yeah. I'm Zoe's husband.'

Fuck. Does Brian know? He knows it's more than favours. Yet what an awful and territorial thing to say over someone who isn't yours anymore. Over someone who didn't even want me. I hope my completely bemused look tells him that much.

'But not anymore, right?' Jack replies.

Lottie smirks but I see her huddled into her brother for support, for comfort, both of them trying to work out this man. Brian looks like he doesn't know what to say. I swear the earth has stopped spinning.

'JACK!' Dom interrupts, sensing the awkwardness has reached its peak. He puts a hand to his brother's arm. 'Uncle Jack, we've got to get these boys in a hot bath.' Barney goes over to get in between them and offers Jack a sweet. He smiles and takes it. The boys run over to me and unsure of what to do, I let them both hug my legs and get my coat smothered in mud. 'See you soon, Zoe,' they say before running off towards the car park.

'Bye kids, see you soon.'

'Dom has a point,' Jack says, his gaze still piercing Brian's. 'Zoe,' he adds, turning to me. Please don't look at me like that. Because it's a look of concern, possibly some confusion to have met the four of us out together like some sort of happy family. But there's also some resigned sadness there that I can't be

honest about who he is to me, what we are, that I can't communicate all the emotion I feel for him, that I can't tell Brian, Lottie
and Dylan that this is Jack. Jack who has loved me, held me and
pieced me back together these last few months. Jack who
communicates with me via emojis and Post It notes in my work
pigeonhole. Jack who I think I may be in love with. 'I will see
you on Monday at school. Lovely to meet you all.'

'See you Monday, Jack. Good to bump into you.'

He puts a fist out. Oh, we're fist bumping. I guess that's
better than me snogging his face off. I bump it back and he goes
chasing after his nephews, his figure shrinking, moving further
away from me. I try to dust off my coat, letting Lottie, Dylan
and Brian walk ahead of me while I try to take a breath.

'Hazards of little people, I am so sorry about the coat.' I hear
a voice behind me. It's Dom, grappling with his football
equipment.

I bend down to take a first aid kit and walk alongside him.
'It's fine. I can throw it in the wash.'

'Could you maybe throw those boys in, too?' he jokes.

I smile. 'Thank you, by the way. That was a little tense, and
it wasn't the place to perhaps explain all the dynamics of how
we all know each other.'

Dom nods. 'I get it, it's pretty complicated. I never thanked
you for enduring Laser Tag either, so I think we're even.'

I laugh and we take that walk back to the car park, quietly.

'Laser Tag was actually very fun. It was nice to see Jack
around his family. He certainly loves those boys, eh?' I tell him.

'Uncle of the decade, really. I guess you know our story?' he
asks me.

'Jack may have talked about it. I am so sorry you had to go
through that. What was your wife's name?' I ask him.

He seems taken aback that I should want to know the
details. 'Amy,' he says proudly. 'That's where the twins get it
from, all of it. She'd have been here today, cheering them on,

most likely shouting at the referee. God, she was a liability. Just in the best ways.'

His eyes glaze over and I feel his grief, all of it. I even understand it a little. We grieve those lives we'll never have with people we once loved.

'Jack really likes you, you know?' Dom says, randomly, as if he's not really sure whether it's his place.

'He does?' I enquire.

'It's just, he came to me a few weeks back to chat about you. That's very rare for Jack.'

'I guess he told you about the new job?' I ask Dom, testing the water. He stops for a moment, his interest obviously piqued, and pretends to fiddle with his football bag.

'There's a new job – a teaching job?' he asks.

I realise he's not told him about it, his beloved brother. I take a deep breath. 'No, his friend, Sarah, offered him a place on a conservation team working out of Borneo.'

His face softens with pride, excitement. 'He didn't tell me about that. Idiot. God, that's amazing, it'll be so good for him.'

'It will, won't it?' I tell him.

'And it'd be such a relief, too.'

'Relief?' I ask him, continuing to walk alongside him.

'Just... Jack's been a complete hero to me and the boys. I wouldn't have survived those early years without him, but I always worried we were holding him back. If he takes this job, it just means he's living his life finally, you know?'

I know exactly what he means. The words pierce my heart completely because since finding out about that job, all I know is that he's not told me about it which makes me think he's turning it down and I think the reason may be me. And as wonderful as that is, there is also something about that which isn't right.

Dom suddenly reads the emotion in my face and realises he may have said something out of turn. 'Oh, I didn't mean that you're holding him back or that you're stopping him from living a life. I phrased that wrong. You'll have to forgive me, I'm renowned for putting my foot in my mouth.'

I smile to put him at ease. 'Dom, please don't worry. I think I know what you mean, and I feel the same, completely. He's quite the person, your brother, and he deserves the world.'

'Has he taken the job?' Dom asks.

'I'm not sure.'

His expression changes and it pains me to see the air of disappointment in his eyes.

'You know, I like your brother very much, too.'

'I'm glad.'

'I'll do the right thing by him, please don't worry.'

And there's a moment where we both look out into the car park to see Jack playing around with his nephews, holding one under his arm and trying to chase the other. We both laugh to see it and share a final look, one of love that we both feel for this man. I wasn't sure what to do with that love, but I think I now know.

Jack

I walk up the path to Zoe's house, looking down at the gift in my hands. I don't know if this is a particularly good idea – the sentiment is there but I hope she gets it. It's just that there really was only so much chicken that I could bring into this woman's house without it feeling like it was starting to get weird. I've only been here once before, post Laser Tag, but there's a familiarity there now. Half a hand job in the kitchen and then a night in her bedroom, her body curled into mine on her bed. It's one of those moments I return to a lot when I'm waiting for traffic lights to turn, when I'm looking out of windows and stirring dinners. To hell, all those small moments are taken up by thinking of her.

I put my finger to the bell, watching her shadow in the glass come towards me.

'Hey,' she says as she sees me, exhaling deeply. She's not in all her football gear. It's that cool casual look I've come to know from her; a floral dress with her trademark big earrings, bare feet and her curls hanging over her shoulders. She leans against the door as I stand on the doorstep, taking her in.

'Is the coast clear?' I say quietly.

She nods. 'The kids are at their mates' houses for the afternoon so yeah... please...' she says, widening the door. 'Please come in.'

I step over the threshold and naturally gravitate towards her, feeling some relief that I can do so without anyone looking or judging.

'Good afternoon, Mrs Swift.' She lets me back her against the wall next to her front door, and allows me to kiss her gently, to let our bodies fold into each other. 'Well, I'm glad I have you for a couple of hours at least. I was very glad to get your phone call,' I whisper into her ear. She curls a leg up around mine, and the sensation makes me drop what was in my hands on the floor.

She giggles. 'You've dropped your package,' she tells me.

'On the contrary.'

She glances down at the box on the floor, the shape of that velveteen box and I see her pause for a moment. Oh. Really? You think that. OK, then. I smile cheekily and she looks me in the eyes, not knowing what to think.

'If I got down on my knees now, would that totally freak you out?' I joke. She bites her lip and I'm not quite sure if she gets the joke. I bend down on one knee, kissing her stomach, one hand at her waist and I reach for the box, opening it up. 'Zoe, would you give me the greatest honour of wearing these paper-clip earrings?'

She looks down at the little silver studs and laughs, but there's another emotion there. I think it may be relief and I am not quite sure how I feel about that. Is that funny? Or such a bad thing?

'They are very cute. Of course, thank you.'

I get up, putting the box on a shelf nearby and then returning to her face, tucking a curl behind her ear. 'Did you really think I'd got you something else that could fit in a box like that?'

She shakes her head. 'No... oh god, no. It's just the romance of my hallway, you know?' She takes a hand and leads me through to the living room where she's lit a fire and laid out a bottle of wine and crisps. She grips on to my fingers and squeezes them tightly, encouraging me to sit down.

'So... this morning...' I tell her as she fills up my wine glass.

'You met Brian.'

'The Brian.' We clink glasses and take a sip of our wine.

'I'm sorry about that. We were both watching Dylan, we were all leaving to get a McDonald's. It kind of took me by surprise.'

'Don't apologise,' I tell her. I can sense she's a little uneasy. I'm not sure if that's because she thought I was going to propose two minutes ago and was freaked out by the prospect or it's because we're on different pages altogether. There's been something sitting between us since Winchester that I can't quite put my finger on. She seems a bit more confused about us, like she may be holding something back. 'Can I ask a question, though?'

'Shoot,' she says, leaning into me.

I place a hand on her thigh, slightly nervous about what I want to say next. 'Not that it was the right time this morning, but do you think there might be a day when you introduce me to your kids and Brian as someone more than just Jack?' I say, looking her straight in the eye.

She leans over the table to put a pretzel in her mouth, her stance changing from someone who was once relaxed to someone who's desperately searching for an answer. 'I think I'm just trying to define what this is... boyfriend sounds so...'

'Don't say the word,' I tell her, putting a finger up into the air.

'I wasn't going to say young. It just doesn't feel... right.'

I sit back. I hadn't realised how jarring those words would feel. I immediately see the panic in her face.

'Oh no, not that this doesn't feel right. It just feels new, and boyfriend seems a little...'

'Then what am I?' I ask.

'You're not a boy. I've found that much out. You're a... manfriend.'

'That sounds like someone who comes in to keep you company and do your shopping once a week,' I say, not really sure how to communicate that bit of sadness that sits in my bones. 'I could be your boyfriend. We could be a thing, no?'

She responds with a laugh before realising I'm being serious. 'Oh, I didn't think that was funny. I guess I just... it's been a very busy six months. I've gone from happily married to this in what feels like milliseconds.'

'Well, not so happily married really,' I reply. She feels the sharpness of that reply and takes a breath to take it in. 'I'm sorry. That was not kind.'

'But true. He was not happy at least. Or else he'd still be here.'

'And I would have just been someone you bumped into at a wedding.'

I take a large sip of my wine, turning my knee away from hers so they aren't touching. I don't know why I'm being so short with her because that's not what I want at all. I want to hold her desperately and take care of her.

'I'm really confused, Zoe. I've let you take the lead on this at every step. I've not pushed it. Ed told me to give you space, go at your pace and I've done that...'

'Ed? You talk about these things with Ed?' she asks.

'Yeah, my brother, too, my housemates because...'

'Because?' she says, curiously.

'I've never felt like this about anyone in my life.' As soon as the words leave my mouth, I feel my voice shake because of the sheer clarity of emotion I feel, and because I rarely allow that vulnerability show to anyone.

'I appreciate that, I do, but...'

'You appreciate it? I'm not a gift token,' I say, trying to lighten the mood. I put my hand back on her thigh. 'What I'm saying is, at the moment, what we have is behind closed doors. It's stolen kisses and it exists in this bubble.'

'Bubble?' she asks.

'Yeah. And I want to burst the bubble. I want to be able to kiss you in public, I want you to have Sunday lunch with my nephews, I want to call you my... ladyfriend...' We both laugh as I say the word. 'That sounds like something you shave your intimate areas with.' And she laughs more, and I love that sound, the way it lights up her eyes. 'I just want to make you laugh like that forever.'

She doesn't reply. She smooths her skirt down with her hands and looks down. 'Jack. I don't know what this is, but I don't know if this is the right thing to do,' she says, struggling to get the words out. I feel them like a punch to the guts.

'I don't think I understand. Then what is this? It's been a couple of months; can't we just see where it goes?'

'Spoken like someone who has time on their side.'

'And there you go with the age thing again,' I reply. 'Please don't patronise me.'

'Twenty-nine, Jack. You are twenty-nine. And I am nearly forty-four. I am only stating facts.'

'Well, age is but an arbitrary label that just denotes how many years we've been on the planet, no?'

'My knees say different,' she retorts, and we both take a

moment, smiling, because that was what I said to her when we first met and she remembers. That has to mean something. She runs a hand through her curls, searching for words.

'It's just I'm not sure you should be here, with someone like me. I feel very landlocked. Here in this house with these kids and work and you... I just feel like you have options ahead of you. I'm not sure I should be allowed to be one of those options.'

'Allowed?' I ask, the hurt starting to churn away inside me.

'I just want you to think about the future. Where would this go? Would you move in here? With me and my kids? What if you want kids of your own? I don't think I can do that for you. I don't think we're being practical.'

'Practical. When is love ever practical?'

She jolts to hear the word, still refusing to look me in the eye. Please look at me so I can understand this. My gaze feels desperate, panicked, just waiting for her to find me.

'It was the Laser Tag thing, wasn't it?' I desperately try to joke, filling the silence.

She half laughs, not answering. I hope the Laser Tag wasn't the death knell to our relationship.

'Is it the job thing?' I ask her.

'What job thing?' she asks curiously.

'The fact I'm just a sub. I'm slightly adrift. I live in a house share and don't drive a car,' I tell her.

'When have I ever placed any worth on those things or called you out for it?'

'You mentioned something in Winchester,' I recall.

'I didn't mean it like that. That says a lot about me if you think I would judge you for those things.' Her eyes well up to be thought of like that and I take her hands in mine.

'I know you think I'm too young, that something doesn't quite match up in real life, but I'm not stupid. I'm old enough to know how I feel about you. I wish you could admit that much to yourself. I wish you had the courage to admit that you have feelings for me.'

And with those words, I see tears roll down her face. I never wanted to make her cry, but I need to know. I am so certain that what I feel for her is love. I am so certain that this is something worth sticking around for. She uses her palm to wipe away those tears and turns to me.

'Jack,' she says, taking a deep breath. 'You're one of the best people I've ever met. I will forever be grateful to you for what you've done for me in these last few months. But I don't know how to do this. I am so sorry.' She puts her head down, unable to look at me anymore and I sit there, once a balloon all buoyant and full of hope, now deflated.

I look down at my hands. They feel empty without her holding them. Maybe I was stupid to think that despite all those wonderful qualities I know she has that she would just change her life completely and that I would slot perfectly into all of it.

'Really?' I say. I almost don't want to believe her but also don't want to appear dickish in the face of rejection. This doesn't feel like her. This doesn't explain the connection I thought we both felt for each other.

'I just... I don't see how this could work.'

And it's like someone taking an axe and just splicing my heart in two. On the one hand, I refuse to believe it but on the other, maybe this was all just one-sided. Maybe she needed me to help her believe in love again, maybe she used me to get back at her husband, maybe she was not as perfect as I thought. Maybe I've been flung a great distance and now I'm landing in a great big heap on the floor.

'I guess that's the end of that then,' I say plainly, and I look over to see a face I remember so well. It was the one I saw when she found out the news about her ex. I can't bear to see it and I reach out to hold her, as she moves towards me, crying softly in my arms.

'I mean, we could just shag casually until the end of our days. That could work?' I joke. Her body shudders again and I hope that's laughter. I kiss the top of her head. 'Just promise me one thing?' I tell her, holding her so she faces me. I rub the tears away from her face with the edge of my sleeve.

'I've never met someone like you. Your light burns so fucking bright. Just if you don't want to be with me, I get that.' The words get stuck in my throat as I say that out loud. 'Just don't stay landlocked. I know how much you adore your kids, and you want to do what's right by them, but put yourself first. Think about what you deserve, too. Put yourself on a pedestal for once.'

She looks at me like she doesn't know how to reply.

'I love you, Zoe. I really think I do. I don't mind saying that out loud even if you don't feel the same way. I think you need to hear it at least.'

And I kiss her, slowly, holding her head in my hands, desperately wanting to be closer to her. But no. I pull away from her, our foreheads touching before getting up. She can't quite speak. Neither can I. I just leave that room, head for the front door and click it shut quietly, tears streaming down my face as I head into the cold winter air.

SEVENTEEN

Three months later

Zoe

'And some wonderful news from one of our ex-students, Gabe Osho, who recently got signed by the Fulham Academy. Congratulations to him on embarking on this very exciting journey.'

There is the sound of applause in this large hall, a few boys who I suspect were asleep during this assembly on the importance of resilience, come alive to hear Gabe's name and the mention of something football related. I smile to myself, looking for Gabe in the room. He did it. He comes and finds me on Mondays, and we have a working lunch and sometimes go through algebra together, but the boy was seen, and is giving it a go, and I feel so incredibly proud.

'Please can we attempt to leave this hall in an orderly manner, Mrs Swift's form first please.' Oh, that's me. I may have also drifted off in that assembly on resilience, but I at least was clever enough to fix my gaze at the board and nod every so often. I don't think these assemblies have changed much since I was in school but at least they don't make us sing together anymore and at least I get a chair to sit on. My form rise from their seats and head over to the door as I follow them. One of them comes up next to me. Hayley. She's in Year Eleven now and I've seen this one through from when she first arrived at this school with knee-high socks and a giant rucksack to now, where her tights are full of holes and her eyebrows are threaded and microbladed to perfection. I could measure angles with those.

'Did you have a good Christmas, Miss?' she asks me.

'I did, thank you.' I stayed at home, ate my weight in cheese and binge watched three box sets. She doesn't need to hear that. I look down trying to work out if she's wearing a skirt. 'Did you read the new school rules on make-up? We want you girls to aim for discretion.'

'You're funny, Miss.'

I'm not but I guess that's how I present my authority in this school.

'I'm just saying, I knew you when you used to come in here with nothing on your face and you were just as beautiful then.'

She pouts and blows me a kiss.

'What have you got next?' I ask her.

'History but Miss Perkins is away,' she says, fist pumping the air. 'Just a shame that fit sub isn't here anymore. Is it true he left?'

'Mr Damon? Yeah. He left at Christmas. You guys must have scared him off.' Was that convincing enough? I can't quite tell. He did leave and it splintered my heart into a million little pieces, but he gave it until Christmas and last thing I heard, he's heading off to Borneo soon. He took the job. It was the right thing to do, the only thing to do, it really was.

'Did they replace him?'

They did. They replaced him with a lady called Magda who has an angular Brigitte Nielsen look to her and who the kids have nicknamed 'Mother Russia.' 'They have. Just be nice, yeah? Attempt to do some work with whoever covers a class.'

Hayley laughs. 'You know me too well, Miss.'

'Unfortunately, I do,' I say mockingly.

'I love your earrings, Miss. What are they? Are they paperclips?'

I nod. 'Have a good day, lovely.'

I continue to walk within this sea of children as the hall slowly starts to vacate. The mixture of young people still amuses me. I think it's seeing their evolution from bright-eyed nervous newbies to rage-filled hormonal dragons to older, wiser, cooler kids in the space of five years that always intrigues, that always makes me realise the importance of my job. Just get them through the labyrinth that is school, get them out of here safely.

I suddenly feel a presence next to me.

'Mrs Swift. Happy New Year.'

Ed. I like how Ed never uses our first names in school. He's sensible and proper, and I see him almost having to adjust himself out of school as well.

'Mr Rogers. Happy New Year. Ready to take on the Spring Term?'

'Always... I have period one off, though.'

'Same. Coffee?'

'I made cake.'

'Then how could I refuse?'

We walk up the stairs to the staff room. I don't think Ed is mad at me after what happened with his friend. Mia was a little more vocal in her disappointment that it didn't work out, but Ed took a step back, maybe anticipating the obstacles ahead of us if we were meant to be a couple. As we enter the staff room, I see a staff member from the site team packing away the Christmas tree. I want to suggest we at least keep it up so its sparkles can get us through January. Ed walks over to the kitchenette, turning on the kettle, and gets a Tupperware box full of impeccably iced sponge squares. I sigh to see it all.

'Mia is so lucky, you know.'

'I know. Keep reminding her of this,' he tells me as he places a square on a plate and hands it to me with a fork and small napkin. This is why you should keep him, Mia; the man thinks ahead to know we may need napkins. Men like that are rare. He makes our tea and then comes over to sit down.

'I need to tell you something. I've not said this to anyone, but I thought you might like to know.' At first, I think he's going to tell me something about Jack and I feel my whole body lurch forward in response. 'Mia's pregnant.'

A smile spreads across my face, a wonderfully happy feeling surging through me. I put my plate down and throw my arms around him. 'Ed, that's brilliant news. I'm so happy for both of you.' Caught unawares as he's still holding on to his cake, he returns the embrace. 'How far along?'

'Not long so please don't tell anyone. We're waiting on a scan. We found out on New Year's Day, and I haven't known who to tell so I just needed to share it with someone.'

'Well then, I am honoured.' I sense him sitting straight up, possibly still in shock from the news as he keeps looking around, unable to process it. It's only the fifth of January so this is all very new. 'Did you have questions?'

'Well, I am a biology teacher, so I know how it happened at least and I teach a module on foetal growth so...'

I laugh, returning to my cake. 'I meant other questions that perhaps you can't research in a textbook? I had my kids many moons ago, though. Perhaps Beth is a better resource these days on parenthood.'

'I'm petrified, Zoe,' he says, spurting out his words bluntly.

'Why?' I say, smiling.

'Because I love Mia so much. I'm a worrier. I want her to be OK. I want the baby to be OK. I don't know if I'll be any good at this. I've not been around a lot of kids. I've only had cats.'

I smirk a little. 'Ed. You're around at least a thousand kids every day.'

'But they're big kids. This is something small that I'll have to grow myself.'

I love how he makes the baby sound like a houseplant, though am slightly saddened how that makes me think of Jack. Jack and his plants, eh? I take Ed's hand and wrap it in mine. 'Ed, you've said it yourself, you love Mia completely. You already care for that baby even though it's the size of a baked bean. You worry because that's a manifestation of all your love, all your care. I can't think of two people who are in safer hands.'

He takes a deep breath, some visible emotion welling up in him. He tries to keep it from showing by stuffing his mouth full of cake.

'You're going to have to make Mia so much cake. I hope you're ready,' I joke.

'Cake? I'm thinking ahead to the labour. She's going to be a nightmare,' he says plainly, and we both laugh. 'This is natural, right? To feel like this?'

I nod, smiling. 'I'd be worried if you weren't.'

'Well, I'm glad I told you. You felt like the right person to tell.'

'You've not told anyone else?' For some reason, I think of Jack in this first instance.

'You're kind. You'd know how to turn that worry around. Just keep it to yourself. If Mia knows that you know then she'll kill me.'

'She wouldn't.'

'But she would.'

I smile and take another mouthful of cake, the hit of coconut suddenly making me realise something. 'Ed, is this the cake you made for your wedding?'

He nods. 'I can't lie, I thought I'd make it for you to cheer you up.'

'To get me through these January blues, eh?' I say, smiling. He's a thoughtful being like that and his brilliant news and this cake will help, for sure.

'Well, that, but also because of what's happening today. You know, right?'

'Know what?'

Ed's face looks sad that I wouldn't have known. 'Jack. He's leaving today. He flies out to Borneo tonight.'

I get home early that afternoon, from school gate straight to front door. Naturally, all the teachers wanted to celebrate first days back with a drink in the pub, but I worried it would remind me too much of Jack. Jack is leaving. I always knew this. Mia told me this before Christmas but ever since Ed told me that today was the day in the staff room, the news has fractured my heart a little. He will soon be over on the other side of the world, there will be huge amounts of land and sea between us. Not a chance to bump into him in the supermarket or through Mia and Ed. Just him jetting off on new adventures, meeting new people whilst I stay here. Landlocked. I do want this for him, though, I always will.

'Hello!' I shout into the hallway as I open the front door. So much has changed in the last month. Brian and I sat down with solicitors and this house now belongs to me. We won't sell it, but he'll buy his own place. We're still chatting about custody and slowly rethreading our lives. Every day, we move into something more civil, coming round to our new sense of normal. I don't think it will ever be a final destination, it'll always be a journey. I don't think Lottie helped by wrapping up a potato and giving it to her dad for Christmas but the initial wounds from our break-up are healing. The air sits cold and stale in the house and I see a school bag at the bottom of the stairs, a pair of shoes kicked off that sit in the middle of the floor. Well, Dylan made it home at least.

'Dylan?' I shout.

I hear a door creak open. 'MUM! SOMETHING CAME FOR YOU ! I DIDN'T KNOW WHAT TO DO WITH IT!'

I mean, he could come downstairs and tell me that to my face. I don't shout back. I kick his shoes to a corner so no one will trip over them, grappling with my school bags and winter coat. When I get to the kitchen, I put everything down, turning on the lights and the kettle. No doubt, if Dylan didn't know what to do with it, it's most likely something that needs laundering or a letter from school that needs my attention. I open the door to the utility cupboard. Nothing. I take a mug out of the cupboard to make myself a cup of tea, have a look in the fridge and walk around our downstairs space. It's then I see it. It's a plant, a small tree sitting by the fireplace. It's wrapped impeccably in brown paper and string with a card sitting on its branches. I stare at it for a few moments. I know who it's from so much so that I'm almost too scared to approach it. I walk over, bending down to carry it and put it on the coffee table. You needed to just leave so my heart could let you go, so I could know I'd done the right thing. The right thing was to let you go. My fingers run along the envelope before tearing it open to find a plain white postcard.

Zoe,

It's believed silver birch trees symbolise new beginnings, rebirth. In harsh conditions and when forests have been damaged, they grow these trees to renew the earth, to offer resilience and protection. I hope it'll offer you shade, protection and be a thing of beauty for years to come. It will no doubt flourish and grow because it has you.

Love, always - Jack x

Jack

'So you're basically telling me you can't be arsed to pay for storage so you're gifting me all your winter clothes?' Ben asks me. 'What if you come back? Do I have to give them back to you?'

Ben looks down at my bed marvelling at my packing system. There is no order here. It's Borneo so I figured I just needed shorts, t-shirts, pants. Go light, go easy. I just hadn't accounted for the nine years of crap that I had accumulated since university. Ben tuts at me. He knows I had two months, including the Christmas break, to sort all of this out but I wouldn't be me without a touch of last-minute spontaneity in my bones. It was why I went to Sarah three weeks after the deadline to ask her if there was still a job on the table. I was lucky it was still there.

'Frank!' he says, as he peers his head around the door.

'I would like to gift you all of these things,' I say, pointing towards the desk in my room. It's a tennis racquet, a screwdriver set, and three rolls of Christmas wrapping paper. 'You can also take any coat you want.'

'What about the box of paper clips?' he asks me.

I look down at them, throwing them in my suitcase. 'Oh, I'm afraid they're coming with me.'

They both enter the room, sifting through this very last-minute jumble sale that is my life. Frank picks up a jumper and holds it to his face, smelling it.

'Frank, I didn't realise you loved me so,' I joke.

He pulls a face at me, but poor Frank has not taken the news of me leaving too well. Ben and I were his first housemates since leaving home. I think he sensed that even though we took the piss out of him constantly, we were fiercely protective of him, too.

'If you're ever out that way, you will come and see me, right?' I gesture to Frank as he goes through some of my old toiletries. He picks up a toiletry set that was my Secret Santa at school before I left. 'Both of you will, yeah?'

'Mate, that's the beauty of friends who move abroad. The perfect excuse for holidays,' Ben replies. He comes over to embrace me, and we usher Frank over to join in.

'My next housemates will likely be mosquitoes,' I tell them.

'I need to make a small prick joke now, don't I?' Ben says.

'Don't cheapen Jack's leaving by making jokes about his penis,' Frank says.

And we all laugh, which is a relief. He's getting the banter, finally.

'Is that why you kept a ruler under the bathroom sink?' Frank asks. Ben doubles over laughing.

'I kept that to help unplug the shower,' I tell them, which is the truth.

'Yeah, whatever,' Ben says. 'Make sure you wash that ruler before you use it, Frank.'

I shake my head at them as they continue to rummage through my belongings.

'Oooh, hangers!' Frank says, distracted, and heads over to the wardrobe. Frank has a work colleague lined up to move in next week, but I hope that we can all agree that I will be forever missed. I reach over to a folder on my bed, stuffed to the brim with visas and travel documents, looking around this small space I called home for a while. Downstairs, I hear the patter of tiny feet running down the hallway.

'JACK?' Dom's voice thunders up the stairs. 'WE'RE HERE!'

I figured. I leave Ben and Frank to continue scavenging and head down to see Barney and George have run straight into the living room and found Frank's PS4 almost immediately, like homing pigeons. 'Lads, shoes off the sofa, yeah?' I say, popping my head through the door. I head down to the kitchen where I find Dom staring at the alarming number of sockets that seem to be held together by gaffer tape.

'Is that safe?' he asks.

'Who knows?'

'Have we got time for a cuppa?'

'Always.'

I turn on the kettle and he takes a seat, balancing at my wobbly kitchen table. If Frank has not taken my leaving well, I'm not quite sure what emotion I'm getting from Dom. It seems to be some sort of push-and-pull feeling where he can't wait for me to leave but every time I hold him in an embrace, I'm not sure he wants to let me go.

'So, have you thought about bringing the boys over to see me in the summer?' I ask him.

He laughs. 'Those boys on a thirteen-hour flight and living in a treehouse? I'm not sure that's a holiday!'

'They would have so much fun. Or you could dump them with me, and I'd find you a nice island resort next door?' I tell him.

'That could work.' He smiles, pointing at me.

I make the tea, bringing it over, and we both hear the boys roaring next door. 'Facetimes and Christmas, yeah?'

'Of course. I mean, you love our Facetimes from the supermarket, no?' he jokes.

I don't think he quite realises it'll be those little inane calls which will make me miss them less. 'By the time I get back, they'll be all facial hair, hormones, proper deep grunting voices.'

Dom mimics how he thinks they may sound. 'Then just like that, they'll turn into you.' I punch him playfully. 'I can think of worse things.'

I laugh under my breath. We quietly sip at our tea.

Dom looks down at the table, his face tense with emotion. 'I never thanked you enough for all you've done for me and the boys. You gave us a lot of your time.'

'You make it sound like a chore – it wasn't. I have good memories. Remember that time when they were babies and we took George to the doctor because we didn't think a baby should shit with that much force...'

'Or volume,' Dom laughs. 'God, the kid was like a sewer. The doctor thought we were mad. Yes, Mr Damon – this is what babies do. They shit like the clappers.'

We both laugh to think about those exact words the doctor told us. We were two blokes absolutely winging it, but we made it. Those children are alive. They are absolutely rubbish at football, but we kept them alive, and they're happy and curious about the world.

'I mean, I'll come back and see you guys. You know that, right?' I tell him.

'You know, you don't have to... right?' he answers.

I look at him slightly affronted.

'I mean, pop in and keep in touch. I won't mind a postcard to know you're alive but just keep moving, yes? Live...' he says, his words weighted with emotion. 'Don't look back wondering how we're doing.'

I don't know how to answer him, so I just punch his arm again.

'I'll expect you to fly back when I need a babysitter, though. Actually, I've got a date coming up with the school-run mum. Finally.'

'Did she ever get a picture of your dick?' I ask.

'She did. That selfie stick you got me for Christmas was very handy.'

I choke a bit on my tea. The boy will be fine. I hope.

'Speaking of gifts, did Zoe get your tree?' he asks me.

Zoe and I didn't exchange gifts at Christmas. It didn't feel right, so I worked out my leave at school quietly and left Griffin

Road Comprehensive without much fanfare, spending the Christmas period with the boys eating my weight in cheese and binge-watching box sets. However, I realised I needed a final gesture. Dom teased me mercilessly that the tree was almost too romantic. No other man would ever stand a chance. But it felt like the right thing to do. I didn't want the last gift I got her to be a pair of paperclip earrings I got for a fiver from Etsy. It still hurts to say her name, to think of the very sudden way that it all ended, but at least she'll know that I wanted to end things on a positive note. I shrug my shoulders. 'Courier said it was delivered but I haven't had anything from her.'

'I'm sorry that never quite worked out,' Dom says quietly.

'Yeah,' I say, picking at a peeling part of our kitchen table, trying to mask how devastating that really was, thinking of the weeks after it ended where I felt like I'd been punched but was still lying flat out, completely blindsided by it. 'I just really liked her, you know?'

'I know. I think she really liked you, too, you know?' Dom tells me. He looks into space, trying to recall something. 'You know, when we bumped into her at football, she said some things. I've been trying to piece it together. But bottom line, I think she never wanted to hurt you, she just wanted what was best for you. You are fucking marvellous, you know that, right?'

'We know that, it doesn't need to be said out loud,' I joke.

He laughs. 'To be fair, she was very nice and actually very pretty. She didn't know that, though, did she?'

'What do you mean?' I ask.

'She didn't think that about herself. With the whole bad husband thing, I just got a feeling that she never backed herself.'

'Pretty accurate, really.' I think back to someone who would just quietly swerve compliments, who never realised how amazing she really was and that still makes me sad. I hope she works that out one day.

The boys suddenly run through the door, Barney jumping

straight into my lap. I inhale the top of his head, gripping my arms around him. George opens cupboards on the hunt for snacks.

'Uncle Jack, I will miss you,' he says and my heart stings for a small moment.

'We can Facetime any time you want. I don't know what my phone reception will be like, but I'll try.'

'Deal. Could you get Dad to get us phones to do that?' he asks.

Ten years old. Wow. Dom sits there shaking his head.

'Well, they're not phones but I did get you some gifts,' I say, reaching in a nearby cupboard.

'Is it that puppy you promised us?' asks George, jumping up and down, clapping his hands. The colour drains from Dom's face. If it's a bloody puppy, I likely won't get my lift to the airport.

'No, it's better.' The boys open the bag and inside are three of the biggest Nerf guns you've even seen. The boys react with roars and cheers and when I say 'boys' I mean Dom as well. They all compare models, and those boys hang off their dad, talking about how much fun they're going to have. I hope so. I really do.

EIGHTEEN

Zoe

I sit there on the sofa, looking out into the room as Dylan goes to answer the front door. 'Everything alright, Dylan?' I hear a voice say.

'Yeah, she's in the living room. I don't think she's OK,' I hear him reply.

Someone's here? Who's here? Dylan called someone? I look as two figures enter the room and, in my daze, I look up to see Mia and Beth both standing there over me. Mia sits down and immediately wraps her arms around me. I know she's pregnant, but I can't say anything. Beth just looks at the many tissues on the floor, wondering how to broach this.

'Is it your ex again?' says Mia, almost seething with anger. Please don't get angry on my behalf. You're growing a baby inside you.

I shake my head, pointing to the tree and showing Beth the note. She gives it to Mia to read who immediately tears up. Dylan hovers by the door. Given Beth lives so close, Dylan and Lottie have sometimes offered their babysitting services to her little ones so it makes sense that he'd call her, but I start crying again to know I've worried him. I usher him in for a hug. All three of them look at me while I sit here sobbing my heart out.

'Dylan, hon. Does Mum have alcohol in the house?' Beth asks me.

'We might have something in the kitchen from Christmas?' he replies.

'Perfect. Can you go fetch it?' Beth replies.

He leaves the room and Beth reaches over, sweeping her fingers under my eyes to wipe away the tears and correct the horrific mess I've obviously made of my eye make-up.

Mia re-reads the note again. 'He's leaving tonight,' she tells Beth and to be reminded of that makes me cry again.

'I'm so sorry that Dylan called you. What about your boys?' I ask her.

'Will has the boys. It's all good. Stop worrying about me. Are you OK?'

I shake my head. I thought I was alright, I really did. Jack was going. Even though I had felt that loss since we broke things off, since convincing myself that this was the right thing to do, the note just cemented how much I have missed him.

Mia looks down at the tree. 'That's quite frigging romantic, isn't it? Have you messaged him to thank him? You should send him a tree emoji,' she suggests.

'She should send him wood?' Beth says.

'Or bush, whatever,' Mia replies and for a moment the laughter, the distraction is welcome.

'I have a question,' Beth asks. 'Tell me to mind my own but why did you break up?'

I take a deep breath, my heart aching. I just remember standing there in that football field thinking that a bright and wonderful soul should be able to do anything he wants with his life. I didn't want the guilt of holding him back. 'I knew that he had been offered that job and I didn't want him not to go, I didn't want him to stay for me,' I tell them through my tears. 'The more I found out about him, the more I realised his life had stood still for his brother, and if he stayed for me then the same would have happened again.'

Beth looks at me, pained. 'So you didn't give him the option. If you weren't an option then he would go.'

'He would have the chance to live his own life. Not be pinned down by me,' I say.

'I don't need to know what you get up to in the bedroom,' Mia jokes and I laugh, snot bubbling out of my nostrils. Beth passes me a tissue. 'That's some "if you love someone, set them free" shit,' Mia continues, eloquently.

She said the word love. I shrug. It felt like the right, mature thing to do. I had to think about us outside of our bubble. I had to think of not only my future but also his and a time ten years down the line where he could look back and not have any second thoughts, no resentment. I had to be sensible because what we had was so heady, so potent that neither of us could think straight.

'Did you love him?' Beth asks me.

I cry. I know I felt something. I was on the floor, and someone offered me a hand, they pulled me up, they danced with me and held me close. No one had done that for me before, but I never understood it. He was so good-looking, so special, that I spent so much time just looking around, wondering what was happening.

'I've never met anyone like him before.'

'How was the sex?' Mia whispers.

'MIA!' Beth shrieks, looking out for where Dylan is in the house.

I laugh. 'Mia, I had an orgasm so strong, my tongue went numb.'

She does a strange little dance next to my fireplace. 'Knew

it. I told him to look after you, by the way,' she adds, pointing at me.

'But he looked after me in so many ways. He was kind and thoughtful and he just made me feel... alive...' I tell them. 'And when he was near, it did feel like nothing else mattered. That's quite a special thing.'

Mia holds Beth's arm near as they stand there bearing witness to this. Dylan suddenly re-appears clutching three or four bottles of half-drunk Christmas alcohol and glasses. Mia examines each bottle, pouring me a small glass of cranberry flavoured gin that Kate gifted me. Dylan looks on at this scene thoughtfully and I catch his eye, glancing down at the card from Jack.

'Dylan, I'm sorry I've worried you. Please don't worry about me. I'm just being silly about something,' I say, wiping at my face.

'Is it something to do with Jack?' he asks. Both Mia and Beth look at each other, taking a step back.

'I guess.'

'Jack – we met him at football and his mates gave me a lift to Birmingham that time,' he says casually.

I nod.

'Were you going out with him?' he asks me. And for a moment, I don't quite know what to say. To be frank, we were kinda just shagging and hadn't put a label on it. But he was someone I cared for greatly, that much I know now. I still don't know what to say but Dylan looks up at me and I realise that he had a parent who lied to him for almost a year, so it's not fair to have another parent do it to him, too.

'Yes. For a couple of months but it didn't work out.'

Dylan seems to exhale a sigh of relief that I've been truthful and smiles. 'I kind of knew.'

I turn to him sharply. 'What? How?'

'When his friends drove me to Birmingham, they thought I

had headphones on and wasn't listening to their conversation, but I was. They were talking about Jack and how he never calls in favours. They said you must be quite special if he was calling this in on his behalf.'

'Oh,' I reply blankly.

'The football thing confirmed it. The Laser Tag excuse was pretty piss poor,' he says, half laughing.

'Jack took you to Laser Tag?' Mia interrupts.

'It was for a kids party,' I try to explain. I turn back to Dylan to hear him continue.

'Then that night I came back from Liam's house, you were sitting in the front room crying, trying to tell me you were watching a sad film, and I just had a hunch something had happened.'

I stop to think about how I never revealed any of this to the kids for fear of how they would react, but Dylan seems so incredibly chilled by this information.

'Does Lottie know?'

'No. She's not as smart as me, you know,' he jokes.

'And how do you feel about it all?' I ask him, curiously.

'I guess he's not who I imagined you with.'

'Too young?' I say.

'Nah, like I know I'm a guy but he's really good looking, Mum. You've got play.'

Mia cackles in reply, pushing my arm.

'But there was a time when I worried I'd never get my mum back. What Dad did hurt you so much, and I saw how sad you were, and I just didn't know what to do. And then Jack came along, and he made you really happy. He brought you back in the room. So yeah...' he continues. 'I'll always miss what we were but I'm happy you had someone to remind you how fucking great you are.'

And at this point, I worry for poor Dylan because there are

three of us sobbing in that room and he looks completely lost to know what to do.

'Don't swear,' I tell him.

'But you are fucking great,' he says, giving me the biggest of hugs. 'Why aren't you going out with him anymore?' he asks.

They all stand there looking for an answer. 'Oh, Dyls. I just... I didn't want him to commit to a life with me. I wasn't sure what I wanted. I just felt too old for all that dating shit.'

'Mum, you're old. You're not dead,' he says, and Beth and Mia explode into giggles. 'If he likes you and you like him, maybe you've got to go for it – not stand back because you're...'

'Scared.'

'Exactly.'

Mia puts an arm around Dylan to signal her approval. 'I like this one. He has a very good point. Did Jack say he loved you?' she asks me.

I nod, tears in my eyes.

'And do you love him?' Beth continues.

Again, I nod. I felt something I'd not felt in a very long time. I felt seen. I felt an emotion so intense that it scared me. To feel it suddenly again after Brian, to think of potentially losing it again. But yes, the way it took hold of me felt very much like love. 'But he's leaving. He's taken that job. I don't want to get in the way of that. He needs to go.'

'But maybe he needs to hear that you feel the same way about him? Maybe?' Mia tells me.

'I don't want to mess with his head,' I say.

'But what do you want?' Beth asks me.

I am Zoe Swift. I want to say I've never done anything spontaneous before in my life, but I kissed Jack first, I invited him up to my room, I made all those first moves because he drew that out of me. He made me experience a joy, a belief in myself that I'd never experienced.

'Do we know what airport he's going from?' I ask Mia, frantically, pushing my hair back from my face and wiping my face.

'No, but I can find out. I'll ring Ed. He can come and pick us up,' she says, her feet jigging from side to side. 'Are we really doing this?'

And for a moment, I look over at Dylan whose face registers an emotion I can't quite read. There was me thinking this would make him sad, that it would change too much in his life too quickly but all I see is excitement, happiness – a boy with this wonderfully calm and empathetic soul. I don't know where he gets that from, not at all. He comes over to hug me and I sob on to his shoulder.

'Thank you, Dyls.'

'It's fine,' he says coolly. 'Was Jack the one who sent us that Nando's the night we came back from Manchester?' he asks when we're in hold.

'Yeah.'

'Yeah, then I like him. He's a real one.'

Jack

'BUT I DIDN'T KNOW THAT SHOES WERE SO HEAVY, DENNIS!'

The woman in front of me in check-in has a suitcase open on the floor. Her husband is refusing to pay the excess luggage fee and telling her she has to dump some shoes. Like put them in the bin because there's nothing else to do with them. Naturally, she's not happy and arguing her case whereas the rest of us in this queue at Heathrow are wondering why we didn't think to check-in online.

'THOSE ARE EXPENSIVE!'

'EXPENSIVE MY ARSE, PATRICIA! THEY'RE HIGH STREET TAT!'

I spy Dom and the boys waiting for me in the corner of the

airport. We had a leaving McDonald's as my farewell meal which felt economical but also fitting. It was always a fancy night out in our books and given I was headed to quite a remote part of Borneo, I did wonder about the next time I'd be able to indulge in a highly processed, deep-fried meal. I don't think Patricia and Dennis are headed to where I'm going. Her suitcase reveals a fair number of sarongs, sandals and suncream and... oh dear, I need to look away. Because it also looks like Patricia has packed some sex toys, which she might need if Dennis decides to go on this holiday without her. Patricia, close your bag. I can see your butt plugs. You didn't look the sort but, hell, I won't judge. She's still sifting through her shoes when I bend down below the barrier. The person at the front of the queue eyeballs me. Please don't worry, I'm not taking your place.

'Hi, Patricia... is it?'

She glares at me with tears in her eyes. Please don't cry. You're headed off on holiday and it'll be a long flight to have an argument simmering like that. Plus, I'm trying to save you your blushes here.

'I just... I do believe that there is a courier in the terminal. Maybe they'll box up the shoes and other items you can't take and maybe you could post it back to your house?' I tell her.

'Really?' she asks me. 'Dennis! This young man said I can post my shoes back to myself.'

Dennis looks over at me with my giant rucksack on my back and hoodie and sneers with an immediate mistrust, like I may be trafficking drugs about my person. I'm not sure who he is to judge, given what I've just seen in his wife's suitcase.

'It's just an option. I'm just trying to mediate another solution to your problems.' They continue to bicker as the line moves on and more check-in desks suddenly open.

'Thank you,' Patricia says, fluttering her eyelashes at me and putting a hand to my arm. I know flirting when I see it and from the looks of it, Dennis isn't too impressed. Happy holidays, you two. I move forward in the queue and head to a free check-in desk.

'Evening, sir,' the check-in agent says as I place my travel documents in front of him. He flicks through the papers.

'So, London to Singapore and then final destination of Kota Kinabalu?'

Final destination. I am not quite sure how I feel about the word final but yes. For now, that's where I will land, and for a moment, I'm not quite sure how I feel about any of it. I nod as he starts keying in buttons on his computer, and checking I match my passport. It's the dream job, it really is, and Sarah has sorted everything on the other end from the accommodation to buying me a new bike with a bell. She was very excited to tell me she'd sourced me a bell. But there's some fear there to be leaving Dom, to be away from everything, and also a very raw ache to be away from Zoe. She doesn't want me. I get that now, but I do worry if I took this job as a reaction to being dumped. Maybe.

'So we have an aisle seat for you today and I've booked all the tickets for you through to Kota Kinabalu. Only one bag to check in?'

'Yep. Travelling light.'

The agent glares down at Patricia and Dennis still squabbling. 'Best way,' he whispers. 'Thank you for being so easy.'

'Yep, usually takes a few drinks,' I joke.

He laughs and Dennis looks over, glaring at me again. 'Have a nice flight, Mr Damon.'

I take my smaller rucksack and exhale a deep cleansing breath, heading over to the boys. I'm not sure I like airports. There really is a collective sense of tension in these places. People rushing around on sprawling shiny floors, their eyes scanning the walls for flight details, eyes widening to hear announcements they can't quite make out, trying to juggle children, trollies, suitcases, their sanity. Even that word – *departures* – holds some sadness. I am leaving, departing, moving on.

'I reckon I just saw David Beckham,' Dom tells me as I relocate them in their corner of the airport.

'Just casually checking in with the peasants, was he?' I joke.

'He's trying to blend in. If you do end up sitting next to him, you'll say hi – yes?'

I know what he's doing. He's an emotional sort so he's just trying to fill the conversation with bad humorous segues to distract from all of that. Maybe this was a bad idea. I should stay here with them and we can play Nerf gun wars until the twins leave home and then we can live together.

He senses the panic in my face. 'It's all good. Let's get you through security and then you don't have to stress.' He starts walking as the boys circle us, super happy that they've discovered they can skid across these floors with their trainers.

'So give me your itinerary,' Dom asks.

'Flying into Singapore to meet Sarah and then we fly onwards to Borneo. Should get there in just over two days.'

'Just let me know when you've landed, yeah? Signs of life and all that.'

I smile. He's taking on some big brother stance. I put an arm around him, grateful for it, completely. 'Of course.' We stop in front of security and he brings me in for a hug, not quite saying a word. Please be OK.

Two heads suddenly squish in this hug and I feel hands reaching around my waist. I can't cry in front of the boys, but I like this octopus-style way of saying goodbye. I look down. 'You two look after your dad, yeah?'

They both look up at me. 'Yeah. We will. Who's going to look after you, though?' asks George.

'Most likely my mates, Sarah and Hakeem – maybe the orangutans.'

'But Zoe will be there, too.'

We never told the boys about Zoe, and it pains me to hear that they liked her. I did. I liked her very much.

'Zoe?' I ask them. 'She's... No, we... She's not coming,' I tell them.

'Then why is she here?' asks Barney.

As soon as he says the words, Dom and I look at each other and then let go, my eyes following Barney's hand as he points towards someone standing away from us. Zoe? She's here? She stands there in a black winter coat and scarf, taking off her hat and ruffling her curls. She puts a hand to the air, and I return the gesture. My whole being aches to see her. Why are you here? Mia and Ed are here, too. I don't quite know what to do but the boys do, and they run towards her.

'Zoe! Why are you here?' George says, stealing my line.

She bends down to hug them. 'How are you, boys? I thought I better come and say goodbye to Uncle Jack. Is that OK?'

They nod as Dom salutes us both. 'Come on, boys. Let's go buy Uncle Jack some sweets for the flight.' I wave at Ed and Mia, keeping their distance as Zoe returns to her feet and we stand there facing each other. I don't know what to say to her. I want to embrace her tightly. I want to say I spend a good portion of every day thinking about you, that all that emotion I felt for you never quite went away. I don't think it has.

'You're here...'

'I am.'

'You could have called, sent an emoji,' I tell her.

'I was told the tree emoji could be too suggestive.'

'This is true.'

I reach up and put a hand to her face as I can tell she's been crying.

'Was it the tree? Did it make you cry?'

'Yes. Very much so.'

'I'm sorry.'

She shakes her head with a smile. 'Never apologise to me.'

All I see is her. In this crowded, rammed departures hall, surrounded by trollies, people, lights and announcements, it feels like I could just stand here and hold her hand in this little bubble, until this place empties and they turn off all the lights.

'Are you all checked in?' she asks.

'Yeah, I have about...' I look at my watch. 'Two hours until boarding.'

Her eyes well up and I take her hands in mine to try and halt all that emotion in its tracks.

'I came here to tell you something. I want you to go. I think it's really important that you go today and that you have the best adventure, but I needed to let you know something first,' she says.

I lean into her to catch all her words, watching the warmth exude from her face, the way I can tell she pauses to carefully select her words.

'I did love you.'

I stop to take a breath as she says that, squeezing my hands tightly.

'I was completely and utterly overwhelmed by you. I didn't expect it. I couldn't quite believe it and I was never quite sure what to do with it. I felt like some very stupid, old...'

I put a finger to the air.

'More experienced?'

I allow her to continue.

'...woman who was battling with so many things and who just didn't want to get hurt again.'

'I'd never have hurt you, Zoe.'

'Oh, you did anything but,' she tells me. She squeezes my hand. 'You rebuilt me. You and your strange magic made me feel again. I felt alive. And I fell in love with you completely.' Her voice shakes, her bottom lip wobbling. 'I am sorry I made you think I didn't love you. I really am.'

I stand there in shock. She did feel all of that, too. All that spark, all that connection. For weeks, I've been trying to work out what had happened. 'But Zoe... I...' I stand there at the security gate, looking at the queues of people waiting to go in.

She follows my gaze. 'In Winchester, I saw a message on your phone about the job,' she goes on to explain, 'and deep down, I felt it would be selfish of me to keep you from that.'

'So you lied,' I tell her.

'You could argue I loved you so much that I just wanted what was best for you.'

'Maybe that's you,' I say resolutely.

'Maybe.'

'I've not crossed over yet. I could stay,' I tell her, slightly frantic, unsure of what this all means.

'Not a chance,' she tells me, kissing my hands. 'Go. Enjoy. I just wanted to tell you that if you've seen my light burning fucking bright, it's only been because of you, Jack Damon.' She shakes her head to be saying it all out loud but only because it feels like a revelation to her, too. I keep looking up at the board, listening to mumbled announcements about boarding gates but also looking at her, feeling that radiance that's always shone from her, wondering where we go from here.

'I really do love you,' I tell her.

'I know. You bought me a tree.'

I pull her into me, whispering in her ear, 'And chicken. Don't forget the chicken.' And she laughs. And it's like music. Our faces meet and I wrap my arms around her picking her up in that airport so her feet skim the floor. I push the hair from her face and kiss her, the closeness of her, the intensity of feeling still flooding every cell. It's still everything I knew I wanted, just this amazing woman in front of me, to be able to hold her for as long as I can.

I rest my cheek against hers. 'I don't want this to be goodbye.'

'I don't think it is,' she whispers back to me, reassuringly. 'Go. Let's see where this takes us, yeah?'

I nod. 'I guess we should try to keep in touch. Can I write to you?' I ask.

'Write?'

'Letters,' I tell her.

'That's old school...'

And I laugh, in the middle of that very crowded airport. 'Seriously? Have I taught you nothing? Less of the old, yeah?'

EPILOGUE

August

Zoe

'I'm just saying, Lottie, it's a Muslim country so it's important to respect their culture, their laws. So less of the swearing.'

'I'm not swearing at a person, though. I'm swearing at a mosquito. There is a huge difference. I don't think even Allah would have objections to that.'

Dylan and I both close our eyes at Lottie's volume and sheer gall. I don't want to fight. It's been a long flight through Kuala Lumpur and onwards to Borneo and we're tired, the thick humidity draining us of good humour and energy. It turns out that it was quite easy to persuade two teens to do an adventure holiday in Malaysia as long as it also included some time on a beach to create Instagram content. I look at them now with their trusted backpacks, supping at fizzy drinks we bought from this small restaurant.

'Hold up,' Lottie tells us, taking her phone out for another selfie. Am I in this one? I guess I am, so I smile in the background. Lottie vets it before saving it. 'Mum, can I just say with the braid and the boots, you're giving me proper Tomb Raider vibes, yeah?'

I pull her in for a hug. The braid is Lottie's work as we both realised at the airport that this humidity was going to kill our curls into frizz. God bless the teenager who learned how to braid on YouTube.

'Are you sure it's here, Mum?' Dylan asks, peering out from his baseball cap. A stray dog weaves around the tables of this place and Lottie reaches down to pet him. Please be a healthy dog. Brian will have a field day if I bring Lottie back with rabies.

Who knows? But I've been following Jack's instructions to the letter. A small truck pulls up outside and a woman jumps out who looks vaguely familiar. We all stand up and head over.

'Sarah?' I ask her.

'Zoe' she says, a broad grin on her face. 'And I know you! How are you, Dylan?'

She comes over to hug all of us. 'This is bloody exciting. Jump in.' We all approach her truck. 'Kids, just jump in the back, hold on to something. It's all a bit lawless when it comes to seat belts and the like.'

I'd like to say the kids are cautious and worried, but they jump in the back of that truck, Lottie with phone in hand to document this in its entirety. I get in the passenger seat, aware that Sarah is tracking my every move, certainly curious.

'I have something for you, by the way,' I say, reaching into a zipped pocket in my bag, handing her a baby photo of little Daisy Rogers.

'Oh, my days, the cuteness. Have you met her?' she asks me.

'I have and the three of them are just gorgeous together. Mia and Ed are besotted.'

'I can't believe our Ed is a daddy,' she says, holding a hand to her chest and putting the photo safely in her visor.

'They send their love and Ed also sent three jars of Marmite.'

'Which is why we all love Ed.' She turns to the back of the truck. 'Kids, just hold on – it's a bit bumpy.'

She starts the engine and the truck crawls to a start, through this small town and onwards through forests and dirt roads. I love how the landscape changes almost immediately, palms stretching over valleys that extend for miles, and I smile to think of the different ways Jack would write about this in his letters. I feel the warm air against my face as the truck picks up speed. I turn to see Sarah smiling at me.

'So you're the famous Zoe...'

'Famous?' I question.

'I've known Jack for over ten years, but I've never seen him write letters for anyone.'

It was a letter or postcard for every week he was away. Sometimes long sprawling notes telling me about his childhood, sometimes rude explicit fantasies written in some detail, sometimes a short note about his days. I read every one. I wrote back. I wasn't sure how much he wanted to read about me teaching maths in a greater London comprehensive, but I wrote back.

The landscape suddenly changes, and we stop at a large building with smaller houses in the canopies of the trees. I look back at the kids, still on the truck but fascinated by it all, heads leaning up to the bright blue sky, the heat bearing down on us. This ain't South London and I think that might be a very good thing for them. For me, though, it feels like much more. Like some sort of homecoming despite only having been here in letters.

'You're here,' I hear a voice say as I get out of the truck. Just hearing his voice makes me smile, despite the heat and the fatigue and I turn to see him standing there, hands in his pockets, casual as ever in loose shorts, shirt sleeves rolled up, buttons not quite done up to reveal a bit of chest. He looks so incredibly well.

'You have a beard,' I tell him.

'Do I look like a pirate?' he asks, smiling.

'It's giving me more castaway.' I walk over slowly, trying to dampen my excitement in front of the kids but as I walk into his arms, he pulls me close and kisses me gently and I swoon quietly to be back here, with him.

I lean my forehead against his. 'Hey.'

'Hey,' he says, his eyes shining. 'And Lottie and Dylan?' he says, looking over to the kids as they climb out the back of the van, bags in tow. Dylan is the first to go up to him and shake Jack's hand. Lottie hangs back, her attention taken by something else.

'Is that a wheelbarrow of monkeys?' she asks Jack.

I hope that's not the heat making her hallucinate but I peer around the van and true enough, it's a wheelbarrow of orangutans.

Sarah intervenes. 'That would be a yes. These have all been rescued from destroyed habitats, some really baby ones. Want to come and feed them with me?'

'Ummm, yeah? Of course. Nice to see you, Jack. Not being rude, but baby monkeys,' she says, pointing down to the wheelbarrow of bright orange fur and sweet baby eyes.

'Not offended at all,' he says, laughing. 'Good to have you here, too.'

'Dylan, go with your sister. Make sure she doesn't steal one?' I ask.

Dylan rolls his eyes but does as he's told. He gives me one final look before he goes, though, a look to say that he's glad he's here, with us. I'm glad you're here, too, kid.

'So those were my kids,' I tell Jack as they walk away.

He laughs. I look around, feeling the sun on my face and take in this place that my boyfriend calls home. Jack's gaze is fixed on me, his hands in his pockets. His complexion is dirty and tanned, my eyes taken by the curve of his legs in his shorts, the line of his jaw beyond his castaway pirate beard. I smile.

'I can't believe we're here,' he says, looking me in the eye and it's some feeling to know he still wants to look at me like that.

'Same.'

He holds out a hand and I take it, interlocking my fingers into his, as he leads me towards the buildings and the thick verdant forest of trees set against that blazing blue sky.

'Let me show you around. You can meet everyone.'

'Then?'

He arches an eyebrow at me. I wasn't thinking of that per se. But I laugh to see his expression.

'Then we'll see what happens, Zoe,' he says, kissing my hand. 'We've got all the time in the world.'

A LETTER FROM THE AUTHOR

Dear lovely reader,

Hello, there! You're bloody marvellous! Thank you from the bottom of my heart for reading *Textbook Romance*. If we've met before then hello again but if you're new – welcome, take a seat... it's a pleasure to meet you. I'm Kristen 😊

I hope you enjoyed reading Jack and Zoe's story. I can never quite decide what genre I'm in – it's romcoms with a little bit extra, certainly quite a bit of innuendo. If that is your thing then do look for my other titles, and keep up to date with all my latest releases and bonus content by signing up at the following link. Your email address will never be shared and you can unsubscribe at any time.

www.stormpublishing.co/kristen-bailey

And if you enjoyed *Textbook Romance* then I would be overjoyed if you could leave me a review on either Amazon or Goodreads to let people know. It's a brilliant way to reach out to new readers. And don't just stop there, tell everyone you know on social media, gift the book to your mates, drop WhatsApp notes to everyone you know.

If you are a long-time reader, you'll know sex seems to be a theme I write about a lot. Why? Who knows? But I don't think I've ever written a book that's made me blush before. That scene behind the key-cutter's (!), I actually had to play through how it would work in leggings, too, so don't tell me I don't do my research. (Note: I didn't go to an alley behind a key-cutter's; I just worked out what angles would work with leggings...) Usually I do try to write about sex from a comedy slant but in this novel, I wanted to have a bit more steam, I wanted to make sure Zoe was laughing but also getting some quality orgasms. In that way, I hope that you also cheered when you read those scenes, too. It was lovely to give Zoe the gift of the handsome, soulful Jack after everything Brian put her through. To anyone who has ever been hurt by love, that's all I ever hope for them, that they get to rebuild their trust in people and remember they are worthy of love. I am so glad Zoe gets a happy ending at the end of the book (and this is not innuendo...)

Essentially, this book is also about challenging how we perceive love, how nothing is really a textbook romance. Like in *Sex Ed,* I like writing about relationships that transcend conventions, defy expectations, that connect different characters who bring out the best in each other. As I've written about younger characters recently, too, it's been a pleasure to write a character such as Zoe. She is my tribute to all women in their forties who find joy in nice earrings and a quality coat but don't quite know how to exist. They have all sorts of labels from mothers to wives to however their professions define them but sometimes they do feel a little lost. They look after everyone else except themselves, they try to exude serenity and confidence but are not quite sure where they are on their journey. It's not quite the beginning, certainly not the end. Know that I see you, I am you. I hope Zoe gives you a bit of hope that you deserve only brilliant things in your life.

I will leave it here. For anyone who's possibly a fan, you get top marks for spotting all the previous book references and I hope you liked seeing Beth, Mia and Ed again. I am in the process of writing a spider/Venn diagram of how all these different characters know each other but, in my head, they all live in their corners of London and England, all existing and living their lives. I love them all like my bestest friends and I hope you do, too.

I'd be thrilled to hear from any of my readers, whether it be with reviews, questions or just to say hello. If you like retweets from Fesshole, then follow me on Twitter. Have a gander at Instagram, my Facebook author page and website, too, for updates, ramblings and to learn more about me. Like, share and follow away – it'd be much appreciated.

With much love and gratitude,

Kristen
xx

www.kristenbaileywrites.com

 facebook.com/kristenbaileywrites

 x.com/mrsbaileywrites

 instagram.com/kristenbaileywrites

ACKNOWLEDGEMENTS

I can't lie, this was one of the hardest books I have ever had to write, during a time when my life was turned inside out and upside down. More on that later but my biggest thanks to all at Storm who supported me during this time. Thank you for the space, the patience and the confidence you've always had in me – I appreciate that human approach so very much. The one person who's really been the biggest prop is Vicky Blunden, my extraordinary editor, who is quietly reassuring, just gets my humour and always gives my books a nudge in the right direction so the prose and jokes can sing. In the bedlam that is publishing, I am so glad we found each other.

Since writing my last books, I've started working in a school and the first thing I need to say is that NONE OF THIS IS TRUE and I really like teaching so if anyone from school is reading this, I am not Zoe or Jack, and I've never seen anyone kiss anyone by the bike sheds. However, thanks to Gemma King who confirmed that it would indeed be possible to fit two people in the cupboard in her classroom. Also, a massive shout out to the team I work with – we are part of an in-house substitute teaching team who float between classes, tearing kids off the ceiling and trying to persuade them to do the work. It's a thankless task but the team make it worth it so thanks and love to Hayley, Åsa, Naomi, George and Karen. And a hello to the kids who can be hilarious and who have given me a lifetime of laughs, material and education. Of course, I work incredibly hard but I will admit to writing this in Year Eleven French so this is me acknowledging Daisy and Michael who asked me to mention them but who should be revising.

To write about kids, it also helps to have your own as a point of reference, though, and Lottie and Dylan Swift are basically an amalgamation of my three teenagers, text for text, hug for hug. Did you like Lottie? Well, I have a real life one and she's just as magical, scary and brilliant. I adore her as she's everything I wasn't at that age. My lads are Dylan, so laidback they're horizontal but, deep down, they're empathetic and big-hearted, despite the fact they hoard all my plates in their room. Three teens but also a little one on the end whose little face and kind soul props me up when the teens have swung into tantrum mode. I bloody love being your mum and the four of you are the reason for everything. Thank you for letting me write alongside our adventures together and for reading through (and correcting) all my teen lingo.

I don't have a Brian. I have a Nick. When I write a book, the first thing he does when it goes to print is flick through to the acknowledgements to make sure I've thanked him. Here you go. Thank you for all that stuff you told me about trees.

Massive thanks also to Sara Hafeez and Ola Tundun whose love and radiance have shone through me for this year, and to Bronagh McDermott and Danielle Owen-Jones who remain my best funny gals. Thanks also to Morgan Hamer, Gemma Atkinson, Katie Blamey, the Lovedays, Andrew Barber, Nicola Davie and two inspirations for this book, Mitch Siddons and Adam Bogdan.

I said writing this book was difficult – it was for a number of reasons but the primary one being I wrote it as my father was struggling with terminal illness that would eventually see him leave us in January 2024. It was quite the struggle to write funny at one of the saddest times in my life, it really was. So many people said some lovely things about my dad when he passed but none more so than my dad's cousin, Joy from

Hawaii, who told me that when she first heard she had an English relative who was a comedy writer, she couldn't quite believe it. None of her English cousins were that funny. They were all a bit grumpy and serious. But then she realised the writer was Barry's daughter. Barry who was one of the warmest people she knew. Barry who could make a whole room light up with his smile, who spent his life laughing, dancing, raising people up with this wonderful brand of positivity and joy. It would make sense that some of that would filter down, somehow. These are the thoughts I now hold on to every day when I sit down to write, when I think about the stories I want to tell, when I think about what I want to put out into the world. Thank you, Dad, for passing that light on to me. I feel it so strongly. I am and was so very, very lucky.

Printed in Great Britain
by Amazon